Dear Reader,

They say that people are the same all over. Whether it's a small village on the sea, a mining town nestled in the mountains, or a whistle-stop along the Western plains, we all share the same hopes and dreams. We work, we play, we laugh, we cry—and, of course, we fall in love . . .

It is this universal experience that we at Jove Books have tried to capture in a heartwarming series of novels. We've asked our most gifted authors to write their own story of American romance, set in a town as distinct and vivid as the people who live there. Each writer chose a special time and place close to their hearts. They filled the towns with charming, unforgettable characters—then added that spark of romance. We think you'll find the combination absolutely delightful.

You might even recognize *your* town. Because true love lives in *every* town . . .

Welcome to *Our Town*.

Sincerely,

Leslie Gelbman
Editor-in-Chief

Jove titles by Carol Card Otten

OUR TOWN: CROSS ROADS
OUR TOWN: DREAM WEAVER

Other titles in the Our Town series from Jove

TAKE HEART
HARBOR LIGHTS
HUMBLE PIE
CANDY KISS
CEDAR CREEK
SUGAR AND SPICE
CROSS ROADS
BLUE RIBBON
THE LIGHTHOUSE
THE HAT BOX
COUNTRY COMFORTS
GRAND RIVER
BECKONING SHORE
WHISTLE STOP
STILL SWEET

OUR · TOWN

DREAM WEAVER

CAROL CARD OTTEN

JOVE BOOKS, NEW YORK

DREAM WEAVER

A Jove Book / published by arrangement with
the author

PRINTING HISTORY
Jove edition / September 1997

ISBN: 0-515-12141-X

A JOVE BOOK®
Jove Books are published by The Berkley Publishing Group,
200 Madison Avenue, New York, New York 10016,
a member of Penguin Putnam Inc.
JOVE and the "J" design are trademarks
belonging to Jove Publications, Inc.

PRINTED IN THE UNITED STATES OF AMERICA

10 9 8 7 6 5 4 3 2 1

This book is dedicated
to:

My editor, Judith Stern Palais,
whose support and guidance I cherish;

My children, Christi and Stephen,
and soon-to-be son-in-law, Rob—
I'm a mother who couldn't be more blessed;

My Human Grammar-Checker and dear
friend,
Jan Dale;

and

A special thanks to all the women at the
Whitfield-Murray Historical Society,
Dalton, Georgia,
whose enthusiasm for this project
spurred me on.

"One vision all my bosom fills,
O village in the Georgia hills. . . ."

—Robert Loveman

❖ 1 ❖

Late Summer, 1895
Atlanta, Georgia

A LIGHT BREEZE crested the open window, bringing with it the sweet smell of night-blooming jasmine. Annabel Lowe sat in front of her dressing table staring at her reflection in the mirror while absently brushing the coppery red hair that fell in loose curls around her shoulders. The room was lit by the soft glow of dusk. She had intentionally forgone turning on the lamps, preferring instead the last remaining incandescence of twilight to the recently installed gas wall sconces her mother had insisted her father have put in their home in Inman Park.

Annabel sighed and placed the silver monogrammed brush back upon the dressing table. At twenty-five, she was bored silly with her life—with the persistent round of parties she was forced to attend, and with the same boring young men vying for her attention.

And tonight would be yet another of those tedious evenings. Her family had been invited to a musicale being held at the home of a society dame whose friendship her mother coveted more than the air she breathed.

Studying her image in the mirror, Annabel wondered if she could evade tonight's entertainments by claiming another headache. If she did, surely her mother would suspect that her only daughter was up to her usual nonsense—begging off attending the gathering because of disinterest. Especially after the headache Annabel had claimed to have had for the last two weekends. In truth, her mother might deem it necessary to have her committed to the hospital for testing, fearing that her prized heifer might be marred by some insidious disease that would make her unfit to marry into a socially prominent family. Not that anyone would want to marry her for anything other than her father's money.

She leaned forward. Light-green eyes with touches of hazel stared back at her from the depths of the silvery looking glass. In Annabel's opinion, she was not a thing of beauty. Her freckled complexion fell short in a society where peaches and cream were considered vogue. To her mother's dismay, Annabel had inherited her father's coloring, his lanky build, as well as his intellect. The latter was abhorred and vastly misunderstood by her mother.

As she stared at her reflection, Annabel questioned what part her mother had played in the creation of the person in the mirror. She saw nothing remotely similar to the petite woman with flashing black eyes and raven hair who'd given her life.

To this day, her mother still captured admiring glances from the opposite sex, and would continue to do so until the day she died. Her father worshipped his beautiful wife and rightly so. Evangeline Lowe was an ornament of beauty that any man would be proud to hang upon his arm. But the redheaded daughter was another story. A sad one, in her mother's opinion, or so Annabel believed— she was the swan's ugly duckling.

Not that her looks really mattered. In her heart, Annabel was her father's daughter—from the top of her red head, down her five-foot-eight length, to the soles of her size eight shoes. Not only were she and her father connected by their looks, but also they were connected by their ambitious natures. Annabel's father's drive had placed his family in the income bracket they now enjoyed. His competence with figures and his dedication to hard work had enabled him to become president of the Phoenix Bank, one of Atlanta's largest financial institutions.

Although her parents had no idea that she planned to use the education they'd provided her with, Annabel intended to seek employment. And soon. The debutante life was not for her, and settling down with the right man was the farthest thing from her mind. She wanted to make her mark on the world, and no better time to do it than now when so many opportunities in the professions were opening up for women. Social work was at the top of her list— Annabel wanted to help those less fortunate than herself.

Jerked from her reverie by her mother's stormy entrance, Annabel watched the elegantly dressed woman as she came through the door. Tonight she wore a dress of iridescent brass satin covered with strips of black lace. The big sleeves and tiny waist brought to mind the image of a bumblebee, and her mother beelined straight to the dressing table where Annabel sat.

She looked from the stormy expression on her mother's face to the piece of linen stationery held in her rigid, banded-agate and gold-jeweled fingers.

Rising from the stool, Annabel faced her mother, fearing the worst. *Had something happened to her father?*

"Mother, what is it?" When confronting her much shorter mother, the extreme difference in their height always made Annabel feel like the parent. To eliminate her cumbrous feeling, she dropped down on the stool.

Her mother waved the piece of paper at her. "This . . . this is the matter. Tell me, please, what gives this—this person the right to suggest such an action of my daughter?"

Annabel followed the movement of the paper with her eyes, trying to make out the writing. When reading proved impossible, she reached for the paper.

"Please, Mother. Give it to me. How am I to address

your questions when I'm uncertain what person and what action you are referring to?"

"It's this letter. From that girl you attended school with in Macon."

Startled by her mother's admission, Annabel swallowed her own anger. "You opened my mail?" She rose again, this time towering over her mother and enjoying the advantage of having her mother look up to her.

"Of course I opened your mail. I am your mother—"

"You have no right. I would never think of opening your or Father's mail. I'd feel awkward, even if you'd given me permission to do so." Annabel squared her shoulders. "Mother . . . mail is a personal thing—"

"Personal, pshaw! You are my daughter. I must make certain your reputation is above reproach. How else will you get a man to marry you?"

How else indeed? Her mother's implication was not meant to be cruel, but it was evident that she didn't hold much hope for her daughter with flaming red hair and freckles attracting a husband any other way than by her excellent reputation as a lady, and by acting as dimwitted as the other young ladies her mother wanted her to befriend. Annabel brushed aside her anger, hiding it beneath a façade of practiced tolerance. An attitude she'd adopted long ago in dealing with her parent.

"Mother, may I please see my letter?"

"Oh, all right." The older woman thrust the letter into Annabel's hand. "I guess you have sense enough not to take her suggestion seriously. Now sit. Let me fix your hair for this evening's entertainment."

Unwilling to provoke her mother more, Annabel did her bidding. She plopped again on the stool in front of her dressing table, allowing her mother to coax her unruly hair into the latest style while she read the letter from Hollie, her best friend from school.

Dear Belle,

 It has been long since we last corresponded. Since that time I've joined my cousin Claire in

Washington, D.C. You may not know this, but she was recently appointed by the Secretary of the Interior for President Cleveland to be one of twenty special investigators for the Bureau of Labor. You do remember hearing about Mary Claire's infamous valedictorian speech in 1865? When I spoke to her of our friendship and our little rallies we'd held for women's rights at Wesleyan College, she said you sounded as insubordinate as she had been at your age.

In her position, she is now conducting an investigation concerning conditions of employment for women and children in the Northeast, in Georgia, and elsewhere. You may have read her recent article in Century *Magazine, entitled "The Georgia Cracker in the Cotton Mills." It is her desire to urge stricter laws in the areas of child labor, compulsory education, housing, factory inspection, and industrial safety. Recently she has had serious complaints about unfair practices in a certain cotton mill in Dalworth, Georgia, only a hundred miles north of Atlanta, and she intends to investigate.*

Since you are still living in the state, I suggested you might be interested in giving her some input. Write me here and let me know.

Until we next correspond, I remain faithfully your friend.

Hollie.

Annabel's heart leaped with excitement. At last she had a purpose. Posthaste, she would write her friend back and inform her that she would be more than happy to help with her cousin's investigation. How to achieve such an undertaking, she wasn't certain, but felt the answer would come to her if she thought on it long enough.

"Annabel?" Her mother thumped her on the head with

the hairbrush to get her attention. "Wasn't Hollie that frowzy-looking girl you brought home from school with you last Christmas?"

"Mothurr, she isn't frowzy. She's really quite lovely when you get to know her."

"From what I recall of the girl, it will take all her father's money, and then some, to find her a mate."

Annabel rolled her eyes toward the heavens before she met her mother's gaze in the mirror. She had to bite her tongue to keep from telling her exactly how she felt about her mother's opinion of her friend. Instead of responding the way she wanted to, she focused her attention on her mother's efforts to make her presentable.

"You'll wear your lime green silk this evening," her mother told her, smoothing the mass of coppery curls into plumped fullness around Annabel's face before securing its length with a knob on the back of her head. "I must say this coiffure complements your face nicely." She tucked a beaded frame of green crystals into her hair. "There now . . . you look almost pretty."

"Almost, Mother?" Annabel's green eyes met her mother's black ones in their reflections.

Evangeline refused to retract her statement and went on as though it were permissible for her to insult her daughter if she chose to do so. "Your coloring is especially high this evening. If one didn't know better one would have to look close to find those bothersome freckles you inherited from your father. You have been using that cream I purchased for you, haven't you?" Not waiting for Annabel to answer, her mother stepped toward the wardrobe and pulled out the lime green gown.

"Mrs. Featherstone's nephew is to be in attendance tonight. I understand he is considered quite a catch in Savannah."

Annabel stood and compliantly stepped into the gown, stuffed her arms through the balloonlike sleeves and allowed her mother to pull the lace neckline up over her shoulders and fasten the tiny crystal buttons that trailed down the back length of the gown's bodice.

"I trust you'll be on your best behavior this evening, Annabel, and not press the young man with your inflated opinions of women's place in today's world."

"Yes, ma'am."

At this point, Annabel would have agreed to anything to be free of her mother's worrisome presence. She needed a few moments alone before she was to depart for Mrs. Featherstone's with her parents. She wanted to re-read Hollie's letter.

Annabel had no idea how she could be of help to her friend's cousin, but she felt that before the sun rose on the morrow her resourceful mind would have arrived at a conclusion that would be beneficial both to herself and to Mary Claire.

A few moments later, with more enthusiasm than she had felt in months, Annabel left her room and joined her parents in the foyer. The sooner she could get this evening over with, the sooner she could return to her room and the letter that her fingers and mind were itching to write.

"Gordy. You're out early this morning."

From atop a three-rung ladder where he'd been dusting bottles of tonic on the hard-to-reach shelves, Coit Jackson greeted his stepbrother Gordon when he stepped through the front door of the store.

Dusting was a chore Coit performed at least once a week, and he usually started in the early hours of morning during the summer months. Upcountry folks knew that by mid-afternoon the buildup of heat and humidity would make the air inside their dwellings sizzle. Work that re- quired any physical effort was best carried out when the air was still cool.

"Saw your light," Gordon Hamil said. "I needed to have a word with you before I headed for the mill."

Coit climbed down from the ladder. Once on the floor, he faced the older man who was four years his senior and connected to him only by their late parents' marriage.

Coit's widowed mother had married Benson Hamil fifteen years earlier.

"I'm in need of a favor," his stepbrother told him.

"A favor?" Coit raised his brows in speculation. "From me?"

"Yes, from you. Believe me, if I had someone else to send in my place, I would."

"Send?"

To curb his impatience at his brother's assumption that he would obey orders, Coit turned his back and walked toward the counter where the cup of coffee he'd poured earlier waited. Even in the early-morning heat, the thick brown brew had turned stone cold. Coit took a swallow, grimacing as the chilled liquid went down his throat, before he answered.

"In case you haven't noticed, I have a business to run right here in Dalworth. I'm certainly not in a position to be going anywhere, for your pleasure or mine."

Gordy wasn't to be dissuaded by Coit's answer. "I happen to know that the third Wednesday of every month you go to Atlanta for supplies. Tomorrow happens to be the third Wednesday."

Coit scratched his chin. "Well, if that don't beat all. Didn't know you were aware of my comings and goings. You got one of your spies watching me?"

His brother ignored his remark. "I've a meeting in Chattanooga that will take me away from the mill for several days—that's why I need you to deliver this for me." He reached inside his suit jacket and pulled out a white envelope. "This money needs to be in the office of the Cotton States and International Exposition Company by the end of the week. Don't know anyone I can trust to deliver this but you."

"Me? Since when have you trusted me for anything?" Coit's gaze locked on his brother's faded blue eyes . . . eyes that could chill even on a hot August morning. "Long as I can remember, you've been of the notion that I was trying to steal your birthright."

Gordon looked uncomfortable. "I'm no longer that person. Besides, you have a vested interest in the mill.''

''The running of this store is my only interest and the one thing that matters to me.''

''Then you'll see that this gets delivered to the right person.'' He slapped the envelope down upon the counter. ''The short-term bonds issued to finance the expo have been slow in receiving subscriptions. Without them, there will be no fair and possibly no northern interest in our products. That means no mill, or this store that you hold in such high regard. Our profits are down, Coit.''

''Yeah, yeah, Gordy, I've heard it all before. What you're really saying is your big pockets may be shrinking and you can't stand the notion.'' Disgusted, Coit turned his back on his brother and slapped the dusting rag down on the back counter and began to rub the worn wood with a vengeance. ''Miser,'' he mumbled to himself, not really caring if Gordon heard his remark.

''If you won't do it for me, then do it for *our* father. He would want us to participate at the exposition.''

Our father? Since when did he belong to the two of us? Gordon must truly be desperate, begging him to be his delivery boy and referring to his father as theirs. For as long as Coit could remember, sharing was not something that Gordon ever did.

The memory of his stepfather, Benson Hamil, surfaced in Coit's mind. A fairer man he'd never known. How in the devil he had spawned such a self-indulgent, money-hungry man like his son Coit would never understand.

Hell, he didn't hold it against the older man for bequeathing the mill to Gordon. The Hamil family, old planters who owned most of the acreage in and around Dalworth, had made certain that any monies or properties were to be entailed to blood heirs only. But why couldn't Gordon be the same kind of person his father had been? Instead of sympathizing with those interested only in the profit margin, why couldn't he feel more compassion for the mill workers and their families?

''Do this for me, Coit, and I'll make it worth your while.''

"Worth my while?" He swung around to face his brother. "I told you a long time ago I can't be bought."

Ignoring his remark, Gordon shoved the white envelope across the counter. "Deliver this to Mr. Benson in Atlanta. The address is on the envelope."

Coit slammed his hand down on the sealed paper. "I'll do it, but only because I'll be in Atlanta tomorrow. This is the last time I'll be your errand boy."

Gordon smiled, but the smile didn't warm the cold eyes. "I knew I could count on you, junior." He turned on his heels and walked toward the exit. "Remember— the contents of that envelope are more important than the stocks waiting in the warehouse in Atlanta. Be sure you deliver it before you do anything else."

The front door slammed, echoing throughout the building. Coit listened until the bell on the door jangled to silence before he took a deep breath. *Junior.* A fighting word as far as Coit was concerned. Why was it that his stepbrother lorded it over everyone, himself included? Gordon might be some four years older, but Coit was still thirty years old.

Picking up his empty cup, he walked to the small apartment at the back of the store where he lived. Once there, he poured himself fresh coffee before returning to the front room that served as his place of business. The store was his legacy from his stepfather, and Coit couldn't imagine doing anything but what he did.

He enjoyed the mercantile business, the customers he knew by their first names; he knew their children. On wintry days, the ornately designed Ward Windsor parlor stove was the gathering place for the mill workers who came to the store to make their daily or weekly purchases. It was from these people that Coit had learned about human nature and life. From listening to his customers, he gained insight into the hardships of the working man, as well as his hopes and dreams. And because of his relationship with his customers Coit had dedicated himself to making their lives a little easier.

After he'd graduated from the University of Georgia in

Athens, he'd taken up the running of the mercantile. He enjoyed the life of a tradesman. Unlike his brother Gordon, who chose management and profits and socializing with the more affluent citizens of the town of Dalworth, Coit preferred mingling with the mill workers and their families. The store and his patrons were his life, along with an occasional afternoon spent fishing in a nearby mountain stream.

Coit walked to the front of the building, opened the door, and stepped outside onto the portico. The air felt hung over with the damp coolness of the fading night. He took a deep breath. The scent of honeysuckle nectar— sweet, warm, and honeyed—filled his nostrils. He loved the fragrance. The soft, green vine, blanketed with creamy golden-orange flowers, was a favorite of his and the pride of most of the gardens in the surrounding mill houses.

Coit thought if he met a woman who smelled like honeysuckle, he would marry her tomorrow. He laughed at his foolish thoughts—marriage. No matter how good a woman smelled, he enjoyed his independence too much to complicate it with a long-term relationship like marriage.

He followed his early-morning routine of watching the sleepy town come to life. It was a scene that Coit never tired of seeing and one he rarely missed.

Because of the lay of the land, which had once been tiered meadows used for farming and herding before the mill was built, Coit could see most of the village from his front stoop. Already the sun had begun to wash the sky in brilliant orange, its reflection glowing like copper off the pressed-metal roofs of the scattered houses. Inside the shaded dwellings, lights began to show. Soon men, women, and children would be rising, breakfasting, then heading out to work in the mill.

As the sun rose higher, taupe shadows turned golden, backlighting the tower and belfry of the Royal Mill building where it stood upon a grassy knoll. The long, narrow, three-story structure looked like a church in the early-morning light. A fitting edifice, Coit thought, for such a pastoral setting.

With his shoulder propped against one of the white-washed Doric columns that fronted the store, he took another sip of coffee. A gentle breeze fluffed his hair, bringing with its playfulness the smell of bacon frying and the clove and cinnamon scent of the sweet peas he'd planted in cast-iron pots on the front portico.

Off in the distance, he heard a baby cry. The tiny whimper was soon silenced by the shrill whistle of the six-thirty-five, the train that traveled daily from Chattanooga, Tennessee, to Atlanta. Coit pulled his fob watch from his pocket and checked the time. Everyone in town set their watches by the coming and going of that train. Tomorrow morning he'd be aboard her when she departed the Dalworth Depot for Atlanta.

"Morning, Mr. Jackson. It's a fine day we've got blooming, now isn't it?"

Coit smiled a greeting at the rawboned woman who passed in front of the store, her baby straddling her hip. "Mighty fine, Mrs. Trilby. Mighty fine. I reckon that was little Joseph I heard crying earlier."

"It was indeed. This little rascal kept us awake most of the night. His teeth cutting is making sleep scarce around our house."

"Did you use the whiskey I recommended?"

"Sure did. Rubbed it on his gums just like you suggested. For a little while it worked fine, but come midnight, he started in again. Leroy finally downed the rest of the bottle so he could get himself some sleep."

Coit chuckled. "Can't blame him much for that."

"Sure can't. Leroy's got to sleep, or he ain't fit for work. I decided a little walk with the wee one here would give him a few extra minutes to snooze." She shifted the baby to the other hip and called, "A good day to you, Mr. Jackson," before moving on down the street.

He watched as more men and women filed past. They waved, and he returned the greeting. Most of them were workers, heading for the gated entrance to the mill.

"There you are, Coit."

He turned to face the young woman entering the portico at the opposite end from where he stood.

"Sara Polk, you're out early this morning."

The Polk family were Coit's backyard neighbors. They shared a fence, along with many hours of friendly conversation, when time and weather permitted.

He studied the petite woman whose energy and enthusiasm always managed to amaze him. Sara was seven months pregnant. She and her husband, Jess, had decided that this would be their last child. They already had two active twin boys, and Sara longed for a girl.

"I brought you the rest of the money like I promised." She approached him and had to look up at his much taller six-foot frame. "I know you're going to Atlanta tomorrow and plan to pick up that dressmaker's dummy I ordered. I wanted you to have the cash before you left."

"Now, Sara." Coit smoothed back his unruly hair. "I told you not to worry about paying me. A nickel a week would suit me fine."

"No. I have all the money. The ladies from the literary society paid me for the tablecloth I crocheted for them. You're to have it all. I want to own the form free and clear."

"Well, I understand, but—"

"No buts about it, this is Jess's and my way. If we can't pay for extras, we do without them." She reached inside her apron pocket and pulled out a handful of coins, forcing them into Coit's hand. "Now I've got to get back to the house before Jess leaves for work. My man's hungry and expecting his breakfast."

Turning to leave, she paused. "You haven't forgotten about that room I have to let, have you?"

"No. The notice is tacked to the back wall."

"Much obliged. I'm starting on the curtains for the windows this morning, and I'm looking forward to sharing some female company. In case you haven't noticed, everything that breathes and eats in our house is male, including the cat."

Sara's plain speaking always made Coit smile. "You know, if you could bottle your energy and let me sell it in the store, you'd make us both rich."

"Pshaw! I'm already rich, Coit Jackson. The good Lord blessed me with a loving husband and two healthy boys. And a lively unborn, if my bruised ribs are any indication." She swung around to leave. "Let me know if anyone is interested in the room."

"I will," he promised.

Coit watched her leave. He knew the extra money she hoped to earn was to be put aside for the twins' education. Also, the dress dummy she'd ordered was to help in her dressmaking business. He'd never met a woman as industrious as Sara, or a man he liked more than her husband, Jess, who was also a hard worker. Jess was a supervisor in the boiler room at the mill and had worked there most of his adult life.

Coit wondered how he was going to help her find a boarder. If Gordy had planned to hire more weavers, it was news to Coit. If anything, he suspected just the opposite, especially if it was true what Gordon had said about profits being down. But then, Coit paid no mind to the running of the mill or how many operatives they hired. Besides, he was under the impression that most of those jobs were filled by word-of-mouth, usually by friends and relatives of those already employed. The new operatives who got a job usually moved in with kin until they could find somewhere else to live or could get mill housing. He doubted that Sara would find a boarder among the newly hired.

Of course, she probably knew more than he did about the hiring at the mill. Coit wanted nothing to do with it—the mill was his brother's enterprise. Only the Company Store was his responsibility, and Coit had insisted that no one in the village know he owned ten percent of the Royal Mill. So far, his brother had kept their secret.

Enough woolgathering, he thought, coming back to the

present. It was time he got to work. Coit threw out the remnants of coffee and walked back inside the building to continue with his dusting. Tomorrow would be here soon enough.

❖ 2 ❖

"THERE," ANNABEL SAID, stripping the lace collar and jabot from the front of her tailor-made shirtwaist. She had worn the frothy Brussels lace for her mother's benefit when her parent had insisted on accompanying her to the train station in Atlanta. Stepping back from the clouded mirror that hung above the dressing table in the ladies lounge on the Dalworth-bound train, she wadded up the jabot and stuffed it inside her traveling bag.

The hardest part of her ruse had been convincing her mother that her sojourn to Dalworth was nothing more than a social visit with an old school chum. And since the town of Dalworth sat in the valley of the blue ranges of the Cohutta Mountains, it was decided that the invitation to visit had been a godsend since Atlanta had been experiencing a record heat wave. Her mother had agreed that a short respite in the mountain climes would do them both good—since tempers had been short of late. But her elder was unaware of the true purpose of Annabel's visit, or that it had been arranged by Hollie Cross and her cousin Claire after Annabel had responded to her friend's letter, agreeing to investigate the labor practices of the Royal Mill.

Excitement rushed through her, blushing her cheeks. The dim lighting of the small private room made her freckles look less pronounced and also dulled her coppery hair beneath the straw boater she wore.

"Yes," she said, eyeing her image one last time in the looking glass. The gunmetal gray ribbon around the hat's brim was the same color as the tailored skirt and jacket of her traveling suit. Her mother had complained bitterly about her choice of dress, claiming her daughter looked like a waif, but Annabel had insisted the outfit was fine for the short train ride. And fine for a prospective mill worker.

Feeling satisfied not only with her appearance, but also with her mission, Annabel opened the door and stepped again into the public coach of the rocking train.

From beneath his bowler and over the top edge of *The Atlanta Constitution*, Coit watched the redheaded woman make her way down the aisle in search of a seat.

The car's windows were open to allow a flow of air through its interior. Usually the last train of the day was not crowded, but this evening it was almost filled to capacity. Coit suspected that most of the travelers were escaping the hot city, their destination the cooler mountains of Chattanooga, Tennessee.

Behind his paper, he eyed his seat companion and cursed himself for not allowing the baggage handler to store Sara Polk's sewing dummy in the compartment with the other baggage. Knowing how hard she had worked to purchase the valued mannequin, Coit had carried it aboard the train with him, to assure its safe arrival home. Now the polished wood, with its curvaceous bust, sat beside him, occupying one of the few remaining seats.

Until this moment, Coit hadn't thought about how personal the form might appear to others. In a society where the practice of covering a piano's legs was carried out so as not to offend the sensibilities of the fairer sex, Coit wished he'd thought to bring something to conceal the dummy's wooden peaks that were as visible as the pinnacles of the Georgia mountains.

He shook his paper, eyeing the redheaded woman who was fast approaching him. Because of the swaying motion of the car, her long-legged stride was less than graceful. Long-legged, he imagined, only because of her relatively tall height. In spite of it, she carried herself with dignity, as though she were proud of the lift of her pert little nose.

He glanced around him, trying to determine her destination. The family with half a dozen children had resettled in the few remaining seats, so it meant that he would have to share his bench with the young woman. Normally it wouldn't have mattered, but his wooden companion was taking up most of the unoccupied seat. Oh, well—under the circumstances, seat sharing couldn't be avoided.

She moved toward him with a purposeful stride that was reminiscent of a schoolmarm's. Having experienced a crack across the knuckles with a ruler many times, Coit hoped this teacher's temperament would be somewhat better than average—in spite of having to share a seat with a wooden dummy. She stopped beside him, her face full of questions as she eyed his seat companion.

It was then that Coit noted the twinkle of amusement in her bright green eyes. He smiled sheepishly, gathered up his newspaper, and stood, removing his hat.

"If I'd known this car was going to be so crowded, I would have stored her in the baggage compartment."

"Your wife?" she asked, raising one coppery brow.

Her question took him off guard. And for reasons unknown to him, it became terribly important that this young woman didn't believe he was married. Groping for a reasonable but unassuming answer, he replied, "She's not my wife."

Her hand flew to her mouth as though to hide her lips' response to his answer. For the first time, he noticed the scattering of freckles across the bridge of her nose and over her high cheekbones. Behind the gloved fingertips, he could see that her lips were turned up in a smile.

"I would hope not," she responded. "She seems a tad stiff."

Coit chuckled, appreciating her humor.

"She's a friend—"

"Ah . . . a friend?" the woman interrupted, looking at Coit, then at the wooden dummy. "Well, madam, it's very nice to meet you."

Realizing that he still had not made his marital status clear, he tried again. "I mean, the dummy is for Sara—a friend. She's a seamstress. I'm delivering it to her."

The way her eyes twinkled and her lips twitched, he knew she'd been teasing him. Coit was charmed by her easy humor. Her next response moved him to action.

"Do you think it would be possible for the three of us to sit together?" She smiled, revealing even white teeth between her rosy lips.

Remembering his manners at last, Coit replied, "But of course. Please forgive me."

As he stepped back to allow her entrance to the window seat, he noted that the woman's height was close to his own. Her shoulders were wide, but were in proportion to her ribs that dipped in attractively at her waist. Its smallness was emphasized by the cut of her gray jacket and skirt.

Beneath her straw boater, her hair was the color of copper and was pinned into the style that was all the rage among fashionable women. Briefly he wondered why a young lady of her apparent station would be traveling alone, but all thoughts of propriety were quickly forgotten when in her maneuvering, the scent of honeysuckle washed over his senses. Taken aback by this last discovery, Coit decided that the wind must have picked up his favorite scent and carried it to him through the open window.

She settled herself on the seat and crossed her hands in her lap. Coit took the seat beside her, Sara's mannequin riding chaperon between them.

Although he knew it wasn't proper to speak to a young woman without a formal introduction, he felt that since she was traveling alone and they had spoken earlier, an introduction was now in store. Leaning forward in his seat, he said, "I'm Coit Jackson from Dalworth."

Dalworth? If the handsome man with the sooty hair and thick lashes hadn't gotten her attention—which he had—the mention of Dalworth would certainly have done so. Annabel looked the gentleman over more closely. He was a looker, no doubt about it, and the mere perusal of him from beneath her lowered lashes made her heart pump a little faster.

Not that Annabel was taken to swooning or given to those heart palpitations experienced by most of her peers; but if she were prone to such conditions, this handsome man would likely cause such reactions. As he waited for a response to his introduction, he studied her with eyes that were darker than dark chocolate; her own gaze strayed to the deep cleft in his chin and the slighter indention at the corner of his naturally smiling mouth.

After a breathless moment, she responded, "I'm Annabel—" She stopped herself before she blurted out her real name and finished with, "Blow." *Anna Belle Blow.* While the alias echoed in her mind, she studied his reaction.

"Annabel?"

"Two names," she corrected. "Anna Belle Blow."

"Well, Miss Blow, I'm pleased to make your acquaintance."

She nodded, the air between them tense, both knowing that good manners dictated they not pry, but both wanting to know more about the other. Finally Annabel decided that her assumed identity gave her license, including the option to voice opinions that would have otherwise been frowned upon by ladies and gentlemen of her station.

Annabel knew that the moment she stepped down from the train in the Dalworth Depot she would be a factory worker and the debutante Annabel Lowe would be nothing more than a memory. The falsified references inside her bag indicated that, so she decided she would use this moment to begin practicing the part she would be playing for the next few weeks.

Clearing her throat to get her companion's attention, although it wasn't necessary because he seemed to be waiting for her next words, she told him, "I'm hoping to be employed by the Royal Mill in Dalworth."

Her explanation appeared to have stunned him because he straightened on his seat, peered around the wooden dummy, and looked her over more carefully.

"Royal Mill? In what capacity?"

She felt herself blush from his close scrutiny. "As a weaver," she replied.

Her new acquaintance mumbled something unintelligible beneath his breath.

In order to catch the drift of his words, Annabel leaned forward on her seat, thinking as she did so that whoever Sara was, she was certainly well endowed with womanly attributes. The mannequin's bosom protruded boldly into voluptuous points, blocking her line of vision. At this discovery of such a personal nature, Annabel felt her skin turn several shades deeper in color and wondered if her seat companion had noticed the provocative mounds of wood that they were trying to communicate around.

"A weaver?" Coit asked. "Now that is a surprise." He leaned back to contemplate her answer.

A weaver in the Royal Mill. That was the last thing Coit had expected of the young woman who shared his bench seat. He recalled that Sara had said they were hiring more weavers at the mill when she had told him about her room to let. But this lady, Anna Belle Blow, certainly didn't fit the picture of a mill worker.

Although her traveling dress lacked pretensions, the garment was finely tailored and of an expensive cloth—not the normal linsey-woolsey fabric worn by the women who frequented his store. And there was something in the young woman's manner that spoke of good breeding. Yes. She was different from the other women who worked in his brother's mill.

Bending forward again, he asked, "You're not from these parts, are you?"

It was several moments before she bent forward again into his line of vision. She began to explain, ignoring the bust between them.

"I'm from Macon. They laid off several workers. I lost my position. I have an ad that says the Royal Mill is hiring. I've come to apply for one of their positions."

Coit nodded his head in acknowledgment. Her story could be true, and who was he to pry? He knew nothing of the young woman, except that he'd been attracted to her sense of humor. She wasn't a beauty, but he'd been drawn to her wholesomeness. Besides, if she were to be a part of the mill family, the least he could do was make her feel as comfortable as possible in her new position.

Suddenly he remembered Sara's room. "Are you staying with friends in Dalworth?"

"No, I'm hoping to rent a room. Since you're from Dalworth, do you know of any respectable boarding houses?"

Their gazes met and locked, the wooden points of the dummy's bosom obstructing their view until they both looked away in embarrassment.

"Oh, for heaven's sake," Annabel mumbled. Lifting her traveling bag from the floor to her lap, she opened it and pulled out the frothy lace jabot. With a deft movement, she fastened the frilly lace around the dummy's neck, allowing the spill of fabric to cover the points of the protruding wooden chest.

Satisfied, Annabel straightened and met her companion's gaze. "Better?" she asked.

Coit couldn't help but laugh. "Better." In that moment, he knew he wanted to get to know the lady with the copper tresses. And what better way than to have her living almost in his back yard? From what he knew of Sara Polk, the two intelligent women would get along famously. "About that room."

His companion looked hopeful. "Yes. Do you know of a place?"

"My friend Sara."

They both looked toward the dummy, at the lacy jabot, and laughed.

"The *real* Sara." He continued. "She and her husband have a room to rent in their home. I believe the two of you would enjoy one another's company. That is, if you're interested."

Her green eyes glistened like rare jewels. "I'd like that," she said, "but of course we both would have to meet and agree to the arrangement."

"Of course, that would be expected."

As the train rumbled closer to their destination, Annabel leaned forward again.

"Mr. Jackson, how do you know Sara?"

"I run the Company Store at the Royal Mill. We're backyard neighbors."

"You don't say," was her only reply before she straightened again.

Annabel couldn't believe her good fortune. She'd been on her way to Dalworth for less than an hour and already she'd made contact with one of the mill workers. If her good luck continued, by tomorrow she would have a place to stay.

The idea of being Coit Jackson's backyard neighbor thrilled Annabel more than she cared to admit. After all, she reasoned, her mission had been made easier by their chance meeting on the train.

Her mind insisted that it wasn't his shiny brown eyes, his winning smile, or the partially hidden dimple at the corner of his mouth that made her skin ripple with goose-flesh. But instead it was the knowledge that she was one step closer to being able to report her findings about the Royal Mill to her friend in Washington.

"Where are you staying?" Coit asked her as they stood on the wooden platform in front of the Dalworth Depot. Their train had arrived some fifteen minutes earlier, and they had disembarked, joining the throngs of other travelers who now shuffled for standing room.

Most of the waiting crowd would proceed on to Chattanooga. Some passengers had left the train to exercise their limbs, but others, traveling with young children, had exited to bolster their patience for the remainder of the trip. The travelers who had ended their journey were met at the station by friends and family, or now vied for the town's two conveyances to take them to their final destinations.

Annabel scrutinized her traveling companion where he stood several feet away with the wooden dummy tucked firmly beneath his arm. Her very own Brussels lace collar and jabot were crushed intimately between the dummy's bulging curves and his manly ribs. The image was unsettling.

Outside the confines of the train, Coit Jackson, with his sooty hair and half-dimpled smile, appeared more devilishly handsome than when she had first made his acquaintance. He was not much taller than she, allowing her to gaze almost directly into the fathomless depths of his eyes. Temporarily spellbound by their chocolate color, she stood unmoving while her heart pounded. A more beautiful man she'd never met.

His voice called her back to the present. "Miss Blow, are you all right?"

Annabel was mortified by her behavior and mentally chastised herself. Regaining her composure, she answered his earlier question.

"I'll be staying at the Hotel Dalworth. I wired ahead for a room."

"A good move, since our little town seems to be overflowing with guests. I'd offer you a ride, but I'm on foot myself. My home is not far, and I enjoy walking this time of day."

Her gaze followed his to where it scanned the rooftops of the business district. The sky was the color of a ripe watermelon. She pulled her eyes away from the glorious reddish hue to get a better view of the town. It was a sleepy little business district, supporting only several streets of shops. Most of the storefronts were made of brick, their edifices changed to the color of ground cinnamon bark as the sun sank lower in the west.

"Nice," she said. "So peaceful compared to Atlanta."

Her remark snatched his attention away from the sky. "I understood you to say you were from Macon."

"I-I am." She felt the warmth travel to her face. "A person would have to be stone deaf not to have noticed the hustle and bustle of Atlanta. I had a stopover there before continuing on my way here."

After a moment, he said, "Of course you did. I don't know what I was thinking." He turned his attention to the departing crowd. "The least I can do is see that you have a ride to the hotel. One of the conveyances will be back any minute. Do you have a trunk?"

Annabel stopped him before he could make good on his offer.

"Thank you, but that won't be necessary. I promised a friend in Macon that I would send her a wire to let her know I'd arrived safely. As soon as I do that, I'm sure someone inside the depot will help me procure a ride."

He appeared satisfied with her answer. "For the next few days will you be staying at the hotel? I can reach you there?"

His question caught her off guard until Annabel remembered their earlier conversation about his neighbor Sara having a room to let. They had been bandying so many words, she couldn't remember what she'd said and wondered if he was as confused by her story as she. If she wasn't careful, she would be caught up in her own falsehoods.

Annabel recalled Cervantes's words on the subject. "The most difficult character in comedy is that of the fool, and he must be no simpleton that plays that part." Right now no one could feel more like a simpleton than she did. Already she'd nearly given herself away by comparing Dalworth to Atlanta instead of to Macon. She needed to slow down and get her lines right.

Realizing she had not answered his question, she said, "Yes, you can reach me at the hotel. I'll be staying there until I learn if the mill is going to hire me." She smiled at him, hoping she sounded convincing. "If they do, I'll be needing your friend's room."

Coit placed his bowler back upon his head. "Sara will be delighted to learn that I may have found her a boarder." He boosted the bulky dummy up beneath his arm, preparing to leave.

"Miss Blow, it was a pleasure making your acquaintance. Now if you'll excuse me, I had best be getting this lady home to her owner."

He glanced down at the lace jabot and collar still secured around the mannequin's headless neck. "I almost forgot—"

"Don't worry," Annabel interrupted. "I'll fetch it later." She couldn't resist one last tease. "Besides, we don't want it said that you were seen escorting a naked lady home."

He chortled. "You're right about that. Enough tongues waggle in this town without giving them more reason to exercise. Good evening to you, then." Bowing politely, he took his leave.

Standing on the station platform, Annabel watched him until he vanished into the darkening landscape.

"What a pleasant man," she mumbled aloud, realizing that her lips were frozen in a silly grin when another gentleman passed her, doffed his hat, and smiled at her as if they were old friends. His forwardness wiped the smile from her face, making her hasten toward the depot's interior.

Adventuresome as Annabel was, she also knew that a young woman traveling alone solicited all kinds of unfavorable attention. This had been a long, nerve-wracking day, and she was eager to get to the hotel. But first she must wire her mother as she had promised.

Later, from the hotel, Annabel would send a message to her friend Merelda Whitcomb who lived in Dalworth. Merelda was part of the network of young women from college who had helped put Annabel's investigation into motion.

Once inside, she walked toward the station attendant's cage. Above the mesh-covered window, *Telegraph Office* was written in bold black letters.

"I wish to send a wire," she told him.

The man slapped a piece of paper down upon the counter and shoved it through the pigeonhole. "Happy to oblige you, miss. You write it, and I'll send it."

Annabel began composing her note.

> *Arrived safely. Train met by Merelda and family. Will write when settled. Miss you.*
>
> *Annabel*

When she had finished, she shoved it back through the opening to the telegrapher. He read it, then looked at her from beneath his green transparent visor before craning his neck to look around her into the now empty waiting room.

"This be Miss Merelda *Whitcomb's* family?"

Annabel nearly choked on her saliva. The last thing she expected was to have her deception acknowledged by a total stranger. She felt the color creep into her cheeks, but she tried for nonchalance by assuming her most haughty stance. Her feigned arrogance went unnoticed by the telegrapher.

He continued to examine the waiting area behind her before his gaze slid back to Annabel. Looking her up and down like a condemning judge, he said, "Don't see the young miss or the rest of her family."

Annabel had never been a good liar, especially when questioned, but she was determined not to allow a complete stranger to thwart her ruse. She squared her shoulders and answered, "I'm meeting them at the hotel."

But the attendant was like a bulldog with his persistence. "Ain't like the Whitcombs. They usually meet their guests in their private carriage, then tote them on up to the big house."

Merciful heavens. What next? All she needed was word

to get back to Merelda's parents about her scheme and their daughter's part in it. The Whitcombs knew nothing of Annabel's planned visit to Dalworth. Unless she could come up with a believable story, and soon, not only would the station agent know about her deception, but by tomorrow morning she suspected the whole town would be informed about her arrival. If that happened, her mission would fail.

She wouldn't allow it. Drawing on her imagination, Annabel plunged ahead, making up a story as she went.

"I'm only passing through," she told him, "and it wouldn't be proper for me to stay up at the big house."

The agent's sensory organs matched those of an insect. If she hadn't known better, she would have sworn his ears had inched higher on his head. The "wouldn't be proper" statement had him leaning toward her, waiting for her next words.

Annabel dropped her gaze from his, feigning nervousness before she began.

"You see, Miss Merelda and I are not of the same station. When she attended Wesleyan College in Macon, I was but a mere serving girl working in the dining room. The lady, Miss Whitcomb, she was always kind to me. We became friends of a sort. When she graduated, she told me if I ever needed anything to be sure and look her up."

"Needed?" he asked, his expression suspicious.

Land sakes, he's appointed himself the town's keeper.

Hoping to correct her blunder before he ran her out of town on a rail, she blurted out, "Not that I be needing anything, mind you. Or, I should say, expecting charity. It's just that I'm to be married soon to a real gentleman and I need me a fine dress to wear."

The agent's bushy brows lifted in question. "How is our Miss Whitcomb gonna help you?" he asked.

Fluttering her hand, she rested it upon her chest.

"While at school, Miss Whitcomb, along with the other ladies, used to give their cast-off dresses to us workers. Since she and I were close to the same size, I mostly got her things. And I hoped she might have something real fancy that I could wear on my wedding day. So I wrote and asked her. She wrote me right back, insisting I come. Sent me my fare, she did. Me being a working girl and all, she knows I don't have much money.''

The attendant continued to scowl at her, but Annabel wasn't about to allow him to intimidate her further. Besides, she was pleased with her story. In school she had always excelled in drama, and she knew when she had a captive audience. The silly little man was falling for her tale, and Annabel almost smiled. But instead of smiling, she frowned.

''I've a mind to pay for my wedding dress, you know. I'll not be accepting charity.''

Beneath his green visor, the station attendant's eyes were still accusing. Annabel waited, holding her breath, until he spoke again.

''It'll cost you twenty-five cents to send this here wire. A working girl like you got that much?''

Annabel reached inside her purse and slapped the required amount down on the counter. ''I might be poor,'' she told him, ''but I certainly have enough to send a wire.''

She didn't waste any time distancing herself from the man, fearing he might make her change the content of her wire to read the way he thought it should. Without a backward glance, Annabel twirled around and headed toward the exit.

So much for asking his assistance in procuring a ride to the hotel. Before she chanced another session with the nosy little man, she would walk the distance. Surely finding the Dalworth Hotel couldn't be that difficult in this one-horse town. But then, she'd never imagined that sending a wire to her mother would have proved so troublesome.

''Land sakes,'' she mumbled to herself, stepping outside. ''Living in a small town is definitely going to take some getting used to.''

❖ 3 ❖

COIT'S STEP WAS light as he left the uptown area of Dalworth and headed toward his store and home in the mill village. As the sun slowly sank beyond the blue-tinted mountains that surrounded the Dalworth valley, he felt quite pleased with himself.

His trip to Atlanta had been very successful. Not only had he purchased the much-sought-after supplies his patrons had asked him to stock in his store, but he had also made arrangements for the shipment to be sent by the end of the week. Sara's dressmaker's dummy would arrive home without a scratch. But most of all, Coit was pleased with himself because he thought he had found Sara her lady boarder.

A real lady. This thought gnawed at his mind. Coit couldn't fit the pieces together. A real lady wouldn't work in a mill.

His gaze dropped to the expensive lace cravat still draped around the mannequin's neck. The fine workmanship of the adornment appeared much too expensive for the salary of a mere working girl. Clutching the dummy tighter beneath his arm, Coit fingered the delicate webbing with his free hand. Even if the ladies who traded at his store could afford such an expensive collar and jabot, most of them wouldn't have anywhere to wear such finery.

Was a mill worker's situation that much better in Macon than in Dalworth? Coit doubted it, but then what did he know about mill wages outside of Dalworth? Or for that matter, what did he know about the out-of-work weaver, Miss Blow?

For a moment, he considered Anna Belle Blow. She certainly didn't fit the usual pattern of the women who worked in the mill. She was single, but the females who frequented his store were usually married and worked beside their husbands and children in the mill. It took their combined wages to feed and clothe their families with nothing left over for lacy frippery.

Of course, Sara was different, but then she didn't work in the mill. Not that she didn't work hard—Coit had never met a woman who worked harder. But any extra money she earned with her piecework and canning she put aside for her children's education. He couldn't imagine Sara spending money on furbelows.

In spite of these differences in the two women, Coit still thought he recognized something of his neighbor in Miss Blow. For that reason, he felt the two ladies would get along famously if Miss Blow was hired on as a weaver and if she decided to rent Sara's room. The prospect of having the newcomer as a neighbor made his blood circulate a little faster.

Anna Belle Blow. It had been some time since Coit had met a woman who interested him the way his redheaded traveling companion had. After he left her at the depot, she had darted in and out of his thoughts like a honeybee courting flowers.

He liked Miss Blow's easy humor and outspokenness. With her red hair and numerous freckles, she would never be considered a beauty, but there was a wholesomeness about her that made her shine, a quality that Coit found refreshing and so different from the women of his acquaintance and status. Lately he'd been more interested

in the running of his store and the few friends he'd made
among the mill families than he'd been in courting social-
climbing women.

Refreshing, yes. Miss Blow was definitely that.

Coit began to whistle. It was a perfect evening for whistling, and he loved whistling as much as he loved to sing.
He did a lot of the latter, joining the other villagers when
they got together for some socializing and good old-time
shape-note singing.

Could Miss Blow sing? As he thought about her, he
recalled parts of her anatomy he hadn't realized he'd noticed—like her firm, high-perched bosom. Yes, he decided, there was a chance that she had a good set of lungs
beneath all that womanly thrust.

His assumption thrilled him, making his step even
lighter, although he couldn't pinpoint what thrilled him
most. Was it the prospect of the lady singing along with
him or was it what stood out above her lungs? He chuckled at the inconsistencies.

As he moved along the street, fireflies streaked the dusk
like miniature shooting stars. Coit continued to whistle,
his tune joining the crickets that were warming up for
their evening serenade. From several of the houses he
passed, folks waved and exchanged hellos from their front
porches.

Up the street and in the fading light he saw his store,
its whitewashed exterior sugar-coating the plainness of its
façade. Home, he thought. It felt good to be back where
he belonged.

Once on the building's portico, Coit took a deep breath,
inhaling the clovey scent of the sweet peas growing there
in iron pots. In the one day that he'd been away, the plants
looked as though they had doubled in size. Their viny
appendages, twisting and curling from their containers,
had already begun to take over the porch. Tomorrow he
would clip them back. But tonight he couldn't wait to
deliver Sara's dressmaker dummy and to tell her about
her prospective boarder.

*   *   *

"Oh, him. I've never met him," Merelda Whitcomb said. "He's the mother's son."

"Excuse me?" Annabel asked, sorely tempted to tell the fashionable miss who sat across from her that they were all spawns of their mothers, but instead she bit back the words and watched her companion and listened to her explanation.

"Coit Jackson's mother married old man Hamil. They both were widowed with sons. Gordon Hamil inherited the mill and all the money with it. I understand there is bad blood between the two brothers. Most believe it is because Coit got nothing from his stepfather."

"But he said he worked in the Company Store."

"Very bitter, I imagine," Merelda added. "He doesn't travel in the same crowd as his older brother."

"He didn't seem bitter to me. He seemed very pleasant."

Annabel recalled how much she'd enjoyed her train ride from Atlanta. She believed now it was partly due to the pleasant company of her traveling companion—er, companions.

Interrupting her thoughts, Merelda warned, "First impressions can be deceiving."

All impressions can be deceiving, Annabel thought as she studied her old school chum.

Merelda Whitcomb, dressed in an afternoon dress of cream satin organza, looked the picture of perfection and nothing like the girl Annabel remembered from school. Her companion sipped tea from a bone china teacup, her little finger crooked daintily while her thumb and forefinger held the delicate porcelain several inches away from her rose-tinted mouth. The two girls were lunching in the Hotel Dalworth's dining room the morning after Annabel's arrival in town.

Merelda's blue eyes were no longer rimmed by the scholarly glasses she'd worn as a student. Perhaps, Annabel thought, she'd forgone clear vision in order to appear more stylish. Whatever her reasons, Annabel wasn't impressed. She preferred the studious girl she remembered from her past to the young debutante who sat across from her today.

"So," Annabel said, "tell me what you know about the workings of the Royal Mill."

Merelda turned several shades of pink deeper than her lip color and looked as though she wanted to gag Annabel for phrasing such a statement. Glancing nervously around the room, Merelda studied the crowd anxiously. Seemingly satisfied that no one but herself had heard Annabel's comment, she replied from the corner of her nearly compressed lips, "They make cotton cloth."

Her eyes fluttered shut as she sipped the steamy brew before her gaze returned to Annabel's. "As far as knowing anything about the workings of the mill, a lady doesn't trouble herself with such things."

Disappointed with her friend's response, Annabel answered, "Even if the *lady* lives in the same town?"

Almost slamming the teacup back upon its saucer, Merelda straightened in her chair. With her friend's abrupt movement, the puff of gauze on top of her hat, shaped to resemble a bird's nest, nearly lost the plump pheasant nesting in the finery.

"Annabel, you always were stubborn with your opinions."

"Stubborn? I beg your pardon, Merelda, but I understood you were to be in on this investigation. I certainly expected more cooperation from you and more information on the mill than what I've received so far."

Her friend stiffened even more in her chair. "You're wrong, Annabel. I'm not in on anything. I agreed only because Hollie asked me to. Because she and I were roommates, I felt I couldn't refuse her. I agreed only to provide you with an alibi if your parents should inquire about you while you're here. Other than that, I want nothing to do with this harebrained scheme of yours."

Annabel felt her temper rising. "It's not my harebrained scheme, and I shouldn't have to remind you of that. Surely you can see the importance of what might be learned because of my endeavors. Aren't you concerned with the conditions of employment for the women and children working in our factories?''

After a moment, Merelda responded. Her shoulders remained frozen in her holier-than-thou pose.

"It's not my problem, Annabel, and in my opinion it shouldn't be yours either. I grew up here knowing there were definite cultural differences between the mill village residents and my group of friends. As children we weren't allowed to associate with *lint heads*,'' Merelda scoffed. "This is not Atlanta, Annabel, this is small town America. And you, as an outsider, know nothing about what goes on in a small town where everyone knows everyone else's business.'' She rolled her eyes heavenward. "I shudder to think what would happen to me if my parents learned that I had any part in this ridiculous undertaking.''

Annabel was miffed. Could this be the same person who'd joined in their rallies during college? Then, they had all been for making the world a better place to live.

Unwilling to allow her friend's opinion to pass without a rebuttal, Annabel said, "Small-town prejudice is a better way to describe what you've just told me. Whatever a lint head is, I'm certain it couldn't be any worse than the good telegrapher who made it his business to pry into mine last night when I wanted to send a telegram to my parents.''

Merelda looked horror stricken. "You mean Mr. Sam? He is the worst gossip in two counties. I certainly hope you didn't mention my name.''

"I didn't have to mention it. I only had to write it, and then he gave me the third degree because the Whitcombs didn't meet me in their private carriage and tote me up to the big house.''

Annabel knew she was being catty, but at the moment she didn't care. Merelda's new attitude was not what she had expected to find in her old school chum.

Merelda practically jumped up from the table, scraping her chair across the floor, the hollow sound continuing to echo throughout the cavernous dining room long after she was on her feet.

"I'm sorry, Annabel. I must leave now. I promise I'll

keep the bargain I made with Hollie. If your parents should inquire as to your whereabouts, I'll swear you're staying with me. But other than that, I won't become involved. You must not mention knowing me to anyone as you go about your silly little disguise. If you do, I'll deny our acquaintance and swear I had no part in any of the scheme. Now if you'll excuse me, I have to go.''

Merelda snatched her purse up from the table, turned, and almost ran from the dining room.

Annabel was flabbergasted. She was so taken aback by her friend's unexpected behavior that she didn't have the energy to protest, much less follow Merelda, which is what she knew she should have done.

It felt as though every pair of eyes in the dining room were focused upon her, drilling right through her. Not knowing what else to do, Annabel took a deep breath then picked up the teapot with as much calmness as she could muster for the moment and poured herself another cup of tea.

For the first time, she realized the magnitude of her endeavor. Without Merelda's support, she was totally alone in this foreign little town. Annabel Lowe no longer existed. Until she returned home to Atlanta, the person she had been must stay buried.

She could count on no one but herself, and it was best to begin right now. Annabel picked up the delicate bone china cup and sipped the hot tea. She was careful not to crook her little finger in the same manner of the stylish stranger, Merelda Whitcomb. Her compeer from school no longer existed.

Annabel's forged references lay on top of the desk that separated her from the manager of Royal Mill, Gordon Hamil. Beneath her black bombazine skirt, her knees knocked so badly that she suspected he could hear them, especially if his ogling were any indication. The administrator's pale blue gaze had traversed her person so many times in the last ten minutes that Annabel swore he could see clean through to her undergarments.

The interview made her feel as anxious as a doodlebug lying in wait for its dinner. Although she had studied cotton manufacturing before leaving Atlanta and had reviewed the information again last night in the hotel, Annabel wasn't certain her crash course would help her when facing the manager's many questions.

Gordon Hamil was nothing like his stepbrother, Coit Jackson. They were as different as night and day. Coit's warmth attracted, and Gordon Hamil's aloofness snubbed. For this reason, Annabel chose not to mention to him that she had met his stepbrother on the train yesterday.

He picked up a pencil and began to tap out a rhythm with its leaded end. "We're a much smaller mill than the one you worked for in Macon, Miss Blow. Here, most of our operatives are women and children."

"I'm of the opinion, Mr. Hamil, that most of the cotton mills in the South are staffed by women and children."

His wooden chair squeaked as he leaned back again. With his arms propped on the chair's wooden arms, he balanced the pencil between his two forefingers. "An advantage, wouldn't you say, Miss Blow, for a working girl like yourself?"

"Indeed, sir. I need to work."

Her answer seemed to please him. He placed the pencil back upon his desk and picked up Annabel's references, scanning them before turning his gaze back to hers. "You were a weaver in your last position?" he asked.

"Yes, sir," she fibbed, waiting quietly while he thumbed through the papers again.

Truthfully, the only thing Annabel knew about weaving was what she had learned from a course she'd taken while in college. When she took the class, it had been her desire to connect with the women of past generations who had spent their days spinning and weaving cloth so that their families could be clothed. Still, that knowledge hadn't prepared her for a position as a weaver in a commercial mill. But she was an intelligent woman and had always been a fast learner. Her familiarity with the shuttles and slats of the looms she had used in her weaving class made her confident that she was up to the task she had set for herself. In Annabel's opinion, one loom was like another. Wasn't it?

Gordon Hamil watched her, almost as if he could see what was going on inside her head. "Are you another Penelope?" he asked, "Do you weave by day and unravel by night in order not to choose a mate?" His eyes narrowed suspiciously.

Caught off guard by his questions, she answered him as a scholar. "I'm sorry, sir, but I can't see the parallels between myself and Odysseus' wife."

"You are an unmarried weaver, are you not? Do you know the myth?"

"Of course. Because Penelope was continuously harassed by men who wanted to marry her, she promised her suitors that she would choose a mate only after she had finished weaving a shroud for her father-in-law. As you stated, she wove by day and unraveled by night, managing to put off her admirers until Odysseus returned to Troy from fighting the Trojan War twenty years later."

Before the last words rolled off her tongue, Annabel realized the error she had made. *Why had he asked her such questions? Was he suspicious?* She might know her looms, but at the moment she felt like a *loon* for almost giving herself away. *How many mill workers would know of Penelope's plight?* Not many, she suspected, and his next statement confirmed it.

"I must say, Miss Blow, your knowledge of the classics astounds me."

Annabel laughed nervously. "Classy? Not me, sir. The gents don't consider me elegant and stylish." Feigning silliness, she chattered on foolishly. "But now I understand about the tale. You were curious as to my unmarried state. I guess you could say I'm a Penelope of a sort, but unlike Penelope, I have no fanciful notions about marriage."

Gordon Hamil propped his elbows on the desk and templed his fingers beneath his chin. "But you did know of the myth?"

"There isn't any law that says a mill girl can't read—is there?"

"No law, Miss Blow, but I dare say that knowledge of the classics is most unusual in my operatives."

"But it's like I told you, I'm not classy—"

"Never mind, Miss Blow. It really doesn't matter. Now then, will tomorrow be too soon for you to begin work?"

Relief washed over her. He was going to hire her in spite of her lapse. "Tomorrow will be fine," she told him.

When he stood, Annabel followed, assuming the interview was over.

"I'll have my typewriter, Miss Whiz, show you through the mill and the weaving room where you will be working. Most of my operatives work five days a week for a total of sixty hours. Some work on Saturday as well. In the beginning, I'll put you on a five-day shift. Your papers indicate you have weaving experience, but for the first month or until I see the quality of your work, you'll receive learner's wages in the amount of two dollars a week. I assume you have a place to stay."

"Yes, sir."

She crossed her fingers and hoped he wouldn't ask where. If Merelda's story about there being bad feelings between the brothers was true, she didn't want her new boss to know about her chance meeting with Coit Jackson. Her wish was granted when after several moments Hamil didn't voice an opinion at all. Instead he ignored her response completely and continued issuing instructions.

"Miss Whiz will answer any questions you may have."

He smiled for the first time, but his expression didn't warm his eyes. Stepping from behind his desk, he came around to usher her toward the door.

"Until tomorrow morning, Miss Blow. Seven o'clock sharp. Have a pleasant day getting settled in." With these words, he left her outside his office door.

I did it. I did it. I got the job. But as Annabel's excitement waned, she worried about how she would pull off her new position. The thought of how her co-workers might react when they found out that she was as green as

spring grass when it came to operating a factory loom,
coupled with the knowledge of the salary she would be
earning, almost made the breakfast she'd eaten that morning make a second appearance.

Two dollars a week. How could she support herself on
such a small amount? When she had decided to take this
assignment she had been determined that she would live
on the money she earned while in Dalworth. For this reason, she had only brought enough of her allowance with
her to pay for several weeks' lodging. If she encountered
no unexpected emergencies, she probably could survive.

But she didn't have long to ponder her situation, or
didn't dare to, because the typewriter, Miss Whiz, was
back at her desk. The woman had been absent when Annabel had arrived for her interview with the manager. But
she was very much a presence now. Miss Whiz resembled
Queen Victoria in both bearing and stature. Not a force
to be trifled with.

Oh, well, Annabel thought, taking the chair when the
woman ordered her to sit. They didn't call this the Royal
Mill for nothing.

❖ 4 ❖

ANNABEL'S EARS WERE ringing from the noise of the machines inside the factory, and her eyes and nose itched from breathing the lint-filled air when she finally left the mill and headed toward Coit Jackson and the Company Store.

Fortunately Miss Whiz, in spite of her regal attitude, had proved to be both enlightening on the weaving process as well as a personable woman who seemed to empathize with Annabel's plight. A single woman herself, Miss Whiz knew the importance of getting and keeping a job, especially in a world where women were only beginning to make a place for themselves outside of their homes.

Not only had Annabel left Royal Mill feeling better about the task she had set for herself, but she also felt that she had made a friend of Gegonia Whiz. In Annabel's volatile situation, she considered her good fortune an omen.

The day was still warm when she left the mill property. Pausing on the rise of a hill, she looked back toward the main buildings and warehouses. A soft breeze rustled the leaves of the many oaks that grew on the grounds, cooling her perspiration-dampened skin. She marveled that a mere flutter of nature's breath could make the memory of the uncomfortable two hours she had spent inside the mill almost diminish.

Almost.

Annabel sighed. Was she up to working twelve hours a day? She knew better than anyone that the soft lifestyle she had enjoyed in Atlanta had not prepared her for the demanding conditions of factory work. Most of the weavers she had seen were women and adolescent girls. They appeared to be a hardy bunch who joked and carried on conversations among themselves although the constant hum of machinery made conversation nearly impossible.

The men she saw were mostly troubleshooters for the many machines and did any heavy lifting that required muscular strength. Of course, her two hours had not given her an in-depth view of the factory, but Annabel was awed by the sheer productivity that turned cotton into cloth.

With Gegonia's instructions in her hand on how to get to the Company Store and her friend's assurance that Annabel would get along fine with her landlord, Sara Polk, she turned her back on the mill and headed up Chattanooga Avenue.

As she walked along, her mind foresaw all kinds of problems with her tentative arrangement to let a room. What if Coit Jackson had forgotten about her since their chance meeting on the train, or more importantly, what if he had forgotten to mention her interest in renting Sara's room to the Polks?

If the room was no longer available, she could always return to the Hotel Dalworth for a few more nights. But returning uptown was not what she wished to do. She wanted to settle immediately into the daily routine of living and working in a mill village. It was the only way that Annabel would feel competent in reporting to Washington.

She stopped and looked across the road. As Gegonia had pointed out before she had left Annabel, the streets in the village were all clearly marked. Matilda Street.

Turning her attention away from the sign, she surveyed the whitewashed brick building that stood on the corner. With its wide portico and Doric columns, Coit Jackson's store couldn't compare with the mammoth emporiums that she had frequented in Atlanta. But, she reminded herself, this wasn't Atlanta.

Taking a deep breath to bolster her confidence, which fell in short supply when she thought about her next interview, Annabel squared her shoulders and crossed the street.

It was pickle barrel day in the Company Store. Coit prided himself on having the best pickles in northwest Georgia, or so he'd been told by the many customers who frequented his market. Even a few of Dalworth's old fogey society people who lived uptown from the mill would come by on occasion to purchase his delicious pickles. Today was his day for freshening the brine barrel where he stored his sour pickles.

Coit was elbow-deep in the briny liquid when the bell on the front door jangled. Without looking up to acknowledge his customer, he told the unknown person, "Look around, and I'll be with you shortly."

Since Coit believed the secret to good-tasting pickles was keeping the brine and vinegar solution fresh, he had emptied out the old liquid and was in the process of adding his special seasonings to the new potion.

A touch of mustard, a dab of dill, a pinch of horseradish, and a tad of clove and cinnamon were a few of the pickling spices he added to create a pungent mixture. And of course peppercorns. He had ground up some of the corns and was in the process of sprinkling the pepper into the barrel when he heard the new arrival say, "I'd be happy to relieve you of one of those pickles, if you're in a position to fish me one from the barrel?"

Coit turned his head, his arms still plunged within the limits of the barrel, to stare into the twinkling eyes of Anna Belle Blow. Inside the store, her eyes looked as green and as round as the fat pickles floating below his fingertips. She smiled at him, and his heart tripped against his rib cage where his chest rested against the rim of the barrel.

"You got the job," he said, knowing from the pleased expression on her face that she had.

Her pickle-colored eyes danced. "I did," she said, "and until I walked into this store and smelled those pickles, I hadn't realized how hungry I was."

"Then I reckon I better fish you out one of these slippery little fellows. No one can say that Coit Jackson sends a customer away hungry or dissatisfied. But you'll have to give me a minute."

She smiled at him. "Oh, take your time. I enjoy seeing people work, especially those who really get *into* their jobs."

"I can see you're as outspoken as ever," he quipped, stirring the barrel's liquid. "If you're not careful, I might deny you the enjoyment of tasting one of the best pickles you'll ever eat."

"Do that, Mr. Pickleman, and I'll spread rumors throughout this little burg of the unfair eating practices one starving female suffered at the briny hands of the storekeeper."

"Sit, woman, and learn patience," he ordered teasingly. "If you can't wait a moment for a pickle, nibble on that round of cheese."

Annabel plopped down on one of the round stools bolted to the floor along the counter. She eyed the wheel of cheese on the counter with an expression akin to lust. For a moment, Coit wondered how it would feel to have that same desirous look bestowed upon him, then quickly brushed aside his absurd thoughts, blaming them on the fumes of the pickle brine instead of the coppery-headed woman.

Coit had thought about Anna Belle Blow for a good part of the night and most of the day. He had enjoyed the easy banter they had shared on the train ride from Atlanta. Coit had been waiting all day for her appearance in his store. And here she was, munching away on his cheese like a hungry mouse. Stealing a sideways glance at the lady, he decided that in spite of her ferocious appetite, there was nothing mousy about Anna Belle Blow.

Finished with his blending, Coit straightened and grabbed a towel to wipe his hands. Annabel smiled at him, her cheeks as plump as a chipmunk's, and said between swallows, "I've come about the room."

"And I thought you'd come to taste my pickles."

"That, too," she added, grabbing a handful of crackers from a nearby tin. She nibbled on one.

"I spoke to Sara last night, and she was delighted when I told her about you."

Watching her lick crumbs from her lips, he said, "Sara told me the moment you appeared on my threshold, I'm to deliver you to the Polks' doorstep immediately."

He would do as Sara asked, but right now the woman seemed famished. Besides, if he admitted the truth, Coit was less than anxious to have Annabel leave.

"So you think Sara will rent me her room?"

"You'll be able to knock me over with a feather if she doesn't."

She let out a long audible sigh. Her womanly attributes lifted, then settled comfortably against his counter as she leaned over to slice another wedge of cheese. Coit swallowed, very much aware of the intimate contact of her breasts against the worn wood.

Yep, she has a fine set of lungs. Embarrassed with the direction his thoughts were taking, he asked the first thing that popped into his head. "Can you sing?"

"Sing?" Annabel laughed, the deep throaty sound kindling a spark that blazed a path straight to Coit's toes.

"Oh, no," she answered, "I can't carry a tune in a bucket. In college, my music teacher absolutely forbade me to join the chorus—"

Too late, Annabel realized the folly of her last words. Coit's dark eyes delved into hers with such ferocity that she shivered. His earlier warmth disappeared.

"I mean secondary school," she quickly corrected. Her untruth made her guilt as unpalatable as the rinds of cheese that lay on the cheese board.

The front door slammed against the inside wall, setting the bell to jingling. Two dwarf-sized knights, each dressed in full warrior regalia, burst through the entrance with wooden swords slashing.

Saved by the bell. Annabel, glad for the reprieve, watched as the two knights advanced toward them. The boys were identical twins and looked to be about seven years old.

"Behead the fing," the one leading the charge ordered. The second boy, an exact mirror image of the first, lunged toward a sack of flour with his homemade weapon. Watching the sword's tip come to rest dangerously against the sack's fullness, Annabel expected at any moment to see the bag's contents spill out upon the floor.

Coit, intent on thwarting the disaster, lunged toward the two young warriors. On his knees, he pleaded, "Mighty knights of the Round Table, please deliver this swine from his death."

The twins' identical brown eyes locked. Several charged moments passed before the leader spoke directly to Coit. "What will thou forfeit for the fing's life?"

Watching, Annabel saw that a yellow crown had been appliquéd to the chests of each gunny-sack covering that cloaked the two knights. Around their waists, a strip of wide, green material served as their belts. The same green material was used for their hats, and each hat resembled a paper sailing boat. She was distracted from inspecting the two warriors when she heard Coit's next question.

"Will raisins save the fiend?"

The two exchanged glances before the appointed one answered. "Naw. Ma says we eat too many—they give us indiscretion."

Annabel bit back a laugh.

"Crackers?" Coit asked, continuing to plead for the safety of his goods.

The twins shook their heads in unison while the second

in command replied, "Naw, we just had crackers."

"Then how about a pickle?"

The boys smiled conspiratorially, this time nodding their heads in approval. "Ma said we're to share one, otherwise it'll spoil our supper."

It was apparent to Annabel that the store's proprietor was familiar with the boys' game. In fact, his pleasure warmed her down to the cockles of her heart. Annabel had never met a man who appeared to take pleasure in such simple things as the active imaginations of two small boys. The look he bestowed upon the twins was one of wonder and approval, not unlike the look she had received from Coit before she had let slip her statement about college. Right now, Annabel wanted more than anything to see that look directed toward her again.

The knight whose sword tip was still buried in the heart of the flour sack asked his brother, "Shall we let the fing live?"

"So be it, Sir Brother. We'll enjoy our spoils and celebrate our victory."

Coit kowtowed to the twins. "Thank you, thank you, mighty warriors, for sparing the fiend."

As they moved toward him, one of the boys fished beneath his gunny-sack uniform. Soon he produced a shiny brown penny. "We brung our own money," he said, offering the coin to Coit. "Ma said to make sure you take it this time."

Annabel, who was still sitting on the stool, watched Coit place a hand on each of the green hats and the curly mops of blond hair. He steered the twins toward her. They stopped several feet away from where she perched, their swords at rest by their sides.

"Lance and Percy, this here lady is Miss Blow." The boys studied her with wide-eyed wonder. "These are Sara's children."

Up close she could see that their eyes were the color of melted chocolate. They were handsome children, and it was evident by their stance that they were also loved.

Lance asked, "You gonna be our ma's hoarder?"

"Boarder," Coit corrected, unable to keep from smiling above the twins' heads.

Unable to restrain her own smile, Annabel replied, "Yes—I am, that is, if your mom agrees to rent her room to me."

"Oh, she'll agree all right. We ain't got any females in our house but her," Lance insisted.

"Unless, of course, our baby turns out to be a girl," Percy added. "But it won't matter. Ma said if the good Lord sees fit to give us another boy, we'll love him anyway."

The gentle knight, Annabel thought as she studied Sara Polk's children. If the mother was anything like the boys, she knew she would like her. Annabel didn't have long to reflect on this last thought because the door opened, and a very pregnant woman walked inside the store. The moment the new arrival spied Annabel, she rushed toward her, her hand extended. "I'm Sara Polk and I thought you'd never get here."

Annabel jumped up from the stool, wiped her palms against her skirt, and took Sara's hand in hers. "I'm Anna Belle Blow. I'm so very glad to meet you. Mr. Jackson has told me so much about you, I feel I know you already."

Sara Polk smiled. "I see you've met my knights, Sir Lancelot and Sir Percival. As a child, I loved King Arthur stories." Blushing, she pulled the twins against her by placing a hand on the boys' shoulders. "I hope they remembered their manners." She removed the large green hats from their blond heads.

"Shucks, Ma. You ain't supposed to remove a knight's helmet."

"Knights, my young man, are supposed to act like gentlemen in the presence of a lady."

"She ain't no lady," Lance insisted. "She's gonna be our new—"

"Boarder," Coit interjected.

"Lancelot Polk, she is still a lady, and you'll treat her as such."

The twins responded together. "Yes, ma'am. We're pleased to meet you, lady." Their manners attended to, they turned toward Coit. "Now can we have our pickle?"

"One pickle, coming up."

Coit lifted each boy and set them on a loafing stool. Reaching inside the pickle barrel, he pulled out a mammoth-sized cucumber and, after slicing it down the middle, placed two evenly cut halves in front of each twin.

"I reckon while you boys attack this, your mother can show Miss Blow her soon-to-be room."

Sara looked at him hesitantly. "Would you mind watching them, Coit?"

"Mind? I'd be delighted to host these two scamps. Besides, it's been awhile since we men had a chance to visit."

For the first time since the store's invasion, Coit looked directly at Annabel, but his earlier warmth was missing. Instead, his expression was marked by doubt as he focused his full attention on Sara. "Take your time, ladies— we warriors have some catching up to do."

"Well, Miss Blow, I guess you can come along with me," Sara said.

"Please call me Anna."

"Only if you'll call me Sara."

Exiting the store, the two women fell into step beside each other. They rounded the corner of the building, and Sara led her along a well-worn path that paralleled the long, brick structure.

"You realize that we're Coit's backyard neighbors."

"Yes. He told me that on the train."

"Coit is such a wonderful man and always willing to offer a helping hand to those less fortunate."

Although Annabel knew it wasn't the right time to begin her investigation, she decided to do a little prying anyway. "I understand his stepbrother inherited the mill from their late father."

Sara looked surprised at her statement. "Did Coit tell you that?"

"No. Today when I applied for the position at the mill, Miss Whiz casually mentioned it."

Annabel hated fibbing to Sara, but she couldn't think of another person to credit her information to.

"I'm surprised that Gordon Hamil wasn't the one that filled you in on his importance. He and Coit aren't related by blood, but I understand for a time they lived as brothers and as a family. But all that happened before my Jess and I came to Dalworth."

Surprised, Annabel asked, "Then you're not from the area?"

"No. We're from south Texas. Our parents owned farms, side by side. For years they tried farming the worthless land, until the heat dried up the only water supply for miles around."

"From Texas how did you ever end up here in Georgia?"

Sara blushed. "My Jess and I were married at fifteen. Soon after the wedding, I discovered that I was in the family way. Jess was determined not to be a farmer, especially in Texas, so when he heard about the cotton-mill boom in Georgia, he decided we should come east so he could get a proper job. We left Texas six years ago and have never been back. We now consider the lush green hills of Georgia our home."

Annabel couldn't imagine being married at age fifteen and a year later having twin boys. In fact, Annabel couldn't imagine being married at her present age of twenty-five. Besides, what man in his right mind would marry a headstrong and independent woman like herself? It was like her mother had always threatened—there wasn't a man in all of Dixie that would take a wife like her.

She stole a sidelong glance at her new companion. If the boys, Lance and Percy, were six as she had first suspected, that would make Sara's age close to twenty-two. Suddenly the very vibrant and young woman walking beside her made her feel very dull and ancient. But her dark mood briskly disappeared the moment they stopped at the white picket fence that enclosed the yard at the back of the store. Annabel took a quick breath in utter astonishment.

"This is Coit's garden," Sara told her.

Edging the inside fence, Annabel saw there were sunflowers ranging in height from three to ten feet tall. The taller ones supported blooms that were as big around as dinner plates with purple-brown seedheads that brought to mind brown-faced ladies wearing golden yellow bonnets. To further support the image, a breeze wafted through the thick, hairy green stems, making the bonnet-shaped blossoms bob a curtsy in her direction.

The long buried words of a poem about the sunflower surfaced in Annabel's mind. She spoke them aloud:

> *"Where the Youth pined away with desire,*
> *And the pale Virgin shrouded in snow*
> *Arise from their graves and aspire*
> *Where my Sunflower wishes to go."*

"What a beautiful poem—did you make it up?" Sara asked.

Annabel focused her attention on her companion and smiled gently when she noticed the shine of tears in her dark eyes.

"Heavens, no, but I've always loved to read poetry. Those words were penned by the poet, William Blake."

Sara stepped closer to Annabel. Grabbing her hand, Sara squeezed it affectionately. "Oh, Anna. I just know we're going to be the best of friends. I, too, love poetry."

"I imagined you would." Annabel entwined her fingers with Sara's. "If you didn't have a love for the written word, I daresay you wouldn't have named your boys after King Arthur's legendary knights."

"And this one," Sara said, placing her small hand upon her stomach, "if she's a girl, we'll call her Guinevere."

"Her name could be nothing else."

The two laughed like old and dear friends before Sara lifted the latch that allowed them entrance to Coit's garden. Once inside, Sara pulled Annabel along behind her.

"Those of us who live in mill housing are encouraged to plant gardens. Of course, my own can't compare to Coit's. He is a natural gardener. Everything he touches flourishes."

Annabel could well understand how everything, including herself, might flourish beneath the handsome store owner's touch. Quickly dismissing her naughty thoughts, she was glad that Sara had turned away and couldn't see her blush.

As Sara pulled her through the beautifully landscaped garden, identifying every plant by name, Annabel thought about her mother and what she might think of Coit Jackson's garden.

Her parent had always claimed that sunflowers grew only beside hovels and were not suitable for stately gardens. But as Annabel drank in the sights and smells of the small yard, she realized that Coit's garden rivaled the most formal gardens of her mother's society friends. And unlike the ladies of her mother's realm who never dirtied their hands in the loamy soil, it was evident to Annabel that Coit's garden was a labor of love.

Giant hydrangeas with flowers as large as a small child's head grew in every shade and color. The heady sweet scent of white, red, pink, and violet roses saturated the warm air.

Everywhere Annabel looked there were flowers. She recognized some of the varieties, like the day lilies, but many were new to her. Beneath a vine-covered arbor, bentwood benches, made from flexible pieces of wood, invited guests to rest in the outdoor parlor. Nearby, an algae-covered basin served as the local watering hole for all kinds of birds.

"That's Coit's kitchen garden." Sara pointed to a corner of the yard not far from a veranda that was identical to the one on the front of the building. "He grows the best vegetables in town and gives away more than he sells."

"Quite the gardener, it appears." Annabel studied the

staked vines that held giant tomatoes the color of blood. "Is there anything the man doesn't do well?"

Sara paused at the fence that divided the Polks' yard from Coit's. "Like I said earlier, Coit is a wonderful man."

Annabel looked back across the stretch of yard they had passed through. It was indeed a fine garden, and somehow it seemed right that the man she'd met on the train would have cultivated his private piece of paradise. From all accounts, he seemed to be a mortal angel, at least in Sara Polk's opinion.

As though her thoughts had conjured up the earthly spirit, Coit Jackson appeared on the back veranda. He stood watching them, his hands tucked inside his pockets. From the distance of several hundred feet, Annabel could see that he scowled when his gaze lit on hers.

"We'll only be a few more minutes," Sara called when she saw Coit. The twins were busy pumping the twigged porch swing where it hung on long, loudly creaking chains.

"Take your time, ladies. I wouldn't want *either of you* to rush into anything."

To Annabel who followed Sara into the adjoining yard, Coit's statement sounded like a warning. Apparently the company store owner was having second thoughts about his introducing Annabel to Sara. Not that his opinion mattered one whit to Annabel. Ignoring his remark, she fell into step beside Sara. As far as Annabel was concerned, he was the last person whose approval she wanted.

Coit watched the two women make their way through the back gate of the connecting yards. In Coit's opinion, not everything about Anna Belle Blow rang true. With one shoulder propped against a white column of the veranda, he watched the gentle sway of her hips and the queenly straightness of her spine as she followed in Sara's footsteps. Even Miss Blow's walk bordered on being regal.

Perhaps if he hadn't caught her in a fib, his willingness

to believe that she was who she claimed to be wouldn't be so hard to swallow. Her statement about her music teacher in college, the expensive lace dickey she had apparently discarded on her trip here from Atlanta, and several other slips of her tongue made Coit suspicious of her identity. It was his feeling that Miss Blow was much too refined for a mill worker.

Behind him, the twins giggled as they swung backward and forward in the old swing. On another day, he might have joined them, but today he was preoccupied with the redhead who followed their mother. The two women paused beneath a big magnolia whose leaves looked like green satin in the late afternoon light. An errant ray of sun fell on Anna Belle's hair, making its color look like polished copper. At that moment, he wondered how it would feel to run his fingers through the coppery strands and felt a tightening in his groin.

Something Sara said to Anna Belle made her laugh. The sound of her deep throaty laughter floated to him on the warm air, along with the bird sounds that issued from the tree's branches, and a honeybee that buzzed the nearby rose bushes.

In spite of his suspicions about the woman, Coit liked her.

Behind him, the boys roughhoused in the swing. His concentration was so tuned to the woman in the adjoining yard that he was nearly knocked off balance when the twins captured his knees. Lance hung on one leg and Percy on the other. Using Coit's legs as a shield, they swayed from side to side in unison, hiding from each other.

Suddenly all motion stopped. Lance, the more outspoken of the two, had stopped swinging and now eyed the front of Coit's britches and the evident bulge beneath the buttoned fly of his pants.

"Mr. Coit, you gotta pee?" the child asked.

Coit who usually wasn't surprised by the words that came from the mouths of babes, especially the twins, felt the weight of his embarrassment. *Just his luck to be lust-*

ing after a woman while in the company of two outspoken little boys.

"Ma says when your dingle gets full, it's a sure sign you need to take a trip to the outhouse."

Percy, who also had discovered Coit's apparent discomfort, stared at his bulging trousers with unabashed innocence.

Coit felt the heat under his collar. "I believe your ma is right, boys. Why don't the three of us take a little hike?"

Without a backward glance at what they considered to be an unremarkable occurrence, the boys sprinted off the porch and dashed toward the outhouse that the two families shared.

As Coit trudged along behind the twins, he said a prayer of thanks for Sara's teachings; otherwise he might have had a hard time explaining his present condition. Heck, he couldn't explain it to himself. But one thing he knew. It would take more than a trip to the outhouse to relieve what ailed his dingle.

Kids said the darndest things. His wonder deepened into jovial laughter.

✦ 5 ✦

ANNABEL'S FIRST NIGHT in the Polks' home was proving to be a restless one. Flopping onto her back, she stared at the pristine white ceiling above her head. The homespun curtains that hung over the open windows swelled like ghosts on the gentle breeze. Suspended between her troubled thoughts and near exhaustion, she lay awake. No matter how many sheep she counted inside her head, she still couldn't fall asleep.

Perhaps it was the strangeness of the environment, or more readily, Coit Jackson's obvious indifference to her that had her in a quandary. When she had returned to his store after touring Sara's room and agreeing to rent it, Coit had ignored her completely, speaking only to Sara. For reasons beyond Annabel's understanding, Coit's scorn had hurt. The realization that their friendship had withered before it had been given a chance to grow brought tears to her eyes now. Disgusted with herself, Annabel hit the pillow ticking to fluff it, then buried her face in the sun-bleached smell of the muslin sheets.

Although everyone she knew in the small town of Dalworth had deserted her—first Merelda and then Coit—she believed she still had Sara's friendship. But the way

her luck had been running lately, the Lord only knew how
long it would be before her landlady turned against her,
too.

No one likes a headstrong, outspoken woman, her conscience reminded her as though her mother had spoken
the words aloud. Could it be that her mother was right?

The thought of her parent brought a heaviness to her
chest. *Mother and Father. I miss them both.* Who would
have believed that Annabel Lowe, independent woman of
the nineties, would long to see her parents? But she did.
She missed her mother's opposition and her father's support. When she rolled onto her back, tears pooled in her
eyes and spilled over, cooling her heated skin as they slid
down the sides of her face and into her hairline.

Disgusted, she sat up and tossed the pillow aside. For
the first time in her life, Annabel was suffering a bout of
homesickness. Not even during her first weeks at college
had she felt as blue as she did at the moment. Could it
be she was going soft at the ripe old age of twenty-five?

"This has to stop," she said out loud as she jumped
up from the bed and began to pace.

Moonlight slipped past the curtains, lighting the small
square room with its whitewashed walls and polished
wooden floors. Sara had done her best to make the room
comfortable for her boarder by adding splotches of color
in the rag rugs strewn about the room, and in the crazy
quilt that served as a spread on the narrow iron bed.

Crocheted doilies covered the bedside table and the top
of the four-drawer chest. There was a solid oak rocker for
sitting, an oil lamp for reading, and a china bowl and
pitcher for washing. Nothing like the rich furnishings in
the Lowe home in Atlanta that Annabel was used to, but
comfortable and eye-pleasing. Knowing Sara, Annabel believed that each piece was chosen not only for function,
but also for its simplicity of line.

Framed samplers hung on two walls, one that Annabel
knew Sara must have completed as a child because of its
date, the other more recently because of its message.

Baby—A sweet new blossom of humanity,
fresh fallen from God's own home,
to flower on earth.

As Annabel reread the Massey proverb in the faint
moonlight, she began to feel better. The sage words
seemed to strike a chord inside her, reminding her again
of her purpose for being in Dalworth. It no longer mattered that Merelda had made it clear she didn't support
Annabel's mission, or that Coit Jackson no longer wished
to be her friend.

But what did matter was her reason for being in town.
She had come to investigate the working conditions of the
women and children of the Royal Mill. If she could fulfill
her obligation, then perhaps her findings would make life
easier for the blossoms Sara referred to in her sampler.

With this resolved in her mind, Annabel crawled back
into the iron bed. She smiled at the sound of the bed's
joints creaking when they accepted her weight. Soon after
returning to the feather mattress, Annabel's soft feminine
snore joined the chorus of other night sounds beyond the
window. Her dreams were filled with sunflowers, each
centered with the face of a smiling child.

Dawn had come too early, Annabel decided, as she
plodded along the street that edged the Polks' and Coit
Jackson's property. Purposely she'd chosen to take the
street to the mill, instead of cutting through the adjoining
yards, presuming that she would have less of a chance of
encountering the company store owner by doing so.

If Mr. Jackson no longer wanted to be her friend, then
so be it. She could be just as cool as the next fellow.

The oatmeal that Sara had prepared for breakfast lay in
Annabel's stomach like a lump of clay. She had forced
down the hot cereal at Sara's insistence, but now she
wished she'd passed up breakfast entirely.

Annabel was so nervous she felt she might spill the
contents of her stomach onto Coit Jackson's pretty picket
fence at any moment. Considering the status of their pres-

ent relationship, she felt the *comeuppance* would serve him right; but, fearing she might soil the edge of her skirt, she swallowed back the nausea and continued on her way.

Gordon Hamil had said for her to report to the mill at seven o'clock sharp. Annabel intended to be there early.

Walking along, she swung the lunch pail that Sara had fixed for her noonday meal. The sun was barely peeking over the horizon, and as the fiery ball climbed higher, its rays gilded the low-lying clouds and the tops of the distant trees.

Last night's dew sweetened the early morning air, making the loamy scent of soil and the musky smell of compost pleasantly stronger. Annabel inhaled deeply of the summer-scented yards and hurried on her way. She planned to cross the street in front of the store and, she hoped, go undetected by the store's owner. Besides, she reasoned, he was probably still in bed.

"Morning, Miss Blow."

Annabel nearly jumped out of her skin. The tin lunch pail that she'd been swinging in time with her springy gait slipped from her fingers and rolled several feet ahead.

"You scared the living daylights out of me," she scolded, scampering to retrieve the errant pail. "What are you doing lurking about in the shadows so early?"

Coit chuckled. "Are you always so cheerful in the morning?" He moved from his position against the column and would have helped her retrieve the pail, but she dismissed him with a wave of her hand.

"Always," she acknowledged, without glancing his way.

Instead of helping her, Coit lifted his coffee cup in a salute. "Beg your pardon, Miss Blow, but it has been my practice now for many years to lurk in the shadows while enjoying my morning coffee. I am sorry if I frightened you."

"I bet you are," she muttered beneath her breath. Just as Annabel was about to regain the pail, her foot bumped it and sent it rolling several more feet beyond her reach.

Coit scrambled to assist her, but again Annabel brushed

aside his offer to help. "I'll get it myself," she told him.

This time Coit ignored her order and joined in the chase. "What do you have in that pail anyway? A 'possum?"

As they chased the rolling bucket, he continued to tease her. "It's my understanding that 'possums like to hide in hollow tree trunks and empty containers. The crafty little critters have been known to roll to safety if the need should arise."

She eyed him skeptically. "Mr. Jackson, since my familiarity with the opossum is sorely lacking, I must admit I know nothing of the animal's habits. But one thing I do know, Sara Polk doesn't strike me as one who would feed her family, or her boarder, opossum."

"A point well made, Miss Blow."

Annabel's fingers closed around the pail's handle just as Coit scooped it up with his hands. They slammed to a standstill, their bodies clashing together like waves against the shore. The intimate contact made them jerk apart as though they had been doused by an icy sea.

For what seemed like hours, they stared into each other's eyes, their faces flushed. Several moments passed before either moved, and it was Annabel who finally broke the spell. "My pail, Mr. Jackson. I need to be on my way."

As Coit watched Anna Belle flounce down the street as though the hounds of hell were nipping at her heels, he believed the only thing that would eliminate his need was to have her impaled on his body. Although the contact between them had been brief, Coit couldn't deny his body's reaction to her curvy softness. He'd had enough experience with women to know that she'd been just as aware of the currents that had flowed between them.

"Damnation," he mumbled, kicking a rock with the toe of his shoe. "Enough of this mooning over a female." Coit swung around and headed back toward the store.

It was bad enough that he'd been awake most of the night because of the redhead. Usually a sip of fine whiskey and a good cheroot would cure his body's yearnings for a woman, but last night neither whiskey nor a smoke had exorcised Miss Blow from his mind.

Not only was his head filled with yearnings he had no right to entertain, but also he was angry with his treatment of her yesterday. Finally, in the wee hours of the morning, before he'd fallen asleep in the swing on the back veranda, Coit had made a decision. He had never been one to judge another, or to be suspicious of a complete stranger who'd been nothing but pleasant since their first meeting. Coit was ashamed of his earlier behavior, his downright rudeness to her without proper cause.

He had awakened this morning in the swing with a crick in his neck and a determination to put aside his doubts about Miss Blow and begin again. Unfortunately the damage had already been done. Today, when he'd tried to tease her about the 'possum, the warmth in her eyes was no longer there.

Coit knew he deserved her cool indifference, but he wanted it to be the way it had been when they first met on the train. He had enjoyed the easy banter they had shared before he became suspicious of her identity. But with this last episode—an episode that had left them both shaken—Coit wondered if they would ever be able to return to the easy companionship. He told himself that he didn't want to bed the lady; he just wanted to be her friend.

Renewed determination accompanied him as he returned to the interior of his store. He would make things right between himself and Sara's boarder. As far as his basic biological drive, he would force out his desire for the woman with physical labor. Before the day was over, every shelf and item in his store would receive a good dusting.

By the time Annabel entered the factory compound, the sun had risen enough to burn off the gossamer patches of early-morning fog that hugged the ground like silky cobwebs. Pausing inside the fence, she took a deep breath to calm herself and reached for the hankie tucked beneath her sleeve. She blotted her perspiring face with the lacy confection. Annabel felt hot all over.

"That man's going to be the death of me," she said to no one in particular before she moved forward again.

"No man is worth the death of a comely woman."

Startled by the intrusion into what she believed had been her unspoken thoughts, Annabel jerked around to face the voice's carrier.

Gordon Hamil tipped his hat and fell into step beside her. Together they moved toward the factory. "It appears that you are not only an intelligent woman," he said, pulling his fob watch from his vest pocket and checking the time, "but you are punctual as well. And if your earlier statement about a man who will be the death of you means what I think it does, someone must consider you attractive."

He looked her over with the same intensity as he had the day before, his gaze lingering long enough to make her feel uncomfortable. "Do I know the local swain?"

Wanting to tell him that her personal life was none of his business, but knowing that such a response might jeopardize her new position at the factory, Annabel bit back the words she wanted to say. "I assure you, sir, there is no swain local or otherwise who considers me attractive."

Gordon Hamil chuckled at her remark.

"I'm pleased to hear it, Miss Blow, but don't sell your appearance short. As I said yesterday, you don't fit the usual mold of the women who work for Royal Mill. I'd hate to lose such a promising employee before she has time to shake the lint from her skirts. Especially to one of our locals."

Not waiting for her to respond, he tipped his hat again and took the forked path that led toward the company office. Annabel squared her shoulders and continued on toward the factory, puzzling over his remarks.

"Mercy," she grumbled. The only men she had met since her arrival in Dalworth happened to be brothers, and it was rumored that they were enemies. Both men left her feeling unsettled, but for entirely different reasons.

Annabel laughed to herself. What would Gordon Hamil think, if he knew the local swain who might cause her death was none other than his stepbrother? It was too much to take in, so she pushed her thoughts aside when she stopped several feet away from the entrance to the main building.

Men, women, and children passed her and nodded a greeting before continuing inside. She responded in kind, but her feet remained rooted to the spot where she had stopped. The Royal Mill workers didn't look like drudges, or even like individuals who were unhappy in their roles. Instead, they chatted casually among themselves while the children accompanying them played a game of tag.

Children, Annabel thought, should be attending school instead of working in a factory. Surely if there wasn't a public school for them to attend, then the mill should provide a place for their education.

She thought of Sara's twins. In a few years, would they also join the other children who already worked in the factory? Knowing what she did of Sara Polk and her husband, Jess, Annabel suspected that Lance and Percy would be attending school.

Although it was nearly time for her to be in the weaving room, she remained where she was for a few more minutes. Gegonia Whiz had mentioned yesterday that she would try to catch Annabel before she started work today. Besides, she reasoned, she needed a few minutes to calm her nerves. Taking several deep breaths, she studied the structure before her.

From her earlier research on industrial mills, the Royal Mill with its traditional architecture was not unlike the other mills that were being built in small towns throughout the South. The exterior was of brick and the building stood three stories high. Segmental brick arches topped the doors and windows. Above the main entrance on the peaked roof was a tower and belfry. As Annabel stood before the leaded-glass entrance, she felt as if she could be entering the urbane walls of a church instead of the rustic walls of a factory where women and children worked equally as hard as men.

Suddenly she was jerked from her reverie by Gegonia Whiz's arrival. "I see you're here already."

Annabel smiled at her friend from yesterday. "I'm here."

"Mr. Hamil told me he'd seen you on the path earlier. You impressed him with your promptness."

"I'm glad I impressed him with something." Annabel patted the twisted knot of hair at the back of her head. "After our interview yesterday, I felt that he thought my qualifications were grievously lacking."

"Believe me, dear, Gordon Hamil makes everyone feel that way. He is a man of little praise and large criticism. You'll hear about your inadequacies long before you hear about your adequacies."

"In other words, I should strive for perfection to keep the hound at bay."

"Precisely. But don't fret about Gordon Hamil's bite overly much. He likes to appear watchful." Gegonia placed her hand on Annabel's arm. "Come, we had best get inside. Birdie, another weaver, has been assigned to help you out today. She's anxious to meet you."

Falling into step beside the older woman, Annabel told her, "I'm more nervous than I thought I would be."

"That's to be expected, sweet. But I'm confident you'll do just fine."

As the door closed behind the twosome, Annabel issued a silent prayer. *Lord in heaven, give me the strength to succeed.*

On the second floor of the building that was designated as the weaving room, Gegonia led Annabel through the long aisles of now silent looms. Since it was not quite seven o'clock, women and a few older girls gathered in small groups, talking among themselves. Everyone Gegonia and Annabel passed greeted them cheerfully and offered Annabel words of welcome. She remembered seeing some of the women yesterday on her quick tour of the factory.

Soon Gegonia reached her destination. She stopped beside a young woman who looked more like a child than an adult.

"Birdie, this here is Anna Belle Blow. She's the new weaver I told you about yesterday afternoon."

The woman called Birdie grasped Annabel's hand in greeting. "May I call you Anna?" she asked.

"Yes," Annabel replied. "I'm pleased to make your acquaintance and want you to know how much I appreciate your consenting to help me through this first day."

"She's a bit nervous," Gegonia added.

Birdie smiled in understanding. "We've all had first days on the machines, and we've all been nervous. That's why we encourage partnering-up with new operatives. Since we started the buddy system, our overall accident rate has decreased."

"Sounds good to me," Annabel told the two women.

Beneath her calm exterior, Annabel suddenly felt nervous. She never considered that she would be putting herself in harm's way by working at the mill. But the announcement of possible mishaps brought home to Annabel just how ill-prepared she was for this experience. She wondered if she looked as queasy as she felt.

The two women exchanged knowing glances, and Gegonia patted her arm. "I had best get back to the office. Mr. Hamil gets nervous if I'm away from my desk too long." Her gaze locked on Annabel. "Perhaps I'll see you at lunch."

"When do we eat lunch?"

"We eat in shifts here."

"Is there a particular place to eat?" Annabel asked.

"Yes. When the weather is nice, we eat outside beside the spring house and reservoir. There are picnic tables under the trees for our use. Most of the time it's very pleasant."

"Sounds good to me," Annabel repeated and felt herself color. *They must think my head is as empty as last year's birdnest.*

For the first time in her life, she felt as though her

command of the English language had completely left her. In school, she had received her highest marks in oration, but today she was reduced to uttering banal statements of no importance. *Respond intelligently, Annabel.*

Suddenly the machinery throughout the long room began to roar, pushing all thoughts from her head. The weavers had taken their places at their assigned looms and had begun the weaving process. All Annabel could do was to gape at the many rows of looms that with the flick of a main switch had come to life. The machinery clamored noisily like an awakened prehistoric beast. She wanted to plug her ears with her fingers.

Above the noise, Birdie shouted. "This morning, these four looms are assigned to us. This afternoon, depending on how you progress, two more will be added. Tomorrow I suspect, you'll be operating four at one time. That's usually what each of us weavers handle."

"Four?"

Annabel nearly choked on the word, or perhaps it was the sizable quantity that took her breath away. In her weaving class in college, she'd had trouble operating one loom. Now she was expected to operate four? All at the same time?

Birdie moved away from her down the aisle. Positioning herself between the four looms, she motioned for Annabel to follow her. "You did work as a weaver in Macon, didn't you?" she asked.

"I did," Annabel fibbed, "but it's been awhile since I've worked."

"Well, it will come back to you, I'm sure. For the time being, you just watch me."

"Yes, that's a good idea. I'll watch you."

Birdie was a study in efficiency. The longer Annabel watched her the more convinced she became that Birdie had received her name because of her looks. She reminded Annabel of a gray-cheeked thrush with her dull gray-brown hair, sallow skin, and the conspicuous rings beneath her large eyes.

She was slender but strong-legged, if the dexterity with

which she darted from one loom to the next was any indication. Above the clatter of the machines, Birdie's voice, thin and nasal, chirped out information to Annabel, explaining exactly what she was doing, and her reason for doing it—almost as though she sensed that Annabel knew nothing about the weaving process.

"It's our responsibility," Birdie told her, "to see that the yarn is threaded correctly and watch for flaws in the weaving process. Basically we oversee the running of the machines. That's why we must be familiar with the entire weaving process so if anything goes wrong, we'll recognize it immediately and can correct the mistake before it turns into a real disaster."

Everything Birdie did, Annabel watched. Lucky for her, she had a quick mind, and only had to be told once about the function of each part of the loom.

As the morning wore on, Annabel was given the responsibility of running one loom. It amazed her how similar the power looms were to the hand looms she had used in her college weaving class. Of course, everything in the factory was automated and worked at a much greater speed.

Soon the parts of the machine became familiar to her. She could identify the shuttle that carried the quill of filling yarn back and forth across the loom. She learned that the shed was a V-shaped opening formed by warp yarns and was controlled by the harness. As for the harness, Annabel couldn't keep track of the rapid movement, for that part of the loom flew faster than the eye could see.

By mid-morning, Annabel could identify the beam, the dobby, the heddle, and the drop wires. She learned that the ends of the warp yarns were threaded through these wires. If an end should break, the wire would drop, causing the loom to stop automatically.

Birdie had emphasized that any stoppage was costly to the plant, and for that reason, any error needed to be corrected immediately. Even when the workers stopped for lunch, their looms were manned by other weavers so as not to slow down the weaving process. The Royal Mill

turned out four thousand yards of quality sheeting a day.
The weaving went on continuously, from sunup to sundown, regardless of the weariness of the operatives.

Only when Annabel felt Birdie tap her on the shoulder,
announcing that it was lunch time, did she realize how
weary she was. Her lungs felt full of cotton lint, her eyes
were irritated from the minute yarn particles floating in
the close air of the weaving room, and her throat was as
parched as a desert. Thankful for the forty-five-minute
lunch break the operatives were allowed, she followed
Birdie from the building.

"Come along, Anna. You'll feel much better after you
drink some water and get some food in your stomach."

Annabel stopped and slapped her hand across her
mouth. "My lunch, I forgot it." She had been so tired
that she had forgotten to retrieve her bucket when she'd
left the second floor.

"I brought it," Birdie told her, holding up the lunch
Sara had fixed that morning.

Gratefully Annabel accepted the pail. "You're a saint."

It seemed like weeks, instead of hours, since she'd bid
Sara goodbye and had confronted Coit Jackson. She only
hoped her lunch had survived being kicked across the
ground like a football, because she felt hungry enough to
eat a horse.

Or so she thought until she flopped down beside Gegonia at one of the many picnic tables. Other mill employees sat in groups under the tall oaks. Outside the
factory, the air was much cooler. A gentle breeze fluttered
the overhead leaves and rippled the water's surface in the
nearby brick-lined reservoir.

Birdie introduced her to the other workers, but Annabel
was too tired to offer more than a polite response. When
Gegonia handed her a tin cup filled with water, she
downed the contents like a man dying of thirst.

"How you holding up?" Gegonia asked, refilling the
cup a second time from a pail that sat in the center of the
table.

"She's doing fine," Birdie answered for her. "Already

she's running one loom, and I expect before the day is over she'll be running more.''

''Or they'll be ruining—running me.'' Annabel was so exhausted she couldn't keep her thoughts straight, and the day was only half over.

''Eat,'' the two women urged her. ''You'll feel better.''

After swallowing two more cups of water, Annabel's appetite had completely fled. The two biscuits with honey and the apple Sara had packed for her lunch no longer had any appeal. All she wanted to do was lie down and sleep for a week.

''Eat,'' Gegonia insisted again. ''If you don't, you won't make it through the remainder of the day.''

''But I'm not hungry.''

Because of the two women's repeated insistence, Annabel finally brought one of the honied biscuits to her mouth and took a bite. It tasted like the lint she had been inhaling for most of the morning. She did manage to force down one biscuit and take several bites of the apple along with another cup of water before she pushed the food aside.

''A short nap is what you need,'' Birdie said. ''I often nap on my lunch break. Lay your head on your arms and close your eyes. You'll feel like a new person when you wake up.''

Again Annabel found herself doing as she was told. She crossed her arms on the table, and propped her head in the square made by her arms. At first she fought the pull of sleep, trying to listen to the conversations going on around her. Her mind told her that she should be gathering information from these folks, but even her responsibility couldn't keep the much needed nap at bay, or the realization of how hard the women and children of Royal Mill worked from sunup to sundown five or six days a week.

Now that the machines no longer thundered in her ears, she heard the birds in the trees. The harsh slurring note of a blue jay's *queedle, queedle* was music to her still ringing ears. Not far from her feet at the edge of the table, a sparrow nibbled at crumbs someone had sprinkled across the grass. She watched the tiny dingy-brown bird until it was startled into flight by someone's loud laughter. The soft murmer of conversation filtered in and out of her head, and her eyelids grew heavier. Soon she gave herself over to the sweet oblivion of sleep.

"Time to go, gal." Birdie gently shook Annabel's shoulder, rousing her from a deep slumber.

Her eyes blinked open. Several moments passed before she sat up. She groped for wakefulness, trying to orient herself to her strange surroundings. Annabel's gaze focused on Birdie who was the only person besides herself still left at the tables.

"We need to get back. Are you up to it?"

Annabel placed her hands at the back of her waist and stretched. "How long did I sleep?"

"Almost a half hour."

"A half hour? I must have been more tired than I realized."

"I would say so. It's my guess you didn't sleep much last night either."

"Now, how did you know that?" She was surprised at how well the little woman could read her.

Birdie chuckled. "Like I told you earlier, we've all had first days with restless nights worrying about first days."

"You all must think me ridiculous. No one else snored away their lunch break."

Annabel felt foolish. Everyone had gone without her even being aware of them leaving.

"Your snoring drove everyone away."

"My snoring—oh!" She covered her face in embarrassment.

"Regardless of what they say about ladies not snoring, you proved it isn't true."

"Oh, no, I didn't," Annabel groaned.

Her friend laughed heartily. "Of course you didn't," she teased. Birdie stood up. "Come along, Miss Anna. We have looms waiting."

*   *   *

When the whistle sounded to announce the end of the day, Annabel had no strength left. Although her short nap had restored her for a few hours, when quitting time rolled around, the minutes seemed to be cast in stone.

She had been on her feet for nearly ten hours straight, standing all day on the hard floors. Her legs and feet ached, and her back, shoulders, and neck were stiff. But as Annabel left the factory with the other women and children she'd worked beside throughout the long day, she enjoyed a feeling of accomplishment.

By quitting time, she'd been in charge of four looms and had encountered no problems with any. Now if she could summon the strength to walk up the hill to her little rented room, Annabel knew that she'd have no trouble sleeping tonight.

"You have a nice weekend, you hear," Birdie said as they exited the fenced-in area. Birdie lived with her family at the opposite end of the mill village.

"Weekend."

"Yes, gal. I won't see you until Monday."

Again Annabel's reasoning had left her. Of course, tomorrow was Saturday. Having arrived in Dalworth on Wednesday, she had only been in town for three days. But with everything that had happened since her arrival, Annabel had lost all track of time.

"You rest up real good these two days, and I'll see you at first light on Monday." Having said her piece, Birdie waved goodbye and left Annabel where she stood.

Forcing her aching bones to move once again, Annabel turned and headed up the street toward the Polk residence.

Two blissful days with nothing to do but sleep. How lucky could a working girl get?

❖ 6 ❖

ON FRIDAY EVENINGS, the Company Store was the gathering place for some of the mill workers who usually stopped in on their way home from the factory to settle their accounts and for some socializing.

This evening was no different from any other Friday, except tonight Coit only half listened to the buzz of conversation going on around him. Instead, his attention was focused on the plate-glass windows at the front of the store and the street that ran by the door. Ever since he'd heard the whistle that announced the end of the work day at the mill, Coit had been waiting and watching, hoping to catch a glimpse of Anna Belle Blow on her way home from work.

He had spent his day dusting and cleaning. The shelves and floors were so squeaky clean that his own mother would have thought nothing of eating off the wooden supports, but God rest her soul that wasn't possible—Lucille Jackson Hamil had met her maker several years past. Coit still missed her today.

The six loafing stools, so-named by the locals, were all filled. The stools with their rotating wooden seats were fastened atop iron posts to the floor and paralleled his oak counter. This evening the worn seats supported both the fleshy and bony rumps of a half dozen loafers.

Most of the women had made their purchases and then hurried home to prepare supper for their men. This last hour before closing was normally reserved for the men-folk to allow themselves to relax and unwind, sip a soda, and munch on salt crackers before they joined their families at home.

"Got a joke to tell y'all," Abner Todd announced to the others.

Coit only pretended interest in the man's story while he served himself a sarsaparilla. As he took a long swallow of the sweetened carbonated drink made from sassafras and birch oil, his gaze never strayed from the front of the store.

Abner began telling his joke: "Elsie the cow was on one side of the fence, and Ferdinand the bull was on the other side. Elsie gave Ferdinand a wink, and he leaped over the fence to her side. 'Aren't you Ferdinand the bull?' she asked. 'Just call me Ferdinand; the fence was higher than I thought.' "

Everyone laughed, and Abner slapped his bony knee. Coit joined in the merriment. He appreciated a good joke as much as the next fellow.

Sometimes the stories the men told got really risqué, but most of the facetious tales were like this one—playfully jocular. Coit preferred this kind, especially if there were still women and children shopping.

Inside the Company Store the talk was easy, relaxed. Men who worked long hard hours throughout the day were gathered as friends along Coit's counter.

A married man by the name of Harve began to tease the only other bachelor besides Coit in the group. All ears were in tune to the baiting.

"Guess that will learn you not to be jumping fences, young Paul. Wouldn't want you to lose your manhood before you got a chance to try it out."

The listeners chuckled, and the tall, skinny youth

known as Paul swallowed, his Adam's apple bobbing like
a cork inside his turkey-neck throat.

"I hear tell that new redheaded warp and woofer has
had you jumping territory all day long." The older man
guffawed. "Heard you'd been in the weaving room more
than in the picking room today."

It was not uncommon among the workers for the young
ones to take the brunt of their elders' teasing. The story-
teller was pleased when young Paul's complexion turned
three shades ruddier. His remark about Anna Belle had
gotten all the men's attention, especially Coit's.

"She's a looker all right." Harve turned his attention
to Jess Polk who was a man of few words, but well liked
by his fellow workers. His easygoing attitude reminded
those who knew him of warm molasses.

"How is it, Jess, that someone as homely as you has
all the luck? Before, you had only one beautiful woman
living under your roof. Now you got two."

Jess took a long swallow from his soda pop. "Like I
told you before, Harve. It's not looks women are interested in."

"Then what the hell is it? Tell young Paul here."
Harve slapped the stringy youth on his back. "Seems
when the boy was born, he thought he heard the Lord was
handing out books instead of looks, and he shouted he
didn't want none. Now, if a fella ever needed to know
your secret, it's young Paul." Harve draped his arm
around the lad who sat beside him on a neighboring stool.

Jess hesitated only a moment. Then he grinned. Coit
knew that grin well. He had seen its effect on Sara, and
all the other ladies Jess chanced to bestow it upon. He
had a smile that could charm the biter off a mosquito.

In his smooth drawl, Jess told them, "It's charm, fellas.
You've either got it or you don't."

"Charm. Shoot." Harve slammed his empty bottle
back down on the counter. "The only charm you know
about is the one hanging around your neck."

Still grinning, Jess fingered the wedding band he wore
on a chain. Men who worked around machinery didn't

wear rings on their fingers. It was too easy for rings to get caught and tear a finger off a hand. But Jess Polk was never seen without his band of gold. In respect for Sara, he wore it like a charm around his neck. "Like I told you before, Harve. You've either got it or you don't."

"Well, I reckon those two ladies we spoke of earlier are awaiting right now for you and all your charm. So I reckon you better be on your way."

Jess placed his bottle back on Coit's counter. "You know, I was thinking that myself. I reckon I'll mosey on home." He grinned again, his slow easy smile lighting up his thin face. "Can't keep the ladies waiting now, can I?"

He strolled toward the front door. Paul, who'd recovered from his earlier embarrassment, called after him as he passed. "Jess, how about putting in a good word for me with that purty lady boarder?"

Abner, who'd been quiet until now, put in his two cents' worth. "Paul, you better wait until you grow some whiskers."

"Whiskers!" Insulted, the youth rubbed his hand across his pimply skin. "I got whiskers. I'll have you know I use the strop and razor at least once a week."

"Once a week," the men echoed.

Harve stood up and scratched his belly. "Take my advice, sonny. Quit that shaving. If you do and you're real lucky, you might grow yourself a beard by the time you're thirty. I hear tell women like men with beards. Especially redheaded women." He elbowed the young man in the ribs.

As though Harve's standing was a signal to the others, they stood as well. The gab session was over.

"Put this here snack on my bill," Harve told him.

The others gave instructions for Coit to do the same with their tabs. But tonight Coit wouldn't do it. On some Fridays he assumed the cost of their snacks. This was Coit's way of keeping the men's bills within a reasonable limit. Besides, he had more money than the most of them, and he enjoyed treating his friends.

Coit followed them. It was nearly eight o'clock and

time for him to close up shop. After seeing the men out the door, he called a good night and flipped the *Open* sign to *Closed*. Leaving the interior of the store, he headed for his apartment at the back of the building.

Once inside his quarters, he loosened his collar and rolled up the sleeves of his shirt. The minute the men had started talking about the redheaded weaver, their conversation had gotten Coit's attention. So much so that he had completely forgotten to watch for Miss Blow's passing. Because of it, he had missed her altogether.

Earlier in the day, he had thought about making a big salad for his supper, but after listening to the men's conversation, his appetite had completely fled. Who would have believed that Miss Blow, who in his opinion wasn't the prettiest woman Coit had ever known, had attracted the young, still-wet-behind-the-ears Paul?

In Coit's opinion, the young whelp had a face only a mother could love. But mother love wasn't the point. If one male was attracted to Miss Blow, that might mean there were others. *Now why in the devil should it matter?* For reasons Coit couldn't explain, it mattered a lot.

Not that he had any claims on Miss Blow. In fact, he didn't entirely trust who she claimed to be. But this morning he had decided to put his doubts about Sara's boarder aside and give her his friendship instead. That was, if the lady would still accept it.

Anna Belle had a wonderful sense of humor, and he felt comfortable in her presence. When he thought about it, she wasn't all that homely either. Even though she had red hair, freckles, and eyes the same color as his pickles. He had never favored copper-headed women, yet Anna Belle Blow had secured his interest from their first meeting. Could it be that he wanted more than friendship from her?

Of course not. He only wanted to be her friend, and since they were neighbors, it was proper that it should be so. In truth, he felt responsible for her after meeting her on the train.

Coit walked outside on his back veranda and stood facing the Polks' house. He imagined old Jess was charming the ladies at this very moment and wished he'd been invited to share in the charming.

Instead, he was alone, listening to the summer night that was alive with activity. Fireflies blinked like the ends of glowing cigars as they floated on the warm current of air. Resident treefrogs had begun their nightly reverberating trill while the hollow mournful *cooo, cooo, coo* of a dove softened the shrill warble. Not far from where Coit stood, an unidentified night creature scurried across the yard, his passage detected only by the rustling of undergrowth.

Coit sighed, shaking off a tinge of loneliness. Tonight the air was redolent with honeysuckle—the flower smelled like nectar—sweet, warm, and honeyed. Like a woman. Or how he wanted his woman to smell.

An image of Anna Belle surfaced in his mind. What was it about this particular woman that had him so intrigued?

If he and young Paul were both infatuated with the new mill worker, what of his stepbrother Gordon? Had he been attracted to her as well? Gordy had a reputation with the ladies. Maybe that was why he hired her.

Fool. Gordy hired and fired women every day.

But Coit recalled several incidents that had occurred with mill girls in their youth, and the girls had always come out the losers. He reasoned that his stepbrother was an adult now and in his position as head of the mill he wouldn't dare become involved with his operatives. Yet Coit trusted his older brother about as far as he could throw him, and that wasn't very far.

For that reason, he would make it a point to keep his eye on Gordy. More importantly, he now had a better reason to keep his eye on Miss Blow.

Annabel lay in the hammock strung between two large maples in the Polks' backyard. Last night, she had slept like a baby in her narrow bed in the Polks' house and had not awakened this morning until long after the sun had risen.

It was a delightful afternoon with moderate temperatures and the constant breeze that ruffled the leaves above her head. Although her muscles ached from the back-breaking hours that she had spent in the factory yesterday, she felt surprisingly refreshed and was enjoying her day off. She listened to Lance and Percy who played in the grass not far from where she lay. They were focused on watching a grasshopper escape the family cat.

Annabel dropped the book she held on her lap and closed her eyes, giving herself over to total relaxation. Sara and Jess had gone into the town of Dalworth to deliver a tablecloth that Sara had crocheted for one of the society ladies, and Annabel had volunteered to watch the twins.

So far, the boys had been no trouble. They had inherited their mother's gift of imagination, Annabel thought, as bits and pieces of their conversation floated on the soft breeze to where she rested. In the twins' minds, King Arthur had changed from a domesticated cat into a ferocious lion that now tormented its prey. Annabel smiled to herself. Before today, the idea of motherhood had never crossed her mind, but she decided, as she listened to the youthful chatter, that if she ever did have children, she would want her offspring to have similar dispositions.

With one leg dangling from the hammock, she pushed her foot against the ground. The movement made her hanging bed rock gently beneath the old trees.

Above her, a bold ray of sun penetrated the thick canopy of leaves and washed her face in warmth. Annabel savored the feeling. Her mother would have a fit if she knew her daughter intentionally invited the sun's attention, scolding her about the danger of freckling. But the way Annabel saw it—what difference did it make? She already had so many freckles that a few more wouldn't be noticed.

Her musing was interrupted by movement on each side

of the hammock. One twin whispered to the other one, "Is the damsel sleeping?"

"Shush! You're gonna wake her."

Annabel remained perfectly still, her eyes closed, pretending sleep. She enjoyed listening to their childish prattle. If the boys thought they had snuck up on her, they were mistaken. Not only had she heard their approach, but she could smell them as well. A combination of earth and grass and the bologna sandwiches they'd eaten for lunch were a dead giveaway to their presence, as well as the bony elbows that jabbed her unmercifully while they anchored their small frames to each side of the hammock.

"Ma warned us not to bother our hoarder."

"We won't bother her none. We'll just rock her a little."

"Yeah! Like we'll rock our baby in the cradle once she gets here."

"Yeah. We're just practicing."

Annabel almost smiled. Two sweeter children she had never known, but then, she hadn't known many children.

What started out as a gentle swinging motion soon changed along with the twins' docility. Instead of the tame back-and-forth movement they had begun with, the activity became wilder. Each twin continued to cling to his side of the canvas hammock, increasing their upward thrust each time his feet came in contact with the ground.

No longer did Annabel dare to pretend sleep. Her fingers grasped the sides of the hammock, and she held on for dear life. At first the exhilarating motion was fun, and she joined in the merriment, giggling along with the boys. They pushed harder and harder, each time their small feet lifted higher and higher off the ground. Annabel knew if the wild ride continued, all three of them could get hurt. She shouted for them to slow down, but the twins' laughter and their screams of delight blocked out her orders to stop.

"We're flying like a bird," she heard one of the brown-eyed angels yell.

And then Annabel did just that. She flew. It happened

so fast that she wasn't aware she was airborne until the hammock flipped her out of its hold as though it had suddenly become a living thing and was tired of suffering abuse. When she stopped sailing through the air, she landed on her back against the hard surface of the ground. The force of her landing knocked the wind from her lungs, and the world turned black. It was a few moments before she came back to consciousness. Two sets of dark brown eyes that floated in her vision had turned into three sets.

"Did we kilt her, Mr. Coit?" she heard one of the twins ask.

"No, boys, I believe she's gonna be fine, but I want to make certain that she has no broken bones." Coit Jackson leaned over her, poking around on her person as if she were a pin cushion.

"If we broke Ma's hoarder, she's gonna kilt us."

"Boarder, Lance, boarder," Coit corrected. "I assure you, you haven't broken Miss Anna, but you see what happens when you forget yourselves. Usually someone gets hurt."

"We didn't mean to hurt her," Lance answered for both twins.

Annabel heard the boys' concern and wanted to reassure them. "Lance, Percy, I'm fine." She tried to sit up, but the three males kept her pegged to the ground, which was just as well because the upward movement made her feel lightheaded. Instead of sitting, she asked from her prone position on the grass, "Are you two boys all right?"

"Yep, we're okay," Percy informed her, "but when Ma and Pa hears we flied you out of that hammock, we won't be able to sit down for a week."

Annabel didn't want the boys to be punished. As the adult, she realized that she should have stopped the game before it got so out of hand. She wanted the twins to understand that she didn't hold them responsible for their actions.

"What do you say, we don't tell your parents? Accidents happen. I know you boys didn't mean to swing me so hard that I'd fly out of the hammock. Besides, now, I'm fine. Really.''

Again she tried to sit up, and this time she accomplished it, but she leaned shakily into Coit Jackson's muscular frame where he knelt protectively beside her.

Still worried about their behavior, Lance said, "Now we'll never be able to rock Guinevere in her cradle. Ma will be scared we'll fly her out, too. Just like we flied Miss Anna out of the hammock."

The twins looked as though they were about to cry. "Come here," Annabel insisted. She opened her arms, and Lance and Percy flew into them.

"We're real sorry we did it." This time, they no longer fought back their tears. The salty excretions slid down their tiny faces, leaving tracks of dirt.

"Boys. I'm not going to tell your mother about this, but in return I must have your promises that when your baby sister is born, you'll be very, very careful with her. Especially if your mother allows you to rock her."

The boys wiped the tears from their eyes simultaneously.

Coit put in his two cents worth. "Miss Anna is an adult and a lot tougher than your little sister will be when she first arrives. A baby probably wouldn't survive a toss from the cradle. That's why you have to promise me that you'll be extra careful with your baby sister. Today we all saw the result of how rocking or swinging too fast can lead to no good."

The twins blew their runny noses on their sleeves. "We're sorry we flied you too fast, Miss Anna. We promise we ain't never gonna rock our new baby so fast that she might fly away forever."

"Good," Annabel said, hugging the boys to her once again. "Now, if you two young men will right that belligerent hammock and fetch me my book, I believe we can put this matter behind us."

The boys scrambled to obey her while Coit helped her to her feet. He smiled down at her, his arm still supporting her weight as she leaned into him.

"I've just made some lemonade and I believe we all could use a glass." He guided her toward the gate that stood open between his yard and the Polks'.

"Boys. We'll meet you in the arbor as soon as you put that hammock to rights."

"Come, Miss Blow. I think you need to sit down." He winked at her. "This time, in a chair."

Annabel smiled up him. The Coit she had met on the train ride from Atlanta had returned. Gone was the Coit of yesterday, who'd scowled at her and treated her with indifference. She liked this Coit much better.

"Yes," she told him, bestowing upon him a heartfelt smile, "I believe a chair would be preferable to the ground."

Once they were inside Coit's yard, he steered her toward the arbor. The shady bower with its bentwood benches looked a sight more sturdy than the canvas hammock she'd abandoned a few moments before.

"Sit, Miss Blow. I'll rustle us up some lemonade and be right back."

Annabel sat down on the twig bench, her eyes never leaving his. Their color reminded her of melted chocolate and at the moment reflected not an ounce of light in their cocoa depths.

Earlier, when Coit had come to her aid, she'd realized how much she wanted them to be friends. To Annabel, now was as good a time as any to begin again. Halting his departure, she said, "I think it only fair, since we are to be backyard neighbors, that you should call me Anna. Every person I've met is calling me by the shorter name. Besides, Miss Blow sounds too formal."

And too confusing, Annabel silently admitted. With all the relevant information she had to remember about her new identity, her work at the factory, she certainly didn't wish to be caught forgetting her assumed name.

Coit's chocolate eyes took on flecks of divinity candy. "I'd like that," he responded, "but only if you'll call me Coit."

"I'd like to call you Coit. Especially since you and the

Polks are on a first-name basis. It makes me feel as though
I belong.''

"Good. Then it's settled. From this day forward, you're
Anna, and I'm Coit. Now if you'll excuse me, I'll get our
refreshments and be right back.''

Coit seemed pleased with her suggestion about the
names, almost as much as she was. But it was his words
"from this day forward" that flooded her with warmth.
They sounded almost like wedding vows.

"You're daft," she scolded, "plumb foolish! Wedding
vows, indeed.''

Since taking on her new identity, her thoughts had become as capricious as her actions. But Annabel couldn't
deny the fluttering of butterflies that took flight inside her
stomach as she watched Coit retire to the house.

A more handsome man Annabel had never encountered, or if she admitted the truth, the only man who
aroused in her more than a curious interest.

As Coit strode toward the store, his long legs carrying
him like an athlete around the many plantings, he cut a
dashing figure. His shoulders were broader than she remembered, but she attributed their increased width to the
slim cut of his vest. The cotton duck material with its tiny
black figures resembled the blue-black color of his thick
hair. In the afternoon sunlight, it looked as lustrous as a
black pearl.

Annabel tried to still her recalcitrant musings by sucking in her breath. But when she did, she inhaled Coit's
scent that still clung to her clothes from when he'd supported her against his chest. For as long as she lived, the
spicy smell of cloves would always remind her of the
storekeeper.

She hurtled back to reality with the approach of the
twins. They returned, carrying King Arthur. One twin told
her, depositing the huge black and gray tabby onto her
lap, "King Arthur is worried about you.''

Once the cat was settled, Annabel stroked his glossy
fur.

"He also wants a drink of Mr. Coit's lemonade," the other twin added.

"Cats don't drink lemonade," she insisted.

"King Arthur drinks everything. Even puddles."

Puddles of the rain variety, Annabel hoped, for the cat's sake as well as her own.

Just as her experience with children was lacking, so was her experience with animals. Her mother had always insisted that people shouldn't keep pets, so consequently Annabel had never owned a dog or cat. But now, as she stroked a purr from the big old Tom, she thought of how unfair it had been that her mother had denied her such a simple pleasure.

With a twin kneeling on either side of her legs, Annabel studied them. Would she ever be able to tell them apart? The boys were mirror images of each other. Unlike their parents and Coit, Annabel doubted that she would ever be able to distinguish between the two boys enough so that she could call them by their given names.

"He likes you," the twins chimed.

"How could he not?" Coit asked, returning to the arbor with a lemonade tray. Her heart turned over at his response. Above the frosty pitcher and four glasses, Coit's eyes met hers and held. It was Annabel who looked away first, focusing her full attention on the boys.

Coit sat the tray on the small table between the two benches. In unison, the boys jumped up, faced him, and shouted, "I'll pour, I'll pour."

"I'll pour." Coit's announcement brooked no further demands. "You two, sit. Over there." He pointed to the opposite bench.

The boys rounded the table and took a seat.

"Yea, cookies. You make these maroons, Mr. Coit?"

"Yes, I made these macaroons. And if you eat more than two, your mother will have my hide."

"We won't, Mr. Coit, we promise. We don't want you to get skinned."

After pouring each boy a glass of the tart drink and

handing each of them a napkin with two cookies, Coit did the same for Annabel.

Her head still reeled from this latest piece of information about Coit. She'd never met a man who baked cookies. Baking was women's work, or so she had always believed.

King Arthur jumped from Annabel's lap when Coit placed a saucer filled with the lemon drink on the ground beside the table.

"He does like lemonade," Annabel exclaimed when the feline began lapping up the sweet concoction. "I thought cats only drank milk."

"King Arthur eats and drinks everything," Coit said.

Annabel paraphrased the boy's earlier words. "Even puddles?"

Coit sat down on the bench and winked at her. "Only of the rain variety."

Bursting into laughter, Annabel said, "My thoughts exactly." It amazed her how two near strangers could be on the same wavelength the way she and Coit seemed to be.

"Can we swing on your swing, Mr. Coit?" one of the twins asked, his mouth stuffed full of cookie.

"I'm afraid, Lance, you'll have to ask Miss Anna. She's in charge of the two of you this afternoon."

"Can we, please, Miss Anna, can we?" Percy begged.

Instead of answering the boy immediately, she asked Coit, "How can you tell these two apart?"

"You mean because they look so much together, when they're apart you can't tell the two of them from both?"

Annabel laughed. "I won't ask you to repeat that."

"It's easy. Once you get to know them." He took a drink of the lemonade and blotted his lips.

"But they're identical. I look at one and see the other."

The twins looked at each other and giggled. It seemed they enjoyed the game that nature had played on everybody but the twosome.

"Oh, you'll learn soon enough," Coit said, "but until you do, maybe I can help you out. Boys, come here."

The twins abandoned their seats and came to stand in

front of Coit. He pulled a Dixon black crayon pencil from
his vest pocket. On one of the twins' forehead he wrote
the letter "P" and on the other one he wrote the letter
"L."

"You branded us, Mr. Coit. Just like a cow gets
branded. But it didn't hurt none," Percy said.

"I'd never hurt you, Percy." With a twang, Coit imi-
tated a cowpoke. "But I figure these here brands will help
Miss Anna identify you young calves until she gets to
know you better."

"Does that mean we don't have to wash ever again?"

"I reckon you'll have to take up the subject of bathing
with your ma, but for this afternoon you're safe."

The boys' eyes twinkled with merriment.

"You need a brand, you need a brand!" Lance shouted,
jumping up and down with excitement.

"You cowboys know your lettering well enough to
mark me?"

" 'Course we do. Our ma taught us."

"Guess that settles it, then." Coit handed the crayon
pencil to the boys.

"We got to brand you twice, cowpoke. First my
brother, then me."

Annabel couldn't keep the corners of her mouth from
turning up as she watched the two boys mark Coit's forehead with the initials "CJ."

Once again she was reminded of the special relationship
that existed between the shopkeeper and the twins. That
special friendship she had witnessed on her first visit to
the Company Store. Coit Jackson was an amazing man,
she thought, the way he communicated with the boys on
their level. He would make a wonderful husband and father. That saddened Annabel when she realized that the
lady in his future wouldn't be her. Not that she was interested anyway—married was the last thing she wanted
to be.

"Now it's Miss Anna's turn." The boys dove toward
her lap, wielding the crayon pencil like a weapon.

"Hold it there, partners," Coit cautioned. "I think you

better give me that branding iron and let me brand this here heifer.''

"Heifer!" Annabel almost choked on the word.

"What's a heifer?" both boys asked.

Caught off guard by their question, Coit looked as though he were searching for an appropriate reply. Annabel waited, as eager as the boys to hear his answer. Finally, after much deliberation, he responded. "A heifer is a young girl cow who is unmarried.''

"You mean cause Miss Anna ain't got a husband and she can't have no babies like our ma?" Lance asked.

Coit's face turned beet red. He must have realized the impropriety of their conversation, because his words stumbled off his tongue. "I . . . I guess you might say that—''

Annabel looked away, hiding her smile. In all of her twenty-five years, she had never been referred to as a heifer. But in truth, that's exactly what she was—in cow language anyway.

Not wishing to subject either herself or Coit to more of the boys' personal questions, Annabel answered their earlier query. "Unmarried ladies are not generally called heifers, but in this instance it's acceptable only because we were playing a game.''

Coit still looked uncomfortable so she took it upon herself to dismiss the boys. "You may go and swing now, but don't swing too high. We don't want another mishap.''

"We won't, Miss Anna. We ain't never gonna swing too high again.'' The children left them and dashed toward Coit's veranda.

Once they were alone, Coit spoke. "I'm sorry, Anna. I should have been more careful with my description. Believe me, there are no similarities between you and a heifer cow. It's just that those boys are too dang smart.'' He grinned and shook his head. "They pick up on things most children wouldn't even notice.''

A smile pursed her lips. "Should I 'moo' my response?'' she teased him.

Caught up in her good humor, Coit moved closer to her on the bench. Playfully he waved the crayon pencil in front of her eyes, his brows wiggling mischievously. "No mooing until this here brand is burned into your hide."

She brought her hand up to stifle a giggle, but Coit quickly pushed it aside. Holding her chin with one hand, he printed a giant **A** in the center of her forehead. His fingers where they steadied her chin burned into her flesh as though he had truly branded her.

Finished, he held his head back to admire his handiwork. "That ought to do you. Moo away."

To *move* away would have been the sensible thing to do, but Annabel felt soldered to the bench. Coit's nearness had burned past her resistance.

Instead of releasing her when he finished initialing her forehead, he continued to hold her chin. He studied every nuance of her face as though seeing her for the first time. His gaze felt like a caress. She heard the crayon pencil slip from his fingers and roll across the ground. In the next moment, his hands had slipped around her neck, and he pulled her toward him.

Coit was not normally given to amorous interludes with women, especially women he hardly knew. He couldn't understand his overwhelming desire to take Annabel into his arms.

He slipped his fingers beneath the coppery knot of hair at the back of her head. The mishap in the hammock had made her chignon slip several inches lower. He wanted to release the fallen coil and run his fingers through the brassy strands.

Angling his face closer to hers, Coit imagined how it would feel to kiss the scattering of freckles across her nose and cheekbones; and then to sample the sweet nectar of her full, pouty lips that at the moment looked like a moist pink bow parted over even, white teeth. He felt her tremble.

Annabel watched as Coit's face dipped toward hers. This can't be happening, she thought. Instead of retreating as she would have in the past when a beau tried to kiss her, she felt herself drawn into a vortex of swirling desire. She, Annabel Lowe, wanted him, Coit Jackson, to kiss her more than she'd ever wanted anything in her life.

His warm breath, tart as lemons, lifted the wispy hairs at her temple, making her heart beat in an exaggerated rhythm. His fudge-colored eyes focused on her lips. Her senses began to flutter in response to his nearness.

No longer aware of the boys' giggles coming from the squeaking swing, Annabel was only aware of the man beside her and the rapid roar of her blood as it coursed through her veins. She could feel Coit's body heat through his shirt and vest. Closing her eyes, she waited for their lips to seal what she imagined they both desired.

His lips touched hers in a whisper-light contact. He uttered a little *mnnh* sound from deep in his throat. The sound was because of her and made her go all mushy inside. His mouth moved over hers taking possession . . .

"Yuk! Sickening!"

Startled by the intrusion, Coit and Annabel's eyes popped open. They jerked apart. The twins who now stood behind the bench where Annabel and Coit were sitting were showing their disgust at the kiss by gripping their stomachs and moaning as though they might lose their lemonade and cookies at any moment.

"Gross! Disgusting!" The twins collapsed onto the ground and rolled around as if they were in the throes of a convulsion.

Coit and Annabel jumped to their feet, embarrassed now because of what had transpired between them and that the boys had witnessed their lapse in proper conduct.

"Oh, no—what have I done?" Annabel moaned into her hands. Her face was flushed with humiliation and anger at herself.

Seeing Anna so distraught, Coit did what any gentleman would do. He apologized. "I'm sorry. I forgot myself. It won't happen again."

She stepped away from him without a response.

"Come, boys," Annabel ordered, rounding the bench

and grabbing each boy's hand. "It's time we leave. Your parents could return at any moment."

Coit's fingers closed around her arm. "Wait, Anna. I believe you're overreacting. We'll explain this to the twins together."

She shook loose of his grip. "I never overreact," she insisted, then stomped toward the Polks' yard, practically dragging the twins through the open gate.

"Never in all my life have I felt so humiliated," she scolded. The boys no longer feigned sickness, but instead they marched obediently behind her like little soldiers.

What in the name of heaven had gotten into her? Annabel worried. Allowing a man she hardly knew to take such liberties. And the boys witnessing all of it.

·Slamming the gate as soon as King Arthur had dashed through the opening, Annabel beat a path to the back entrance of the house, the boys still in tow behind her.

"Wash up before you go inside." She barked out orders like a sergeant. The boys stopped in front of a washstand on the back porch where an enameled pitcher and bowl were filled with water. Sara had placed it there for them to wash up before entering the house.

Sara. What would Sara think of her when she found out about the kiss she and Coit had shared? *And it was certain that she would find out.* Lance and Percy would be the first to enlighten their mother on what had gone on between her *hoarder* and their neighbor, Mr. Coit.

This thought upset her more.

"Inside, boys, now," she ordered.

Suddenly, the anger left her. She leaned against the porch column. How could a perfect day turn into such a disaster? The twins weren't at fault; she was. She shouldn't be taking her anger out on them. Realizing this, on a much softer note, she added, "After I wash up, I'll read you a story. Please wait for me in the parlor."

They were as quiet as mice when they left her. Only the slam of the screen door broke up the silence beneath the eaves.

Annabel was alone now with her thoughts. She tossed

the dirty water the boys had left into the yard and poured more from the pitcher.

Her face still burned with embarrassment. How could she ever explain her actions to Sara? What if Sara asked her to move out, believing that she was a loose woman? Then where would she go and what would she do? Would her lapse in conduct ruin her investigation?

After dousing her hot face with the cold water, she straightened and studied her image in the mirror that hung above the washstand.

The letter "A" was still visible on her forehead. Although the "A" stood for Annabel instead of adultery, she likened her situation to that of Hester Prynne in Nathaniel Hawthorne's book, *The Scarlet Letter*.

"Mercy. Whatever am I to do?"

Annabel scrubbed away at the hateful initial until nothing was left but a red blotch on her skin.

She leaned toward the mirror and examined her face, fully expecting to see someone different staring back at her. But on the outside she looked as she did every day when she faced her image in the mirror: coppery-colored hair, green eyes, and a scattering of freckles.

The only visible difference was the chafed skin on her forehead that still burned from her hard scrubbing. But deep inside, she knew that Coit Jackson had left more of a mark than the one made with his crayon pencil. He had branded her with his lips as well.

It was time she explained her actions to the twins and put this business behind her. Tossing the Turkish towel over a hook, she drew in a deep breath. Lance and Percy needed to hear an explanation for her conduct, and she knew she could no longer delay going inside. Doubting that she would ever be the same again, Annabel straightened and moved toward the back door.

With hushed footsteps, she entered the kitchen, closing the door softly behind her. Perhaps, by not making her presence known immediately, Annabel could get a better feel for the boys' mood, that way knowing better how to explain her actions.

The kitchen and parlor were separated by a wall with double doors that were always open. Where Annabel stood it was impossible for her to see the boys, but it wasn't impossible for her to overhear the conversation taking place with their parents in the front room.

"Just like you and Pa do. They were kissing."

❖ 7 ❖

ANNABEL'S HEART PLUNGED to her stomach. Oh, no! It wasn't fair that Sara and Jess had returned before she had a chance to speak with the twins about her indiscretion. Her knees felt as wobbly as rubber as she propped against the wall for support. After hearing the tittle-tattle about her from their angels, would the Polks demand she leave immediately? Oh, Lordy—whatever was she to do?

The soft mumble of conversation floated to her where she remained hidden behind the wall between the kitchen and parlor. One of the boys exclaimed, "Yuk! Why would they want to suck each other's lips?"

She heard Jess tell his son, "When you're an adult, Lance, you'll understand. Who knows, you might even enjoy kissing."

"Not me. I ain't never gonna suck someone's lips— especially some sissy girl's."

Sara and Jess laughed companionably. Then she heard Jess say, "Believe me, sons. When you've grown into yourselves, I'm sure you'll agree that lip sucking isn't so bad—especially if the lips are attached to a beautiful woman like your ma here."

Annabel heard what sounded like a loud smack and

decided that her landlords were practicing a little lip sucking of their own.

"Ma and Pa . . . not you, too? Gosh, that's disgusting."
Annabel heard the muffled sound of bony knees thumping
against the front-room floor. She pictured the twins rolling
about, much the way they had when they had discovered
her and Coit kissing.

"If you boys carried on in such a way when you saw
Miss Anna and Mr. Coit kissing, you must have shocked
them both."

"Naw. Only Miss Anna. She looked as though she
needed to visit the outhouse."

"Boys. You should be ashamed of yourselves," their
mother scolded. "Poor Anna. Where is she now?"

"Last we saw her, she was washing away Mr. Coit's
suck." The twins' tumbling had stopped, and the room
was quiet except for their loud whispers. "She told us
she'd read us a story when she finished washing."

"Well," Sara said, "I believe your father will have to
do the reading. But first I think you boys need a lesson
in lip sucking. You hold them, Jess, while I give them
their instructions."

From where Anna stood hidden, it sounded as though
the boys were rolling around on the floor again. Loud
screeches and giggles rent the air while elbows and knees
thumped against the floor. The sound of loud, smacking
kisses, along with the little boys' merriment, reached Annabel's ears.

She could only imagine the family play taking place in
the parlor. The merrymaking tugged at her heartstrings.
Never in all her life could she recall having shared a similar experience with her parents. The absence of such an
event only added to her already restless mood.

Tears that had threatened to fall since the incident with
Coit stung her eyes. Unwilling to cry or to add any more
eavesdropping to her list of crimes, Annabel fled through
the screened door. Once outside, she paused, uncertain
where to run. A moment later, the decision was made for
her.

"Anna, are you out there?" Sara called from inside the kitchen.

"I am, but I wish I weren't." Annabel's pride was seriously marred by her behavior. Reluctantly she swung around to face Sara. "I'm sorry, Sara. I'll pack my things immediately. Please believe me. I never meant to be such an embarrassment to you and your family."

"Embarrassment? To my family? Lawsy, child, don't be ridiculous. The way I see it, witnessing a little spooning goes a great distance when teaching little ones how to show their fondness for another."

"But my conduct . . ." Annabel's face reddened as she remembered her unladylike act. "I was in charge of the boys. They should never have seen me and Mr. Jackson kiss—" Annabel's voice broke on the last word.

"Did you enjoy it?"

"Enjoy it?" Sara's question caught her off guard. "Well, I never thought about it . . ." Her voice trailed off. For the first time since Sara had stepped outside, Annabel made eye contact with her landlady.

"Whether I enjoyed it or not is not the point, and you know it."

"It's my point exactly."

Sara lowered her cumbersome frame down upon the back stoop and patted the wooden step beside her. "Anna, dear, I think it's time you and I had a good old-fashioned girl talk."

"But I acted like a ninny." She flushed miserably. "Kissing a grown man in daylight while your boys watched me. I don't know what I was thinking. What must you think of me?"

"Come sit a spell," Sara told her again. "As for what I think of you, I think it's perfectly normal that a young unattached lady like yourself should kiss a grown man if she has a notion to. Especially if Coit Jackson is that man."

"But, Sara, your boys—what must they think?" Defeated, Annabel dropped down beside her friend on the stoop.

Sara draped her arm around Annabel's shoulder. "You'd have to be blind, deaf, and dumb not to know what Lance and Percy think of kissing." The boys' antics seemed to amuse her because she smiled. "They think kissing is yuk, disgusting, and sickening! And if I thought for a minute that I could get up from the ground once I got down there, I'd demonstrate to you exactly how yuk, disgusting, and sickening the act really is."

In spite of herself, Annabel laughed. "I guess they don't think much of lip sucking, do they?"

Sara rolled her eyes heavenward. "You heard? Give them a few years, honey, and they'll be trying to lip suck the bloomers off all the girls. And God help me, if they are like their father, they probably will succeed."

"Sara!" Annabel tapped her friend on the knee playfully. "You are so candid."

"No, I just believe in telling it how it is."

Sara's outspokenness never failed to amaze Annabel, but then she had never had a married friend close to her own age. Sara was different from the girls her mother wanted her to befriend in Atlanta. Annabel enjoyed Sara's bluntness. In fact, the few women she had met since her arrival in Dalworth didn't have a pretentious bone in their bodies. She found their honesty refreshing.

"I'm so embarrassed," she told Sara, burying her face in her hands. "How will I ever face your Jess, or more importantly, Coit?"

"My Jess won't be a problem, believe me. As for Coit, I don't see him as a problem either. He's as mild as a moonbeam."

"Moonbeam indeed? I'm not so sure about that." She would equate his kiss more with the sun.

"You must feel something for the fella or you wouldn't have allowed him to kiss you. And although I've been married nearly seven years, I can still remember courting. The attraction is there before the touching begins."

"There's nothing between us," Annabel insisted. "Besides, we're too different."

"You certainly are. He's a male and you're a female."

"Oh, Sara, that's not what I mean. We come from two entirely different worlds. Our social standards are not the same."

Fool, idiot, you blundered again.

For several moments, Sara said nothing. To Annabel it seemed as though she were wrestling with her thoughts. Had her last statement made Sara question that she wasn't the mill worker she claimed to be? How could she be so careless? Social standards indeed. Annabel stole a sideways glance at her friend, wondering as she did how she could right this last mistake without sounding totally like an idiot.

Instead, Sara righted it for her. "Just because Coit's stepfather owned the mill? Coit would be the first to tell you that his family's position in the community means nothing to him. He is perfectly satisfied being a working man and running the Company Store. Gordon would prefer his brother take his rightful place in uptown society, but Coit wants nothing to do with the social elite of Dalworth. An honest, hardworking girl like yourself is exactly what he needs and, in my opinion, what he wants."

Honest? Hardworking girl? That was exactly what Annabel wasn't. In fact, until last Friday she had never worked a day in her life. Unless of course one considered charity work as work. In truth, she was of the socially elite not unlike the young ladies of Dalworth, and she came from the same kind of uptown society that Coit wanted nothing to do with.

What would Mr. Mild Moonbeam think of her, if he knew the truth? But because of Sara's reasoning, he wouldn't have to know. For the moment, anyway. It seemed that heaven had favored her by allowing Sara to assume that it was Annabel's low birth that was causing her concern with Coit's and her relationship.

Land sakes! If Sara knew the truth about her and her real purpose for being in Dalworth, would she be so forgiving?

Sara's words brought her thoughts back to the porch. "If I were you, I'd just act natural when I saw Coit again.

Act as though nothing untoward happened between you. Since I live in a houseful of males, four to be exact if you count King Arthur, believe me I know how they think. It will be Coit who makes the first move to apologize, and when he does, I'm certain the woman in you will know the right response.''

"But I'll die of embarrassment when I see him again."

"No, sweet, you won't die. You'll live, and I promise you'll come out the winner." Sara stood up and stretched. "Now I think it's time I hustled up some dinner for my menfolk. You want to help me?"

Missing Sara's warm bulk beside her, Annabel stood also. She was still worried about her encounter with the Polk men so she was slow in responding.

"I promise this incident won't be mentioned again," Sara said. "As far as my family is concerned, it's over with—forgotten."

Having Sara's assurance that all would be fine made Annabel more determined to put this incident behind her. She certainly couldn't go into hiding, which at the moment was exactly what she wanted to do. Instead, she drew on her mettle and answered while following Sara inside, "I'd love to help you prepare dinner."

Sara looked over her shoulder. "We could invite Coit to join us."

"You wouldn't," Annabel challenged, her spirit wilting.

Sara's bubbly laughter floated up from deep within her chest. "I would, but since I don't favor losing my favorite boarder from heart failure, I'll wait awhile before issuing such an invitation."

"Thank heavens you're a reasonable woman."

"Oh, I'm very reasonable. But I must warn you, Anna, every happily married woman alive wants to see her unmarried friends as happily married as she is."

"Please don't tell me you're one of those."

"A matchmaker? Of course not," Sara replied contritely.

It was fortunate for Annabel that she couldn't read the

thoughts that were swirling around inside her friend's head. If she could have, she would never have trusted Sara again.

On this bright and sunny morning the Mill Village Church was packed to overflowing. Annabel had wanted to plead illness so that she wouldn't have to attend the Sunday service, anticipating a chance meeting with Coit Jackson. She was not granted a reprieve, however. Sara Polk had a suspicious mind and because of it Annabel was now stuffed into the crowded pew between Sara and a mere stick of a woman whose family of lookalikes filled up the remainder of the bench.

All eight members of the Twigg family were pencil thin and reedy. Seeing them standing beside one another, shoulder-to-shoulder, when Sara had first introduced her to the family, Annabel had immediately decided the new-comers looked like fence stakes in graduated sizes.

At first the elder Mrs. Twigg seemed amiable enough. But once the service started and she took her seat beside the woman, Annabel soon learned that Mrs. Twigg's sole purpose in life was to ride herd over her brood in church, and anyone else who took a notion to fidget during the long service.

If Annabel moved an inch, she was instantly awarded a sharp jab to her ribs by Mrs. Twigg's bony elbow. After the woman's third poke, Annabel was sorely tempted to return the woman's stab. Instead, she focused on keeping her bruised dignity, by reminding herself that she was in God's house, and that her parents had brought her up to respect her elders.

The service began. The choir filed in behind the preacher, and Annabel realized that bruised ribs were the least of her problems. Coit Jackson stood in the front row of the choir box looking like one of God's chosen angels in his white robe trimmed with gold. As she watched him, his voice raised in song, Annabel wondered which group of angels he belonged to: those spirits who lived in heaven with God or the devils of hell, who had fallen from goodness. If the havoc he caused to her composure was any indication of his purpose here on earth, she knew he'd been sent to execute a personal punishment to her.

The preacher raised his hands heavenward, intoning, "Let us pray."

Annabel dropped her head so fast her neck snapped, but even a misplaced vertebra would be better than having to face Coit Jackson this morning. When the reverend finished delivering the opening prayer, she opened her eyes to find Coit's brown eyes burning a hole into her.

Merciful heavens. It was stifling inside the crowded church. Or was it the fallen angel's scrutiny that had her near to scorching? Whatever it was, she knew it would take a miracle to get her through the service intact. Annabel slumped lower on the bench and tried to hide behind the lady directly in front of her.

It seemed that her personal tormentor didn't approve of slumping in church either, because Annabel felt another quick stab to her ribs.

The minister announced, "Let us stand and sing the next hymn."

Once on her feet she jerked the hymnal in front of her face. The congregation began singing the familiar lyrics of "Blest Be the Tie that Binds," while Annabel only mouthed the words. Not that she could have sung if she'd wanted to—her mouth and throat felt as charred as the stones of Hell. Even on a normal day her voice sounded more like a frog's than a human's, and today was certainly no exception.

But that didn't seem to be Coit Jackson's problem. He had a fine baritone voice that rang out as clear as a bell, distinguishing it from all the others. His voice was higher than a bass and lower than a tenor, and each note he sang sent perplexing vibrations running unchecked throughout Annabel's body. The experience was not unlike what she had felt when he had kissed her the day before.

She got hotter. She squirmed. Expecting at any moment to experience God's divine intervention for thinking such thoughts in church, she looked toward the cross behind the altar. The only intervention that occurred came from Mrs. Twigg's elbow, and there was nothing remotely divine about the offensive woman.

Ignoring Mrs. Twigg, Annabel escaped into her thoughts. No wonder Coit had asked her if she knew how to sing. It was evident that he did and that he enjoyed the pastime very much.

When the song was finished, the congregation sat down with a heavy clumsiness that echoed throughout the chamber. The wooden pews creaked, feet shuffled against the floor, a baby whimpered, and the reverend cleared his throat, preparing to deliver his sermon.

Annabel shifted restlessly in her seat and once again was poked in the ribs by her seat companion.

"*Who is my neighbor?*" the minister shouted. Finishing on a quieter note, he asked, "Who is my friend?"

At this very moment, Annabel believed she had too many neighbors. All of the unfavorable kind. Mrs. Twigg and her bony elbow and Coit Jackson whose gaze was again drilling into her.

She breathed in an exasperated sigh. The clean smell of soap and the musky odors of too many people in a crowded room invaded her senses as the minister went on to tell the story of the Good Samaritan, reiterating that "Good Samaritans" are persons who go out of their way to perform acts of kindness to others, especially strangers.

In spite of Annabel's resolve to ignore Coit completely, she admitted she hadn't been successful. From their first meeting, he'd gone out of his way to perform acts of kindness toward her—he had helped her find a place to live and had introduced her to the Polks.

From being kind to strangers, the reverend moved on to the topic of friendship.

"It's in the sweetness of friendship that we find laughter and pleasure. And it is in the little mundane things we share with others that our heart finds its reward."

Annabel decided that since meeting Coit she had enjoyed both laughter and pleasure in his company. And, as a little voice inside her head reminded, humiliation.

She dared to sneak a peek at him, wondering if he, too, had found pleasure in their friendship. He still held her captive in his gaze. Fearing that her thoughts were readable, she quickly looked away and concentrated on the preacher's words.

"As humans we love passionately. And often our soul is the battlefield where rational thoughts and judgment wage battles against our powerful appetites. You, my children, must learn to be the peacemaker of your soul. You must turn the elements of your passion into a pleasing melody."

Annabel's judgment lately had certainly been warring with her passion for the storekeeper. She still couldn't believe that she had allowed him to kiss her. Or worse yet, that she had enjoyed it. But unlike the reverend, Annabel was a realist. She knew it would take more than a peacemaker to settle the dispute between her normally good sense and the out-of-control behavior of her heart whenever Coit looked at her as he was doing now. The heat of his look burned all the way down to her toes.

"When we think of passion, we think of love."

Love was the last thing Annabel wanted to consider, especially the love between a man and a woman, but as the preacher warmed to his subject, so did she. She listened, studying her hands that were clasped in her lap.

"Love is giving as well as receiving. Love is not selfish, but self-absorbed with satisfying the one you love. Your own happiness comes from loving. When you love, you must melt and be as a flowing stream. You must give all of yourself to that love, and by so doing, you will know the pain of too much tenderness. For your heart's chosen one, you must bleed willingly and cheerfully."

When Annabel looked up this time, Coit smiled at her, and even after the smile faded, the emotional response it triggered lingered. His glance made her wonder how it would feel to be loved by a man such as Coit Jackson, how it would feel to love so deeply that you would bleed willingly and cheerfully for that person.

The absurdity of her thoughts jerked her from her musings. Love, indeed. Annabel had no time for such fancy. Besides, she had always believed that love was a man's excuse to own a woman and her property, and she wanted no part of it. In fact, she was getting fidgety. She was anxious for the service to end so she could be on her way.

On and on the preacher's voice droned. Was his sermon never going to end? She was so hot and uncomfortable in the cramped pew that she felt as though she might melt and be like the flowing stream the preacher had mentioned earlier.

As for tenderness—her bruised ribs could certainly attest to the tenderness of too much pain. Her nerves formed a tight knot in her stomach. She took a deep breath and tried to relax, but her efforts were useless, especially when Mrs. Twigg punched her again.

Annabel had had enough. She was fed up. And she was tired of being her seat companion's personal punching bag.

Intentionally she wiggled and waited for Mrs. Twigg to strike. This time, when she did, Annabel was prepared. She fended off Mrs. Twigg's blow with a thrust of her own. Leaning toward the woman, she whispered, "If you dare jam me one more time with your bony elbow, I swear I'll rip it off."

Mrs. Twigg sucked in her breath. The skin of her cheeks sank deeper over her angular bones. Her complexion turned several shades whiter than its normal pallor. "Well, I never," she criticized Annabel, scooting as close to her skinny husband as was possible on the already crowded pew.

Annabel lifted her chin in triumph and stared straight ahead. A smile of pure pleasure tickled her lips while her victory tickled her mind. Finally she'd put the old biddy in her proper place, and she wished she'd done it sooner. If nothing else, it would have saved her ribs some bruising.

Annabel's gaze met Coit's. He was fighting a smile. Had he witnessed the ladies' confrontation? If he had noticed her unladylike behavior, then that must mean that everyone in the choir, including the preacher, had noticed.

Oh, Lordy. Poor Sara. What must she think of her boarder now? Loose with men one moment and beating up an old lady in church in the next. For the second time in two days, Annabel's actions had jeopardized her reputation, and this last act might have her permanently blackballed from the community.

Sara nudged her with her shoulder. "Don't worry," she said, leaning toward her and whispering in her ear. "Most everyone at one time or another has suffered sitting next to Mrs. Twigg in church."

Annabel looked at Sara with surprise. "You mean I— you knew?"

Before Sara could respond, the sermon suddenly ended. On the preacher's instructions everyone lumbered to their feet as the organist pumped out the first refrains of the final hymn. Whether or not the congregation sang so robustly because they were feeling the heavenly spirit, or because they were as glad as she was that the service was over and they could go home, Annabel couldn't say. But had she been a betting woman, she would have put her money on the latter. They had been inside the hot little church for nearly two hours.

The congregation began to file out. Jess steered the twins toward the aisle, and Annabel caught Sara's arm and held her back.

"Tell me," she said.

Sara looked sheepish. "You're not Mrs. Twigg's first victim, but you're the only one who gave her back some of her own medicine."

"Lord in heaven. Did everyone in this church know that I was to be the sacrificial lamb?"

"Oh, Anna, you do have a way with words." Sara covered her mouth, trying to hide a smile. "Not everyone knew."

"Sara. Why didn't you warn me about the woman ahead of time? At least I could have worn my armor."

"Armor?" Sara giggled like a young girl. The church was nearly empty now. The Twiggs had gone one way and the Polks the other. Annabel followed the Polks, determined not to encounter the woman again. Not today anyway.

"What shall I say to her when I see her next?" she asked Sara. "That I'm sorry I defended myself and that I threatened to rip her arm off?"

"You said that?" Sara looked at Annabel with amused wonder. "If you said that, I don't believe you'll have to worry about sitting next to her in church again. Most bullies don't get along well with other bullies."

"I'm not a bully."

"No, you're no bully at all. You did something I wanted to do a hundred times, but I never had the nerve." She hugged Annabel to her. "You're my hero."

"A knight of the Round Table?" Annabel teased.

"No. I believe the ice cream parlor tables in town are more suitable for our modern-day heroine."

"Ice cream? Now that sounds like a reward I can't pass up. Especially after what I've suffered for the last hours."

"Exactly. You can tell all of us about your ordeal on our way to the Ice Cream Saloon."

"What do you mean *all* of us?"

"Oh, didn't I tell you that every Sunday after church Coit joins us on our outing to town?"

❖ 8 ❖

Outside the church Coit was waiting. He stood beneath a large sweetgum tree with several other parishioners, soaking up the shade. A soft breeze fluttered the star-shaped leaves above his head, their movement mottling his face with ethereal shadows. Shadows, Annabel thought, that God reserved for his special immortals to make them look more celestial.

He looked heavenly even without his choir robe. Dressed now in a chocolate-brown suit and pristine white shirt, he was too devilishly handsome for his own good. She knew his eyes would match the color of his suit perfectly, if and when she dared to gaze into their liquid depths.

I can't do this, meet you and act as though our lips never touched.

But she had no choice in the matter, because Sara jockeyed her along the path, holding her arm as though she feared at any moment Annabel might bolt.

As they approached him, she felt his eyes upon her. He looked so spiritual standing there in the sunlight and shadows that she expected, at any moment, for the trumpets of heaven to sound. She prayed the heavens would open

up and swallow her completely, but instead only the
crowd around him disappeared, and she could do nothing
but face him. Her heart thudded in her throat, and she
shifted her gaze to his shiny brown shoes when the twins
darted forward and grabbed him around the legs.

Thank heaven for little boys.

"Mr. Coit, Mr. Coit! Now we can get our ice cream."

Coit patted the twins on their tow-colored heads. "You
got that right, fellows. I thought that preacher's sermon
would never end."

"Me, too. I was so hot I nearly melted," one of the
twins responded.

Last night's bath had removed the brands from their
foreheads, and Annabel was uncertain which one spoke.

Sara told her sons, "If you want to, you may remove
your jackets."

"Amen. We want to."

Annabel watched as the twins tore off their coats and
almost threw them at their mother. Dressed in their Sunday suits, Lance and Percy looked just like little grown-
up men. As Sara had predicted when she and Annabel
had talked last night, the kiss was never mentioned again
by the boys. They had welcomed her back into the fold
as though the lip-sucking had never occurred. Now if her
encounter with Coit could only be as easy, she might enjoy their outing to the Ice Cream Saloon.

"Ladies. Jess." Coit's eyes were on her. "Are you up
for the hike into town?"

Annabel met his gaze briefly, then switched her attention to the twins who were jumping up and down, swat-
ting at leaves on a low-hanging branch.

"I'd walk a hundred miles for an ice cream," Sara
answered.

Jess moved toward his wife, and she locked her arm
with his. "I could roll you more easily," he teased.

Annabel couldn't help but overhear Jess's remark or
avoid the smile it solicited from her lips. Her landlords
seemed so comfortable in their love.

Sara playfully tapped her husband on the arm. "I'll

have you know I'm still capable of moving about on my own, Jess Polk." With a slow secret smile that Annabel suspected only Jess understood, she rallied the boys into movement. "Lance, Percy, you two ready?"

"We've been ready," they shouted, dancing with excitement.

It was apparent to Annabel that this was a routine her friends followed most every Sunday. The boys walked ahead, and Sara and Jess fell in behind them. Annabel's presence had probably taken Coit from his place at Sara's opposite side. Today he offered Annabel his arm, and they brought up the rear of the promenade.

"About yesterday," he said. Coit spoke so softly that Annabel would have missed his words if he hadn't slowed his steps to allow them more privacy.

The mention of the incident was inevitable, but Annabel wished it could be avoided. It was far too lovely an afternoon to have to discuss such unpleasantries. The mere mention of the occurrence made her ears and neck burn with embarrassment beneath her high, white collar.

But Coit wasn't about to let the subject drop. "I acted ungentlemanly and I apologize for my behavior."

She didn't respond immediately. Instead she stared straight ahead and studied the sunbeams bouncing off Sara's dark hair. After several moments had passed, she said, "I was as much at fault as you."

Coit exhaled in relief. "I'm not sorry it happened, but I am sorry I upset you."

His concern spoke well of him. Annabel cocked her head to the side and for the first time since they had begun their stroll, she dared to meet his gaze. "You mean because I overreacted?"

His lips twitched with humor. "You told me you never overreact."

Her reserve thawed. "I lied. Sometimes I—"

"Then you agree that you overreacted?"

She loved it when his eyes sparkled the way they were doing now, and she decided to tease him. "Don't press your luck, Mr. Jackson."

"Coit," he corrected. "Remember, we agreed."

"Coit," she repeated. "And while we're agreeing, I guess I'll have to accept your apology."

The remainder of the walk to town was very enjoyable. It was a good half mile, but the lane they traversed was shaded by trees and free of traffic. Along the way, they passed several houses that for the most part were modest, one-story frame structures. A few were built in the same style as the Polks' bungalow, with a gabled roof, a single centered front door, and a hip-roofed front porch. Some families relaxed on their porches and waved at them, calling out friendly greetings.

Annabel had not been to town since her arrival last Wednesday, and she was anxious to view the business district in daylight. She and Coit moved closer to Sara and Jess. The conversation between them was easy, focusing first on the weather and then shifting to the episode involving Mrs. Twigg.

"I can't believe my friends would allow me to be that woman's personal punching bag." Annabel scolded the now three chuckling adults.

Coit informed her, "We figured you had enough sass that you could survive her harassment."

"Sass? Now why did you think that? After all, we were in church, and that was no way for that woman to act."

Sara laughed. "You know Anna told her that she would rip her arm off if she elbowed her again."

Jess and Coit hooted. "You told her that?" They shook their heads in amazement.

Grinning, Coit ran his fingers through his dark hair. "No wonder the woman turned whiter than a ghost and practically tried to crawl into Bemas Twigg's lap."

Jess turned his head and winked at Coit. "Probably the first time old Bemas got a good feel since before their last babe was born. Not that I'd want to be feeling Mrs. Twigg. In my opinion, she's so ugly she has to sneak up on a glass of water."

"Jess Polk," Sara scolded, "the boys will hear you. And don't you be forgetting there are ladies present."

"You're no lady, you're my wife," he teased, hugging her closer to him with his arm.

Sara pushed him away playfully. "Church sure didn't do you much good this morning. And quit hugging me— we're gonna be the neighborhood scandal if you keep carrying on in such a way."

"Now, Sara, there is nothing wrong with a man hugging his beautiful wife on Sunday morning."

"In public there is. Now, you behave yourself before you embarrass Anna with your shenanigans."

He turned to look back over his shoulder. "I apologize, Anna. Besides, I'm not wishing to have my elbow ripped off."

Joining the others, Annabel laughed in sheer joy. "I'll try to control myself, Jess." She couldn't remember a time when she had enjoyed herself so much.

Soon they reached the business district. The Ice Cream Saloon was on the same street as the Hotel Dalworth where Annabel had stayed her first night in town. Although the shops on both sides of the main street were closed, the Ice Cream Saloon and the hotel appeared to be doing a grand business.

Promenaders were everywhere. Fashionably dressed families in their Sunday finery strolled the boardwalks that lined the streets. Annabel wondered if the Polks noted the difference in dress between these folks and those they had left behind at the Mill Village Church.

Her friend from school, Merelda Whitcomb, would belong with this group of townspeople, she thought. And so would her parents back home in Atlanta. Instead of wearing homespun and going hatless to church, these churchgoers were decked out in the latest fashions made from the best fabrics. Annabel's own wardrobe would rival those of the amblers. She stole a quick peek at Coit. He, too, could belong with the fashionable set, if good looks and expensive clothing were your invitation.

At the moment Annabel felt very comfortable dressed in the same white blouse and tailored skirt that she'd worn on the train from Atlanta. And she certainly liked her new friends better than the strollers they passed on the street who looked at their small group with disdain—a disdain that made her angry, especially when she thought of how kindhearted and loving Sara Polk was.

"Here we are, ladies. I believe we've arrived in time to beat the crowd." Jess pushed open the shop's front door.

Once inside, it took several moments for Annabel's eyes to adjust to the softer light. What she saw pleased her.

At the end of the long airy room, she recognized what she thought must be the soda fountain. Soda fountains were becoming all the rage just as eating ice cream was fast becoming an American pastime.

The Saloon was like a small indoor conservatory. The ceiling was glass supported on high wooden beams that were held in place by polished wood columns. Ferns, in every shape and size, hung from the rafters. Potted palms decorated the encaustic-tile floor.

Coit led them to a small table with an iron pedestal base and marble top. Annabel and Sara sat down on green cast-iron chairs, and while the twins hopped from one foot to the other, Coit and Jess confiscated extra seats.

"We'll decide on what we want in a moment," Coit told them. "Remember, today it's my treat."

The Polks didn't protest, and neither did Annabel. After all, she was an invited guest and she wanted to do what was expected of her. Her friends came here every Sunday, and they already knew the rules.

Eyeing the milling crowd, Annabel felt like a schoolgirl on her first outing. The biggest treat of all was the pleasure she received when she closed her eyes and inhaled deeply of all the different kinds of syrups: Vanilla, lemon, sarsaparilla, strawberry, pineapple, ginger, and chocolate.

Coit plopped each twin in a chair and pushed each in turn beneath the marble table. "Now, what will it be, ladies?" he asked.

Annabel's eyes popped open. "A taste of every flavor."

"Yeah, every flavor." The boys mimicked her request and licked their lips.

Coit leaned toward Annabel, and his warm breath tickled her cheek when he spoke. "You're a bad influence on these here young'uns."

"No," she corrected, "this place is a bad influence on me. So I'll compromise. Bring me a scoop of vanilla."

"Vanilla?" everyone said together.

"A giant scoop and an ice cool lemon soda water."

"You're a greedy little thing," Coit teased her.

"I'm far from little and I'm certainly not greedy. I'm hungry and thirsty. After all, I've just done battle in church, then marched nearly a mile in the heat. It's only fitting that I should receive my just deserts."

"Literally said, literally said." Coit sounded like a traveling medicine man hawking his tonics in the street. She enjoyed his wit.

Everyone placed their orders. Coit returned to where Jess waited in the long line of customers, and Annabel watched his retreat.

"It's like I told you," Sara said, interrupting her observation. "Everything is just fine between you two. I can't remember ever seeing Coit so happy."

Annabel leaned toward Sara. "He's naturally happy."

"Silly. How can someone be naturally happy?" Sara asked.

"It's in their outlook—their disposition. I believe your words were, 'He's as mild as a moonbeam.' "

"I reckon what you say is true. Today he's naturally happier."

"Oh, Sara. What am I to do with you?" They giggled companionably.

The boys started wrestling, and Sara had to intervene. Anna looked at the wall where a sign declared: "Ice cool soda water is a healthy drink."

Only since carbon dioxide had appeared commercially, she thought. In the early years of soda water, she'd read that druggists mixed ground marble with sulfuric acid to make the bubbly liquid. Such a concoction wouldn't cure you; it would kill you first.

The door to the shop swung open, and a group of young belles and beaus entered the saloon. Their laughter floated above the heads of the other customers already seated, demanding everyone's attention.

Sara nudged Annabel, singling out one of the young ladies in the group. "What a beautiful dress," she said.

The lady's gown was made from a white lawn fabric with embroidered lemon-yellow flowers scattered over the skirt and bodice. A froth of white lace draped over the shoulders and the large full sleeves. Yellow bows danced saucily on the girl's shoulders when she moved, and an identical ribbon and bow accented her tiny waist. One side of the skirt was tacked up to reveal an underskirt of the same lace as the cape-like collar.

It was a beautiful dress, but much too fancy for Annabel's taste. Her mother would have adored it, especially with her daughter wearing it.

Sara broke into her thoughts. "My biggest pleasure in coming here on Sundays is seeing all the latest fashions. Someday I'm going to make a dress just like that one and I just might keep it and wear it myself."

"Speaking of making dresses," Annabel said. "I could use a few more skirts and waists to wear to work. Would you make them for me if I bring you the material? I'll be glad to pay whatever you charge."

"Of course I'll make them. We'll talk about price later. But, Anna, haven't you ever wanted a dress as fancy as that one? I shudder to think what it must have cost her."

Guilt as heavy as iron settled on Annabel's shoulders. She had a wardrobe full of such dresses, and never once in her life until this moment had she thought about their desirability. Especially by someone less fortunate than herself. She had always taken her wealth for granted. The realization that she had made her feel ashamed.

"And look at that bonnet. I'm sure she bought it specifically to go with her dress."

It was a white straw hat with a turned-up front brim.

A posy of yellow flowers, the same shade as those on the girl's dress, was attached to the bonnet's crown. The wearer turned toward Annabel, and their eyes locked.

"Merelda," Annabel mumbled beneath her breath. *Why didn't I consider that I might run into her in town?*

Sara turned to face Annabel. "What did you say?"

Uncertain how to respond, she said the first thing that popped into her mind. "Merelda. She's the milliner whom I believe designed that hat. You've heard of her, haven't you?"

Sara turned back to inspect the hat again. "No. I can't say that I have. But she does beautiful work."

Merelda Whitcomb was the last person Annabel wanted to see, especially under these circumstances. She still hadn't forgiven her old school chum for her attitude toward the Dalworth mill workers.

She wondered what Merelda would think when she saw Annabel sitting with her new friends—the *lint heads*. Recalling the disrespectful slur, she became angry. In truth, it didn't matter anymore what Merelda thought. But if she dared to insult the Polks in Annabel's presence, then she would do battle to defend Sara and her family.

Sara interrupted her musings. "The men are almost at the front of the line. I can't wait to get my ice cream. I'm starving."

The twins echoed their mother's words. With their short legs swinging to and fro, they bounced in their seats like toy jumping jacks.

Annabel glanced curiously around the room. No other families from the mill village were present, and that made their little group stand out among the finery like a teapot without a spout. Curious, she asked, "Why don't more families from the village frequent the Ice Cream Saloon?"

"Some do. But most of them prefer to stay at home on Sunday. As you can see, it's mostly the society folks who come here after church."

Annabel wasn't certain if Sara had noticed, but everyone in attendance seemed to keep their distance, Merelda Whitcomb included. Instead of ignoring Annabel as she would have expected, Merelda held her gaze as though she were silently trying to communicate a message to her.

She ignored her. If Merelda could snub Sara, then she could snub Merelda. Annabel gave her attention back to Sara who continued to talk.

"Most of the uptown society believe the mill workers are lazy, ignorant, and that we don't pay our debts. I intend to prove them wrong."

Sara's remark revealed yet another facet of her personality. Her kindhearted landlady was the real heroine—she believed in life, liberty, and justice for all. It amazed Annabel that Sara should be so courageous, but when she considered what she had learned of Sara since their first meeting, her friend's views no longer surprised her.

"We're not all like that." Sara brushed a piece of lint from her skirt. "When Coit first invited us to join him here on Sundays, I felt very strange, like I didn't belong. But after several visits and thoughtful observations, I decided coming here was a lesson my boys needed to learn.

"I've been in some of these people's houses," she continued. "I crocheted tablecloths for their tables and bedspreads for their beds. Even done a little mending on their fancy dresses."

Annabel glanced at the fancy dresses, then returned her attention to her friend.

"Then one Sunday as I sat here feeling all uncomfortable, it came to me. I realized as humans we are all alike. We all feel pain, rejection, pleasure, and acceptance. They're no different than we are, except the lot of them were born into a more comfortable life. But what's important is that in God's eyes we're all equal. I bring my children here each Sunday to show them the diversity of the world. And I plan to raise my youngsters to believe that they should never feel like lesser people because they aren't wealthy. If my boys have a mind to, they will be able to go anywhere and do anything they want."

Annabel was impressed. Sara never ceased to amaze her with her intellectual ideas. "You, my friend, are a princess."

Sara covered her mouth with her hand, quelling a laugh. "Do you really think so? I always wanted to be a princess."

"You're much wiser," Annabel told her.

At that moment the men returned with trays laden with soda water and ice cream, and the women's conversation ended. Annabel couldn't help but wonder if a much greater power than Coit had placed her in Sara's keeping. It seemed that she and her new friend were of the same opinions. Sara's statement about people being alike, no matter what their backgrounds, confirmed her beliefs. She and Sara were that proof. Whose backgrounds could be more dissimilar than theirs? Yet they each believed in equal rights for everyone.

Feeling very satisfied, Annabel plunged her spoon into the dish of ice cream in front of her and dug out a huge bite. It felt velvety smooth and delectably cold, and its creamy sweetness made her feel as though she might die from the sheer pleasure of eating it.

"Heaven," she exclaimed, savoring the ice cream's cool richness.

Coit watched Anna devour her dessert. Hell would be a more apt description of what *he* was experiencing.

He tried not to stare at her, but the way her little pink tongue licked the spoon each time she emptied the utensil of its contents was driving him to distraction.

Before he met the copper-haired woman with her green eyes, Coit had never thought the act of eating could be so erotic. Watching her now, he was reminded again of the day when she had first eaten crackers and cheese in his store. Even then, as a near stranger, her uninhibited manners had awakened something inside of him. Until now, he'd never bothered putting a name to that something. Until her spoon-licking had his noodle feeling as stiff as dried dough. Thank God the twins were preoccupied with their ice cream. He didn't need them to announce to the whole room that he needed to make another trip to the outhouse. He reached beneath the table and adjusted his jacket over his thighs.

Sara corrected the twins. "Don't lap, boys." They were busy scoffing down their treats like hungry puppies.

"Why?" Lance asked. "King Arthur laps, and you don't say nothing to him." He took another bite and made a loud slurping noise as he licked the last remnant of ice cream from the spoon.

"Don't argue with your mother, son," Jess said. "Just do as she says."

Percy giggled merrily. "Miss Anna slurps. I just heard her. And Mr. Coit, he can't stop looking at her licking her spoon."

If Coit could have strangled Percy at that moment, he would have, but since murdering children wasn't in his nature, he winked at the boy and took a long swallow of his soda. The liquid coolness of the root beer tempered his own embarrassment, but not Anna's. She turned several shades pinker than Sara's strawberry ice cream.

"Percy," Sara scolded.

Anna quieted Sara with a look before she straightened her shoulders and spoke. "If I slurped, Percy, I'm sorry. I guess I didn't pay much attention to my mother when I was your age. She, too, cautioned me against lapping. But as you noted, I'm still practicing bad manners. But I'm going to stop right now."

Coit watched as she focused on the dish in front of her. In a more mannerly fashion, she resumed eating her ice cream. She held the spoon between her thumb and third finger, her little finger crooked, and brought the spoon's contents daintily to her lips.

After placing the bite into her mouth, she raised her eyes ever so slowly and nearly choked when she discovered that everyone at the table was watching her.

"Much better," Coit teased, making everyone laugh. Soon the twins were mimicking Anna's mannerisms, holding their spoons the same way she was with their tiny pinkies crooked.

"See, Anna, you're a good influence on my little heathens," Sara told her. "I'm on them constantly about their manners, and they still eat like pigs."

"Oink! Oink!" the twins sounded together.

A stern look from their father quieted their antics, and they returned to eating like gentlemen.

No longer forced to watch Anna lick her spoon, Coit relaxed. Soon he was able to enjoy the Sunday outing again.

"Not to change the subject," Jess said, "but, next Saturday evening we're having a sing-along on the mill grounds."

"Oh, Anna, you're going to love it," Sara said. "All the ladies bring a covered dish, and the food is delicious. Some of the menfolks bring their musical instruments. You'll hear banjos, guitars, mandolins, and harmonicas. And best of all is the singing."

Anna pushed back her now empty ice cream bowl and picked up her drink. "Well, if they expect me to sing along, they can forget it."

"Oh, you don't have to be an accomplished singer to sing," Sara said. "If you can't read music, like most of us, there will be people to lead us in shape-note singing. You can follow along as best you can." Sara motioned to Coit as though presenting a star. "And, of course, our very own Coit is a wonderful singer and leader."

"I don't know how wonderful I am, but I do enjoy singing."

Coit wanted Anna to go to the sing-along, to share in the festivities that he enjoyed so much. "What do you say, Anna, you think you'll join us?"

"I'm not much for singing," she offered, "and if a note had a shape, I wouldn't recognize it."

"It's like reading pictures," Sara said. "Even Lance and Percy enjoy singing along with the pictures."

The twins confirmed their mother's response by nodding their heads. Their mouths were too full of ice cream to answer properly.

Anna breathed deeply, and Coit was distracted by the upward thrust of her bosom before she exhaled. Good lungs, he thought again, trying not to ogle. "If you don't do anything but listen," he said, "I'm sure you'll enjoy yourself. It's one of the few occasions when all the mill families get together and socialize.''

"She'll be there," Sara assured him. "What else does she have to do?"

"I guess I'll—"

Someone bumped against Anna's shoulder. It was a young woman dressed in a white gown embroidered with yellow roses. A nice-looking woman, Coit thought, but not his type. She traveled in different circles than he chose to travel in. He dismissed the girl, interested instead in Anna's reaction.

She stiffened in shock. Her face had turned flaming red, and she acted very nervous. Her composure seemed as fragile as a shell. This in itself was unusual for Anna.

The young woman stooped to pick up something she had dropped, apologizing as she did so. "Excuse me, I'm sorry. I'm not usually so clumsy."

Both Coit and Jess stood in the young woman's presence. Coit had been ready to retrieve whatever the lady had dropped between Sara and Anna's chair, when Anna bent to assist her.

Once the mystery item was retrieved, both the women's heads appeared above the table again. "My purse, I dropped it," the young lady said, eyeing the purse still clutched in Anna's hand.

Sara looked at the girl. "I was admiring your hat earlier. My friend here tells me that a hatter by the name of Merelda designed it. It is really a lovely creation."

The girl looked panic-stricken when Sara mentioned the designer's name. As for Anna, she looked like the cat who had swallowed the canary and gotten away with it. The young woman snatched the purse from Anna's fingers and turned to leave, but caught herself.

She looked down her upturned nose at Sara and replied, "Thank you, but I'm not certain who designed it. If you'll excuse me, my friends are waiting." Without a backward glance, she flounced toward the group of people who were waiting at a table several feet away.

The men took their seats again, and Sara bent toward

Anna and whispered, "Imagine owning a hat like that and not even knowing who designed it."

"Imagine," was Anna's only response.

After the girl bounced away, Anna visibly relaxed, but that earlier cat-and-canary look had vanished. She suddenly looked ill. Her face had turned from strawberry red to fish-gill green.

It was time, Coit decided, that they end their sojourn to the Ice Cream Saloon.

❖ 9 ❖

IT HAD BEEN a lovely day except for the chance meeting with Merelda Whitcomb. It had been a day that Annabel had hated to see end. After leaving the Ice Cream Saloon, they had strolled home in much the same fashion as they had strolled to town earlier—the twins leading and she and Coit bringing up the rear.

Once home, the six of them had spent the remainder of the afternoon beneath the shady trees in the adjoining yards. Then they had enjoyed a cold supper outside, supplied by Coit and the Polks. The dinner consisted of last night's roast "beast," as the twins called it, on crusty white bread as well as pickles and cheese, and potato salad that she and Sara had hastily stirred together. Coit's macaroons and lemonade topped off the delightful meal.

When the twins had begun to show exhaustion, Sara and Jess had rushed them off to bed, leaving Coit and her alone. Uncomfortable in his company, Annabel had pleaded a headache. Now, hours later, she couldn't dismiss her new neighbor from her mind.

It was well after midnight, and the Polks had long since retired to their beds. Unable to sleep, Annabel sat in the rocker in her room. Because of the moonlight that slipped past the windows, the interior was bathed in a pearlescent glow. The vellum stationery that lay open on her lap looked like a sheet of pearl in the lustrous darkness.

The house settled comfortably on its foundation, sighing peacefully as the sun-baked wood cooled with the evening temperatures. Annabel wished she could feel as tranquil. The encounter at the Ice Cream Saloon with Merelda had left her emotions in a turbulent state. She worried that Coit and the others had seen through her school chum's ruse.

When Annabel had bent down to help recover Merelda's purse, she had slipped the envelope into Annabel's hand. Fortunately her skirt had large pockets, for she was able to hide the secret message in the material's soft folds. It wasn't until much later, when Annabel had retired to her room, that she had discovered the envelope contained a letter from her mother. According to the postmark, it had been delivered to the Whitcombs' home by the Saturday morning post. She reread the words:

> *Dearest Daughter,*
>
> *You have been gone only three days, and already I am questioning my judgment in allowing this visit. I cannot understand why you have to be so headstrong.*
>
> *You knew I didn't favor your leaving Atlanta at this time, especially with the Expo festivities planned by my friends. But as always, you and your father rallied to champion your cause against my wishes. Instead of being where you belong, you are off visiting that country bumpkin friend of yours from school. Tell me, dear, what chance do you have of meeting an eligible man in that backwater town?*
>
> *I suggest you shorten your visit and return home immediately. With the Cotton Expo beginning in less than two weeks, all of Atlanta is abuzz with preparation. I need you here to help*

with the Women's Exhibition, and it is unfair that you should be missing all the soirees and the bevy of rich young men from all over the country who are arriving every day.

I expect you to be an obedient daughter and write to me soon, telling me when you plan to return.

Your loving mother.

Would her mother never learn? The bevy of rich young men she spoke of weren't interested in her redheaded daughter with freckles and a *brain*. Evangeline knew she had planned to be away from Atlanta for at least two weeks, and if her mother would admit the truth, she knew Annabel had no interest in working alongside her parent in the Women's Exhibition. Annabel knew her rightful place in society, and it wasn't at some man's side. Even if her mother didn't realize this, her letter of demands was ridiculous. *Return home immediately.* Impossible. Annabel had a job to do.

And although she wasn't that very fond of Merelda, or her change of faith, the girl certainly wasn't a country bumpkin. Annabel was angry with her mother not only because the useless letter had placed her identity at risk in front of her friends, but also because she didn't want a husband—especially one of her mother's choosing.

She crumpled up the letter and tossed it aside. In the moonlit room, the paper resembled a discarded gardenia blossom where it lay on the floor.

Spurred on by determination, Annabel moved the rocker beside the window. Tucking up the curtains to allow in more moonlight, she placed a piece of crisp white paper on a book in her lap and picked up a pen. She began to write:

Dear Mother,

It was so nice to hear from you. I appreciate your concern over my missing all the gay par-

*ties going on in Atlanta with the approach of
the Expo, but I am having a wonderful time
here, making new friends. Country bumpkin?
Mother, really! Must you be so unkind with your
reference to Merelda?*

*In truth, I am finding Dalworth's social cli-
mate anything but dull. The town has a lovely
resort hotel, an Opera House, singing schools,
and a fine bookstore. I take it you aren't aware
that Georgia's first women's literary club was
created right here in this backwater town.*

*As for eligible young men, I'm meeting plenty
who are not only well placed in the community,
but who are very entertaining as well. And the
mountain air is delightful. For now I have no
intentions of cutting my visit short. Please co-
operate with me on this, and I will be home
before you know it.*

Give Papa my love.
Your loving daughter,

Annabel

She reread the letter. Although Annabel didn't like mis-
representing herself to her mother, her circumstances demanded she do so. Nothing she had said in her letter had
been an all-out lie. To support her cause, she had simply
bent the truth.

So far, Annabel was having a wonderful time. She had
made many new friends, but not the kind that Evangeline
Lowe would approve of. As far as the eligible young men
she had mentioned in her letter, there was always Lance,
Percy, and Coit. All three were unwed, and she had never
met more entertaining males than the twins. And the boys
were well placed—they ranked very high in their parents'
hearts.

Coit's status in the mill village community would have
to be sufficient for her mother. God forbid that she should
learn that Annabel was being courted by a mere store-

keeper. If she did, her mother would be on the next train bound for Dalworth to personally escort her only daughter back to Atlanta.

Courted. Did a kiss and a stroll to the Ice Cream Saloon constitute courting? Of course not, Annabel's rational side insisted, but as she looked past her window in the direction of Coit's house, her irrational side maintained—*maybe.*

She leaned forward in the chair and placed her elbows on the windowsill, propping her chin on her hands. The window was open to allow for the flow of fresh air into the tiny room.

In Atlanta Annabel always slept with her windows open even when the temperature dropped to near freezing. She was a firm believer that fresh air not only kept one's physical constitution healthy, but it kept the brain alert as well. Breathing in deep gulps of the night air, she stared across the moonlit yard and recalled lines of a poem she had composed:

> *I am acquainted with the night;*
> *On windless breeze my heart takes flight.*
> *Entwined in depths of ebon lace;*
> *Caressed by silence, my holy place.*

Annabel had always loved nighttime, especially when the moon was full. With the plants and trees washed by the moon's luster, the yard took on an ethereal look. Mist hung in pockets above the silvery yard. The beauty of the scene almost took her breath away.

The air was heavy with the smell of growing things—plants, trees, and flowers. Each distinct scent meshed together to make an ambiguous whole.

A symphony of sound filled the night. Crickets trilled. Cicadas whined, their pitch rising and falling, and the katydids protested the behavior of someone named Katy with their calls of *katy-DID*, and *katy-DIDN'T*. Annabel wondered, with a smile in her heart, if the insects followed

leaders that held up shaped-notes that helped the creatures
to sing along.

Singing made her thoughts return to Coit. She had
never known a man who could sing, much less one who
sang with such gusto. Scanning the glistening brightness
that separated the Polks' house from Coit's, she searched
the shadows of the veranda. She didn't expect to find Coit
there because everyone in the village, except Annabel, had
been asleep for hours. But a red glowing dot about as big
around as a penny caught her attention. At first she believed the vivid spark belonged to a firefly. But as she
studied the small orange-red light, its contained movement, Annabel knew it must be Coit.

To calm her rapidly beating heart, she inhaled deeply.
The aroma of cigar smoke drifted to her nostrils. It was
him. He must be sitting in the swing that hung from the
porch's rafters. Peering deeper into the darkness, she
tracked the spark's movement—back and forth it went
like a child waving a Fourth-of-July sparkler.

The idea that he could be so close yet so inaccessible
made her question her sanity. Never in all of Annabel's
life had a man affected her so. Knowing that sleep would
be doubly impossible now, she slumped against the
chair's high back and began to rock. Mesmerized, she
watched the cigar's movement, spellbound by the man she
imagined held the stogie clamped between his even white
teeth.

Anna Belle Blow was a puzzle, Coit thought, gliding
lazily in his back-porch swing. One long leg bent at the
knee, then repeatedly straightened, created the smooth ef-
fortless motion.

He drew deeply on his Cuban cigar. It was one of the
finest made and not the same brand as those he sold in
his store. Coit reserved the expensive, imported smokes
for his own personal use. Although smoking was not a
habit he often indulged in—except when he was in a re-
flective mood. Tonight was one of those times.

And a beautiful night it was. The darkness was full of

light because of the white-icing moon and the sporadic twinkling of faraway stars. Coit looked across the pale spread of lawn to the shadowed windows of Sara's back room where he imagined Anna lay sleeping. Perhaps she was dreaming—maybe of him? Until he'd met Anna, Coit had never given much thought to a woman's dreams or his role in them.

Had she enjoyed the day as much as he had? A better time he couldn't recall. Anna seemed so comfortable with the Polks, and with him, especially after he had apologized for his behavior of the day before. By the time the day had neared its end, the four of them were acting like old married friends, sharing stories and light banter.

Not that Coit wanted to be married. He enjoyed being his own man without the responsibility of a wife. But lately he'd been suffering from what he called Sunday-afternoon loneliness. Even now he was feeling the lingering effects of his solitary lifestyle and he had had a wonderful day.

Most of his Sundays followed the same routine. First he attended church, then he and the Polks enjoyed their weekly jaunt to the Ice Cream Saloon in town. Afterward, weather permitting, he would return home and spend the remainder of the day puttering in his garden.

Although it had been Coit who had instigated the weekly trips to town, lately the outings had made him feel like a crusty old bachelor with nothing better to do on a Sunday afternoon than tag along with his married neighbors. Today, however, had been special. With Anna beside him, he had felt as though he truly belonged.

His nighttime musings were suddenly attacked by a wave of common sense. He wasn't looking for a wife. But if he had been in the market for a partner, a woman like Anna Belle Blow might suit him fine. She was witty and had a sense of humor. *And a hardy set of lungs.* He quickly pushed aside the image of her high, rounded breasts, fearing that such ruminating might disturb certain parts of his own body. Instead, he concentrated on her intangible attributes. Anna laughed easily, and she appeared to love the twins.

Even knowing all the good things about her, he still thought she had an aura of mystery that ate at him. No matter how hard he tried, he couldn't see Anna in the role of a mill worker.

Heck, he thought crankily. It was lunacy to worry so about a woman. Lunacy even to care if she was telling him the truth.

Today's incident with the young woman at the Ice Cream Saloon had fed his earlier suspicions. Coit still believed the two women knew each other. Both had acted as though they were scared to death that one might reveal the other's identity to everyone present.

The name Merelda tormented his mind. Coit had never heard of a hat designer by that name, but then he wasn't knowledgeable about women's millinery since he didn't stock a line of designer hats in his store. But the name Merelda did have a familiar ring.

Merelda. He jerked the swing to a stop. "Merelda Whitcomb." Coit spoke the name aloud. Suddenly he realized why the girl had seemed familiar and why her name had haunted him. She was the daughter of one of Dalworth's finest families. Her father, Melvin Whitcomb, practiced law in town like his daddy before him. The Whitcombs were an old family with plenty of money and clout.

"No. It couldn't be. A mill worker from Macon and a debutante from Dalworth? Impossible."

He set the swing into motion again. Inhaling deeply on his cigar, he relaxed, allowing his thoughts to ramble. Was Anna who she claimed to be? Were she and Merelda friends from a past Coit knew nothing about? If that was the case, why would Anna be passing herself off as a weaver in a cotton mill?

Doubts about her identity assailed him. For some shapeless reason, Coit couldn't believe Anna was only a mill worker.

She did not fit the usual mold of a mill hand. He tallied

up the points: There was the expensive Brussels lace jabot that she just happened to have in her valise and had pulled out to cover Sara's dummy. Then there was her slip that day in the store about her music teacher in college forbidding her to join the chorus.

But there was more than the above reasons. Anna exhibited a refinement that was not common among most mill operatives. There was more to Anna Belle Blow than appeared on the surface. His doubts would never give him peace until he had delved beneath her outer layers to discover who she really was.

Maybe she was only a mill worker. He liked Anna and wanted her to be no more than she claimed to be. Until he found out the truth, to him she would remain simply his Anna.

His Anna. The thought made him grin, imagining what her response would be to his indication of possession. The Anna he had only begun to know would never allow herself to be owned by any man. She was much too willful and stubborn. He had witnessed traces of that obstinacy in his few dealings with her. What would it be like to be married to such a woman? An inner voice warned him it would be like being stabled with an ornery mule. No matter how much he might like the mule, Coit wanted no part of such an impossible arrangement.

He puffed several times on the cigar, then flipped the glowing ash to the floor. Exhaling, he blew a series of cloudy rings into the night air.

He saw movement beneath his gardenia bush several feet away. King Arthur vaulted from beneath the satin leaves then sauntered toward the swing where Coit sat. Coit patted his lap, inviting the cat to join him. Once the animal was settled, Coit gently stroked the big tom's back.

"You old reprobate, you been out spooning with the local females?" King Arthur's shaggy-soft coat held the faint scent of honeysuckle. It was understandable that the animal would smell like the heady blossom because the vine climbed nearly every fence and trellis throughout the village and grew wild in the surrounding woods.

He rubbed the cat's ears. "You know I love honeysuckle." The cat's rumbling purr warmed the moment. "If you were a woman, I just might marry you."

With the haughtiness of an insulted guest, the cat's purring ceased. Green cat eyes peered arrogantly into Coit's as though the man who held him had suddenly taken leave of his senses. The royal beast then stood on Coit's legs and hunched into a perfectly arched bow. No longer interested in his bachelor friend's opinions or company, the cat vacated Coit's lap. As sleek as jam, King Arthur disappeared into the deep shadows of the yard.

Coit threw back his head and laughed. He wasn't certain which of his remarks had insulted the cat's dignity—Coit's claiming that the old Tom smelled like honeysuckle, or that Coit had mentioned that if he were a woman he might just marry him.

Whatever was the reason for the cat's swift departure, it didn't matter. But what did matter was that Coit's night was again empty of companions except for Anna who had taken up permanent residence in his thoughts.

It was pointless to deny his attraction to her. She was a bewitching young woman he intended to exorcise from his mind. Coit knew it would take more than words or sounds recited in an incantation to make her disappear completely. Instead he would find out who the real Anna Belle Blow was, and the truth would set him free.

⋄ *10* ⋄

Annabel's SECOND WEEK at work was uneventful. Her position as weaver, running six machines at once, no longer seemed the challenge it had been on the first day. Instead she found the work boring and terribly exhausting. Standing in the realm of her six machines, for nine hours straight, took its toll on her back, legs, and feet.

At the end of each day, she dragged herself home from the mill. Forgoing dinner, she fell into bed and didn't move until daylight awakened her. Still half asleep, her muscles aching, Annabel pulled herself out of bed, dressed, and began her day again.

At night her sleep was haunted by the noisy machines and the faces of the men, women, and children who toiled daily at their jobs. With every passing day, she began to admire their unwavering fortitude more. Each one performed his odious task without complaint. To them, working in the factory was as natural as drawing a lint-filled breath.

She lived daily with the deafening shriek of the machinery that started each morning with the flick of a switch. Her ears roared constantly with the noise of the clamoring, howling machines. In self-defense, she stuffed her ears with raw cotton from the picking rooms. This softened the noise somewhat, but she felt completely isolated from Birdie and the other women who worked the looms. It didn't take Annabel long to learn that conversation was near impossible in the weaving room unless one cared to shout. Shouting and constantly inhaling the humid, lint-filled air irritated her throat. Soon she gave up trying to converse.

There were advantages and disadvantages to being isolated from the other women. Annabel had time to observe the working conditions of the Royal Mill. So far, her biggest discovery was that all the operatives worked shifts that were far too long.

To Annabel it seemed inhumane to work twelve hours a day, breaking only once for a forty-five-minute lunch. At least her fellow workers were not coal miners, working grueling hours deep beneath the earth's surface. The weaving room had plenty of light, and fresh air circulated throughout the many windows. It was tolerable even if the environment was tainted with floating fiber and fluff.

What struck her as unusual in the room were the many plants and flowers that decorated the windowsills. The operatives tended them faithfully. The greenery, unlike the workers, seemed to thrive in the humid atmosphere, but then the plants weren't susceptible to lung disease. Not that the laborers appeared to be unhealthy. Annabel only imagined that after working years in the mill, their health would eventually fail.

The plants made Annabel think about Coit Jackson's garden. Isolation was definitely a disadvantage in this respect; the quiet time gave her too much time to think. Something she preferred not to do because her thoughts were always filled with Coit.

Three days had passed since their Sunday outing, and she had found it was impossible to escape him. In person or otherwise. Not that she wished to miss their chance meetings every morning. In truth, Annabel looked forward to seeing him. She believed this was a bane, an impairment to her normal, rational sense. Her attraction to Coit Jackson was as toxic as any poison.

Every morning when she passed the Company Store on her way to the factory, Coit was propped against the front column of his veranda as though he were waiting for her. His greeting was always friendly, and their brief communication made her heart take wing. As he had on their first morning encounter, he claimed to be there specifically to watch the sunrise, but Annabel suspected his motive ran much deeper.

Once she had passed him, she could feel his chocolate-colored eyes burning into her back, making her insides feel as scalding as hot cocoa on a wintry morn. But she believed Coit's close scrutiny went beyond mere attraction. Had he somehow found out that she wasn't who she claimed to be? It was as though he wanted to delve beneath the layers of her being to discover who she really was.

Not that he ever would. In the last few days, she had perfected her act and had become so convincing in her role as mill worker, she almost believed it herself. Annabel Lowe, the debutante from Atlanta, no longer existed. Except in her unconditioned body. Her aching muscles protested daily against the rigors of hard labor. Recently every movement was a painful effort, and today was no exception.

When the noontime whistle blew, she had followed the women who worked her shift outside. A spasm shot up her legs to her back, and she winced as she plopped down on the bench beside Birdie.

"You'll get used to it," Birdie reassured her.

They were having lunch at one of the many picnic tables beside the reservoir pool. Because of Birdie and Gegonia, Annabel had been accepted by the other women operatives. She now knew most of them by their first names.

Since her arrival that morning at the mill, the sky had become veiled in gloomy clouds, and the wind had picked up, spiraling leaves from the trees and scattering them across the yard. Off in the distance, thunder rumbled.

Annabel shivered. After leaving the hot, humid air inside the factory, the sudden coolness chilled. Fall was not far away. Soon the mature season of summer would meet its decline in the form of autumn. It was a time of year she looked forward to as well as dreaded because winter usually danced on the coattails of the brilliant fall color.

She watched a group of girls, the youngest a pretty eleven-year-old named Billie Jean, who also worked in the mill. They had wolfed down their lunches and were skipping rope on a nearby grassy mound. Because Annabel felt comfortable with the women who surrounded her, she decided today was as good as any to make a few inquiries.

Annabel directed her question to no one in particular. "Shouldn't those children be in school?"

A woman by the name of Fanny whose face was as shriveled as a dried apple, and who Annabel suspected was years younger than she looked, answered, "It's summertime, gal. Young'uns don't usually go to school in summer."

Annabel felt foolish. She hadn't thought out her question before she asked it. *Of course, children didn't attend school during the summer months.*

Another woman by the name of Mona laughed. "Our young'uns don't attend school any other time of year either. What schooling they get begins and ends at home. All a body really needs to know about learning is the alphabet so they can sign their name. Besides, most of them will stay right here, working in the factory like their mas and pas afore them."

Annabel was appalled by Mona's answer. "Surely you must want more for your children than working in the factory?"

She thought about the Polks. Sara and Jess wanted so much for their twins. Had she been wrong in assuming that the other families in the mill village would feel the same as the Polks? When Fanny answered, Annabel realized that she shouldn't assume anything.

Fanny leaned her elbows on the table. "Beats working in the fields. Before the cotton mill came to town, my family eked out a living by dirt farming. Instead of getting paid twice a year, we now get paid every two weeks. We earn steady wages and we ain't worried about crop failures. All the vegetables we grow feeds our bellies and we live in a nice little company house. The way I see it, it don't get much better than that."

"Working in the factory is fine, but surely you want your children to be able to do more than just sign their names. How about reading?" Since Annabel was an avid reader, she couldn't imagine not being able to enjoy this pastime. "There is nothing as wonderful as being able to read a book or the newspaper."

Fanny assured her, "If'n they have a hankering to read, they'll learn themselves. My Billie Jean, she can read every piece of news that's pasted on our parlor walls."

Annabel had heard that people less fortunate than she papered their walls with newsprint, but she'd never seen the finished product. She also knew who Billie Jean was. She watched Fanny's daughter who appeared to be as quick at jumping rope as her mother claimed she was at reading. Billie Jean worked in the spinning room.

The child's thick brown hair hung in soft curls to her knees. As she jumped, the undulation of hair looked like swells on a stormy sea. Billie Jean was a beautiful child, and Annabel's heart went out to her. In a few years, after working nine-hour shifts in the mill, would she, too, look as haggard as her mother?

"Couldn't the mill provide schooling for the children? Or couldn't they be allowed time from their work to attend school in town?"

"Ain't you been listening, gal?" Fanny's earlier friendliness turned cool, and she stood to leave. "I know you worked in a factory in Macon, but you don't seem to know how it is for most of us. I've five children to feed, two of them younger than Billie Jean. It's family labor what keeps our family going, just like it got work done on the farm. Each of us had chores to do, same as now.

But the difference now is we all get paid for our labors. You can be sure when it comes to choosing between money or starvation, there ain't no choice. We got no time for schooling.''

Fanny's mouth tightened into a thin line when she'd said her piece.

Drat. This was not the way Annabel wanted their discussion to end. The last thing she wanted to do was to alienate herself from any of the women workers. She struggled with what to do next. Hoping to ease the woman's tension, she apologized. "Fanny, I'm sorry, I didn't mean to offend you.''

"Oh, I'm not offended, gal. I just want you to realize I ain't hankering to change a good thing. Now, if'n y'all will pardon me, I'll be heading back to work.''

Fanny turned on her heel and started toward the mill. "Come along, Billie Jean,'' she called to her daughter, "we've work to get back to.''

"Oh, Ma, it ain't time yet.''

"I said now, Billie Jean, and no arguments, or I'll have your pa get the strop to your backside when we get home.''

Reluctantly the child followed her mother, and Annabel watched them disappear into the doors of the mill.

Birdie shifted restlessly on the bench beside Annabel. "Don't you worry yourself none about Fanny. She doesn't mean to sound sharp. She's only doing what she has to do to survive. Her old man doesn't do anything but sit at home all day. I understand he guzzles whiskey as fast as she can make money to buy it.''

"Why would she stay with such a man?''

Mona pinned Annabel with a look of astonishment. "Why would she not? It's a woman's lot to stand by her husband—through good and bad times.''

"Mona. Certainly you don't believe that women should be slaves so their husbands can stay home and drink whiskey all day.''

"I believe what goes on between a husband and wife is their own business, and it isn't my place to interfere.

You'd do good to believe the same thing.''

"I'm not trying to interfere, I'm only expressing my opinion."

"Your opinions might be best kept to yourself." Mona stood. "I had best be getting back to the looms, too."

Birdie pushed herself to her feet. "You coming, Anna?" she asked.

Annabel's face flamed. She hadn't meant to insult anyone, or more importantly, make enemies among the women. "I'll be along shortly," she told Birdie. "Give me a few moments to collect myself."

"Don't worry yourself about those two. Their parents worked in the factory since its beginnings. As factory offspring, they followed in their parents' footsteps without question. It's as natural as breathing for them to be here. For them, the system gives them what they want."

"And what about you, Birdie? How do you feel about the system?"

"There's nothing much that I see needs changing. I'm happy to have a steady income that allows me to contribute to my family's welfare. And I enjoy working in the factory—my work gives me pleasure." She smoothed back a piece of hair that had come loose from her bun. "Don't tarry overly long. You have about ten minutes left."

As Birdie departed, Annabel watched her, recalling the first day she had met her. Birdie might look like a little wren, but she was the strongest woman Annabel had ever encountered, doing the work of three operatives and never complaining. She was the kind of "slave" the mill owners loved.

Annabel sighed. Some investigator she'd turned out to be. Already she had upset two women with her outspoken opinions. She never meant to upset anyone. Her purpose for being in the mill's employ was to improve the working conditions for those same two women and their children. Certainly there was nothing wrong with wanting to help those less fortunate than herself. Was there?

Annabel didn't have time to ponder her question, because the sky opened up, spilling rain with a vengeance. She dashed the long distance toward the mill entrance and rushed inside. Her clothes and hair were drenched, and her feet sloshed inside her only pair of boots. By the time she reached her place on the weaving floor, the humidity inside the building made her dress steam.

Once again she plugged her ears with cotton, blocking out the roar of the machinery whose sound eclipsed the rumbling thunder overhead. With nothing but her thoughts to entertain her, Annabel felt as isolated as an oyster.

Coit sat in front of the huge rolltop desk where he kept his books and ledgers and looked toward the store's plate-glass windows. The gully-washing rain that had begun on Wednesday still continued to pour down in a steady stream, wrapping the surrounding countryside in sheets of dismal gray water and making pumpkin soup out of the red clay streets.

Coit had devoted the afternoon to bringing his ledgers up-to-date. He traded two ways—he bought and sold goods from wholesalers and exchanged goods with his local customers. Most of his patrons bought on credit and would turn over the contents of their mill pay envelopes to him every other Friday. Since a lot of the families supplemented their incomes with cash crops, they also bartered eggs or butter for credit, along with vegetables, nuts, lard from butchering, natural bee honey, and fruit.

In Coit's opinion, the majority of the mill workers were underpaid, especially since his brother's latest cost-cutting efforts were put into effect. So Coit had taken it upon himself to supplement their salaries. He did so by pinching a little off their bills. Making huge profits didn't interest Coit. He lived very comfortably without price gouging.

Coit checked his pocket watch. From all appearances, it seemed that his Friday night regulars, instead of stopping by the store for their usual gab session, had hurried straight home from the factory, escaping to the dry, warm interiors of their houses. Not that he could blame the men.

A nice warm hearth and a woman to go with it would feel right cozy on such a miserable night. It had rained so much in the last three days that Coit's skin felt as though it might sprout mushrooms.

He was alone inside the store except for the Polks' cat. King Arthur had chosen to spend the wet afternoon in Coit's company, and now the big tom sat on one of the "loafing stools" that were normally occupied by the men from the factory.

Alone tonight, Coit welcomed the cat's company. Besides, King Arthur was a good mouser when the need arose, which wasn't very often. Coit was meticulous in rooting out all rodents and dispensing with them immediately upon discovery, but occasionally King Arthur's services were demanded, and he rewarded the hunter with some juicy treat. If eyes could portray thoughts, the signal the cat's gaze sent his way at the moment said he was demanding back pay, or maybe credit for some future kill.

Unable to resist the furry feline's demands, Coit got up from his desk chair and walked toward the counter and the round of cheese. First he sliced off a big wedge for himself and then a smaller one for the King.

He placed the morsel on the stool in front of the cat. "Does that suit you, Your Royal Highness?" Apparently it did. The cat tore into the cheese, attacking it as if it were some wild animal. "Glutton," Coit scolded.

Carrying his snack to the front window, he looked up and down the rain-soaked street. He was of the opinion that even ducks wouldn't enjoy such a wet day. If the rain kept up through tomorrow, the "shape-note singing" scheduled for the evening would have to be canceled. This thought frustrated him. All week long, he'd been looking forward to the event that included dinner on the mill-grounds. If the affair was canceled, it would ruin his chance of seeing Anna.

He heard the barking first. When Coit looked out the window, he saw a rain-drenched mongrel running up the street toward his store. Watching the mutt's progress, Coit wondered what had the dog in such a fit. Every few feet he would stop and turn around as though he were about to attack. Then he would bark and lunge at whatever was trailing him.

Assuming it was another dog, he was about to turn away from the window when he noticed the object of the mutt's displeasure. On first seeing the sodden black form, Coit didn't recognize it as being human. If the apparition hadn't been wielding a broken umbrella like a sword at the disorderly mutt, Coit would have believed the unusual sight was evoked by the blowing wind and rain. But then he recognized the straggly spill of coppery-red hair that fell wildly around the wraith's shoulders.

It was Anna.

Annabel was in a tiff as she slogged up the quagmire surface of the road. She had to contend not only with the rain and mud and being soaked through to the bone, but also with the fleabag mongrel that had dogged her passage from the moment she had stepped outside the mill's walls.

All the workers had disappeared so quickly when the whistle had announced the end of the day that it seemed to Annabel as if they had evaporated into the liquid air. Not in a hurry to face the elements, she had tarried at the factory longer than usual, hoping the rain would let up before she started home. When it didn't, she had stolen an abandoned umbrella that she had found by the entrance door. Now she could add the word thief to her list of deceitful pursuits. Not that a thief would have stolen such a nefarious umbrella. The moment Annabel had whipped it open, she'd discovered that one of its ribs was twisted like a pretzel. By the time she had reached the perimeter of the grounds, the wind had sucked the black silk mushroom inside out.

But, Annabel decided, if she hadn't had the hateful object, the mongrel dog might have eaten her alive. He'd nipped unmercifully at her ankles until she had turned the useless umbrella into a weapon. Because of it, she had become the pursuer as the twosome made their way up the street.

Never in all of Annabel's days could she recall feeling

so humiliatingly miserable. She suspected she looked like a wild woman with her black bombazine clothing clinging to every sodden curve of her body. When she was wielding the umbrella at her attacker, one of its rib tips had snagged on the knot of hair at her nape. After struggling to free the umbrella from the entanglement, she had freed her hair as well. It now hung around her shoulders like a rusty wet blanket.

To make matters worse, her only pair of serviceable boots had given up service. The rain of the last few days had taken its toll on leather and sole. Annabel didn't have to look at her feet to know that her stocking-covered toes sank into the oozy mud as she walked.

Before her perilous journey could end, Annabel intended to purchase a new pair of boots at the Company Store. She had her trusty pay envelope in her wet pocket. The envelope contained the whole dollar plus some change that she'd earned for her week and a day of work at the mill. The pittance was disgraceful when she compared it to the large allowance she received from her father for doing nothing but being his daughter. She wished now that she had brought that allowance with her from Atlanta instead of being noble and insisting that she would live on her weaver's salary.

The dog attacked again. This time he seemed to have recovered his earlier valor, or had he realized just how useless her umbrella was? He lunged for her ankles. Annabel whirled away from him, nearly stumbling. Their positions had changed. Now she was the hunted. She walked backward, nearly tripping on her dragging skirt, striking out at the dog that suddenly seemed more deadly than lightning.

"Shoo! Get," she shouted, almost near hysteria. The carnivorous dog parried as well as any trained fencer. Growling, the animal dove again for her ankles, then retreated. Annabel's feet tangled in her skirt. She started to fall. But before she hit the ground, strong arms caught her around the waist.

❖ 11 ❖

COIT SET ANNABEL beneath the veranda. Clapping his hands and stomping his feet, he shouted at the dog, "Go on, get! You unruly mutt!"

To Annabel, his man's voice sounded as threatening as thunder, but the mutt wasn't frightened. He held his ground, baring his teeth at his new tormentor. It was only after Coit hurled a piece of uneaten cheese toward the street that the animal turned tail and followed it. When he did, Coit grabbed her arm and shoved her through the store's open door. He slammed it shut behind them once they were inside.

Annabel sagged against the door frame, laboring for her breath. Her fingers still clutched the broken umbrella while her clothing dripped a big puddle onto the floor.

"Are you all right?" Coit asked, still watching the dog outside the window. "I don't remember seeing that pup around here before. He must be a stray."

Now that the ordeal with the dog was over, she realized how frightening the incident had been. Shaking, she answered him. "Stray or not, he must be rabid."

"Oh, I doubt that. I imagine he's just hungry and feeling misplaced. Poor little fellow."

Poor little fellow? She wasn't hungry, but she sure as the devil felt misplaced. Not that Coit had noticed; he seemed more concerned with the dog's welfare than hers. His indifference stung. She didn't belong in this little *backwater* town where rain came down in buckets, and where wild dogs attacked lone women walking down the street.

Anger shot through her all the way down to her wet toes. Annabel had had more than she could contend with for one afternoon. Imagine a man showing more compassion for an animal than a woman. Her temper exploded.

"Must you see good in all things? Even in a rabid dog? If you hadn't grabbed me when you did, that . . . that . . . mongrel you're so concerned about would probably have eaten me instead of that morsel of food you tossed his way."

Surprise furrowed Coit's brow. "I'm sure you'd taste better."

"Can't you be serious for one moment? He wasn't interested in tasting me, he . . . he wanted to eat me. He followed me all the way from the mill. I would have been dog food long before now if I hadn't had this sorry excuse for an umbrella to protect me." She shook it in his face.

Coit smiled. "Your umbrella is in pretty bad shape. But step right this way, and I just might be able to fix you up with a new one." He sounded like a huckster, peddling his wares. Coit winked and moved to where several black umbrellas, similar to the one she still clutched, stood in a stand by the door.

She eyed the umbrellas with disdain. "You're probably the hawker who sold this one to the poor sucker I stole it from. Look at it—it's not worth a hoot." She tossed it at him. If he hadn't deflected it with his hands, it would have hit him square in the chest. In her present mood, the thought gave her extreme pleasure.

"Now, don't get violent—"

"Violent?" She glared at him. "I didn't drop in for a friendly visit. I came here to do business."

"Business? I don't usually have to drag my customers off the street."

Annabel completely ignored his remark. Instead she lifted up her sodden skirt and showed him her feet. Mud-covered toes peeked from the ends of the misshapened, worn-out boots. "I've come to buy new boots," she told him, fighting back tears, "but I don't have much money."

He looked her up and down. For the first time since she had entered the store, Coit seemed to notice her soaked condition. "You are a mess, aren't you? From the looks of you, you'll be needing some dry clothing as well." He reached for her elbow and tried to steer her toward a long rack of men's and women's clothes. "I have a nice supply of readymades. If you'll just step over here, I'm sure you'll find something that will accommodate you until—"

"Didn't you hear me, sir?" Exasperated, Annabel shrugged loose from his hold. "I just told you I don't have much money. I'll be lucky if I can afford to pay for a pair of shoes." Reaching inside her skirt pocket, she pulled out her soggy pay envelope. "I assure you there isn't enough money in here to purchase a whole new outfit."

"Don't worry about it," Coit said. "I'll put it on your account."

"My account?" Surely she hadn't heard him right. "I don't have an account in your store."

"Well, you can open one. Everyone else in the mill village purchases from me on credit."

His statement was like a bell going off inside her head. So that was how it was.

In her research on cotton mills, Annabel had discovered that some mills paid their employees with scrip. At least at the Royal Mill the operatives were paid in cash. She'd witnessed the transaction today with her own eyes. The mill hands, herself included, were given small manila envelopes that contained their pay.

But she wondered if there was a difference between being paid in scrip and surrendering your wages to the

Company Store. In Annabel's opinion there was not. And the worst thing about this latest discovery was that the man whom she had begun to like and respect was no better than a robber baron!

Appalled, she turned an icy stare on Coit. "Doesn't it bother you that these mill people live on the margin of subsistence? Or that they live from week to week, payday to payday? What do they do when they get their pay envelopes, come in here and hand it to you unopened? I bet you grin all the way to the bank. You . . . you robber baron!"

Anger flared in Coit's dark brown eyes. But it came and went so quickly that Annabel wasn't certain if she had imagined it or not.

Coit grabbed her arm again. "At least allow me to get you some towels to dry off with. I'd hate for you to catch pneumonia on my account. Besides," he added on a controlled note, "the towels are free. They won't cost you a red cent."

Annabel jerked away from him, throwing words at him like pebbles. "How dare you jest when we're discussing such a serious topic?"

"Discussing?" This time Coit's voice was loaded with censure. "I wouldn't exactly call this an exchange of ideas and opinions. So far it's been one-sided. Oh, yes, and Anna, weren't you the young woman who told me just the other day that you never overreact?"

"I'm not overreacting," she assured him.

"Well, you could sure as hell fool me."

His response silenced her. If she hadn't been in desperate need of a new pair of boots, she would have stormed back into the gale rather than endure his rudeness a moment longer.

Taking advantage of the quiet, Coit said, "Now, if you'll excuse me, I'll get those towels."

He left her dripping in the middle of the store. Now she understood the expression "mad as a wet hen." In a few moments, he returned. Instead of handing the towels to her, he tossed them at her.

"Maybe while you're drying off you'll cool down as well. And since you seem so all-fired opposed to the way I run my business, consider this a loan." He thrust a flannel shirt on top of the towels. "You need to get out of that wet clothing, or some of it, before you catch your death. Now tell me your shoe size, and I'll see what I can find that might fit you."

Annabel was tempted to throw the towels and shirt back at him. It would serve him right if she died right here in his store. But she was freezing, and since she had a purchase to make before she left, she answered him sarcastically. "A size eight. I don't suppose you would have a ladies' size eight among your humble stock, would you?"

This time there was no mistake. Coit's expression darkened with anger. The air between them was so charged it was almost palpable. They faced each other like two animals ready to charge. Finally Coit broke the tension. "Thank you," he said curtly. Then he left.

She watched his retreat. He mumbled beneath his breath as he made his way to the far corner of the store. Annabel strained to hear his words.

"Women," he grumbled, "they're all hopeless."

"We're not all helpless," she informed him.

Coit didn't take the bait, so Annabel began rubbing one of the towels over her hair, sponging out as much moisture as she could. Next, she wrung out the hem of her skirt. The sight of the water pooling on Coit's spotless floor gave her a rush of satisfaction, but her pleasure quickly dimmed in view of their heated words.

Skeptically she eyed the dry shirt. Since she had no money to purchase it, she decided she would take Coit up on his loan. Besides, she was freezing to death. Never taking her eyes from Coit's position, she quickly unfastened the buttons on her waist. Removing the wet garment, she tossed it aside and slipped into the flannel shirt, buttoning it up to her neck. It felt like heaven next to her chilled skin.

From where she stood, she watched Coit rummaging through a wooden barrel. Several pairs of discarded shoes clunked against the floor. As he searched the container, his broad shoulders beneath his white shirt stood out like a beacon in the deepening dusk. Although Annabel believed she truly hated the man and what he stood for, the sight of his muscles rippling against the taut white fabric played havoc on her already run-away emotions.

She wouldn't allow such thoughts. Determined to purchase her boots and leave, she looked for something to sit on so she could remove her ruined shoes and stockings. A small stool sat near the potbellied stove. Annabel moved toward it, sat down on it, and began removing her rain-soaked articles.

As Coit rummaged through his shoe barrel, Anna's snide remark ate at him. If he had to empty out the whole barrel, he would find something in his paltry stock that would suit the lady's taste.

No longer was Coit unsure that Anna wasn't a lowly mill worker; he was dead set convinced she wasn't. Anyone who could speak so resolutely in the face of anger had to have some formal training in debate.

In fact, it wouldn't surprise him one whit if the eloquent Anna turned out to be one of those prominent suffragettes who traveled around the country stirring up trouble, while claiming they wanted to make things better for all people, women in particular.

Harpies was how Coit saw them. Some folks predicted that if women ever got the vote, they would become "large-handed, big-footed, flat-chested, and thin-lipped." He considered those attributes for a moment. It would be a long time in coming before Anna Belle Blow became flat-chested, but then, she already did have big feet. A size eight was large for a woman.

Maybe it wasn't suffrage at all that Anna was mixed up with. Coit had recently read about the national federation of the Knights of Labor. He knew the union that had been established in 1869 had begun to organize women in 1881. Maybe Anna worked for this union and had been sent to the Royal Mill to try to get a foothold in the industry.

Not that Coit would be opposed to any organization that could make a mill worker's life a little easier. In his own way, he did what he could toward this end. But it annoyed him that Anna would believe the worst about him: that she would believe he felt no more compassion for the mill hands than her statement implied. *A robber baron.*

Maybe he was mistaken. If Anna was all the things he thought she could be, then surely she would have come to town with some funds. She had claimed to have no money, and the boots she wore had definitely seen better days.

No, Coit reasoned, still wanting her to be who she claimed to be, Anna had a tirade because she was upset over being chased by the unruly pup in the frog-choking rain. Under similar circumstances, any woman would have overreacted.

After finding several pairs of boots for her to try on, he straightened and headed back to Anna. When he didn't see her, standing where he had left her, he thought that she had sneaked away. He searched the front of the store, then the middle. Disappointment assailed him. She had gone. But then he spotted the top of her coppery-red hair on the level with the top of the wood stove. His frustration on believing that she had slipped away disappeared. No matter how much he wanted to, he couldn't stay annoyed with Anna.

He approached her where she sat on the low stool. "Here we are."

Coit was taken aback by how childlike she looked in the green plaid flannel shirt and with her hair spread around her shoulders. The image of a Christmas angel he had once carried in his store flashed through his mind. Her skin was flushed, making her freckles less noticeable. Before that moment, Coit hadn't considered Anna Belle Blow to be a beautiful woman. But in the soft glow of twilight, his earlier notion no longer held true.

He took a deep draft of air, suddenly aware that the two of them were alone in the store with the rain outside providing a barrier from intruders. Alone with the woman who had been in his thoughts, both night and day, since their first meeting. Alone with the woman whose kiss had set him on fire like no other woman before her. The knowledge of their isolation did manly things to his body.

"I'll need some stockings as well," she told him, her flush turning to a deeper shade of rose.

Her statement brought Coit back to the present. "Of course you will," he replied. "Do you have a preference?"

"Cheap," she responded.

Coit fought a smile. He left her again. A few moments later, while thumbing through his stock of women's hosiery, he pictured Anna's slim ankles encased in stockings fashioned of the finest Paris silk. The image brought other images to his mind, like him removing them.

Holy catfish! What was the matter with him anyway? Coit sold stockings to women nearly every day, but until today, he had never entertained such visions with his customers. The woman had him crazy. Pushing all thoughts of silk stockings from his mind, he searched through his supply of "cheap." He had plenty of that brand in his inventory. When he had found the proper size, he returned to where Anna waited and handed her the merchandise.

In his absence, she had been examining the shoes. From the expression on her face, he suspected that the boots didn't meet with her approval. Coit had brought her one pair each of the two styles of ladies' boots that he stocked in his store. Both were reasonably priced and durable.

He pulled up a stool in front of her and picked up the boots and began to unlace one pair and unbutton the other.

"What are you doing?" she asked him.

He met her stare. "What does it look like I'm doing? I'm preparing these shoes so you can try them on."

"And just how am I to put these on with you sitting mere inches away from my knees?" The woven cotton stockings dangled from her hands like black snakes.

Coit couldn't resist teasing her. Besides, he wanted to wipe the frown from her face and replace it with the smile he'd gotten used to. "How about if I close my eyes and promise not to peek?"

"And you think I can trust you?"

In spite of the hardship of her trying to keep a stern face, the corners of her full mouth turned up a tinge.

No thin lips there. The slight movement heightened Coit's hopes. Maybe she wasn't mad at him any longer.

"Even if I pledge my honor not to look?" he asked, arching his brows playfully.

"There is no honor among thieves."

"Well, I figured since you had filched an umbrella, we might consider a truce among thieves."

Anna gasped. "Surely you're not comparing my crime to yours."

"I'm not comparing anything to anything. I'm only saying that in this country before one is charged with guilt, he has the right of a fair trial."

She considered his statement before she responded, "I'm not the one robbing these poor people blind."

"I'm not either."

Coit stood up so fast the stool tumbled backward. The sound of its falling echoed throughout the quiet room. Anna jumped. Apparently she wasn't going to let her charge against him rest until she had beaten it into the ground. If they kept at each other's throats the way they were going now, they would end up enemies. Coit didn't want that.

"Anna, put on the stockings and try on the boots. Then you better get the devil out of here, or I might be charged with murder."

He heard her gasp as he whirled away from her to give her some privacy.

"You, Anna Belle Blow, are the most frustrating woman I've ever known. You may believe you know what's best for these folks, but in my humble opinion, you don't know squat about them or where they are coming from."

"Believe me, I know," she insisted.

He felt her presence behind him before she began tapping his shoulder like a woodpecker tapping a tree. When he swung around to face her, she continued the tapping against his chest.

Her eyes were dilated with outrage. "I know what it's like to stand for twelve hours on hard floors without any breaks except for a forty-five-minute lunch in the middle of the day. I see children not much older than the twins, working the same twelve hours as their parents. Those same children are denied schooling because they have to work in the mill to help support their family. To put food on their tables.

"Also if people like your brother who owns the mill would pay their parents more money, then maybe the children would be able to attend school. And maybe, with those same increased salaries, every cent those poor folks earned wouldn't be owed to the Company Store."

Her last statement made her sound too cocky. Coit was fed up. He was tired of her pounding a hole through his chest with her forefinger, and more importantly he was tired of her insults.

In one swift motion, he grabbed her by both arms, picked her up, and carried her back to the stool. "It's closing time, my sweet, and I have more important things to do than argue with you all night. I suggest you pick out the boots that please you, then be on your way."

Stunned, Annabel found herself being thrust back on the stool she'd vacated earlier. Coit righted the one he had knocked over, pulling it in front of hers again, and sat down. Jerking the laces through the holes, he readied the boot for her foot. Anna tried to stand, but he effectively stopped her from rising, using gentle force to keep her seated.

He ordered, "Give me your foot."

"I'll give you nothing but a swift kick if you dare to touch me."

"Anna, give me your damn foot." His voice held a threat.

"No. I don't want your ugly shoes."

"Anna, you're acting like a spoiled brat." Coit grabbed

both of her feet and held them in a viselike grip on his lap. "You can try these shoes on in a civilized manner, or I can resort to force. It's your choice, Anna. Make up your mind."

"I told you, I don't want your ugly shoes." She kicked out at him. "Let go of me," she ordered. The stool wobbled. The armless seat tilted sideways. Too late, she tried to steady it, but instead she felt herself airborne. Since Coit held her feet, her bottom hit the floor first. Stunned, she flopped backward, no longer bothering to struggle. She lay without moving, staring at the ceiling, studying all manner of implements hanging from it—lanterns, pails, saws, chains, dinner bells.

He let go of her feet and bent down beside her, one hand on each side of her shoulders. Coit's worried face peered above hers, blocking out the paraphernalia. "My God, Anna, I'm sorry."

Even if she had wanted to move, she couldn't have because she was pinned between his two arms.

"Believe me, Anna, never in all my thirty years have I ever manhandled a woman. I don't know what came over me."

Coit continued to apologize, and she could only stare up at him. It seemed that her will to move had fled with her fall, taking her tantrum with it.

"Can you ever forgive me? My God, Anna, are you hurt? Should I fetch a doctor? Please speak to me."

Anna didn't speak. Instead, she recalled the twins' words, when they had flipped her from the hammock. *"Have we kilt her, Mr. Coit?"*

In the last week, her body had suffered more abuse than it had in all of her twenty-five years. For the second time in less than five days, she had found herself tossed to the ground on her backside, and had Coit staring down into her face, inquiring if she was all right. *Hell, no, she wasn't all right.* Not only was she in pain, but she was also out of control of her own destiny.

The entire situation had become ludicrous, absurd really. Instead of answering Coit, she laughed. Her giggles started deep inside of her chest, then shook her convulsively as they escaped her mouth.

Coit stared at her in disbelief. His puzzled look only fueled her merriment. She laughed harder. With her laughter, her anger fled. What an afternoon. Her experiences had her in a near hysterical state. First a mad dog had chased her through the rain-soaked streets, and now this crazy, infuriatingly handsome man had taken unrivaled liberties with her feet before throwing her to the floor.

The same infuriatingly handsome man who looked at her now with so much concern in his chocolate brown eyes that he made her insides feel as formless as uncooked fudge.

Stroking her mussed hair back from her face, Coit asked, ''Anna, you're not delirious, are you?'' Worry filled his voice.

''No,'' she reassured him, ''I'm not delirious. I think you could better describe my condition as illusional.'' She laughed again.

''How's that, my love?'' He continued to stroke her forehead, trying to calm her.

His love. His endearment left her speechless.

Maybe she was suffering delirium and didn't know it. But at the moment, it didn't really matter. All that really mattered was that Annabel wanted Coit to kiss her. She wanted to feel his lips pressed against hers. She wanted the two of them to practice a little lip-sucking, as the twins had so aptly put it.

It was as though Coit had read her thoughts. He dropped down on one elbow and stared deeply into her eyes. ''I think I need to kiss you, Anna,'' he said.

She swallowed the lump that suddenly closed her throat. ''I think you need to, too.''

''This time you won't overreact?''

She replied breathlessly, ''I never overreact.''

He chuckled softly and pressed her nose with his finger. ''Oh, my sweet, Anna, whatever am I to do with you?''

She wiggled more comfortably beneath him, accepting

his weight on her chest. "Kiss me now, or I just might die."

His dark eyes sparkled with mischief as he leaned his face closer to hers. "What a scandal that would be—you lying dead on my floor. No, we can't have that now, can we?"

"Not with the list of all your other crimes—"

"Shush! Let's not talk about that any more tonight, Anna."

"But—"

Coit silenced her with his lips.

An hour later, after practicing every kind of kiss known to mankind, he escorted her home. It was still raining, but with her new Dongola Box Toe Button Boots, her dry cotton stockings, and Coit's flannel shirt, Annabel practically floated the distance between the two houses.

This time the umbrella that sheltered her from the elements wasn't a force to be reckoned with. And instead of a mongrel dog nipping at her ankles, King Arthur trotted along between them, sharing the shelter of Coit's big umbrella.

Once they reached the overhang of the Polks' back porch, Coit pulled her into his arms again. Annabel welcomed his embrace, returning his kiss with as much ardor as the one he gave her.

"Until tomorrow," he whispered, stepping back, holding her hand until only their fingertips touched.

"Tomorrow," she whispered back. Their fingers parted, and he drifted away. Annabel watched him until his long form melded with the surrounding darkness and was no longer visible.

Feeling beautiful for the first time in her life, Annabel turned and slipped inside the back door. Tonight she had learned how it felt to be kissed by a man. Coit's kissing was beyond heavenly, almost spiritual, she decided, recalling all the wonderful ways he had kissed her and how his kisses had made her feel.

Stripping out of her clothing, she donned a nightgown

and crawled into bed. Her last rational thought before she drifted into a deep contented sleep was that there was much more to lip-sucking than just puckering up. Already Annabel was anticipating her and Coit's next session.

❖ *12* ❖

THE FOLLOWING MORNING, when Annabel took a chair beside Sara on the Polks' back porch, the crystal-bright morning felt more like fall than late summer. Sometime during the night, the infernal rain of the last three days had ceased. The overhead sun shone with such brilliance that the rain-soaked trees and plants sparkled as though they were adorned with jewels. Annabel deeply inhaled the fresh, clean air. The world always seemed brand new after a long, hard rain, and today the landscape looked as spiffy as her shiny boots.

"New shoes?" Sara asked, examining Annabel's feet.

She held her feet out in front of her. "And not a moment before I needed them. The leather and sole of my old ones had parted company days ago. I was almost barefooted."

Being barefooted made her recall last night. She gloried briefly in the remembrance; Coit holding her feet in his lap, then Coit holding her. This last thought made her blush. Had Sara noticed how Annabel had changed? She felt every bit as lively and vivacious as the dawning of this brisk day.

"You seem different this morning," Sara said, studying her. "You almost glow."

"Glow?" Fire stole into Annabel's cheeks, making Sara smile.

"I suppose it was the purchase of those brand new shoes that kept you so late at the store?"

Annabel swallowed. "Why, Sara Polk, whatever are you implying?"

"I'm not implying anything, Anna, but I am dying to hear all about what happened."

"Happened?"

"If that glow on your face comes from the purchase of new boots, then perhaps I should buy me a pair." Sara studied Annabel's face. "I haven't had a glow like that since Jess and I were courting."

Annabel could no longer retain her indifference. Covering her mouth, she giggled like the besotted girl she was.

"Oh, all right. I did purchase these boots from the Company Store. But because it was raining so hard, Coit and I visited."

"And?" Sara leaned closer. "You visited, and then what?"

"What do you mean what?" Heat flashed from the top of Anna's spine to the ends of her knotted hair. She imagined her face, scalp, and ears were the same awful color as her tresses.

"Practicing a little lip-sucking, were you?"

"Sara Polk—where do you get such ideas?" Anna tapped her friend's knee playfully.

"I knew it—the two of you are perfect for each other."

Sara's statement darkened the bright moment, causing a deep pain in Anna's chest. There were no two people in the world less suited for each other than she and Coit Jackson. But without revealing her true identity, she couldn't tell Sara why.

Also, she couldn't afford to entertain romantic notions about the storekeeper. "Believe me, Sara, Coit and I are only friends, nothing else." After all, she rationalized, they had only shared a kiss. A lot of kisses, a little voice reminded her, but then men and women exchanged kisses all the time.

"Don't be so modest, Anna. You're both unwed and both in need of a mate."

"Sara, neither of us are looking to get married. Must you be such a matchmaker?"

"I'm only doing what comes natural," Sara quipped.

The conversation was getting far too personal for Annabel. Besides, if she didn't think of Coit Jackson in the way Sara suggested, when the time came for Annabel to leave Dalworth and return home, the leaving would be so much easier.

"Please, Sara, let's talk about something else. Like where are the rest of the Polks on this bright, sunny morning?"

"Aren't you just dying to tell me all?"

"Sara, please!"

"Oh, all right, if you insist. Jess is at the mill, and Lance and Percy are in the garden, picking butter beans. I'm going to cook up a mess of them and bake a spice cake to carry to this evening's festivities."

"Sara, you do too much," Annabel insisted.

"No, I don't. Besides you and the boys are going to help me. While I'm whipping up the cake batter, the three of you can shell the beans."

"Shell the beans?"

Annabel had about as much experience with shelling beans as she had with kissing. Until last night. As far as whatever it was you did with the little green things, that chore had been left to their cook back in Atlanta. Annabel only ate them.

The twins came running from the side of the house and screeched to a stop several inches away from the edge of the porch. "Morning, Miss Anna." Each boy carried a metal pail, filled to the brim with the unshelled butter beans.

"Ma said you and us are going to break them," one of the twins told her.

She eyed the boys skeptically. Their clothes were caked with red clay and wet grass. It looked as though they had been wrestling with the beans instead of picking them.

"See," said one of the boys as he pointed to his forehead. "We already marked ourselves so you won't have no trouble telling us apart."

Sure enough, on each boy's forehead the first letter of their name was written in dried clay. "We wrote it just like Mr. Coit showed us." Each boy grinned, baring several spaces of missing teeth.

Sara stood up. "That was mighty thoughtful of you boys to help Miss Anna out." She raised one eyebrow as though questioning the twins' actions. Lance winked at his mother when she reached for a big pan that hung on the wall behind her. Then the twins helped her spread a piece of oilcloth over the floor. Handing Annabel the pan, Sara told the boys to put only the shelled beans in the pan and the hulls on the cloth. "Now, I'm going inside to stir up the cake. You two mind your manners and do your share of the work."

"We will, Ma," the twins answered in unison. They giggled mischievously when their mother went inside.

Okay, Annabel thought, how does one shell beans? Maybe if she stalled long enough, the boys would answer that question for her.

"You gotta work, too, Miss Anna," Percy told her while she watched them. His tiny fingers snapped off one end of the long green pod. The popping sound made both the boys laugh. Annabel continued to watch as Percy then peeled back one side of the bean's hull. Three butter beans clung to the shell's inner lining. With a flick of his fingers, the beans *pinged* into the tin pan that now sat on the floor between the threesome.

It looked easy enough, Annabel decided. If a six-year-old boy could do it, so could she.

She picked up a green pod, snapped off one end, then tried to peel back the bean's side as Percy had done. The stubborn little sucker refused to be peeled. Only after several digs with her fingernails did she finally manage to open the hull and pluck out its contents. She tossed the three tiny beans into the huge pan.

As the sun rose higher, the twins challenged each other to races. Beans snapped, popped, and pinged from their short fingers. Some beans missed the pan, but the boys were careful to retrieve the runaways and put them where they belonged.

As the boys' fun grew rowdier, King Arthur joined them. If an errant bean flew his way, he'd swat it with his furry paw. Soon he owned several of the beans that he continued to bat and chase across the wooden floor. In fact, to Annabel it looked as though the cat's pile was growing faster than the supply inside the pan, especially when the boys kept tossing beans his way.

Lance and Percy opened five pods to Annabel's one. Never would she have believed that snapping beans could take so long. It didn't take that long to eat them. At the rate they were shelling, dinner on the grounds would come and go before they finished.

"You boys are good at this," she told them, admiring their deft fingers.

"Ma always says 'practice makes perfect,' and we sure get a lot of practice." Lance watched her struggling to open the same bean she'd been wrestling with for the last few minutes. "I guess because you ain't married like our ma, you ain't very good at snapping beans."

"Don't say ain't, Lance," his brother disciplined. "You know ma hates that word."

"She ain't here to hear it, is she, Mr. Know-It-All?"

"Oh, she'll hear it okay. And then she'll box your ears."

"You're the one that's going to get boxed."

"Oh, yeah?"

"Yeah! And I might be the boxer."

"Boys," Annabel interrupted. "I'm sure your mother is more interested in getting these beans shelled than in you two boxing each other's ears."

Although her fingers were starting to cramp, Annabel was getting better at shelling. She tossed several more beans into the pan with the others. The twins were glaring at each other. Hoping to divert them from their earlier disagreement, she asked, "Why don't you boys tell me how they make butter out of these beans?"

"Butter?" Percy and Lance stared at her, their small mouths gaping open.

"Yes," she said, "they are butter beans, aren't they?" Annabel tossed a handful of beans into the pan. The *ping, ping, ping* was a welcoming sound because it meant she was making progress.

Lance slapped his forehead, smearing the red clay letter. "I guess because you ain't married like our ma, you don't know where butter comes from either?"

"Well, why don't you tell me."

"Our ma makes it," he answered impatiently. "It comes right out of that mixer." He pointed to a butter churn, sitting next to the house.

"It's a churn," Percy told his brother, before adding, "Miss Anna, how come you're so dumb?"

Annabel stifled a laugh. "I guess it's because I'm not married like your ma, and I don't have two smart little boys to tell me all I need to know."

"Oh, we don't tell our ma. She tells us. That's why we're so smart."

Percy leaned toward Annabel and whispered, "But you're right about the butter, Miss Anna. Ma does put these beans in that churn and she beats the daylights out of them. Best butter this side of the Mason-Dixie line."

"Is that a fact?" Annabel couldn't hide her smile this time.

"That ain't true, Percy Polk, and you know it," Lance said. "Pa's going to whoop your backside for fibbing. Butter comes from cows."

"We ain't got no cow. So how come we got butter?"

Lance pondered this question for several moments, his face puzzled. "Maybe it does come from butter beans. But to be sure, we better go ask Ma since Miss Anna don't know nothing."

The bean-shelling forgotten, the twins headed for the back door.

Now I've done it. Setting those boys on Sara when she's so busy.

"Boys," she called. "Maybe you should wait and ask her later. She's working right now."

"She ain't never too busy to answer our questions," the boys echoed.

Annabel looked first at Percy then at Lance, addressing each twin by the letter written on their foreheads.

"Percy, Lance, you know your ma expects us to shell all of these beans. She needs our help."

"Yeah, we know, but first we gotta find out where butter comes from."

"Lance, if you'll wait a moment, maybe I can tell you. I seem to recall—"

"You can't tell us, Miss Anna, cause you don't know about things like our ma does."

Annabel started to protest again, but the twins interrupted her. "Oh, yeah, we almost forgot." They pointed to each other. "He's Lance and I'm Percy. We swapped letters so we could trick you." Giggling, they ran inside.

Shaking her head in amazement, she kept snapping beans. If she stayed around the twins much longer, she would really be confused.

Surprised by the boys' admission, she now understood the questioning look Sara had given the boys before returning to the kitchen. She knew the boys were trying to trick her, and they had succeeded.

"How clever those two are." She'd only known the twins for a little over a week, and already they had wormed their way into her heart. The thought of not seeing them again saddened her.

Annabel knew if she stayed around this town much longer, she would need her own initial tattooed on her forehead. Not only would she need to remind herself who she was, but also she needed to remember her purpose for being here.

*   *   *

From his vantage point outside the mill's red brick office building, Coit could see the back of the Hamil family home and the front of his store that sat diagonally across the street. He had closed the store at two o'clock this afternoon in order to help ready the mill grounds for tonight's festivities.

His stepbrother, Gordy, had just exited the back of the house and now sprinted across the gently sloping yard toward where Coit stood waiting. Earlier, Gordy had forgotten the building's keys and had returned home to fetch them. Although Coit was forced to wait for Gordy, after the pleasant evening spent with Anna he felt benevolent toward his older brother. Besides, he wanted to ask him about Merelda Whitcomb. His brother prided himself on knowing and socializing with Dalworth's elite.

As Gordy approached him, he jangled the keys in his pocket. "Sorry, Coit. Don't know where my head was earlier. If you'd take to carrying your own key, then you could have let yourself in."

"Since when do you want me to carry a key to your domain?" Coit asked.

"A key to the building and a key to the safe are two entirely different matters." He entered before Coit and bade him follow.

Although Coit owned a ten percent, non-voting interest in the mill, he wanted nothing to do with its operation, especially with Gordy holding the other ninety percent of shares. Gordy had always resented Coit's ten-percent interest in the mill as well as his title to the Company Store. As Benson Hamil's only child and rightful heir, Gordy had wanted it all. The fires of contention had been fueled even more between the two men when his stepfather had named Coit in his will.

Gordy inserted the key in the lock and opened the front door of the mill office.

Coit had to bite his tongue to keep from responding to his stepbrother's sarcastic remark. But why belabor the issue? The deadlock between them would never be resolved as long as Gordy kept cutting costs at the mill, at the expense of the workers.

Once inside, the two men headed for the large storage room at the back of the building. Extra benches and tables, along with shelves full of company records, were stored in the area. After unlocking the huge swinging doors, Gordy pocketed the keys. Together they propped open the doors, allowing sun and fresh air to flow into the otherwise closed space.

"You setting this up alone?" Gordy asked.

"No. Several men from the mill will be meeting me here in about an hour. We'll set up the extra tables beside the others near the reservoir pool."

Gordy looked him over. "You really get into this sing-along, don't you?"

"I enjoy it, yes. You ought to try it sometime. You might enjoy it, too." Coit couldn't resist a little dig. "It's a good way to get to know the people who work for you."

"Believe me, I know enough about the people who work for me. I admit most of them are good workers and dependable, but that doesn't mean I want to socialize with them like you do."

Or pay them more for their good work and dependability. Anna's argument had stayed with Coit long after he'd left her on her doorstep last night. He understood her concern for the workers, but it was Gordy who ran the mill, who had reminded Coit numerous times that he knew nothing about profit and margin.

Gordy swiped a white handkerchief over his receding hairline. "You know I always put in an appearance. And since I don't enjoy these socials as you do, I'm sure your presence will make up for my absence. Besides, this evening there is an engagement at the Opera House in town that I can't miss."

Won't miss, Coit thought, but didn't voice his opinion. Instead he grabbed a rag hanging from a nearby hook and began dusting off benches and tables. "There is something I've been meaning to ask you." Coit paused in his dusting and looked at his brother. "What do you know about Merelda Whitcomb?"

His question had clearly surprised his brother. Gordy folded his arms across his narrow chest and looked as though he was debating how to answer it. Finally he responded with the sarcasm that Coit had gotten used to through the years.

"My, my, little brother, don't tell me Miss Whitcomb has attracted your fancy. She's a bit out of your league, is she not? I was under the impression you weren't interested in hobnobbing with the 'uptown society.' Because you're my father's stepson, I'm sure doors in town would be open to you if you should go calling. But I'm not so sure old Melvin would want his only daughter marrying a mere shopkeeper."

"Dammit, Gordy. I'm not asking about the woman because I'm interested in marrying her. I ran into her at the Ice Cream Saloon the other day, and she acted as if we knew each other."

Coit lied about their meeting, but then Gordon wasn't interested in the preliminaries. He was more interested in driving home the point that it was the Hamil name that carried weight in Dalworth. It didn't matter to Gordy that Coit's mother had been born into the same kind of society that Gordy coveted so much, but in Nashville, Tennessee.

Gordy shut his pale blue eyes as though he were trying to recall Merelda Whitcomb. "Now, let me see. . . ."

Such theatrics, Coit thought. He'd swear on his dead mother's grave that Gordon Hamil knew everything there was to know about the girl, and more. Not only would Gordon be knowledgeable about her female attributes, but also her monetary worth as well. Close to losing patience, Coit waited for his brother's reply.

"She's not a looker in my opinion. She's not my type. Although, with her daddy's money, she has spruced herself up quite nicely and she is now a presentable escort. Before she went off to Wesleyan College in Macon, the girl was much too scholarly for a gentleman's taste. Could be why she hasn't married."

Coit watched as Gordy folded his handkerchief and placed it back inside his pocket.

"I hear tell," Gordy continued, "that her father has plans for a match between her and his new law clerk. I understand young Dewey is after a partnership in the Whitcomb firm. Old Mel wants to keep it in the family, so to speak."

Gordy smirked. "Doesn't sound good, little brother, for your suit, now does it?"

"My suit? Believe me, Gordy, I'm not interested in courting Merelda Whitcomb. I'm just trying to recall if we've met."

Wesleyan College in Macon. Here was a possible connection between Anna and Merelda that Coit hadn't thought about before. Anna was certainly eloquent and articulate enough to be a college graduate. And wasn't Wesleyan an exclusive, all-female college? All Coit would have to do was shoot off a letter to the registrar's office to find out if an Anna Belle Blow had ever attended the institute. Providing, of course, that was her real name.

Breaking into his thoughts, Gordy asked, "You're certain you're not interested in this girl? As long as we've been brothers, you've never once asked my opinion about a woman. Considering my experience—"

"No, I'm not interested in her. I was only inquiring about her."

Gordy studied him with an arrogance that Coit had come to expect from his stepbrother. Why, after all the years of sharing parents, hadn't a connection formed between them? Neither had any family left to speak of except each other. In the beginning, Coit had worried over it, hoping they would become closer like real brothers, but time had proved that such a relationship was impossible—he and Gordy were too different.

When a shadow darkened the shaft of sunlight that spilled through the open doors, Coit was relieved. Gordy had given him the information he'd asked for, and now he was glad to see Jess Polk standing in the doorway.

"Howdy, Mr. Hamil, Coit." Jess smiled at the two

men. "Harve and the others will be along shortly. I told the twins to send them on in here when they arrived."

Gordy walked toward Jess. "I guess your presence here means you've finished up at the mill."

"Yes, sir, everything is locked up good and tight until Monday."

"I'm glad to have a man like you to depend on, Jess. Miss Whiz tells me Miss Blow, our newest weaver, is boarding at your house."

"Yes, sir, she is. Anna's a very nice lady and a good companion for my wife, Sara. The twins like her as well."

Coit listened to the exchange. Now why in the devil would Gordy be concerned about Jess's boarder? He sure wasn't concerned about the other people who worked for the mill. In all the years that Gordy had managed the mill in his father's place, Coit couldn't recall hearing Gordon inquire once about a worker's personal life. Was his earlier suspicion about Gordy true? Did his interest in Anna go deeper than what appeared on the surface?

Damn and blast. White-hot anger sizzled in Coit's veins. If his brother dared to lay a finger on Anna or take advantage of her because of his position, he would beat him within an inch of his life.

Gordy's response brought Coit back to the moment and the conversation between Gordy and Jess. "That's good, that Miss Blow found a nice place to stay. I like to see my operatives happy. She was lucky the room was available when she needed it. How did she hook up with you so quickly?"

"Coit knew Sara was looking for a boarder. When he met Anna on the train ride home from Atlanta, he told her about the room."

"Is that right?" Gordy said, brushing back his almost nonexistent hair with his hand. "Nice of you to be so accommodating, Coit. Miss Blow is a right comely-looking woman and an interesting one as well. I found her knowledge of the classics most unusual for a lady of her status."

"So she likes to read," Coit replied. "Nothing wrong with that."

"Nothing wrong with it, but most unusual in a mill operative, wouldn't you say?"

Coit's temper flared. He looked at Gordy with heated disgust. How could anyone be so insensitive to another's feelings? Here he was talking about the mill workers as though they were all illiterate, and with Jess listening. Coit would never understand his stepbrother, but he wouldn't stand by and let him continue his insults.

"It's like I told you earlier, Gordon, you should get to know your employees better. It's surprising what you might learn about them."

Smiling thinly, Gordy responded, "Maybe, little brother, I should take your advice. Who knows, maybe Miss Blow would make a delightful companion. But I don't suppose you would know about that, would you?"

Coit returned Gordy's smile. "Jess here knows more about Miss Blow than I do. But what I've seen of her, I'd say yes, she is a pleasant woman."

With a quick snap of his shoulders, Gordy turned toward Jess. "You agree?"

"Pleasant enough, I'd say. Sara likes her."

"I understand she performs her tasks in the mill with the highest efficiency. It's nice to know I hired a good weaver."

Gordy shuffled his feet. "Well, I'll be leaving you to your work. Perhaps tonight I will see you. Always do enjoy the wonderful food the ladies prepare for these occasions. An old bachelor like me doesn't often get a chance to enjoy home cooking." He looked pointedly at Coit. "Don't worry about locking up when you're finished, I'll be by later. Jess, it was nice seeing you."

Coit and Jess exchanged a knowing look as Gordy disappeared through the front office.

You bastard, Coit thought. There was no doubt in Coit's mind that his brother wouldn't make it a point to show up this evening. But if he did come, it wouldn't be for the food and the entertainment, but out of downright curiosity. Now that he knew Coit and Anna were acquainted, Gordy would suspect the worst. He judged others by his own twisted actions.

"I'm sorry about Gordy," Coit apologized.

"No need for an apology," Jess said. "Gordon and I have an understanding. I learned a long time ago, it isn't how you play the game, but how you finish it. Your brother knows I'm one of his most dependable employees, and my position as supervisor proves it." Jess winked at him. "He also knows I can read."

"He's damn lucky to have you. Now we better get to moving these tables, or we won't be ready for this evening."

Jess nodded. They hoisted a table onto their backs and carried it toward the pool area. Harve and the other men joined them on the return trip to the storage area.

Although Coit tried to put the conversation with Gordon out of his mind, he couldn't. Of all the rotten luck.

The last thing he wanted was for Gordy to be sniffing around Anna like some stray following a she-dog in heat—which was exactly what Gordy would be doing if he returned this evening. Now Coit wished that he'd kept his suggestions to himself. Especially if Gordy's getting to know his employees better was to begin with Anna.

❖ *13* ❖

I**T WAS LATE** Saturday afternoon, and Annabel and Sara were in Annabel's room after each had enjoyed a long soak in the hip tub in the kitchen. Jess was at the mill, helping set up the tables for this evening, and the twins had willingly accompanied him. Sara and Annabel had the whole house to themselves.

"You shouldn't have, Sara," Annabel said, staring at her reflection in the looking glass.

She held a spring green, checked blouse with tiny coral rosebuds printed on the fabric up to her torso. Sara had given it to her only moments before. Since Sara didn't own one of Isaac Singer's wonderful sewing machines, Annabel knew her friend had sewn it by hand. Sara's effort had been one of love.

In the short time the two women had known each other, Annabel marveled at the nature of their relationship. They were more like old and dear friends than landlord and tenant. Sara's big heart never ceased to amaze Annabel. She was a woman who worked with everything she had in order to supplement her husband's meager income. Instead of using the cotton for something for herself, she was presenting Annabel with a gift—a new waist for Annabel to wear to the "sing-along." If there was gift-giving to be done, Annabel should have done the presenting.

Annabel smoothed her hands over the handmade garment, admiring the box-pleated front and the leg-o'-mutton sleeves. "When did you have time to make this with everything else you do?"

"In case you haven't noticed, my friend, I have nothing but time these days. I usually spend the day setting like a hen waiting for her egg to hatch. Sewing keeps my mind and hands busy, and, besides, I enjoy it."

"But the material, it's so pretty. I'm sure you made this from piece goods you purchased for yourself. You should have saved it for that female chick you'll soon be hatching."

"A babe wouldn't look pretty in a check that large, and you know it. Since the fabric was a gift given freely, I decided you should have it. Coit gave me the material for baking him a pie."

"Coit. I should have known he would figure in this somewhere." Every time the man's name was mentioned, Annabel felt like a teapot whose contents were about to boil. Today it was no different. Hoping to stop the burning sensation, she asked, "How will Coit feel about me wearing a gift he gave to you?"

"A penny he won't remember. It's been well over a year. If he does recognize the fabric, I'm sure he'll agree it is perfect for you. That shade of green was meant to be worn by redheads. The color almost matches your eyes."

Annabel studied her reflection with indifference. After a moment, she said, "If green was meant to be worn by a redhead, it should be worn as a shroud to hide her hair and freckles."

Sara's lips twitched with amusement. "Listen to you, Anna Belle Blow." Her fisted hands rested on her nonexistent waist. "I take it you don't consider yourself a striking woman, but you are, you know! You have a certain glow—"

"Oh. I thought that glow was caused by the purchase of my new boots." She arched her brows.

"Shame on you. You know I never believed those boots caused that radiant glow."

"Really now, and I thought I had you convinced."

Their gazes locked in the mirror, and both giggled like young girls.

When their laughter had subsided, Annabel said, "You can just call me a glowworm. Or more appropriately, the grublike female firefly."

"Anna," Sara scolded, "how you do carry on. There is nothing grubby about your looks. To me, you're beautiful and I'm not the only one who thinks so."

"I won't even ask who the other who is. Sara dear, you're matchmaking again."

Sara ignored Annabel's remark and continued to pull a hairbrush through her long, damp hair. Both women had washed their hair earlier and now waited for it to dry so they could style it.

There was a lull in their conversation, and the room felt comfortably quiet. Annabel listened to the sound of the hairbrush as Sara pulled it through her long dark locks—the motion made her hair crackle. Outside birds sang in the trees, and the drowsy sound of a bee buzzing around a flower floated through the open windows. The room smelled of fresh air, soap, talcum, and Honeysuckle Rose perfume. Earlier, Annabel had doused them both with the scented water she had brought from home.

A contemplative look replaced the whimsical one that Sara usually wore. "You know, I reckon I am matchmaking," she told Annabel, breaking the earlier quiet. "It's only fair that the godparents of my unborn child should be hitched, wouldn't you say?"

Godmother! To have such an honor bestowed upon her brought a mixture of pleasure and regret—pleasure that Sara had accepted her as a friend and regret that she had been dishonest about her identity.

"Sara." Annabel turned from the mirror and faced her friend. "I'm flattered that you wish me to be Gwinevere's godmother, but that doesn't mean Coit—I'm assuming he will be the child's godfather—and I have to be wed in order to accept the honor. Besides, Sara, we've just begun to know each other. All of us. We must not rush too quickly into things.''

''I'm a yesterday girl, Anna. Besides, if you marry Coit, you'll always be close by. The seven of us will be backyard neighbors and friends forever.''

Annabel put her arms around Sara and hugged her close. ''We'll always be friends. Although we may not always live close together.''

''I know,'' Sara replied, ''but until you came here, I had no close woman friend. When I was growing up in Texas, I always wanted a female sibling, but God didn't see fit to bless me with one. But then he dropped you on my doorstep like an angel sent from heaven. I hope I'll be as lucky with this new babe I'm carrying inside of me. Do you know how lonely it gets being the only female in a houseful of men?''

''No, but I do know it can be very lonely growing up an only child.''

''So you see, if you were lonely and I was lonely, don't you think it was meant for us to meet and become friends? My mother always said, 'God works in mysterious ways.' ''

Sara smiled, and her face sparkled like sunshine. The pensive Sara had fled, and the usual optimistic one had returned. Her reappearance was confirmed by her next words.

''I'm sure everything will work out for all of us. Now I'm going to get us a nice cool glass of tea, and you can tell me all about your family and your lonely childhood.''

Leaving Annabel, she walked toward the kitchen, calling over her shoulder as she went, ''You've never spoken of your family. When I return you can tell me all about them.''

All about them. All three of them counting herself. Annabel didn't believe anything she had to say about her family would take all that long. She loved her parents, but her upbringing was so different from Sara's. Sara's memories of her youth were sowed in warmth, while Annabel's were sowed in apathy.

Not that her parents didn't love her, she knew they did. But Annabel had been reared as a possession and had never experienced the warmth and companionship that she expected Sara had received. That love was carried over into the Polk family. The realization that Annabel had missed something made her feel as though she had been cheated.

"I'm back," Sara said, interrupting her thoughts. Returning with a tray and two large glasses of tea, she handed a drink to Annabel before settling down in the rocking chair. "I'm listening."

Considering Annabel's reason for being in Dalworth, she had to be careful what she said about her past. The worst part of telling Sara about her family would be that she would have to tell more lies. It would be a relief to have this assignment finished so she wouldn't have to continually fib to those she cared about.

"Well," Sara said after taking a big swallow of tea, "I'm just dying to know everything."

"If you had died as many times as you've claimed you were going to while trying to solicit information from me, I'd be talking to a corpse."

Sara dismissed her comment with the wave of a hand. "I'm still waiting."

Annabel began. "There's not much to tell, really. I grew up in Macon as an only child." Suddenly the image of Billie Jean from the mill popped into Annabel's head, giving fuel to the fib she was about to tell. "I was eleven years old when both my parents were killed in a carriage accident. My mother's sister took me in, and I went to work in the mill alongside of her. It took both of us working to support our small family."

"And what about your schooling? You're so smart and so well read."

"My parents," Annabel continued, "wanted better for me than they themselves had. Kinda like you, Sara. While they were alive, they insisted I attend the local school. I was a quick learner. Books soon became my favorite companions. Without siblings, one turns to other entertainments.''

"Yes, yes, I can understand that. I was much the same way as far as reading. I read everything I could get my hands on.'' Sara finished her drink and set the glass on the floor.

"It's like I told you earlier, Anna, God has plans for us. You trust me on this. You'll see. Now we had best get dressed before my menfolk return to fetch us. I'll help you dress your hair, and then you can do mine.''

While Anna was struggling to put Sara's hair into the latest Gibson style, Jess and the twins returned. Sara had whipped Annabel's tresses into place with the same efficiency as her mother did in Atlanta. But when it was Annabel's turn to style Sara's hair, they both discovered that Annabel was all thumbs.

Only the males' return had saved them both. While the men quickly bathed in the leftover bath water, Sara had pinned her own hair in its usual neat style. When they were ready, the five of them left the house and headed toward the mill. Jess carried the basket of food that Sara and Annabel had prepared earlier.

As they neared the mill grounds, the sun had begun to set and looked like an overripe tangerine. The air was redolent with the same washed smell that had been present that morning, but instead of the scent of lush dampness, it smelled like sun-dried earth. Annabel inhaled deeply, not only to enjoy the mingling scents that flowed around her, but also to calm her tripping heartbeat.

Soon she would see Coit again. After last night's kissing episode on the floor of his store, things had changed between them. What would happen now—would tonight find them practicing more lip-sucking?

Imagining it left her breathless. She wanted him to kiss her; she wanted him to press his brawny length against her own. She wanted to experience again the heady sensations his kisses inspired.

Why was she so obsessed with this particular man? Before meeting Coit, she had never entertained such hussy-like imaginings. Nothing could come from a relationship between her and Coit. They were too different.

But throughout the day, her rational side had argued with her irrational side—the one leaning toward reason, the other, championing her sentiments.

Coit was not her reason for being in Dalworth. She had been sent here to study the working conditions of women and children in the Royal Mill.

With her discovery yesterday, she had learned that most of the employees of the mill turned their paychecks over to the Company Store. Even now the idea angered her. Coit was only doing his job like everyone else, her conscience told her. Recalling their conversation on the train ride from Atlanta, she remembered Coit had told her that he *ran* the Company Store. If this was the case, then his position made him less guilty of robbery than if he owned the business outright.

She had wanted to question Sara about last night's findings, but their discussion this afternoon had not afforded her the opportunity. But soon she would have to ask. All she really knew about Coit Jackson, other than that the mere sight of him took her breath away, was what she had learned from Merelda Whitcomb on her first day in town.

What was it Merelda had said? "Gordon Hamil had inherited the mill and all the money with it." Surely the store had been part of that inheritance.

As they neared the mill property, music drifted toward them on the soft evening air. Already the grounds were dotted with groups of people—men, women, and children who had come to join in the festivities. A musician tuned his fiddle, and with the twangy sound flavoring the night, Annabel decided to put aside all her doubts. Tonight she wouldn't think about anything but having a good time. After all, this was the first social gathering that she could remember looking forward to with happy anticipation.

And why shouldn't she anticipate it? She certainly felt

pretty in her new green-checkered blouse and the brown serge skirt she had brought with her from home. Her hair looked almost presentable after Sara had washed and styled it. Maybe she did glow as Sara had suggested.

Recalling Coit's kisses of the night before, Annabel decided that maybe she wasn't as plain or as uninteresting as her mother had always claimed she was. As giddy as a young girl going to her first dance, Annabel's feet fairly floated inches above the ground.

The sound of the fiddle grew louder as they entered the compound. A harmonica player had joined the fiddler, and Annabel recognized the tune written by Stephen Foster, "Hard Times Come Again No More." She thought it an odd tune to be played by people who lived with hard times every day, especially when this was supposed to be an easy-time gathering.

Sara took her arm and leaned toward her ear. "Usually these events last the whole weekend and are tied to a revival."

"The whole weekend? Revival?"

Somehow the merrymaking she anticipated didn't lend itself to the more serious side of worship, unless it was associated with rejoicing.

"Yes," Sara answered, "but I understand this is to be more of a social evening and a practice session. Besides leading those of us who aren't very talented, some of the better Sacred Harp singers will probably perform a few pieces." Sara clasped her chest in excitement. "And since there are musicians present, it wouldn't surprise me in the least if we weren't here all night."

"All night?"

Annabel hated parroting Sara's words, but everything her friend said about this evening's entertainments sounded new and strange. The musicales she had attended in Atlanta were nothing more than social gatherings held in her friends' homes. Young ladies usually played the pianoforte and sang classical songs, hopeful that their talent impressed the gentlemen who were present. Since Annabel had always been a listener instead of a performer, she had found those evenings terribly boring. But she didn't believe that would be the case tonight.

As they neared the tables and the group of women who were spreading cloths on their surfaces, Sara turned toward Jess and the twins. "Give us the basket, Jess. You go join the menfolk who are already gathered around the punch bowl."

Jess winked at his wife. "I reckon if I'm going to have to bellow the night away in song, my whistle might need a thorough dousing."

"As long as you don't douse it too much, Mr. Polk."

"Now, baby, you know I wouldn't do that." Smiling, he handed the heavy basket to Annabel and sauntered toward where the men stood.

Right now, Annabel could use a small drink herself—her throat felt as dry as a bone.

Sara cautioned the twins. "Lance and Percy, you are not to act like wild Indians, understand me? You may romp with the others, but I want you to stay within my sight."

"Yes, ma'am. We'll stay where you can see us. Promise." After a quick nod from Sara, they loped across the lawn to where a group of children were playing tree tag.

"I don't know why I insisted they bathe and put on clean clothes," Sara said, shaking her head. "Before the night's over, they'll be as grimy as moles."

They both laughed, then headed toward the tables and the other women.

Annabel scanned the crowd for Coit, but he was nowhere to be seen. Maybe he hadn't arrived yet or maybe he was involved in busywork that had taken him out of sight.

"What a unique tablecloth," she commented when they passed a candlewicked design on muslin.

"Looks like Catherine Evans's work," Sara said. "She made her first spread from flour sacks."

"Flour sacks?" Again, Annabel mimicked Sara's words.

Just like all her new experiences of the last week, her

experience with flour sacks was also limited. Their cook
back home collected the empty sacks, but until now, Annabel hadn't thought about what she did with the fabric.

Sara had no time to answer because they met up with
a group of people. Annabel greeted those she recognized
from the mill, including Birdie and Gegonia, and those
she didn't know Sara introduced. Her fears on seeing the
two women whose feathers she had ruffled at lunch yesterday were unfounded. Instead of holding a grudge
against her as she expected, Fanny and Mona welcomed
her with open arms and hugs.

Standing beside Sara, she admired the grounds being
readied for the party. The area looked nothing like it had
when she took her lunch there every day.

Of the dozen or so tables, most were covered with
patchwork quilts or candlewick spreads. Mason jars
placed on each table overflowed with bouquets of mixed
flowers—zinnias, daisies, and roses—from the many gardens around the mill houses. There were no fancy linens
or exotic flowers like those used in the grand dining
rooms of Atlanta's most wealthy, but to Annabel these
simple adornments were far more beautiful. The table
coverings represented the handiwork of the ladies present
or cherished heirlooms handed down from one generation
to the next. Instead of exotic hothouse bouquets, these
ordinary flowers were grown in the women's yards.

"Anna," Sara said, "here is a young lady you must
meet."

The girl who had approached them looked to be in her
middle teens. She smiled sweetly, first at Sara and then
Annabel, and said, "Miss Sara, it's nice to see you."

Sara linked her arm through the girl's. "Anna, meet
Catherine Evans. She is partially responsible for all these
beautifully tufted spreads we've been admiring. Catherine,
this is Anna Belle Blow, a new weaver at the mill and
my boarder."

"Nice to meet you, Miss Anna," Catherine replied nervously. "Miss Sara always makes me blush with her
praise."

Anna smiled. "I know what you mean. But your work is lovely, and it should be praised. I've never seen such an interesting technique. Sara was telling me earlier that your first spread was made from flour sacks."

Catherine's blue eyes sparkled. "Yes, ma'am. I got flour sacks and seamed them together. Then I embroidered the Irish Chain quilt pattern in squares. After I finished the stitching, I clipped the yarn to make tufts. Soon everyone I knew wanted one just like mine. Some made their own or asked me to make one for them."

"Then your endeavors have turned into a lucrative business?" Annabel asked. She always enjoyed hearing success stories involving independent young women.

"I reckon you could say that," Catherine answered.

Sara confirmed it. "I would say you have a successful business. She is one busy young lady."

"Maybe I should order a spread from you now before I leave."

"Leave?" Sara asked, her dark eyes questioning Anna.

Drat, Anna scolded herself. Her slip of the tongue had upset Sara, and that was the last thing she had meant to do.

"I mean before I leave tonight. Catherine, I would love for you to make me one of your beautiful spreads."

"I'd be pleased to make you one. Why don't you and Miss Sara drop by my house sometime? My sister-in-law, Addie, and I are doling out work like crazy to friends and relatives. We have more orders than we know what to do with. Besides, you might like to see some of the other patterns we do before you choose your own." Her glance skirted the crowd, and she waved at someone. "Now I gotta run. I see Emma Lu has arrived. I'll talk with you later. 'Bye."

After Catherine had departed, Sara turned to Annabel. "What did you mean when you said, 'before you leave'?"

"Sakes alive, Sara. It was a slip of the tongue. Believe me, I'm not going anywhere."

Lying to Sara made Annabel feel as guilty as sin. What would Sara think about her when she finally learned the truth? Surely she wouldn't still want Annabel to be the godmother of her unborn child.

Annabel was determined not to dwell on this topic a moment longer. The thought of leaving saddened her, and she had come here this evening to enjoy herself. She touched Sara's sleeve. "Shouldn't we put this food down somewhere before my arms are pulled from their sockets?"

Sara's hand flew to her mouth. "Oh, Anna. I'm an ungrateful hag. I forgot all about it. Come on. Follow me. It looks like they're spreading the food out over there on those tables."

Grateful for being saved from answering more of Sara's questions, Annabel followed obediently along behind her friend. They headed toward a copse of trees where someone had hung Chinese lanterns in the lower branches. As they neared the area, the evening breeze swayed the brightly colored globes, making them look like giant butterflies. At any moment Annabel expected the collapsible coverings to lift and take flight.

Coit spotted Anna standing among the other women beneath the trees, like a flower among weeds. She made him think of the rose set in the buttonhole of his shirt. He had picked the flower because its coppery-apricot bloom and long elegant bud had reminded him of Anna.

Ever since last night, Coit's thoughts had been filled with Anna. He was like a drunken man. Her kisses had been as potent as any wine, and the psychological effects made him feel dizzy as he thought about them.

What was he to do about Anna? Coit recognized that what he felt for her was different than what he'd felt with the few women from his past who had eased his bodily urges. Last night's kisses had fueled his desire, and now it burned like a raging inferno. He was no longer sure he could control the urge to take her if they should enjoy another kissing session.

After leaving her last night, his body had ached long into the morning hours. Even now he wanted Anna beneath him, her long legs wrapped around him, their bodies joining. And when he took her, he wanted to see her desire for him mirrored in her eyes.

Besotted fool. Coit shook his head to clear it. If he kept thinking the way he was now, he'd embarrass himself in front of everyone. Why did she possess him like some bogy, causing him more worry and annoyance than any woman he had ever known? And what did this annoyance mean?

One thing he did know. He didn't want the obligation or responsibility that would go along with bedding a woman like Anna Belle Blow. She was a lady—an innocent—not a woman who would enjoy a one-night affair. A woman like Anna would expect a commitment, and Coit wasn't ready to commit to any woman, especially one whose identity still remained a mystery.

Be sensible, a cowardly voice warned. *Maybe I should ask her some questions about her past, instead of ignoring the issue. Maybe if I was truthful with myself, I'd realize that I don't want her to be anyone but who she claims to be. And maybe it wouldn't matter anyway.*

Coit didn't have time to argue the maybes, for a moment later Anna turned, spotting him. His heart beat a wild tattoo against his ribs as he walked across the grounds to meet her. When they were separated by only a few feet, he stopped. She smiled shyly into his eyes.

"Good evening, Mr. Jackson," she said, with all the formality of a lady.

Her use of his surname surprised Coit, but he decided to play along with her. He returned her greeting with the same formality. "Miss Blow, how nice to see you." But he couldn't resist teasing her. Taking her hand in his, Coit leaned toward her. "So formal, after last night?"

His teasing had the desired effect. She blushed all the way to the roots of her coppery hair, making her skin glow like ripe peaches. The heat of her response also made the fragrance of her perfume waft warmly around him.

Honeysuckle? Had she and King Arthur been wallowing in the same bush? Coit inhaled deeply. The essence of her perfume seemed to emanate from her marrow. She had the coloring of the rose and she smelled like his favorite—honeysuckle. What more could a man ask for?

Their gazes held fast and would have remained stuck like a burr to a sock if Sara hadn't interrupted.

"Oh, there you are, Coit." Sara's eyes darted from Anna's back to Coit's. "How are you on this fine afternoon?"

Reluctantly he tore his eyes from Anna and looked at Sara. "I'm fine, thank you. And yourself?"

"Myself is fine," she answered, "and so is Anna. I was telling her only this morning that she glows. Don't you agree?"

"Sara, please," Anna begged, her expression disapproving.

Coit leaned toward her and peered into her face. "Like a glowworm," he acknowledged. When both ladies burst into laughter, he puzzled over their response.

Sara said, "Must be those new boots she purchased from you last night."

"Boots? Oh, yes, they did look nice on her legs—feet!"

When Anna's face turned from peach to apple red, Coit realized his blunder. His starched collar felt as though it had shrunk several inches. Perspiration popped out on his forehead.

"I meant feet," he insisted.

Sara swallowed another laugh. "If you two will excuse me, I believe I see Lettie Barkley and I've been meaning to ask her about canning." Leaving Coit and Anna alone, she made her way toward the older woman.

After Sara left, Coit said, "I'm sorry. I didn't mean to embarrass you."

"You mean embarrass us?" she corrected. "I think we both know Sara is a hopeless romantic."

Coit agreed, then extended his arm to her. "Will you walk with me?"

Together they strolled toward the reservoir pool where a makeshift platform had been set up and now served as a low stage for the fiddler and the harmonica player.

When they were out of earshot of the others, Coit said, "You look mighty pretty this evening, and before I forget, I brought you something from my garden."

He fumbled with the rose still stuck in his buttonhole. When he had finally worked the flower loose from the tiny slit, he handed it to Anna. "It reminded me of you."

Anna's throat felt as though she had suddenly inhaled the lint-filled air she'd been breathing for the last week. Her eyes stung as she fought to hold back tears. No one had ever given her such a beautiful flower, especially one with such sentiment attached to it.

They had stopped moving, and Coit faced her. "You should wear it in your hair. You know it's almost the same color?"

"Orange?" she croaked, still fighting to get her emotions under control.

"Silly. Only clowns have orange hair, and, my dear, there is nothing remotely buffoonish about you. In truth, you're a very lovely woman."

"Me? Lovely?" Anna laughed. "My mother will be very glad to hear that someone thinks I'm attractive."

Coit looked at her strangely, making her wonder if she had given herself away. Anna couldn't remember what she had told him about her parents.

Only this afternoon she had told Sara her made-up story about how her parents had died in a carriage accident. No, she remembered now. Sara was the only one she'd told about her past. Angry with herself, she feared she had spoiled the moment. Oh, why couldn't she learn to keep her lips buttoned? Flattery wasn't something that Annabel received often, and she wanted to savor it because it came from Coit.

"Give me the flower," he told her.

"You're not taking it back?" Trying to determine if Coit was angry, she kept her fingers clasped around the flower's stem.

"Of course I'm not taking it back. Give it to me," he ordered.

Reluctantly Annabel handed the rose to him. Once he held it in his strong fingers, he threaded the stem through her hair just behind her ear.

"There," he said, standing back and admiring his handiwork. "It's as perfect as I expected it would be."

"Stop it, Coit, you're embarrassing me." Annabel glanced around as several people passed them, heading toward the musicians.

"Evening, Mr. Jackson," they greeted. "We're looking forward to hearing you sing."

"Thanks," Coit replied, "I'm looking forward to hearing us all sing." He extended his elbow, and when Anna's fingers curled around his arm, he pulled her closer, and they began to move along with the crowd. "Even this lady is going to sing," he told the others.

Annabel whispered, "I can't sing, and you know it."

"You'll sing like a Spanish diva with my flower tucked behind your ear."

She slapped his arm playfully. "Believe me, it will take more than a flower to make me sing like a diva."

"Trust me."

From behind they heard someone approaching them at a fast pace. The person seemed determined to overtake them. Coit slowed their speed, and a man rounded Annabel's side, skidding to a stop in front of them.

"I knew it," the man said. "When I saw that orange hair, I said to my Hilda, 'Hilda,' I says, 'I know that little gal.' " He looked Annabel up and down. "You ain't so little, but no sirree, I never forget a body once I meet them."

He scratched his head in contemplation while viewing Coit. "This here ain't the fella you're planning on marrying up with, is it?"

• 14 •

THE TELEGRAPHER FROM the depot. Oh, Lordy, whatever was she to do?

To make matters worse, her head felt as empty as a balloon. Not only did she feel faint, but also absent of all rational thought. It was as though her brain had gobbled up her tongue, then both had disappeared into thin air.

"Sam," Coit asked, "what the devil are you talking about? Anna—I mean Miss Blow isn't getting married. You might pride yourself on your good memory, but this time you're mistaken." He looked to her for confirmation.

Bless his soul. Coit had given her an out. She would deny knowing the telegrapher and maybe she could convince him they had never met before tonight.

Finding her voice, she said, "I'm sorry, sir, but you must have me mixed up with someone else."

"No, ma'am, I don't. I never forget people once I meet them. Or the telegrams they send." For further emphasis, he added, "Or the stories they tell me." His eyes peered into hers as though searching her soul for the truth.

Coit interrupted. "I'm sorry, Sam, but Miss Blow says she doesn't know you."

"Ain't saying we was formally introduced, but we sure

did meet. Ten days ago, it was. A Wednesday, I believe. She came into the terminal, right after the arrival of the Atlanta train. Said she wanted to send a wire to Atlanta. I remember her because she said she knew Miss—''

"Mr. Sam," Annabel interrupted, "surely you must be mistaken. If we did meet, I'm certain I would remember a handsome gentleman like you."

Her flattery received the focus of both men. Coit looked at her as though she had taken leave of her senses, and the telegrapher, who was far from handsome with his bald head and big ears that had hair like dandelion fluff growing inside them, preened like a proud peacock at her unexpected flattery.

"You probably saw me at the station, but I never sent a wire to Atlanta. I don't even know anyone in that big city."

For the second time since Mr. Sam's arrival, he scratched his head. Squinting, he looked her over again before asking, "You didn't tell me you were getting married and that Miss—''

"Married? Merciful heavens, no." Anna nodded her head so zealously her brains rattled. "Marriage is the last thing on my mind. I'm employed at the Royal Mill and, although I'm new to the area, I plan to be here for a long time." Annabel shook her head again and laughed. "Me, married? Never in this lifetime."

"If that's the case, I'm supposing you ain't never met the right fella." He studied her curiously. "You sure you ain't the young woman who visited my depot? You look just like her, and we don't get many orange-haired ladies in these parts." He crossed his arms, eyeing her as if she were posing for a portrait. After a moment, he continued. "Stands to reason you ain't her, if what you say is true. She already had herself a fella and had come to town to get a wedding dress. I thought it was right nice of Miss—''

"Coit, Sam, come on over here," the fiddler called to the two men. "It's time to begin the fasola."

"Excuse us, Sam, I need to help Anna find a seat."

"And I need to find my Hilda. She'll be claiming neglect if I'm not careful." The telegrapher left them and headed back in the direction he had come to search for his wife.

Anna sighed with relief as Coit led her toward the platform and the rows of benches that had been placed in and around the area.

"Over here, Anna," Sara called from where she sat with several other women. When Anna and Coit approached them, the ladies scooted over to make room for her on the bench.

Before Coit left, he leaned close to her ear and whispered, "Like a diva, remember."

"Like a diva," she confirmed.

Annabel was so thankful that her duplicity had not been revealed by Mr. Sam that she vowed to sing grateful praises to the Lord in spite of her incapability. It mattered not one whit that her song would be delivered in her discordant voice.

As Coit took his place on the stage, his enthusiasm to lead the singing had waned. Instead, he wanted to take Anna aside and demand answers to the many questions Sam Toby had raised.

Coit had known Sam for as long as he had lived in Dalworth. He also knew that the telegrapher and station manager could coax tomatoes off a vine with his gossip. Not only did Sam love to gossip, but he also had a knack for remembering; he never forgot a name, a face, or everyone else's business.

If Sam believed that Anna was the same young woman who had sent the wire to Atlanta some ten days back, then Coit would wager his best cigar that Sam was correct. The timing was right. It would have been during the same period when Coit had met Anna on the train ride from Atlanta. Sam could have easily encountered Anna at the depot, but unless she was trying to hide something, why would she deny their meeting?

Damn Sam anyway. Meddling old fool. He should have kept his comments to himself. Now Sam's tale, coupled with the conversation Coit had had earlier with Gordy about Merelda Whitcomb, doubled his suspicions about Anna.

As the last strains of the tune being played floated into silence, the fiddler turned to Coit and asked, "Are we ready to get started?"

"I suppose we should," Coit answered over his shoulder. "Have you seen the lead singers?"

"Saw them earlier. I expect they're socializing."

Coit searched the crowd, and his gaze connected with Anna's. She smiled at him, and his heart flipped like a griddlecake. Despite the aura of mystery surrounding her, Anna was too damn good to be true. Besides being physically attracted to her, he liked her as well. He delighted in her quick wit and her warmth. If whatever was blooming between them could grow into something deeper, he needed to root out his doubts once and for all. It was time he learned who Anna was and what her reasons were for being in Dalworth. Later tonight, he would pose the questions of her identity to her and he was determined to get answers. Now it was time to round up the lead singers and get started with the singing.

Coit placed three fingers in his mouth and whistled. The shrill sound sliced through the murmur of conversation taking place on the grounds. All chatter ceased. Coit called out, "Leaders, we need you up here now. It's time to begin."

Annabel watched as a man and two women broke away from the crowd and headed toward the raised platform.

The man took his place beside Coit and said, "That whistle of yours probably shattered my singing ear." Coit chuckled good-naturedly, and the singer poked him playfully in the ribs.

One of the two women stepped upon the stage and joined in the banter. She said, "Everyone here knows, Willie, that those ears of yours ain't good for nothing but keeping that hat out of your eyes."

Her comment made everyone laugh, Annabel included.

She wondered if their lines were rehearsed, because the jesting seemed to flow so smoothly.

True to the woman's words, Willie's ears did appear to be holding up his shabby straw hat. It rested right above his eyes, almost swallowing up his small head. The overalls he wore looked better suited for working in the fields than attending a social, but what did Annabel know about anything? She did know that the sing-along had only begun, and already she was enjoying herself more than she had in a long time.

Next, the second woman joined the others. Coit extended his hand toward her and guided her to his side. When he smiled down at his much shorter companion, Annabel watched the exchange with more than mere curiosity.

"That's Dora," Sara whispered. "She *also* has a beautiful voice."

When Dora turned to face the crowd, Annabel recognized her as one of the ladies who worked in the spinning room at the mill. She had never met Dora, but she knew immediately what Sara had meant when she had used the word also.

The petite young woman resembled a porcelain doll, but there was nothing hard about her appearance. With her silky blond hair hanging in loose curls down her back, and with her big, luminous blue eyes twinkling, she was so femininely captivating that even Annabel was charmed. Standing together, Coit and Dora made a breathtakingly attractive couple. Coit could have been the prince of darkness and Dora the princess of light. Their coloring complemented one another and made Annabel feel as attractive as a warty toad.

As her resentment toward the woman grew, Sara divulged more information. "Sometimes she and Coit sing together. Maybe they will tonight."

A flood of emotions rushed through Annabel. At that moment, she wanted to jump up on the stage and snatch out Dora's silvery hair, then jab out her fathomless blue eyes. No matter how hard Annabel tried to control the jealousy that threatened to consume her, the green-eyed monster lingered, inspiring horror and self-disgust.

"You don't have to worry," Sara said, studying Annabel as though trying to gauge her reaction. "Coit's not interested in her—"

"Sara, please. Spare me the details." Annabel fidgeted in her seat while her hands smoothed the wrinkles from her skirt. "I told you a dozen times that Coit and I are only friends."

"Oh, I see . . . then you're kinda like kissing cousins?"

"Yes, I suppose you could say that."

Coit laughed at something Dora said, and Annabel wished for all the world that Sara would shut up and Dora would disappear. But her wishes were futile. Dora remained, and Sara continued her annoying chatter.

"Then you aren't interested in knowing that she's set her cap for him."

"Not in the least," Annabel answered. Sara's words made her feel as though an arrow had lodged itself in her heart. "They make a beautiful couple."

She watched Sara's expression. It seemed to Annabel that Sara was having a hard time containing her mirth.

"Anna, you're such a ninny and so flimsy that I can see right through you." She grabbed Annabel's hand and squeezed it affectionately. "You know, it's natural to feel jealousy for your man and be willing to fight for him if it should come to that. First you must admit to yourself that you're every bit as pretty as Dora. Then you must learn to sing like a nightingale."

Annabel sputtered. "Me? Sing like a nightingale? Humph! Surely, you know . . ."

Her voice trailed off. For the first time this evening, she noted the I-told-you-so expression on her friend's face. Annabel shook her head in disbelief.

"Sara Polk, you've been baiting me, haven't you? You knew the moment that flaxen-haired goddess stepped on that stage and took her place beside Coit that I was sick with envy."

A soft gasp escaped Sara's lips. "Me? What makes you

think I would do such a thing as bait you? Honestly, Anna, I'm shocked. Besides, I've decided to take your advice and stop playing matchmaker.''

"You're lying, Sara. And I should tell you that you don't do it very well.''

"I never lie." Astonishment touched her features. "I'll admit I've been known to twist the truth a little, but I don't tell falsehoods.''

Annabel pretended not to understand. "Does this mean you'll no longer interfere in Coit's and my friendship?"

"Tonight, yes," Sara answered.

"Well, I'm certainly glad to hear it.''

Annabel relaxed, pleased that Sara had agreed to let nature take its course. She felt peaceful until Sara's meaning sunk into her brain.

"Tonight?"

But any further arguments were silenced when the four voices of the lead singers rang out in song. The mellifluous sound raised the tiny hairs on the back of Annabel's neck and sent chills rushing across her spine like Saint Elmo's fire.

As if by common consent, the audience grew silent. Coit stood before them, his manner poised, his handsome face serious. When there was complete silence, he breathed in slowly then hummed one clear, perfect note. While he held the pitch, the tenors and altos scattered throughout the audience sounded a tone a third above Coit's. Seconds later, the sopranos added their voices a fifth above, and the simple chord that resounded in the night was as sweet and pure as any Annabel had ever heard. She was reminded of angels.

Annabel knew enough about music to recognize the four classes of the singers; Coit sang tenor, Dora soprano, Willie bass, and the second woman whose name she didn't know sang alto. Their voices blended together in harmony, sounding as one. The music was so lovely it made tears spring to Annabel's eyes.

When they had finished several numbers, Coit stepped to center stage and waited for the applause to die down.

When it did, he said, "Now it's y'all's turn. Those of you who know what range you sing in, group yourselves accordingly. Those who don't, stay where you are and follow along as best you can."

She knew Coit's speech was meant for her. In college, her music instructor had classed her as an alto. But after her several failed attempts to sing in a lower key with the other altos, he had rolled his eyes heavenward, pleading for mercy.

When he had taken her aside and told her he wanted her to sing solo, Annabel had been flattered—until she learned the true meaning of his request. He wanted her to sing *so low* that no one else could hear her. At the time, his words had stung, but now the memory brought a smile to her lips.

"I have an alto voice," Sara told her. People stood and shuffled back and forth in search of their respective groups.

"Me, too," Annabel said, "but I should warn you we will all enjoy the music more if I keep my lips sealed."

"Never. You must sing with the rest of us." Sara looked beyond her, and an amused expression lit up her face. "But I bet you won't move an inch while you're doing it."

"What do you mean, I won't move an inch?"

Sara's glance was bright with merriment as she watched someone approaching them. She heard Sara say, "Mrs. Twigg, how are you this evening?"

Annabel kept her eyes fastened on Sara and mouthed the name *Twigg!* Now she understood Sara's remark about her not moving an inch. Surely after Annabel had threatened to rip the woman's arm from its socket, Mrs. Twigg wouldn't dare approach her with the intention of sitting next to her. Would she?

God must be punishing her for her untrue declarations of the last ten days—first with Mr. Sam and now with Mrs. Twigg. Fearing the woman had sought her out for retribution, the words of the Twenty-Third Psalm surfaced in Annabel's head. *Yea, though I walk through the valley of the shadow of death, I will fear no evil, for Thou art with me; Thy rod and Thy staff . . .*

When it was not possible to ignore the woman, Annabel swung around to face her. "Why Mrs. *Staff*, it is you?" Annabel smiled as though she were greeting an old and dear friend instead of the woman she had threatened to do bodily harm to last Sunday in church.

"I see, young woman, you're as impudent as ever," Mrs. Twigg replied. "My name is Twigg, not Staff."

Merciful heavens. Twigs, staffs, and stakes all looked alike.

"I know, Mrs. Twigg, I'm sorry, I don't know what I was thinking—"

"It's obvious you weren't thinking. And your actions when last we met were a clear indication to me that you aren't used to practicing goodwill toward others either. It's my Christian duty to forgive those who are not of the same mind while teaching them to become more charitable toward all."

Oh, Lordy, does this mean what I think it means?

"I think," Mrs. Twigg said, "that we should begin again. I'll try not to discipline you as I would my children, although in God's eyes we're all His children."

She smiled, and the result softened the stolid expression that Annabel associated with the woman.

"If I should forget, Miss Blow, you'll have to promise me that you won't rip my arm off. If I am without an arm, my brood would starve to death, not to mention the little darlings would all turn into ruffians."

Annabel couldn't believe it. It was too good to be true. Mrs. Twigg didn't hate her after all. She was offering Annabel her friendship in her own roundabout way.

"I promise," Annabel replied, extending her hand to seal the agreement.

Mrs. Twigg's slim fingers gripped Annabel's tightly. "Good," she said. "Now that that's settled, we'll begin again by singing our praises together."

Sara added, "Oh, Anna, I forgot to tell you. Mrs. Twigg sings alto, too."

Feeling lighthearted and gay, Annabel quipped, "Then we can sing *alto*gether."

Good humor warmed the moment, and the threesome sighed with pleasure. If Mrs. Twigg could practice civility, Annabel decided, then she could, too. Her position in this town was precarious enough without adding a list of enemies to her sins.

In the next few moments, the serious business of singing took precedence. Four more people joined the others on stage, and each of these four brought with them a large card with a geometric shape drawn on its front. There was a triangle, an oval, a rectangle, and a diamond.

What Sara had told Annabel about shape-note singing came back to her. The singers used a four-shape notation for the notes *fa, sol, la,* and *mi.* When the cardholder held up his card, the crowd would sing the designated notes on the scale. *Fa* was the triangle, *sol* was the oval, *la* was the rectangle, and *mi* was the diamond.

Annabel held her breath, anxious for the singing to begin. She didn't have long to wait. Soon the music swelled toward the heavens, bringing with it an eerie and primitive sound that was also harmonious and melodious. To Annabel it was spellbinding, and she wondered if this was how the angels of heaven would sound on Judgment Day. Her heart swelled to near bursting, and once again her eyes brimmed with tears.

Throughout the repertoire of songs, Coit's gaze continually sought out hers. No words were needed to convey the feelings that flowed between them with a caressing gentleness.

The night was filled with magic, enchanting all with its scent of life and with the many fireflies flickering like lightning against the velvet darkness. Her heart was filled with the same magic and with the man whose voice and being embraced Annabel's soul.

This last realization stunned her.

She was in love. When had it happened? When had Coit stolen a place inside her heart, stonewalling her will to remain detached? She was caught in this helpless state of emotional turmoil as surely as the fly that was snared in the spider's silken web, looping between the branches above her head.

Annabel studied the fly that battled for its freedom. Her love for Coit was as futile as the insect's struggle. She was hopelessly in love with a man she hardly knew; and now she had to figure out what to do about that love.

❖ *15* ❖

AFTER A COUPLE hours of singing, and grappling with her latest dilemma, Annabel was still at a loss about what to do. The way she saw it, she had two alternatives, neither of them pleasant. She could confess her love for Coit, and if her feelings were reciprocated by him, she would have to give up her family because her mother would never approve of her marrying a shopkeeper. Or she could leave Dalworth when her assignment was finished and walk away, never to look back. Either choice would leave her the loser. The music ended, jarring her from her preoccupation.

Coit announced to the crowd, "We'll break for dinner and begin again later."

Sara stood and turned toward Annabel. "You never began the first time—why didn't you sing?" she scolded.

"Sing." That was why most people had come to the fasola, but after Annabel realized that she was in love with Coit Jackson, she couldn't have sung one note even if she had wanted to. Her vocal cords, like her brain, had shut down, leaving her unable to do anything but worry over her situation.

"Anna, are you okay?" Sara asked her.

"Yes, yes, I'm fine. I guess that I'm still under the spell of the music. I've never heard anything like it before."

Mrs. Twigg spoke. "Beautiful, ain't it? I bet before the night is over you'll get the hang of it and be belting out notes like the rest of us."

"I hope so," Annabel answered, her eyes fastening on the spider's web again.

"Soon you'll be singing like our Dora here." Mrs. Twigg turned toward the soprano who had left the stage and joined them. "Have you two met? I understand you both work in the mill."

Annabel's heart plunged into her stomach. As she faced the blond goddess up close, she saw that the woman was lovelier than she had appeared from a distance, if that was possible. Drawing on all her reserves to remain civil to the newcomer, she smiled and said, "No, we haven't met, but I'm very pleased to meet you, now. You have a lovely voice."

"Thank you," Dora replied, "I do so love to sing." She returned Anna's greeting, revealing even white teeth when she smiled. "I've seen you at the mill, but it seems we are always going in opposite directions. It's nice to meet you, too." She turned toward Sara. "How are you this evening?" she asked.

"I'm fair to meddling—middling," Sara replied, coloring when Annabel's gaze lighted on her.

Annabel fought her need to laugh. Sara's first comment couldn't have been closer to the truth—she was always meddling.

"Dora is my second cousin," Mrs. Twigg informed them. She placed a bony arm around the much smaller woman and hugged her.

Surprised by this revelation, Annabel searched the two ladies for some resemblance. When she found none, she turned her attention back to Mrs. Twigg and heard her say, "You and your young man going to sing us a duet later?"

Her young man could only be one person. Coit still stood on the stage engrossed in conversation with the other singers. Annabel and Sara exchanged glances while Annabel fought to control the jealousy that threatened to overcome her.

Instead of denying that Coit was her young man, Dora beamed at the reference, making her ethereal beauty even more breathtaking. It wasn't fair, Annabel thought. If Coit was the moonbeam, then Dora was its silvery shimmer. They looked beautiful together, and Dora could sing. Some people had all the luck.

"We might sing later," Dora said. "You know how Coit loves these things. I'm always ready for anything he wants to do."

I just bet you are. Annabel steamed. She imagined what the *anything* could be, then pictured the twosome lip-sucking on the floor of Coit's store as Annabel and Coit had done the night before. This thought was as disgusting to Annabel as it had been to the twins. *Blast his fickle hide anyway.*

"Well, ladies," Mrs. Twigg said, "if you'll excuse us, we promised Miss Whiz we would make sure everything was ready to serve before we got started. We'll see you later."

As the two women left them and headed for the food tables, Annabel felt Sara's gaze on her. "Don't say a word. I don't want to hear it." She held up her hands to ward off Sara's arguments.

"Why, Anna Blow, I hadn't planned on saying anything. After all, I gave you my word. I'm not meddling tonight." She stretched up on her tiptoes to look over Annabel's shoulder. "But I think you should know that Dora's young man is heading our way right now."

Sara's announcement sobered Annabel. After all that she had discovered about her feelings in the last few hours, how could she face Coit without revealing herself? With the mere mention of his approach, her heart impaled itself on her tonsils, and she felt as though she might faint. How does a person act casual and nonchalant toward a man who had claimed her love and wasn't even aware that he had done so?

You foolish, lovesick girl, she scolded herself. *You don't have to do anything—Coit doesn't know how you feel.*

He approached her from behind. "What happened to my diva?" Coit whispered, his warm breath brushing the rose tucked behind her ear, expelling the bud's intoxicating scent into the air.

"I think your diva retired," Sara informed him. "She didn't utter one note throughout the whole session."

Anna looked at them pointedly. "I told you both repeatedly that I'm not a singer."

"Well, you should learn," Sara scolded. "Look at Dora and what a beautiful voice she has."

"Sara," Annabel warned.

"Oh, never mind. Come along, and let's see if we can find my brood. I'm sure they're all starving half to death." The threesome fell into step, and together they walked toward the food.

"I imagine my Jess has drowned his whistle by now," Sara told Coit.

He chuckled. "I saw him earlier with the bass singers. His whistle seemed to be alive and well."

"I certainly hope so. Speaking of the devil—"

"There you are, my sweet." Jess joined them and squeezed his wife affectionately. "I missed being close to you during the singing. I reckon that means you're gonna have to learn to sing bass."

"Jess Polk, you know I couldn't sing like a bullfrog even if I wanted to. Which I don't." She swatted him playfully on the arm that had surrounded her large waist. "Have you seen the boys?" she asked.

"I was rounding them up for supper when I became distracted by the prettiest gal here. They'll be along shortly."

"Good, because I purely don't have the energy to search them out. Singing takes a lot out of a body."

Jess slowed their progress. "Are you feeling okay, baby?" he asked.

"Yes, I'm fine," Sara replied. "I guess I'm hungry."

"Eating for two is tough, isn't it, baby? I'm gonna sit you down at a table and do the waiting on you for a change. How does that sound to you?"

"Like you've been drinking too much punch."

"Not me, baby—not tonight."

They all laughed at the stricken look on Jess's face.

"I believe you, Mr. Polk, and I just might make good on your offer. Tonight, you can be my slave," Sara teased.

"I'm already your love slave," Jess whispered. Although his words were meant for Sara's ears only, Annabel heard the exchange, and the idea it conjured up made her tingle.

The Polks' playful banter made Annabel wonder if a man would ever love her the way Jess loved Sara. In her mother's world, husbands put their wives on pedestals and kept them there like prized possessions. But here in the mill village, there was not much evidence of female worship. What Annabel had learned from the few women she knew who worked in the mill was that they were slaves all right, but not of the love variety.

Except for Sara. Jess Polk was a fine man, a devoted father and husband. Annabel imagined there were other men like Jess who lived and worked in the village, but so far she hadn't met them.

She stole a quick look at Coit. In Annabel's opinion, he, too, was fine, and someday he would make some woman a wonderful husband. The thought that she probably wouldn't be that woman saddened her and she wondered how it was possible for someone whom she had known for less than two weeks to cause her so much confusion.

When they reached the picnic area, dozens of people were already milling around the tables. True to his word, Jess found Sara a seat and ordered her to sit. Then, accompanied by Lance and Percy, he joined Coit and Annabel, and they all got in line.

Annabel had never seen so many different kinds of food in one place. She had been to covered-dish suppers in

Atlanta, but those feasts couldn't rival the food spread out on the long tables. Most of the dishes were prepared by the women present, not by their cooks, and were a reflection of true Southern cookery and hospitality.

Her mouth drooled as she scanned the many dishes. There was corn bread, black-eyed peas, collard greens, ham, fried chicken, corn, grits, and okra. And, of course, the butter beans she had helped shell.

There were many dishes she didn't recognize and wasn't about to try. She didn't have to ask the names because as people moved through the line recognizing the mystery fare, they oohed and aahed their pleasure by calling out the names of the dishes: cracklins, liver pudding, 'possum, and sweet potatoes.

When they reached the dessert table, the waistband of Annabel's skirt felt tighter, and she hadn't eaten a bite since early this morning. There was every kind of dessert imaginable—ambrosia, cobblers, pralines, cakes, and sugar cane. Several watermelons, round and plump, floated in tubs of iced-down water.

After filling the plates that Sara had brought from home for their use, the five of them filed back to the table where Sara waited. The twins plopped down beside their parents, and Coit and Annabel sat opposite them, leaving room on the long bench for other diners to join their group.

Once Anna was seated, Sara looked at her and said, "I told you these two would be as dirty as moles." She eyed the smudged faces and clothing of the twins. "Why I insisted you two bathe before we left home, I'll never understand."

Both boys grinned. "It's like we told you, Ma, when you make us bathe, we're just gonna get dirty again."

"People bathe not only to wash away the dirt, but also so they won't smell."

Lance lifted up his arm and sniffed. "I can't smell nothing so I mustn't be dirty." He leaned toward his brother and took in a deep whiff. "Phew! Percy smells like a skunk."

"Do not."

Percy shoved Lance, and Lance shoved him back. Soon the twins were tussling with one another to the point of upsetting their plates of food.

"Boys. That's enough," their father ordered. "If you two can't behave yourselves, we'll be heading for home and bed."

"Ah, Pa, we're just having fun."

"The dinner table isn't the place to roughhouse. Settle down and eat."

The wrestling stopped, and the twins exchanged contrite glances and began eating their dinner without uttering another sound.

While Annabel watched them, she hid her smile behind a glass of lemonade. The boys were so transparent, she could almost read their minds. They were going to eat their dinner and escape before their father changed his mind and took them home anyway.

Gordon Hamil approached their table. "Evening, folks. Mind if I join you?"

With the arrival of his stepbrother, Coit nearly choked on the piece of ham he had been about to swallow. Although Gordon was being polite, his position as mill owner guaranteed him a seat anywhere he felt like sitting.

Only Coit would dare refuse him. Under different circumstances he might have, but tonight he didn't wish to make a scene. So he swallowed his averse feelings, along with the last chew of ham, and watched his stepbrother settle on Annabel's opposite side.

Once seated, his brother turned on the charm. "Nice to see you again, Miss Blow."

"Nice to see you, too, Mr. Hamil," Anna responded.

He watched his brother's gaze take in his full measure of Anna, or the part of her that was not tucked beneath the tablecloth, and he felt Gordy had overstepped his bounds. He wasn't looking at Anna as though he were her employer; he was looking at her as though he were about to plough new ground.

Beneath his stiff collar, Coit's anger burned. He found himself wanting to tussle with his brother the way the twins had tussled earlier. Instead Coit pretended politeness and watched Gordy's every move.

He spoke to Sara. "How are you this evening, Mrs. Polk? I understand Miss Blow here is your new boarder."

"She is. You can't believe how happy I am to have her." Sara smiled at Anna reassuringly, and Anna smiled back.

"Jess tells me that the both of you get along famously. I like to hear that my mill workers are like one big happy family."

This time Coit did choke, only it was on the liquid that he accidentally inhaled. Anna thumped him on the back while Sara and Jess looked more uncomfortable by the minute.

"Must have bones in it," Lance told him, watching Coit struggle to catch his breath. "That's what Ma always tells us when we 'bout strangle to death."

"Your mother is probably right." Coit glared at his brother around Anna's profile. "A bone of contention," he mumbled beneath his breath. If Gordy heard his remark, he ignored it. Instead, he gave Anna his full attention.

Not that she seemed to mind. She listened to everything he said, made comments, and tried to draw everyone into the conversation. Coit's annoyance with his brother continued to grow. He wasn't certain if it was because Gordy appeared to have Anna's undivided attention, or because he kept ogling her like she was the prize dessert and he had just won it.

"Wonderful food, don't you think?" he asked no one in particular. "I swear you ladies outdo yourselves with the meals you prepare for these functions. I never saw or tasted so many different kinds of food."

Both Anna and Sara smiled at Gordon's compliment.

His next statement was directed solely to Anna. "Old bachelors like myself don't get many home-cooked meals."

Anna cleared her throat and responded matter-of-factly.

"Then maybe, Mr. Hamil, you should find yourself a wife."

This time it was Gordy's turn to choke. His face turned red, and he gulped for breath. Apparently the idea of marriage didn't go down as easily as the food had. Trying to make light of the situation, Gordy looked at the twins and said, "This food does seem to have a lot of bones."

"Could be cause you ain't chewing it proper," Percy informed him.

"You might have something there, young man." He swabbed his forehead with his napkin.

Coit watched his brother's face turn redder and couldn't hide his grin. The twins never minced words, and Gordy was finding out his new employee didn't either.

Lance decided to put in his two cents' worth. "Could be you was talking with your mouth full. That's what happens when you stuff your mouth too full, ain't it, Ma?"

Sara looked embarrassed. "I think the two of you should finish your supper and let us adults do the talking."

"Leave them alone, Miss Polk. I love children."

Sure you love children. Coit looked at his brother with disgust. *You and I both know you only love bullion, and not bouillon soup that comes from beef or chicken.*

Anna's next remark got everyone's attention. "If you love children," she said, "that's another reason why you should consider getting married."

Gordon ran his finger beneath his collar. He laughed good-naturedly. "You seem awfully interested in my marital state. You keep it up and you'll have me believing you're in the market for a husband."

"Me? No, sir. I guess I'm trying to get a point across. Sometimes those of us who aren't married don't realize how expensive having a family can be." As an afterthought, she added, "or the disservice we as adults do to children by using them as laborers instead of seeing that they go to school."

Coit wanted to stuff a biscuit into Anna's mouth. He

knew where this conversation was leading and he wanted
to stop it before it got there. He also recognized the same
gleam in her eye that he had seen last night when she had
gotten on her high horse about the unfair labor practices
at the mill. If Anna believed that she could tear into Gordon the same way she had torn into him, she was in for
a big surprise. Come Monday morning, she might find
herself without a job or a proper reference.

Her next statement proved Coit's earlier thoughts.

"I imagine it is quite a drain on most of the families
here to have furnished this wonderful spread. It's kinda
like taking food off their tables so they can feed you.
Don't you agree, Mr. Hamil?"

Sara laughed nervously and sent Anna a worried look.
"Anna, dear, where do you come up with such ideas? Mr.
Hamil is very generous to his employees. We have good
housing, nice yards, and we can grow our own food. We
enjoy sharing with others. I'm sure most of the food we're
all enjoying tonight was homegrown."

"Or came from his Company Store," Anna added, dar-
ing him to deny it.

Damnation. She wasn't going to let the paycheck issue
die.

Coit immediately recognized the anger that flashed in
Gordy's eyes with Anna's last statement. Had the woman
taken leave of her senses? A mill social was no place to
bring up such issues. Granted, Coit didn't agree with a lot
of his brother's policies at the mill, but he didn't agree
with Anna's timing either. Again, a niggling suspicion
poked at Coit's mind. An ordinary mill worker would
never challenge Gordy so.

Fearing that nothing good could come from this discussion, Coit tried to direct the conversation elsewhere. If
the truth were known, instead of directing, he wanted to
drag Anna away, using her hair if need be.

"Have you finished your meal?" he asked. "There is
a woman who asked me if I would introduce you to her.
It seems she worked at the Macon mill, also. I told her
I'd bring you over after dinner."

Coit stood, and the other two men followed suit. With any luck, Anna would seal her lips and not say another word.

She looked to the trees across the way where a group of men and women were gathered. For a moment, it seemed she had lost some of her gusto. She searched the distant crowd for the elusive woman that Coit knew didn't exist.

"Miss Blow," Gordy said, drawing her attention, "as I told my brother earlier today, you are an unusual woman. Not like most of the women who work for me. I'd be interested in speaking with you further about your opinions on my mill and its workers." He looked at her with a snide expression. "Your attitude makes me question your real reason for seeking employment at the Royal Mill."

Annabel swallowed. Gordy's statement made Anna look ill at ease, but not for long. Instead of backing down as Coit expected her to do, she answered Gordy, surprising everyone with her boldness.

"I'd like that, Mr. Hamil," she said. "Maybe at that time you could enlighten me as to why there aren't more women in supervisory positions at your mill—"

"Anna, really," Coit interrupted, seeing disaster approaching. "I don't believe this is the time or place to discuss such things."

Gordon dismissed his intervention with a wave of his hand and spoke directly to Anna. "I'll answer your question now. Most of the women who work at Royal are not capable of holding such a position and probably wouldn't know what to do with it, if they had it. Ask Jess. He works in that capacity."

Not giving her a chance to respond, he continued, "We'll talk again, young lady. Now if you'll excuse me, I see someone I need to speak to."

Everyone watched him until he disappeared into the crowd. Then Coit turned to Anna and said, "Are you stupid or just plain dumb? You are aware that Gordon is your boss, and he does the hiring and firing at the mill."

Sara stood up next to Jess. They both looked uncomfortable until Sara broke the silence. "Anna, I'm going to take the twins to the necessary. Would you care to join me? If not, I'll see you back in the stage area once the singing begins."

"I'm fine, Sara, thank you. I'll see you there later."

After the Polks had left them, she looked at Coit and squared her shoulders. In answer to his earlier question, she replied, "I'm neither stupid nor dumb, and, yes, I'm very much aware of Gordon Hamil's position at the mill." She folded her arms across her chest, challenging him. "Now, where is this woman you wanted me to meet?"

"Woman?" Coit was confused by her reference until he recalled his ploy to distract her. "You mean the woman from Macon?" He looked in the same direction that he had earlier, searching the crowd. "Looks like she got away. I don't see her. But I'm sure she'll show up later."

Anna looked at him chidingly. "There is no woman, Coit Jackson, and you know it. You made up that story because you didn't like what I was saying to your brother."

Coit heard his heart pounding against his ribs. *No, she surely wasn't dumb.* "You're right, Anna, there was no woman. Because your remarks made everyone present uncomfortable, I thought it best to guide the conversation in another direction. Tonight wasn't the proper time or place to discuss such matters."

She cocked one coppery brow in question. "Will there ever be a proper time?"

"Yes," he answered, "and you and I will talk about it later. But for now, you'd do well to remember, if it ain't broke, don't fix it."

"But it is broken—"

"Later." He placed a finger on her lips to silence her. "Right now I see Dora and the others summoning me to return."

A belligerent look shadowed her face. "Well, we can't keep Dora waiting, can we?" she said.

"Dora? Why, of course not." Coit steered her toward the platform. When he left her at her seat, she was as stiff as a stick. "I promise you we'll continue this discussion later."

"I'll be waiting with bated breath." She dropped onto the empty bench and smoothed her skirts, not even acknowledging his departure.

As Coit walked toward the platform, he knew Anna was mad enough to kick up stumps, but he wasn't sure what it was that had her so riled—the abrupt end to their conversation or his mentioning that Dora was waiting.

He preferred it to be the latter. Was he correct in detecting a hint of jealousy in Anna's tone? If so, it would do her good to experience some good old-fashioned jealousy. Those were the kinds of feelings a young woman should have, instead of worrying over factory children attending school, and why there were no women employed as supervisors in the Royal Mill.

Recalling the conversation between his brother and Anna, Coit chuckled. To his surprise and pleasure, she had effectively thwarted any intent Gordy might have had to woo her. Her indifference to his stepbrother's charm must have been a real blow to his ego. But Coit couldn't have been happier with the outcome, except he didn't want her to lose her job.

In fact, he no longer had to worry about Gordy trying to court Anna. The knowledge that his stepbrother was completely out of the picture made Coit so high on his pleasure that he could have jumped over the moon.

❖ *16* ❖

For Anna, the night had lost its magic. Although the music still continued to entertain her with its haunting sounds of notes sung with no words, she felt as though she no longer belonged amongst the happy group of singers.

Once again, her outspokenness had alienated her from those she cared about. Not only had she earned Coit's censure, but also Sara's.

Several hours later when Sara whispered that she and Jess were leaving to take the twins home, Annabel chose to stay instead of accompanying them. She refused their invitation so she wouldn't have to explain her actions to them on the walk home.

Too late, Annabel recognized her breach of etiquette. She should never have questioned Gordon Hamil as she had done. Had her outspokenness placed her dearest friends, Jess and Sara, in a bad light with the mill owner? She prayed it had not. Maybe it was as Coit had said. "If it ain't broke, don't fix it." To people like Jess and Sara, whose livelihood depended on their jobs at the mill, maybe they didn't see the system as being broken.

Oh, Lordy, whatever was she to do? Was it time for

her to pack up and leave Dalworth? The only thing she had found out since her arrival that was of any significance was that she loved Coit Jackson. Her love for him, she admitted sadly, was as impossible as this whole undertaking. Labor investigator indeed.

Annabel was snapped from her thoughts when the crowd starting shouting, "Duet, duet, duet." She had been so removed from the group she hadn't noticed that the singing had stopped.

She looked toward the stage. Coit and Dora were standing together, their arms linked, both of them smiling beautifully at their adoring audience. Again Annabel was reminded of what a handsome couple they made.

The other leaders had left the stage, and now the fiddler and the harmonica player had returned. While Coit and Dora waited for the musicians to warm up, the audience made several song requests: "Greensleeves," "Wildwood Flower," and "Barb'ra Allen."

Once Coit and Dora started to sing, Annabel's spirits dropped even lower. Not only were they beautiful to look at, but also their voices blended in compassion and conviction. The sound left Annabel feeling breathless, and she felt a twinge of disappointment because of her own inadequacies.

The performers sang most of the audience's requests before singing a repertoire of their own choosing. It was apparent to Annabel that Coit and Dora were a well-known twosome, a detail that was almost more than she could bear.

No longer able to contain herself, Annabel gulped back her tears. She had to escape before she started bellowing like a fool in front of everyone. Excusing herself, she walked steadily toward the ring of darkness that surrounded the lighted stage and sitting area. Beyond the lantern and candlelight, and the rows of benches holding warm bodies, the night air felt almost chilly.

When she reached the compound's outer gate, the last refrains of "Beautiful Dreamer" drifted into silence. She paused to catch her breath while hiding in the shadow of a large tree. For one not normally given over to tears, tonight Annabel didn't have the usual iron control over her emotions. Tears gushed forth violently like water freed from a dam. Deep sobs shook her body. Rocking back and forth, she wept aloud, drawing in deep snorts of air that sounded like the resonant honk of a goose. A goose was exactly what she was, carrying on in this manner. Fearing that someone passing might hear her, she pulled up the hem of her skirt and buried her face in its folds to muffle her sobs.

What seemed like a lifetime later, but was only a few minutes, her tears ceased, leaving Annabel drained and empty. She straightened and leaned back against the tree. The singing had stopped. She recognized the sounds of the fiddle and the harmonica. This realization sent panic flying through her. If Coit was no longer singing, then he could at this moment be searching for her. He wouldn't want her walking home alone in the dark. The last thing she wanted was to face Coit in her exposed state.

But then she recalled Coit and Dora together—he wouldn't be thinking about her. At this very moment, he was probably holding Dora's arm, escorting her the way he had escorted Annabel earlier this evening. This deduction brought both relief and disappointment, and then a determination not to worry about either of them.

In spite of Annabel's resolve to dismiss Coit and Dora completely, she couldn't control her curiosity. She expected the pain of seeing them together would feel like having a stake driven into her heart.

No, she didn't want to know, she told herself. *Don't look.* Annabel took a deep steadying breath and inched away from the tree, intent on going home. But she had only taken a few steps when she stopped dead in her tracks. Several minutes passed while she continued to argue with herself not to look, but soon the desire to do so won out.

Groaning aloud, Annabel swung around and practically ran back to the tree. Once there, she clung to the trunk as though they were old lovers. *It's best to know,* she reasoned. With her front pressed intimately against the cool bark, she dipped her head to the side and glanced back toward the halo of light.

Annabel almost jumped out of her skin. Instead of viewing the crowd as she had expected, her line of vision was blocked by the silhouette of a man. It took only a moment for the man's identity to register in her brain.

"How dare you sneak up on me," she scolded, her hand flying to her chest. "You scared me speechless."

Coit's eyes squinted in what looked like amusement. "That will be the day when you're scared speechless. And I wasn't sneaking up on you. I heard you blubbering and thought you might like some time to yourself."

"Blubbering? I never blubber."

"Just like you never overreact."

"Exactly." She moved away from the tree and strode toward the gate. "Now if you'll excuse me, I'm tired and I want to go home."

"Good. Me, too," Coit answered, falling into step beside her. "Since we're both going in the same direction, I think it only proper that I should escort you home. I wouldn't want the bogyman to get you."

Annabel choked back her laugher. Earlier she had equated his hold on her to that of a bogy. And he was a man. The idea that Coit had almost read her mind irritated her. Annoyed she said, "You, Mr. Jackson, are the biggest bugbear to date."

"Me?" His dimple deepened, marking a comma on one side of his mouth. "Am I really a continuous source of irritation to you?"

Wearily she considered his question. "On most days," she answered.

He fell into step beside her, took her hand, and tried placing it in the crook of his arm. Annabel resisted but soon realized it was fruitless when his much stronger grip won out. They strolled several more feet in silence, but finally her curiosity got the better of her again. She asked testily, "Who is escorting Dora home?"

"Dora? I don't—" A flicker of a smile twitched his lips. "You're jealous, aren't you?"

"Me, jealous?" Annabel harrumphed her displeasure. "Don't flatter yourself."

"I like flattering myself," he teased. "When I first came upon you trying to drown that tree you were hiding behind, I thought you were feeling out of sorts because of your rudeness. But now I think it was entirely something else. You think Dora and I have a thing going."

Annabel snatched her hand from his. "I told you I wasn't blubbering. All I can figure is that lint from the mill must have escaped the windows and made my eyes burn and my nose run. That's why I left the singing early."

"Anna," he said gently, taking her hand and pulling her toward him. They stopped moving. With one finger, he lifted her chin and looked deeply into her eyes. "We both know the mill is closed and it wasn't lint that made your eyes red and puffy. And if it wasn't Dora who made you cry, what was it?"

"I'm not crying."

"Now you're not, but you were earlier." He pulled her closer. "If you're worried about losing your job, don't. Although Gordy and I don't see eye-to-eye on most things, I won't let him terminate you."

"I'm not worried," she lied. She wanted to tell him the truth, wanted to tell him she loved him, but she didn't dare do either. Instead, she said, "The music was so beautiful it made me weepy."

"Yes. It does that to me sometimes as well." He brushed back from her brow the hair that the soft breeze had teased loose. "What do you say we go to my place and have that chat I promised we would have?"

Annabel hesitated. "It's late. I don't know if it's such a good idea."

"What's the matter, you scared of the bugbear?"

Scared senseless.

"Of course not," she answered. Her spirits had lifted now that she knew Coit preferred her company over

Dora's. "Do you have any of that lemonade at your house? All that singing gave me a powerful thirst."

"Singing? You didn't utter a note. I know because I watched you."

She feigned surprise. "Watched me! How could you watch me when your eyes were glued to Dora the whole time?"

"Aha!" He beamed. "I was right. You *are* jealous."

"I most certainly am not." Annabel realized too late that she wasn't any good at keeping her feelings for Coit to herself. She pushed away from him and began walking.

Coit caught up with her in two long strides. "I'm glad you're jealous. And if you won't tell anyone, I'll tell you my secret."

"Tell anyone? Who would I tell? After tonight and the way I conducted myself in front of Mr. Hamil, Sara is not likely to speak to me ever again. I imagine she and Jess both rue the day I appeared on their doorstep."

"Well, then, if Sara is no longer open to hearing bits of gossip from you, I guess it doesn't matter if I tell you my secret or not."

Annabel whirled around to face him. "Tell me," she insisted. "Maybe I can bribe myself back into her good graces."

Coit stepped closer until he was mere inches away. His proximity made the points of her bosom feel as though she had suddenly stepped into a magnetic field as the tips of her nipples strained against the fabric of her chemise. Not only did it seem that she couldn't hide her thoughts from Coit, but also her seditious body had betrayed her state as well.

"Bribe *me* back into *your* good graces," Coit whispered as his arms encircled her waist and pulled her closer.

Annabel knew she should run, but her feet in her shiny new boots seemed snarled with his. She couldn't move an inch. And, she admitted, she didn't want to run.

The night was filled with the scent of freshly mowed lawns and gardens newly sowed. The heat of their bodies straining toward each other loosened their individual scents.

To Annabel, Coit smelled like the spicy fragrance of cloves. To Coit, Anna smelled like honeysuckle and the rose she still wore in her hair. Their lips met and played until their kissing made it difficult for them both to breathe.

Breathless, Annabel said, "Someone will see us."

"Let them." Coit nibbled on her earlobe.

"We had best be on our way," she insisted, stepping back, but then slammed against him again when the air between them felt cold and empty.

Coit pulled her closer and mumbled in her ear, "I was jealous of Gordy tonight. I didn't want him within a hundred yards of you."

His warm words breathed into her ear made Annabel's legs feel as weak as a baby bird's. Or maybe it was his confession.

"You were jealous of your brother? But you have no—"

"I have every reason. I don't trust him, especially around you." He trailed kisses down her neck and up again. Then he squeezed her so tightly she thought her bones might crush into powder. Just as suddenly, he released her, except for her hand.

"Come on," Coit said. Pulling her behind him, he strode toward the store.

The moon was still bright enough to light up the street, its pearly glow gilding the tin rooftops of the houses and sugarcoating the trees and shrubs they passed. As they hurried along, Annabel wondered if Coit was as eager as she was to be in his arms again. Was that why he hurried so?

When they reached the store, its white façade with its classic portico and Doric columns gave the appearance of a temple in the moonlight. It was a fitting image and place for Coit to take her because, in Annabel's mind, she had usurped Dora's place as goddess.

Instead of entering through the front door, he led her

along the building's side toward the backyard garden. Coit pushed open the gate, and it clanked shut behind them, interrupting the critters' symphony that was taking place before their arrival.

Pausing, Coit plucked a dangling pink flower from the tall stems leaning against the fence.

"Kiss-me-over-the-garden-gate," he said, pulling her into his arms again and handing her the blossom.

"Now, how am I to kiss you over the gate, if we're both standing inside?" she teased.

His lips brushed her forehead lightly. "Anxious for me, are you?" He grinned and tapped her nose. "My greedy little maiden."

Yes, she was greedy for him. Also, she was thankful for the cover of darkness that didn't allow her blush to show.

Coit ended their embrace and led her toward the back portico. When they walked through the lushly planted yard, a lingering richness of flowers, mingling with grass and mulch, spiced the night air. For Annabel, the magic had returned with all its enchantment.

"Sit," he said, directing her to the porch swing. "I'll get us some lemonade and be right back."

Left alone, Annabel set the swing into motion. The grating squeak that accompanied any worthwhile swing creaked out its familiar sound. It wasn't long before King Arthur, his eyes shining like jewels in the moonlight, made his appearance beside her feet.

"Your Royal Highness, how are you this evening?" Annabel patted her lap in invitation. The big tom hesitated only a moment before he was lured by her summons. He jumped up on the swing, then settled in her lap. Soon his rumbling purr joined the other night sounds.

The screen door banged shut. Coit returned with a tray and two glasses. He pulled up a small twig table and placed the tray on its top, then settled himself beside Annabel in the swing.

"I see I've been replaced," he said, reaching to stroke the cat that filled Annabel's lap. His fingers accidentally touched Annabel's stomach, and the caress, although innocent, sent fire rushing through her.

I should leave, she thought. A proper lady didn't keep company with a man unchaperoned, but then when had she ever followed proper decorum? Her mother would be the first to attest to her daughter's usual negligent behavior, and Annabel wondered briefly why she should be concerned with it now. So instead of fleeing, she stayed, allowing her eyes to feast on the man she loved.

Coit had removed his starched collar and unbuttoned several buttons of his shirt. The movement of his arm as he caressed King Arthur's back made his shirt tabs flap open, giving Annabel a better view of his chest and the dark hair that covered it.

Until that moment, Annabel had not considered the difference between a man's chest and her own. But with Coit sitting several inches away from her, his body warmth seeping past her clothes, the idea suddenly fascinated her. She imagined that Coit's chest would be hard and smooth like a plain, while hers would be soft and rounded like mountains. And with all that grassy hair covering that flat plain, she wondered how it would feel to press her smooth mountains against it.

Merciful heavens. How the man possessed her. Here she was in the middle of the night, sharing lemonade with a near-stranger, and entertaining lustful thoughts that made her feel all wet and juicy in the oddest places.

Annabel shifted uneasily on the swing. When she did, Coit's fingers accidentally brushed the apex at her thighs. The brief contact took her breath away. Coit looked embarrassed, especially when he jerked his hand away from King Arthur's back as though he'd been scratched by the feline.

Suddenly Coit seemed shy. Reaching for the glasses of lemonade, he said, "Here, drink this. It will cool you off and quench that thirst you complained of earlier."

"I am warm," Annabel replied, taking the glass he handed her. Although she didn't believe for a moment that the icy liquid would banish the out-of-control fire growing inside her, she took his offering with shaky fingers.

Silently they each downed almost the entire contents of their glasses before they dared to look at each other again. When they did, they quickly looked away.

Coit licked his lips. "Good, isn't it?"

"Very," she replied, sounding like some stodgy old lady taking tea. The image of Merelda Whitcomb holding her teacup in the Dalworth Hotel surfaced in her mind. She wondered if perhaps she should crook her little finger the way Merelda had done on that long-ago day.

Coit took her glass and placed it on the tray. Then he settled back on the swing, staring at her as though he had something more to say but wasn't sure how to say it. Instead of talking, they glided back and forth with only King Arthur's purr making conversation between them.

After several more stilted moments had passed, Coit stood, saying, "I'll get us more lemonade."

Annabel knew she couldn't drink another drop, but answered him, "Yes, why don't you."

Moving to pick up the tray, he stopped. "Damnation. Who cares about more lemonade?" He swung around to face her, dropping down on his knees in front of the swing.

"Anna, you have me acting like a nervous schoolboy."

His eyes latched on hers, and she felt a hundred heartbeats throbbing in her throat.

"I'm crazy about you, Anna. I've never felt this way about another woman, and I'm not even sure there's a name for what I'm feeling."

He leaned toward her, placing a hand on each side of her lap. King Arthur's eyes opened to half mast before drooping closed again.

Coit's sudden, unexpected movement and announcement left Annabel without a response. She stared back at him, her heart beating so fast that if he couldn't see it trying to jump out of her chest, he most surely could hear it. Did Coit care as much for her as she did him? He leaned toward her and said, "I want to kiss you again. I

want to hold you like I held you out in the street, but this
time I don't want to stop with holding.''

Annabel had a good idea what came after the holding
but wasn't certain that she should divulge this knowledge
to him. Although she imagined that she wanted the rest
as much as Coit claimed he did, she didn't want to sound
too eager. But when Coit only stared at her, not saying a
word or making a move, she decided that maybe he was
waiting for her response or for her to make the first move.
Feeling totally out of her element, she said, ''You may
kiss me if you like.''

''I'd like and I probably would have done it anyway in
a few more moments.'' He leaned toward her, pressing
his weight against the swing. His maneuver moved her
backward and farther away from him, instead of closer.

After several failed attempts at reaching her lips, Coit
straightened. Frustrated, he loosened his grip on the
wooden seat. When he did, the swing swayed forward,
and Anna's knees slammed hard into his midriff, forcing
most of the air from his lungs. Gasping for breath, Coit
doubled over, his head now even with Anna's lap, which
King Arthur had claimed as his own and clung to like a
magnet.

Eye to eye with the feline, Coit read the message that
shined from the depths of the cat's yellow-green eyes. It
said, *From one old tom to another, tonight this one's
mine.*

Why was it that cats believed everything belonged to
them? Coit pushed back on his knees, rubbing his midriff.
''You're going to have to choose between that cat and
me,'' he complained.

''There's really no contest,'' she said, ''I'll stick with
the King.''

In the low light of the moon, he could see she was
smiling and knew she was teasing him in the way that he
loved. Then she slipped from the swing onto her knees
directly in front of Coit. Her movement sent King Arthur
sliding to the ground. He meowed his displeasure then
sulked away into the shadows of the lawn.

When Coit took Anna into his arms, this time it was as though they both realized that nothing would keep them apart. There was no one in the street to happen upon them embracing and no one to care that they embraced. Even King Arthur had left them.

It was as though they were the only two people in the world.

They were alone in Coit's garden that had appealed to Anna as a small Eden from the first time she had walked through it. With their arms surrounding each other, their kisses became heated and more demanding.

Coit stood, drawing her up with him. Gently he placed her back on the swing and sat beside her.

"May I take your hair down?" he asked, reaching for the pins that held the high knot of hair in place.

His voice sounded husky, his chocolate-colored eyes lazy with desire.

Never had Annabel taken her hair down in front of a man, except in front of her father. *Mother. Father.* What would her parents think of their only daughter if they could see her now?

The pins dropped, pinging as they hit the bricks and bounced like tiny unwound springs. Soon her hair fell around her shoulders like a sheath of coppery threads.

"It's more beautiful than I imagined it would be," Coit whispered, running his fingers through the silky strands. The rose he'd given her earlier he tucked again behind her ear. "You're my diva."

Annabel wasn't sure about the "diva" part of his endearment, but she sure as the devil was certain about the "my." She was his and would soon truly belong to him. It was as Coit had jested earlier; she was greedy for his body.

Although Annabel had never been with a man, she had read books on the subject at Wesleyan and had had many midnight discussions with the free-thinking women who had been her friends. She knew fornication was a sin, and if she and Coit should fornicate, in the eyes of the world she would be a fallen woman. But none of that mattered now. The consequence was not important. If Annabel was going to sin, she wanted to sin with Coit. Besides, she already knew she loved him. That knowledge made her hope that her wickedness wouldn't be quite so bad.

Coit kissed her neck beneath the fall of hair. She smelled like honeysuckle and all woman. Hadn't he boasted once that if he ever met a woman who smelled like his favorite flower he would marry her tomorrow? Is that where his crazy, topsy-turvy feelings were leading him? Down the aisle? Was Anna the woman he wanted to spend the rest of his life with? Right now, as his body grew more heated by the moment, all he wanted to do was to take her to his bed. He wanted to love her all night long and then into the morrow. Was his desire to possess her body enough to build a marriage on?

His fingers fumbled with the small buttons at her nape. He wanted to kiss her neck, kiss her pulse points, and feel the rhythm of her heart synchronized with his. And he didn't want to do it in this back-breaking swing.

"Anna," he murmured huskily, "you're driving me crazy." He fought to get a better grip on her, to draw her closer, but their position in the swing made it impossible. He couldn't recall the last time he'd kissed a woman in such uncomfortable surroundings. Anna was a decent woman and one who wouldn't take his next suggestion lightly. But his desire for her overruled all his reason. He would either have her or he would not. This necking in the swing had to come to an end before they broke their backs.

Pushing back from her and holding her shoulders in his hands, Coit said, "I want to make love to you, but I want to do it right. Not like this with both of us twisting like pretzels to get closer." He released her and ran his fingers through his hair. "I want to take you to my bed and pleasure us both."

Their gazes collided. Her eyes looked luminous and wet in the pale light. Had his request insulted her, hurt her, and now was she straining to hold back her tears? God, he hoped not. He had never meant to hurt her or embarrass her with his request.

Suddenly Coit felt foolish. Had he been presumptuous in assuming her needs were as strong as his?

"I know what I'm suggesting might seem forward." He paused. "If you refuse, I'll understand, but damn it, Anna, a man can only take so much."

She chewed her lower lip in indecision.

"I won't think less of you—"

"I thought you'd never ask," she answered, her determination as visible as a rock.

Had he heard right? Had she said what he thought she had said?

"Are you saying yes?"

Anna laughed, a deep warming laugh. "I'm saying, Coit Jackson, I'm greedy for your body."

"Oh, Anna." His heart swelled on hearing her answer. The swelling didn't surprise him in the least. It was his body's natural response to her, and had been almost since their first meeting.

He stood and pulled her up with him. Then he lifted her, weightless, into his arms. Anxious to get her into his bed, he carried her toward the back door and his apartment.

Anna giggled and wiggled like a young girl. "Put me down before you break your back or injure us both."

"Not a chance, my sweet," he told her. "I've got you now and I don't intend to let you go."

❖ 17 ❖

ONCE INSIDE, COIT set her on her feet. Pulling her close against his body, he buried his lips against the warm flesh below her ear. Where his mouth touched the pulse point hidden beneath her hair, Anna's heart beat as erratically as a frightened bird's. Her skin against his mouth felt as hot as embers, and he cooled it with the touch of his tongue. Her skin tasted of salt and the lingering sweetness of perfumed water.

He realized his wet caress was a mistake when lightning desire streaked through his belly, fueling his need for her. His heart thundered against his ribs, and he wasn't sure which of them trembled the most.

She felt soft and all woman against him. He wanted to drive his hard need deep into that softness until his craving for her was sated. But as badly as he wanted her, he knew this would be Anna's first experience with a man, and he wanted to make it as pleasant for her as he knew it would be for him.

As his fingers fumbled to release the back buttons on her blouse, he was reminded of the many things still unsaid between them. Coit wanted answers from her about her true identity, and he had wanted those answers before things had progressed this far. He had meant to have the conversation he had promised Anna they would have, but because they were carried away by their need for each other, his questions and answers no longer seemed important.

Soon he had the buttons trailing down Anna's back unfastened. Gently he peeled away the covering that would reveal her womanly secrets to him and him alone. His fingers trembled when he accidentally brushed her satin skin.

When Anna felt the cool air wash against her skin, she felt as though she'd been doused with icy fire.

What am I doing in this strange bedroom, allowing a man to take such liberties? Especially with a man who believed she was Anna Belle Blow. She had wanted to have that talk with Coit that he had promised they would have, but her need for him had outwitted all reason. When she should have insisted they have their discussion, she had remained silent, and her deceit weighed heavily on her already guilty heart.

There is still time, a voice cautioned. But the wonder in Coit's eyes as he stared at her naked shoulders was Annabel's Waterloo. Any resistance she might have summoned was crushed by his near worshipful gaze. She could no more have denied him his pleasure than she could have denied herself.

She allowed Sara's handmade gift to slip from her arms and fall to the floor. In only her chemise and skirt, Anna stood before him, hoping that what he saw pleased him.

They stood hip-to-hip with his arms encircling her waist. "You are a feast, my love," he said, caressing her with the intensity of his look. His perusal made her feel uncomfortable and shy once again.

Never sure of herself as a woman, Annabel wondered if her mountains were too lofty for Coit's taste. In the past, when she had thought about her breasts, she had wished for much smaller ones instead of the plump variety God had seen fit to bless her with. She dreaded the final unveiling when her chemise would be removed and all of her imperfect parts would be revealed to him, the man she loved and wanted to be perfect for.

He kissed her lips, exploring her mouth with his tongue. Soon all thoughts of her imperfections flew from her mind as her body responded to his kisses. Coit bent his head to nibble at the juncture of her neck and shoulder. When he laved her skin with his tongue, it was his arms that kept her anchored to him and to the floor. His kisses made her feel lightheaded and weightless. Only gravity kept her from soaring straight to the ceiling and reeling out of control.

He had to stoop to nuzzle her cleavage. It was lucky for them both that his bed was only a few feet away when they teetered, almost losing their balance, as Coit's exploration of her breasts became more ardorous.

Annabel fell backward onto the plump feather mattress, bringing Coit with her. Frolicking and laughing like children, they bounced to a standstill half on and half off the bed with Coit's legs tangled in Anna's heavy skirts. After several attempts to free himself, he finally found his purchase between Annabel's spread thighs.

She soon learned that Coit was as well endowed with manly parts as she was with a woman's. She felt his manhood pressing against the juncture of her thighs. She had never been touched between her legs by a man, and the sensations that rippled through her were so enjoyable that she couldn't resist moving against him.

Her motions brought a low moan from Coit's throat. Had she overstepped propriety with her forwardness? Her face burned from the thought, but the heat quickly vanished when Coit's gaze collided with hers and he smiled his pleasure.

"You're one desirable woman, Anna," he told her. "But if you keep wiggling like that beneath me, I'm not sure how much longer I can maintain my control."

His words conjured up all kinds of images, and she wondered if she was close to being his love slave. Suddenly she was anxious to explore the mysteries of intimacy that a man and woman shared—anxious for them both to be naked, lying in each other's arms.

Boldly she wrapped her arms around his neck and nuzzled beneath his chin. His whiskers felt scratchy against her kiss-swollen lips. She breathed deeply, committing to memory his scent of spicy cloves and tart lemonade. They kissed and explored, their temperatures soaring for several more moments before Annabel finally asked when he didn't, "Shouldn't we be naked?"

His grip tightened around her, and she could feel his uneven breath against her cheek. "To have you naked is my greatest desire."

She felt the tenderness of his gaze. "But, Anna," he asked, "are you certain you want to do this? It's not too late if you wish to change your mind."

Coit's concern pleased her. At that moment she felt cherished, and her heart fluttered wildly in her chest. His desire was evident, yet he was willing to stop if she chose to do so.

"I've come this far, and the delights of the flesh intrigue me."

Coit chuckled then whispered in her ear, fluffing her hair with his warm breath, "Now, what do you know about the delights of the flesh?"

"Only what you've taught me so far."

Her remark was all the encouragement Coit needed. He clamped his arms tighter around her waist and drew their bodies so close that her breath fairly left her lungs.

With his mouth he fondled her breasts through her chemise and teased her nipples into tight little buds. His fingers delved beneath her still-constricting garments, seeking her skin and making her cry out her desire.

When he thought he might die from his need of her, Coit slipped off the bed and stood, pulling her up with him. Once they were on their feet, he began to disrobe, pulling his shirt from his trousers and unfastening the row of buttons down his shirtfront.

Annabel watched, fascinated, while Coit undressed. He wasted no time with the preliminaries. Before all the buttons on his shirt were unfastened, he ripped the garment off and tossed it to the floor. A rush of heat stained her cheeks as she gazed at his muscled chest covered with thick black hair. The silky pelt swirled around dusky nipples before arrowing downward and disappearing inside the waistband of his pants. With his masculinity exposed, she thought him more beautiful than it was possible for a man to be.

"You're next," he teased, pulling her closer again.

Since Annabel had already shed her waist earlier, he helped her to unfasten her skirt and petticoats. Her courage wavered as the loosened garments slipped below her waist to ride her hips before dropping to the floor.

"Must you look?" she asked, suddenly feeling unsure.

"How can I not?" he teased.

How could he not? She knew herself that it would have been impossible for her not to have watched him when he had removed his shirt. She reasoned that turnabout was fair play. Besides, by giving up an article of her own clothing, she would be rewarded in turn when he gave up another piece of his. She pushed her skirt and petticoats lower until they landed in a puff around her ankles. She faced him wearing only her chemise, her bloomers, her cheap black stockings, and her shiny new boots.

Coit's breathing sounded raspy when he spoke. "You remind me of Botticelli's painting, the *Birth of Venus,* standing with your skirts fluffed around your feet."

Annabel recalled the painting of the goddess Venus merging from the foamy sea, her coppery hair reminiscent of Annabel's own. Coit's comparison made her feel beautiful for the second time in her life.

Until that moment, Annabel hadn't realized how nervous she was. Here she was on the brink of an experience that she never imagined she would be taking, offering her body to a man to use and pleasure as he chose. The idea of lying totally naked with Coit left her feeling less sophisticated and sure of herself than when they had first begun to disrobe.

Stalling for time, she asked, "Should we remove our shoes?"

"Shoes?" he repeated. After a moment, he smiled. "Yes, my Anna, we should remove our shoes."

Standing on one leg, he bent the opposite knee and removed his shoe and sock, then, shifting to the other leg, he repeated the action. Each shoe clunked heavily to the floor, shattering the only other sound in the room, that of the ticking dresser clock. A lamp on a nearby table cast a golden circle of light on the floor, and Annabel saw that the top of Coit's bare toes were covered with a sprinkling of black hair.

The man is an ape. She could only imagine how the rest of him, the still hidden part of him concealed beneath his trousers, must look with the same furry hair that covered his chest and toes. She shivered.

"You're cold?" he asked.

She shook her head in denial, although she suddenly felt as though she might freeze.

"Come here," he said, "let me help you undress, and then we can get beneath the covers and get you warm."

She replied hesitantly, "Is that how it is done?"

Coit's heart went out to her. He wasn't certain how to answer her question. Did she mean was it proper for him to help her undress, or did she mean to ask if people made love beneath the covers. Her innocence in matters of the flesh pleased and excited him. He would teach her all the things she needed to know and more. Answering her question as best as he could, he said, "My sweet Anna, it's done however two people wish to do it. But right now it would give me great pleasure to undress you."

She agreed with a weak smile.

Guiding her back on the bed again, Coit removed her boots, unlacing them as he had laced them only last night.

"Nice legs," he teased, reminding them both of his earlier slip in front of Sara.

His remark eased some of the tension that had accumulated beneath Anna's ribs. Before she had time to worry about what would come off next, Coit pulled her to her feet again and undid the ribbons that held up her drawers. The white cotton fabric slipped to the floor, revealing the nest of coppery curls at her thighs.

She and Coit both inhaled. Coit's response was caused by his awe of her perfection, and Annabel's was caused by her nakedness and her sudden vulnerability.

She squinched her eyes closed and fisted her hands at her side. Although Coit didn't touch her for several moments, she could feel his gaze sweeping over her.

"My beautiful Anna," he crooned, drawing her close so she wouldn't feel as though she were on display. With deft fingers he untied the ribbons on her camisole and peeled away the flimsy garment.

She wore no corset, but then in Coit's opinion she didn't need one. Her breasts were high and firm, her waist tapered and small, her hips rounded with nubile curves.

Coit's breath soughed between his teeth. It was as he had always suspected. Anna did have a magnificent pair of lungs.

It didn't take much longer to dispense with her stockings and his trousers. And before she had more time to grow self-conscious, he had them both back upon the bed, beneath the cotton sheeting, embracing.

Soon her timidity turned to passion as Coit fondled her breasts, laving the budded tips with his tongue and tracing a path of kisses down her stomach. Her body was perfection, all and more that he had dreamed it would be. With her coppery-colored hair flowing around them, he was reminded again of Botticelli's painting. Anna was his very own Venus.

Anna twisted beneath him, murmuring his name, basking in his maleness and his touch. His kisses, his caresses, his turgid hardness against her thighs made her blood flow like a raging, out-of-control river. Coit's hard grassy plains felt wonderful pressed against her satin smooth mountains, and Annabel felt as close to heaven as she believed it was possible to feel and still be alive.

They played and explored each other's bodies, sating themselves with touches and kisses until those failed to satisfy.

When Coit thought he could no longer hold back his

need for her, he poised between her thighs, above her. As he guided his sex to hers he found her body wet and ready for his entrance.

He swallowed, wanting to explain and to apologize before he hurt her.

"Anna, do you know what to expect next?" he asked.

She wiggled against him, almost causing him to lose what little control he had.

"You know when I enter you, it may hurt. If it does, it won't hurt for long. Then it will feel good again."

She replied languorously, "How could anything that feels so good hurt?"

"I'll try to make it as painless as possible," he promised.

He moved toward her entrance as she awaited his entry. It was slow and easy admission until she thrust upward, impaling herself on his sex.

"Oh, Anna," he uttered, slipping deeper into her womanly warmth.

They fit perfectly together as though God had made their bodies to be a perfect match.

What Coit found lacking in her experience she made up for with her eagerness to please.

Annabel found him incredibly gentle for such a strong and virile man.

For a woman who claimed she never overreacted, Coit found her eager exaggerations of movements titillating. Beneath his driving thrusts, she responded to his silent requests with a fever that matched his own.

Together they practiced the age-old dance of lovers everywhere, until their passion hurled them over the brink, shuddering. Both satisfied completely, they floated back to earth at a snowflake's pace to meld gently together. They lay exhausted with limbs entwined, blissful, in the sweet pleasure of their combined efforts.

Afterward they languished, replete, touching, and nibbling softly on noses, ears, and shoulders with neither confessing the love that bloomed in their hearts.

Spooned together, they drifted into a light sleep and

woke again with a ravenous hunger. For the second time
in less than two hours, they reached for each other and
made love again. When their desire was sated, they lay
abandoned of all strength on Coit's feather bed, listening
to the night sounds outside the window, and hearing the
ebbing thunderous heartbeats inside the room.

It was hunger of the stomach that forced Coit from
Annabel's arms and out of bed. As naked as the day he
was born, he left their love nest for sustenance of the food
variety. Propped against several downy pillows, the
mussed sheet tucked beneath her arms, Annabel watched
Coit exit the room.

If she loved him before their coupling, it was understandable why she worshipped him afterward. Coit had
been a gentle and caring lover, making sure she received
as much pleasure from their joining as he did. The only
thing lacking in their union were the words her heart had
longed to hear Coit say, words that would have bound
them together throughout eternity and the same words her
heart cried out silently to him.

It was best, she reasoned, that no promises were made
in the heat of passion, especially if those promises
couldn't be kept in the cool light of day. Besides, no one
knew better than she that there were too many secrets
between them—her identity and her purpose in Dalworth.
If Coit and she were to have a future together, all those
things needed to be discussed.

While Annabel waited for his return, she looked around
the long room that was Coit's home. It was a very mas-
culine room that served both as a study and bedroom.

On the opposite wall from where Annabel sat in the
big bed was a brick fireplace. Two large brown leather
wing chairs and a matching ottoman were grouped together in front of the hearth. A mahogany table between
the chairs held a lamp for reading.

For a moment, Annabel allowed her imagination to
wander. She envisioned herself with Coit, sitting side by
side in front of a blazing fire on a cold winter's evening.

It was a cozy picture and one she wanted to be a part of.

Above the fireplace hung a huge painting, depicting mountains with a silvery blue stream running through them. A man in fisherman's gear waded knee deep in the water, casting his fishing line. Her gaze wandered to the shelves on each side of the hearth. A big fish mounted on a wooden plaque sat among the many leather-bound books that lined the shelves.

Other things that suggested this was a man's domain were placed around the room. Certificates framed in dark wood, pictures of hunting dogs, a gold-handled cane propped against the wall, and a humidor for cigars.

The furnishings in the room made Annabel realize how little she really knew about the man she loved. Did Coit like to fish? Did he smoke? The twins had said he liked to cook, and she knew he enjoyed gardening. Besides his love of singing and working in the Company Store, what else gave him pleasure? She wanted to know what made him happy and what made him sad. Would he remain forever in Dalworth, making his home at the back of the store? If he took a wife, would they live together in these same rooms and raise a family here?

She noted the interior was tastefully furnished from the silk swags that hung above the windows to the twin Persian rugs that were spread on the floor beneath the leather chairs and the bed. The heavy Victorian bed she lay in was of museum quality, just like the Tiffany lamp that sat on the table across the room. The furnishings spoke of refinement and reminded her of her father's study back in Atlanta.

How could a man of Coit's means, a mere shopkeeper, afford such luxuries? Unless, of course, his apartment had been furnished with pieces he had acquired from the Hamil family home. Even a stepson would be allowed a few family heirlooms, wouldn't he? This room suggested a different sort of person than the Coit she had come to know. Her Coit wasn't a man of means or even education. Her Coit was a simple man who was at home among his pickles, tonics, leathers, and all the other paraphernalia on the shelves of his store.

Her gaze shifted again to the certificates on the walls. Because the distance was too great for reading, she couldn't see who had given the awards or the person who had received them.

Annabel would have gotten up to read them if she hadn't heard Coit returning. He came back through the door that led to his kitchen and the front of the store, carrying a tray laden with food.

She couldn't help but laugh at his image as he made his way toward her. He carried the tray with one hand, on a plane even with his shoulder, still naked as a new-born babe.

"You look like a statue of a Greek warrior," she told him when he neared the bed. "Except the warrior carried a shield, instead of a tray of food."

It seemed strange to Annabel that his nudity no longer made her feel embarrassed. In fact, she loved looking at his muscled body.

Coit placed the tray on her lap and crawled back beneath the covers beside her. Once he was settled, he positioned the food tray on their combined laps.

He had prepared quite a snack, and until Annabel smelled the food, she hadn't realized how hungry she was. There was cheese, clusters of deep purple grapes, an assortment of crackers, pickles, cookies, and four sarsaparilla sodas.

Coit fed her several grapes, downed a few himself, then recited a line from *Alice in Wonderland*. " 'The time has come, the walrus said, to speak of many things—' "

While he paused to chew the hunk of cheese he had plopped into his mouth, Annabel finished the next line. " 'Of shoes and ships and sealing wax, of cabbages and kings.' "

"I see you're not only beautiful, you're also well-read." He paused in his eating, studying her impassively for some moments before he continued. "If I didn't know better, my sweet,'' he said, ''I'd believe you were one of those intellectual college girls.''

''Do you object to women being educated?''

''I don't mind them being educated, I just don't like them meddling in affairs they know nothing about.''

Color rushed to her cheeks. Annabel downed a gulp of soda, hoping to wash away her growing uneasiness. If this was the conversation that Coit had promised her they would have later, it wasn't how she envisioned it would be. She was supposed to be the one asking questions about the mill; instead, Coit was getting dangerously close to the truth about Annabel Lowe.

He had almost described her perfectly. She was working toward an accepted place for women in a man's world. He couldn't possibly have found her out, could he?

He stuffed another grape into her mouth, saying, ''I'm impressed with your knowledge of literature and art. I know people gain knowledge from books, but your recent conversation with me and then my brother about the mill has me wondering if my beautiful Venus couldn't be one of those infamous reformers.'' He looked at her long and hard. ''Never had a fancy for those society types with too much time on their hands.''

Society types? Dear Lord, that's exactly what I am. Uncertain how to respond, Annabel was glad when he stuffed a wedge of cheese into her mouth and she couldn't say anything.

''But I did promise you that we would talk before the evening ended. I'm still confused as to why you chose to bring up the topic of the mill with Gordy, but since you did, I believe there are things you need to know about the Royal Mill and the people who work there. In this area, you appear ignorant.''

''Ignorant? I assure you I'm not ignorant.''

''Don't overreact,'' he cautioned her, tapping her on the nose. ''I'm not saying you are ignorant, I'm only saying there are some things you are less informed about than others. As I said earlier, if it ain't broke, Anna, don't fix it. ''

In defiance she crossed her arms against her chest. "And as I told you earlier, I see things that are broken."

He studied her intently. "Granted this is not a perfect world, and there are things that can always be improved, but you must understand that the people who work in the mills are so much better off economically than they were before my stepfather built this mill back in 1884."

"And is he not wealthier?"

Coit ignored her rebuttal and continued with his explanation. "Benson Hamil, my late stepfather, established the Royal Mill at a time when farmers in the valley were becoming less self-sufficient and more entangled by poverty, tenancy, and a declining cotton market. The economy was so bad it plunged farm families into deep and abiding poverty, pushing many into the ranks of landlessness and near starvation.

"The move to mill work was a family affair, and most workers came from the rural areas surrounding the town. These folks tried to hedge against economic disaster by sending family members to work in the mill. Today it's decent work, and it puts food on tables and feeds families."

With a stubborn set to her chin, Annabel asked, "And why does the mill employ more women and children than men?"

"A lot of the women are working at Royal to help support their families while their husbands work at other trades. Some of the women are widows, while some have been deserted by their husbands. The children, like their parents, work out of necessity."

"But those children should be in school instead of working in a mill."

"Someday maybe they will be. That was my stepfather's dream. He was a man of vision. He wanted to establish schools just as he provided decent housing. Those things don't happen overnight, Anna. Like everything, you get there by taking one step at a time."

"I know that," she said.

"What truly puzzles me about this whole business,

Anna, is why you're so concerned about these people."
He took her chin in his fingers and turned her face toward
his. "Who are you, Anna, and why is this business at the
mill so important to you?"

She lowered her eyelids so he couldn't see the truth.
"In case you haven't noticed, I work in the mill. I'm one
of those women—"

"Anna . . ." His voice trailed off.

Tell him now. Tell him the truth. Annabel wanted to
tell Coit, but from what he had said earlier about women
like herself, she didn't believe for a minute that he would
be responsive to her answers, or her meddling in something he had already claimed she knew nothing about.

Until ten days ago, Annabel had never given a thought
to the women and children working in the Royal Mill.
But she admitted that those women she had met since her
arrival didn't seem unhappy. In fact, Birdie had said she
enjoyed working in the mill.

"You've grown quiet, my love." Coit kissed her forehead and brushed her hair back so he could better see her
face. "Won't you answer my question, or am I to take
your silence as an indication that you've grown tired of
conversing and would rather practice more lessons of the
flesh?" Playfully he wiggled his brows up and down like
a villain.

After his remarks about women who sounded exactly
like herself, Annabel believed that instead of her being in
bed with the villain, *she* was the villain. If Coit knew she
was one of those society women he claimed to hold in
such little regard, then he would never consider a future
with her.

This piece of knowledge tore at her heart, not only because he wouldn't approve of such causes, but also because it seemed to her he wasn't interested in the rights
of women or children. Working for the rights of women
had always been Annabel's desire.

After graduating from college, she had been forced to
bow to her parents' wishes, but she'd been bored to tears
with her debutante role. The only thing she had enjoyed

in that status was the charity work she and her friends did for the less fortunate of Atlanta. Then her dreams had finally seemed within reach when she'd been given the opportunity to come to Dalworth. If her work here proved successful, who could say what opportunities might open for her. She had even entertained the idea of moving to Washington, D.C.

She had deliberately defied her parents to come here with the purpose of gathering information that she hoped would make life better for women and children forced to work in an industrial world. But she hadn't planned on meeting Coit Jackson and falling in love with him.

His opinions mattered to her, and he certainly knew more about that mill than she did. She worried over her ability to determine what was right or wrong for these people. What did she, Annabel Lowe from Atlanta, know about almost starving to death or, for that matter, anything else in Coit's world?

"Anna, do you have something you wish to tell me?" His chocolate brown eyes held so much tenderness it almost took her breath away.

"I—"

Thump, thump, thump.

The loud blows on the store's front door interrupted her words.

Coit grumbled, rolling from beneath the covers, "Who the devil could that be at this time of night?"

Again the thumping rumbled through the building like thunder.

Annabel's heart lunged to her stomach. Heaven forbid if she should be discovered in Coit's bed. She slipped lower beneath the covers, pulling the sheet up over her head.

Coit reached for his discarded clothes and began dressing. "You stay right here. I'll see who it is and hurry them along. You'll be fine. No one will know you're here."

What kind of a fool did he take her for? At the moment, she wasn't going anywhere. The last thing she wanted to do was draw attention to herself. In fact, she wished she could disappear between the cracks in the floor. She wasn't about to move an inch, in or out of the bed, while Coit entertained customers in the front of the store.

Several tense moments passed. Fragmented conversation drifted beyond the interior walls. The visitor sounded like a man. Minutes dragged by, seeming like hours before the conversation ceased and she heard the front door close and Coit returned. From beneath the sheet that covered everything but her eyes, she peeked at him.

"That was Jake Gilmore," he said, tucking in his shirttail. "It seems his mother has taken sick, and I happen to be out of the laudanum she needs. He is very worried about her. She's got a bad case of dysentery, and nothing she's taken has helped. I told him I'd run in to town and fetch some from Doc Larson. He knows me, and I'm sure he'll give it to me, regardless of the ungodly hour."

Coit sat on the side of the bed and wrestled with his shoes and socks. "We'll have to finish our talk when I return."

He stood and squinted at the clock on the dresser. "It's two-thirty now. I shouldn't be gone for more than an hour." He walked to the dresser and ran a brush through his mussed hair, then came back to the bed. He pulled the sheet away from her face and kissed her full on the mouth. "I won't be long, I promise."

✦ *18* ✦

ANNABEL WATCHED COIT leave. She was torn. Should she stay as he expected her to do, or should she leave? With all the things she had learned about herself tonight, and the things that Coit had told her about the mill people, Annabel felt confused. She needed time alone to think.

She heard the front door close. No longer was the dresser clock a soothing sound, instead it annoyed her with its loud ticking. The moments dragged by.

With her nerves on edge as they were, Annabel knew she couldn't sit here half the night doing nothing, waiting for Coit's return. She needed to distance herself from him. She needed time to examine what he had told her about the mill people and draw her own conclusions. But most of all she needed time to lick the wound he had inflicted to her heart with the statement he had made about women like her. Her decision made, she threw off the covers and slid from the bed. Once she was dressed, she slipped out the back door.

For the second time this evening, the night had lost its magic for Annabel. Her deception plagued her as she walked through the moonlit yard. She was tired of being someone she wasn't, tired of deceiving Sara, and so afraid to tell Coit who she really was.

Especially after their lovemaking. She didn't regret those moments they had spent making love because Annabel knew that if Coit couldn't accept her the way she was, she would at least have the memory of the passion-filled hours they had shared. She would leave here, knowing how it felt to be pleasured by the man she loved and with the knowledge that she had given him a part of herself that no other man would know. She loved Coit. He was the only man she would ever love.

Sadness overwhelmed her. The reality of her leaving traveled with her when she closed the gate separating the two yards. It was funny how much happier she had been here than she had ever been in her life. The many people she had met in her short sojourn here had touched her heart, especially Sara. How could she leave behind the closest friend she had ever had?

Tears stung her eyes as she glanced around the now familiar yard. Bathed in moonlight, she saw the hammock that had tossed her to the ground, and a toy shield and sword belonging to the twins. When she left, she would miss her extended family. That was how she had come to think of the Polks.

From beneath the porch's overhang, she heard movement. At first she thought it was King Arthur milling around in the dark until she heard Sara speak. "Anna, is that you?" she called.

"Sara? What are you doing up at this late hour?"

Annabel hesitated at the bottom of the steps, wishing for the second time in the last hour that she could disappear into thin air. She hadn't expected to encounter anyone. She had hurriedly thrown on her clothes, and her hair hung in tangles down her back. With Sara's keen insight, it wouldn't take her a second to figure out where Annabel had been, what she had been doing, and with whom she had been doing it.

Sara sat on the porch floor, her legs dangling over the edge. She wore her nightgown, and it was rucked up to her knees, revealing her white calves. She patted the floor beside her, indicating that Annabel should join her.

"To answer your question, I'm up because of my earlier gluttony. I don't think the babe enjoyed all that wonderful food as much as I did."

Annabel scooted backward on the porch beside Sara, allowing her own legs to dangle. "Is there anything I can get for you that might make you feel better?"

"Just your company. Nights like this when I'm so restless, it's nice to have someone to talk to."

"Even your vocal boarder?"

Annabel hated herself for having embarrassed Sara and Jess with her outspokenness in front of Gordon Hamil. She would understand if they were angry with her. They had every right to be.

"I'm so sorry about the way I spoke to Mr. Hamil. How you and Jess must wish I'd never set foot on your doorstep."

Sara's body stiffened, then relaxed before she spoke. "Don't be silly, Anna. I'm not saying I agreed with the timing of your complaints, but there are times I've found myself having the same thoughts that you expressed aloud." Sara stretched as though she were uncomfortable.

"Are you sure you're okay?" Annabel asked. When Sara assured her she was, Annabel continued. "I feel so awful putting you and Jess in such a position. I only hope I didn't jeopardize Jess's job at the mill with my big mouth. Mr. Hamil might believe you both empathize with me."

"Jess empathize with a woman taking his job?" She laughed that bubbly laugh that had become so familiar to Annabel. "Never! I love my Jess, but he believes if it's humanly possible, a women's place is in the home, raising children. He is not as up-to-date in his thinking as you and I are."

Sara rubbed her lower back while Annabel looked on in concern.

"What will I ever do without you?" Annabel asked. The tears that had threatened to fall earlier burned her eyes. "No matter how often I blunder, you stand beside me, always urging me back on track."

Swallowing her despair, Annabel blinked back her tears. This time there was no holding back; she choked on her voice. "You know, I've never had a friend like you." She dropped her head into her hands and sobbed. "I don't know who I am anymore or where I belong."

Sara's arm encircled her shoulders. "Anna, don't cry. Is it Coit who made you so sad? If he's hurt you in any way, I swear he'll have me to reckon with."

"My circumstances are no one's fault but my own. Coit has only added to my problems, but it's not his fault." She stopped speaking, yielding to the compulsive sobs that shook her body. Finally, when she could speak again, she said, "Sara, I'm not a very nice person—"

"I don't believe that for one minute, Anna. No matter what you've done or what you think is so awful, it doesn't change my opinion of you one bit."

Annabel knew her appearance was a dead giveaway that she'd been tumbled in someone's bed. Sara knew. How could she not?

"Then you know? You know where I've been and what I've been doing?"

Sara looked smug. "I know where I think you've been and what I hope you've been doing." She smiled like a kitten that had stolen the last lick of cream.

"It doesn't bother you that you have a fallen woman living under your roof, and an outspoken one as well?"

"Not as long as you took the plunge in Coit Jackson's arms."

"Sara, really, your choice of words—"

"I've told you all along that he is the man for you."

"If it were only that simple."

"It's simple as pie. He'll have to marry you now and make an honest woman out of you."

"Sara, listen to me. It isn't simple. There is so much that you don't know about me. So much that Coit doesn't know about me."

Her heart squeezed in anguish. Annabel couldn't live

with her deceit a moment longer. If nothing else was gained from her mission here, she at least wanted Sara to remain her friend. It was time she told Sara the truth.

Taking a deep breath, she began. "My dear and trusting friend, I'm not who I've claimed to be. You don't even know my real name. Can you understand why I feel my identity and reason for being here is a mockery to our friendship?

"I'm not Anna Belle Blow, mill worker from Macon. Instead, I'm really Annabel Lowe, the spoiled rich daughter of an Atlanta banker. Before I came to Dalworth and posed as a weaver, the closest I had come to a loom was in a college course I took at Wesleyan College in Macon, Georgia."

With a moan of distress, she added, "I'm nothing but a fraud."

Sara didn't say anything for a few moments. She allowed Annabel to rave on about her deceit, never interrupting once. Finally when Annabel fell silent, she said, "I'm not surprised at all. I always knew you were different. I sensed it at our first meeting. But whoever you are, it doesn't change the fact that we met and are now friends."

"Stop it, Sara. Don't you understand? I've done nothing but lie to you—to all of you. How can you still like me?"

"How can we call ourselves friends if we can't forgive each other's little failings?"

"Mine are not little failings."

"Surely they are not as great as you think. Why don't you tell me your reasons for lying and let me decide from there."

Exasperated, Annabel threw up her hands. "Sara, you are impossible, but maybe that is why I love you so. But I shall tell you, because I want to set the record straight between us. Your friendship and your respect mean so much to me."

"And yours to me."

Annabel was quiet for a few moments. "Have you ever heard of Mary Claire de Graffenreid?"

Sara shook her head. "Is she a friend of yours?"

"Not a personal friend, but we did attend the same college. Miss de Graffenreid graduated from Wesleyan in the summer of 1865, shortly after Macon had fallen to the Union Army and the day after General Lee had surrendered in Virginia."

"It's hard for me to comprehend a woman graduating from college during those troubling times," Sara added. "I guess it's hard for me to comprehend a woman graduating from college any time. Did you graduate?"

"Yes, I graduated, but I don't know what good it did me. Attending an all girls' college was the socially accepted thing to do for some of the girls in my circle. My mother hates it that I'm intellectual instead of beautiful and dumb."

Sara looked at her questionably. "Your mother is alive? You told me both of your parents were killed in a carriage accident."

"I lied, Sara, remember? Please let me tell you everything about me and why I'm here. When I'm finished, if you're still interested, I'll answer all your questions."

"Okay." Sara winced as she steadied her hands against the porch.

Annabel noticed the pained movement. "Are you certain you're feeling all right?"

"Yes, yes, I'm fine. Continue with your story."

She watched Sara for several more moments before she began again.

"Miss de Graffenreid's cousin, Hollie Cross, attended Wesleyan at the same time I did, and we became friends. There was a group of us, Merelda Whitcomb included, who were rebels of a sort. Our little group of intellectuals took an oath among ourselves that after we graduated and made our place in the world we would work to make it a better place for women."

"Merelda Whitcomb? You two are friends?"

"Were. We're not any longer. Miss de Graffenreid's

cousin, Hollie Cross, who now resides in Washington, wrote me a letter a month back, informing me that her cousin is a special investigator for the Bureau of Labor in Washington, D.C. It seems that someone from the Royal Mill had written a letter to Washington, complaining of the unfair labor practices for women and children working in the mill.

"Hollie knew how I always wanted to work for women's rights, and because Merelda still lived in Dalworth, she asked us both to snoop around and find out if there was a legitimate complaint. Supposedly we were doing this for Miss de Graffenreid, although we are not officially employed by the Bureau, but because Merelda and I were from the same general area, Hollie told her cousin that we could find out the information without appearing too obvious. Having a flare for the dramatic, I came up with the idea of impersonating a mill worker.

"When I arrived here, I thought that Merelda was going to help me. But when I saw her, she told me she wasn't going to have any part in the scheme and that I was on my own—"

"That's why you two are no longer friends."

"Yes, that's part of the reason, but the other part isn't important."

There was no way in the world that Annabel would tell Sara that snobby Merelda thought all mill workers were "lintheads" and below her in station.

"Merelda did agree to be my contact person in case my parents inquired about me during my visit. You see, I'm supposedly visiting Merelda who they knew I had been friends with in school. That friendship is the only reason they allowed me to come to Dalworth."

"Now I understand why you looked as though you might faint that day in the Ice Cream Saloon when she approached you."

"That day she gave me a letter that had come from my mother, demanding that I return home." Annabel dropped her head into her hands. "I'm so ashamed of deceiving you. Can you ever forgive me? I'm not a weaver from

Macon—I'm not anything but an idle debutante of the kind that Coit Jackson abhors.''

"Coit despises you?'' Sara's look reflected disbelief. "Then you told him who you are?''

"No, I didn't tell him who I am. And, yes, he loathes me. He told me earlier he couldn't tolerate women like me. Well, he didn't say me in particular, but he said intellectual women, women with money and time on their hands.''

"Now I understand,'' Sara said. "Coit still believes you are who you said you were, but you really aren't, and because he doesn't like women like who you are, you have to be who you're not and you can't be who you really are?''

For some reason, Sara's words had a familiar ring. Almost sounding the way Coit had sounded that long-ago day when he had described how much alike the twins were. No wonder Coit and Sara got along so well. They had the same kind of minds, along with the same sweet dispositions. And she loved them both.

"So now you understand my dilemma. It's bad enough that I lied to him, went willingly to his bed, while all the time he believed I was something I'm not. Not only did I deceive him, I'm the very kind of woman he could never love.''

They sat quietly side by side, listening to the crickets and frogs whose songs, in spite of the late hour, were still going strong.

"Anna, I know you see this as a problem between you and Coit, but I think you're making more of it than you should. We all have secrets, little ones and big ones, but if you truly love someone all these secrets can be explained away. You do love him, don't you?''

"With every inch of my soul.'' Tears flooded Annabel's eyes again. "When I leave him to return home, I'm sure my heart will break. But the regrets I'll feel will not come because I lay with him as his wife, but because I deceived him with my lies.''

"You must tell him everything just like you told me,''

Sara said, sitting up straighter. "He will understand because he loves you, too."

"He didn't say he loved me."

"Did you tell him you loved him?"

"No, but how could I?"

"With your big mouth, my outspoken friend. Since we've met, I can't recall a time I've known you to mince words."

"But this is different, Sara. I don't know anything at all about love. It seems to me that if you can't trust someone you love, that love will never have a chance. I've already deceived him, so how could he ever trust me? I don't think I could stand it if Coit rejected me because of my lies." She reached over and took Sara's hand. "Or you either," Annabel reminded her. "Sara, can you ever forgive me? Will you still be my friend now that you know the truth about me?"

"Mercy. What kind of person do you take me for? It's like I told you yesterday, you and I were destined to meet and become friends. Since I don't have any other girlfriends or sisters, I've claimed you as my own."

The two women hugged each other.

"Now, before my poor back breaks from sitting here half the night and before I go in for bed, I want to say I'm so happy we met. Even though we're from different backgrounds, we still became friends. That says something about how really special our friendship is. Do you have siblings in your real life?"

"No, what I told you about having no siblings was the truth. I was a very lonely only child. I'm still lonely, but I'm all grown up."

"Good," Sara said. "Not good that you're lonely, but it's good you have no brothers or sisters. Not only will you be Guinevere's godmother, but also I'm officially adopting you as my sister. You and I won't be lonely ever again."

Sara slid from the porch to her feet, then suddenly she doubled over, gasping in pain.

Annabel jumped up and grabbed Sara, cradling her in

her arms. "My God, Sara, are you all right? Is it the baby, should I call Jess?"

"No, no," she reassured, "it's not time for the baby. Just steady me a moment until I can catch my breath."

"Sara, you are scaring me. When is this baby due? I've never really heard you say."

"On All Hallow's Eve." After taking several deep breaths, Sara's pain appeared to subside. She straightened up slowly but still clutched her stomach. With her normal good humor, she said, "Instead of being a pumpkin for the holiday, I'll be shedding my pumpkin shape for a baby. Won't that be a trick?"

"Sara, let me get Jess, please."

"No. I don't want to worry him. I assure you I'm fine. The baby turned a somersault is all."

"Whatever happened, you're going straight to bed. And unless you want me to scream at the top of my lungs for Jess, you'll give me no argument." She helped Sara up the steps. "You're going to sleep in my bed the rest of the night."

"You're overreacting, Anna. Don't forget that I birthed twins. I assure you this is a natural occurrence in the later months of pregnancy. I'll be fine."

"Yes, you will be fine. But it's like I told you before, you do too much for a woman in your condition. Tomorrow you're going to stay in bed all day and let me take care of you. If you're not feeling better in the morning, I'm telling Jess, and we're going to call the doctor."

Annabel closed the door behind them and led Sara into her rented room.

"You know," Sara whispered, "you're going to make Coit Jackson a wonderful wife because you're already a terrible nag."

"So how is Sara?" Coit asked Anna.

It was mid-morning the next day. They stood opposite one another separated by the fence. He thought of how beautiful she looked today with her hair gathered low on her neck with a black ribbon. A light breeze played with the loose strands hanging halfway down her back, lifting them gracefully like rolling waves. Her skin glowed with an alluring warmth that he knew he had put there the night before when he had made her a woman. He wanted her again, right now, so badly that his body ached for her.

Unaware of her effect on him, Anna told him, "Dr. Larson left a few minutes ago. He said there is nothing to worry about. Both the baby and Sara are fine. He suggested that Sara stay off her feet for a couple of days."

Anna's knuckles were white where she clutched the fence. Coit wanted to reach out and touch her, to ease her tension. No, he wanted to break down the fence that separated them and pull her into his arms and never let her go.

"Why didn't you wait?" he asked, recalling his disappointment when he'd returned home last night to find that she had gone. Without a note, or an explanation, she had left. Her absence had left a void in his heart, making him feel lonely, friendless.

Anna avoided his gaze. She picked at the leaves of the nearby gardenia bushes before answering him. "I don't know," she said softly. "Things between us had progressed so fast that I guess I got frightened. I needed time to think."

"You don't have regrets—"

"No, of course not." Her flush deepened when their eyes locked. "I need to go back inside and check on Sara. I promised her I'd stay around today. Tomorrow, while I'm at work, the neighbors will sit with her and help look after the twins."

"When will I see you?"

Anna turned to leave. "I'm not sure, Coit. Right now while Sara needs me, I want to be here for her."

"What about my needs?" Once the words were out, he hated himself. He knew he was being selfish. But Anna affected him that way. "I'm sorry, Anna. I know you're concerned about Sara. Jess said you were up with her all night. You must be dead on your feet."

"I'm fine, but I'm concerned. You understand, don't you?"

"Of course I understand. I'm concerned, too. Before you go, I have something for you, for both of you." Coit squatted down, disappeared behind the pickets, then stood up again. In his arms was a huge spray of flowers that he'd picked from his garden. "Here," he said, handing the bouquet over the fence.

Anna took them and buried her face in the flowers' center. "They're lovely," she said. Above the blossoming show, the many colors reflected against her dewy skin like a rainbow.

He pointed to the middle of the bouquet and a deeply hued flower. "That one I picked especially for you," he told her. "It's called love-lies-bleeding."

Their eyes met and held. "That's the way my heart felt when I returned last night and realized you were gone."

Anna's eyes filled with tears. There was desperation in her voice when she finally spoke. "I can't talk about this now," she told him. "Please, I've got to go."

Before he could respond, she turned and ran toward the house. Coit watched her until she had disappeared behind the closing door.

Frustrated, he hit the fence with his hand. "Not only am I waxing poetic, you have me busting out of my britches if I get within a foot of you."

Between the two gardenia bushes where he stood, Coit felt movement next to his legs. King Arthur sprinted away from the bushes as if the hounds of hell were on his heels. Then he heard giggling.

"Lance, Percy, come out of there this minute."

Two towheads popped from beneath the bushes, and identical brown eyes looked up at him.

"What were you doing under there? Eavesdropping?" Coit asked.

"No, sir, Mr. Coit, we ain't easy dropping." They crawled from below the greenery and stood. Mischief lit up their faces.

"You were spying, weren't you?" Coit said, trying to keep a straight face.

"No, sir, Mister Coit. We'd never do that."

"Well, it doesn't matter anyway." He tousled their hair. "You boys going to the mill later with your pa to help clean up the grounds?"

"Yes, sir. Pa said he needed our muscles to help him do all that heavy work." Both boys flexed their scrawny arms, showing their strength.

Coit squatted down between the twins. First, with his thumb and forefinger he felt Lance's muscle, then he felt Percy's. "Not much bigger than a bird's egg," he teased.

"Oh, they'll grow bigger," the boys assured him. "Pretty soon we'll be bursting out of shirts just like you said you was bursting out of your britches."

Coit couldn't help himself. He laughed aloud.

The twins dashed toward the fence opening, no longer interested in anything but bursting away from Coit.

Monday morning, bright and early, Annabel passed Coit's store on the way to the mill. Sure enough, he was waiting in his usual spot, claiming he liked to watch the sunrise. He leaned against one of the whitewashed columns that looked more gray than white in the defused morning light.

"Morning, Miss Blow," he said when she rounded the block and passed in front of the store.

Annabel's heart thwacked against her ribs with a vengeance on spying him in his usual spot, with coffee cup in hand and with his beautiful smile in place. Coit had a way of doing that to her. More so now than before, especially when the pleasures of the flesh were so fresh in her mind.

As always, Coit looked meticulous in his pressed, white shirt, his creased trousers, and with every dark hair in place. It amazed her to think that he could look so perfect when she knew for fact that he had rolled out of his big feather bed only minutes before. From her window she had watched his lights go on in his apartment right after she had rolled from her narrow cot.

"Morning, Mr. Jackson." They were back on formal terms, or maybe closer, Annabel thought, to more personal ones. She had heard Sara address Jess as Mr. Polk and vice versa.

"How's Sara this morning?"

"She had a restful night after her duty in bed yesterday. It's like Dr. Larson said, 'She's gonna be fine.' "

"I'm glad to hear it. So maybe that means you and I can see each other this evening and finish our little talk."

Annabel swallowed. She knew she couldn't keep refusing to see Coit. More importantly, she knew she had to tell him the truth about herself. She and Sara had talked of nothing else the whole of yesterday afternoon, but talking about it and actually doing it were two different things.

"Maybe tonight," she responded, "only after I see if Sara doesn't need me."

Coit stepped off the porch and grabbed her hand before she could get away. "*I* need you," he told her, and before she knew what he was about, he had pulled her hard against him and kissed her smack dab on the lips. When she came up for air, sputtering about what people would say, the taste of his coffee was strong on her lips.

"I've something for you," he said, keeping her fingers entwined with his, forbidding her to escape.

Although she was determined to keep her distance from Coit until she told him the truth about herself, she couldn't help but respond to his charm. Her heart wouldn't allow it.

"You're always giving me gifts," she said.

"It's because I like you."

Coit searched her thoroughly before bending down to fetch something from the floor beside his feet. When he stood again, he said, "I was right. You did forget your lunch."

Seeing the pail he held toward her, Annabel's hand flew to her mouth.

"I was correct in assuming your head would be filled with everything but food."

If he only knew what my head is filled with.

It was best he didn't know because if he felt the same way she did, he would be worrying about feeding the cravings of her body instead of worrying about what she should eat for lunch. *You, Annabel Lowe, have turned into a very wicked woman.*

Coit squeezed her fingers. "I can't have my favorite girl going without lunch, now can I?"

Annabel hesitated, uncertain how to respond to his familiarity. She licked her lips and replied, "Thanks."

"I'll collect my reward later," he whispered, releasing her hand and allowing her to continue on her way.

Annabel moved forward on numb legs and turned around once to see if he was still watching her. He was. Maybe if she were his favorite girl, she thought, he could find it in his heart to forgive her deceptions. Maybe it was like Sara had said—although Coit hadn't told her he loved her, he still might. Hadn't she kept her feelings for him to herself? Maybe it was possible for the two of them to make a life together.

Her steps felt lighter as she approached the entrance to the mill grounds. She noticed that all traces of Saturday's festivities were gone. Today the grounds and mill looked exactly like before. Dalworth's Royal Mill was an impressive sight. It was a place where men, women, and children worked to put food on their tables so they wouldn't starve.

She met Birdie at the front door, and together they went inside. The conversation that buzzed among the workers revolved around the fasola on Saturday night and how much everyone had enjoyed the singing and the wonderful food.

Annabel soon learned how fast news traveled in the small community. Everyone knew of Sara's setback and inquired as to how she was convalescing. Most of the women promised they would check on her in the next few days, and some of them promised to bring a covered dish of food to help sustain family appetites until Sara was back on her feet again. Annabel was amazed by their charity. These people who seemed to have so little were willing to share what they did have with those in need. Again she was humbled by their benevolence.

Like the other weavers, she took her place in front of her six looms just as the main switch was turned on and the machines began their daily roar. With the loud, clanking noise, all conversation between them ceased. But this morning Annabel didn't mind the forced solitude. It gave her time to relive in her mind every moment she had spent in Coit's arms and in his bed.

She performed her routine task like a professional, watching her machines and checking on the weaving process. About an hour later the main switch in the room was thrown, and the machines suddenly came to a dead stop. The quiet lay heavily in the room until a bloodcurdling cry sliced through the silence. Fear tread up and down Annabel's backbone—a woman was screaming hysterically somewhere in the building.

"What is it?" she asked Birdie who had come up to stand beside her. The eerie-sounding wail continued and was soon joined by what sounded like a child's cry of pain.

Uneasiness masked the faces of the other weavers who quickly gathered in small groups across the floor of the long hall, their curious murmuring spreading like wildfire throughout the interior.

"Accident, there's been an accident," a woman shouted from the doorway that led to the stairs. Before her last words were uttered, everyone rushed toward her.

Above the excited babel, a woman asked, "What happened, and who was involved?"

"It's Fanny's daughter, Billie Jean."

"That will be upstairs in the spinning room," a woman Annabel hardly knew announced.

Everyone swarmed toward the stairs like an army of ants and Annabel was carried along in the advance.

Please, God, don't let it be a fatality. She prayed silently for Billie Jean, the beautiful little girl who only days before Annabel had watched jumping rope with the other children who worked in the mill.

The spinning room was on the third level. Everyone raced up the stairs, and Annabel recognized two brawny men standing before the entrance that led into the spinning area. They worked in the carding department where they prepared the raw cotton for spinning.

"Better stay back!" they shouted to the approaching women. "Mr. Hamil is with the little girl now. There's nothing you can do."

"No, you can't keep us out," Birdie told the man. "Fanny needs us."

Annabel had been on Birdie's heels from the moment the throng headed for the stairs. She was right behind her now when she pushed through the opening and approached the circle of women, children, and men who had gathered around the accident victim and her mother.

"Dear Lord in heaven, is my baby going to die?" Fanny wailed as they approached. She was on her knees beside Gordon Hamil who also knelt, holding Billie Jean. Gordon held a white towel, soaked with blood, pressed against the child's head.

As Annabel came to a stop at the circle's inner edges, she saw immediately that Gordon Hamil wasn't the same, self-assured man he usually presented to the world.

The accident had clearly upset him. His hands shook so badly that he could hardly hold the towel in place on Billie Jean's head. She whimpered like a wounded puppy. There were tears in Gordon Hamil's eyes.

"Get my brother," he ordered. "Someone go for Coit, now."

"Jess Polk is summoning him, sir. He'll be here shortly."

Annabel was astonished by Mr. Hamil's order. Coit? Why would he want Coit, especially when it was a well-known fact the two brothers were at odds with one another and that Coit had nothing to do with the running of the mill?

"What happened to the child?" someone whispered.

"Billie Jean's hair tangled in the steel spinning frame. Ripped her hair and scalp right off her head."

A woman standing beside Annabel buried her face in her hands, moaning, "Dear Lord, no."

The circle of somber-looking workers, clad in dark working garb, reminded Annabel of a flock of crows. She looked toward the spinning frame. It took her several moments to distinguish the child's hair from that of the yarn tightly wound around the spindles. The bloody clump of flesh that had been part of Billie Jean's scalp was still attached to the once wavy tresses.

Poor Billie Jean. What pain she must be suffering. Annabel felt sick, woozy. She clutched her stomach to still the squeamish motions that rocked her insides.

Looking back at the little sufferer, Annabel realized that there was still plenty of hair left covering the child's head. This gave her hope for Billie Jean's recovery. It looked as though only a clump of her hair had been ripped out by the machine. Her thoughts were interrupted by pounding footsteps trampling up the stairs.

Coit and Jess muscled their way through the crowd. Both men kneeled by the stricken child and the others gathered around her.

"She's going to die," Gordy moaned. "Please, I don't want her to die, Coit. She's just a little girl."

Gordy's announcement made Fanny wail louder. Mona, kneeling behind her, kept her arms around Billie Jean's mother while reassuring her that Billie Jean wasn't going to die.

"Gordon," Coit assured, "Billie Jean's going to be fine." He smiled at Fanny, trying to comfort her as well. "We're going to take Billie Jean to Dr. Larson in town. In a few days your daughter will be as good as new. Trust me."

Coit moved to Gordon's side. "Here, Gordon, I'll take her now. A runner was sent into town to notify the doc that we're coming. I have a wagon waiting outside."

Gordon ignored Coit. He kept holding the child, rock-

ing her. "She's so young, Coit. And all that beautiful hair.
Scalped like an Indian's victim. Only I'm the Indian who
dealt the blow."

"Gordon, we'll talk about this later. Now isn't the
time." Coit sounded like the one in charge when he ordered Gordon to change places with him. "Billie Jean is
going to be fine. Now give her to me."

When Coit, with Jess's help, had finally maneuvered
Billie Jean into his arms, Gordon sat back on his
haunches.

With a vengeance he attacked Coit with his words.
"You're as much to blame for this accident as I am.
Everyone here knows you're part owner in the mill."

The gathered crowd looked embarrassed by their employer's outburst. To Annabel, Gordon Hamil was only a
shadow of his former self—a nervous, insecure man who
looked for someone else to help shoulder his blame.

He appealed to the onlookers. "Y'all know my brother
shares the blame as much as I do. Don't you? Just like
me, he owns shares in the mill, pays your salaries, and
receives his share of profits. We're in this business together."

Annabel winced as though she had been struck. *No, it
couldn't be true.* But if Gordy had spoken the truth, then
Coit was as guilty as his stepbrother. No wonder Coit had
tried to sway her into seeing things his way. It was true.
Coit was a partner in the Royal Mill.

She almost stopped breathing. Had he intentionally deceived her into believing that he only ran the Company
Store? What a fool she had been. She was an intelligent
woman. She should have put two and two together and
realized that if he ran the Company Store he probably
owned it as well since he was Gordon Hamil's stepbrother. How could she have been so naïve?

Coit scooped Billie Jean up into his arms while Jess
helped the child's mother to her feet. "We'll go to Doc
Larson's now, Miss Fanny. I'll have someone find your
husband, and have him meet us there."

As the crowd parted to allow the small entourage

through, Coit's eyes locked on Anna's. Instead of awarding him with her admiration for his take-charge attitude, she looked at him with contempt. He tried to convey a message to her with his eyes as he passed, but she ignored it, looking right through him.

Resolved that this wasn't the time or place to explain himself, Coit pushed past her and hurried down the stairs. Jess, Fanny, and Mona followed in his footsteps.

To Annabel, Gordon Hamil appeared to be in better control now that the responsibility for the injured child had been taken from his hands. He turned toward his employees and said, "Billie Jean's going to be okay. For the rest of the day, the mill will be closed. It will give us all some time to pray for young Billie Jean's recovery. I'm real sorry this accident happened. . . ." His voice trailed off, and tears welled in his blue eyes. "Report for work tomorrow at the normal time, and we'll try to put this unfortunate accident behind us." He turned and followed the others. Another man accompanied him to the stairs, patting him on his back in reassurance.

Annabel wanted to run after him, but instead of patting, she wanted to pound her fists into his back. At that moment, she hated him, hated Coit Jackson. Billie Jean had been injured because she was too young to be working around the dangerous machinery. A child shouldn't be expected to work like an adult no matter how much her family needed the money.

She heard someone ask, "How did it happen?"

A man began to explain. "I understand Billie Jean was combing her hair. She turned about to get her little friend to braid it for her, and the ends flew under the two small rollers on the spinning frame." The teller shook his head in sympathy. "Pulled her down, it did, before it tore that plug of hair right out of her head."

Annabel saw Billie Jean's actions as a childish act and not an unusual one. She had done something that little girls everywhere did—she had played with her hair, probably wanting to look beautiful as all little girls dreamed of being.

Everyone expressed their sympathies for the child. "She'll be okay just like Mr. Hamil told us she would be," someone else said.

A man laughed. The same one that had accompanied Gordon Hamil to the stairs. "Don't know about that machine, though," he said. "It'll have to be taken apart to unwind that hair from around them rollers."

Annabel wondered how they could speak so casually about such a freakish accident, or express concern over the machine. How could they begin to consider Mr. Hamil's opinion, especially after he had conducted himself like a weakling? The realization hit her. These people, whom she had believed she knew, were nothing more than strangers. She didn't belong here.

Annabel wasn't aware of returning with Birdie to the weaving room or retrieving her things to leave. Before she realized where she was, she had passed through the fancy entrance doors of the Royal Mill and was standing outside in the fresh air. Like a zombie, she walked beside Birdie and the others and said her good-byes at the gate.

Coit Jackson was a partner in the mill. This knowledge of his betrayal almost overwhelmed her. She trudged toward home, glad that Coit wouldn't be in his store when she passed. How could she face him, knowing he was no better than his stepbrother? Their relationship had been built on nothing but lies—hers *and* his. Her love for him had been nothing more than a farce. Annabel could never love a man who used people less fortunate than himself to further his own gains.

The sign on the Company Store window read, CLOSED, when she passed. Just like this chapter in the book of her life was closed.

There was only one thing left for Annabel to do, but first she had to talk with Sara.

✦ *19* ✦

"Gone? What do you mean gone?"

Coit stood in Sara's bedroom at the foot of her bed where she sat propped against the headboard. There was an open book on her lap and a twin on each side of her. Mrs. Twigg, who had apparently come in to lend her help, stood beside the bedroom door like Sara's self-appointed watchdog.

Sara looked none too pleased. She glared at him, her lips puckered in annoyance. This surprised Coit because he and Sara had always been the best of friends.

She snapped, "Anna went back to Atlanta where she doesn't belong." It was evident that Sara had been crying, and she blotted her red eyes and nose with the hankie she'd been twisting in her hands seconds before.

Coit suspected she held him responsible for Anna's departure and wished he could be anywhere but in this bedroom where all four occupants glared at him as if he had just committed a mortal sin.

Uncertainty crept into his bones. "Atlanta? Why the devil did she go to Atlanta?" he asked. "We were supposed to talk tonight."

Even as he spoke, he heard the departing whistle of the

eastbound train. Anna could be on that train, leaving town this very moment. All he wanted to do was run to the depot to delay her departure. Instead he stood before his jury of four, already condemned by their votes as the train whistle droned in the distance. His shoulders sagged in defeat. His Anna was gone, and he didn't know why.

"Why did she go?" he asked.

Choosing not to answer, Sara told the twins, "Boys, will you please give Mr. Coit and me a few moments alone? What I have to say won't take long."

Taking Sara's request as a cue, Mrs. Twigg walked to the bed, helped the boys to the floor, then ushered them toward the door.

As both boys stopped in front of Coit, they looked up at him. "You hurt our Anna," Lance said.

"Yeah, you made her cry," Percy added. "We saw her."

"I made her—"

"Seems it ain't above Mr. Jackson," Mrs. Twigg said, squaring her bony shoulders, "for him to take advantage of *all* the ladies. Come along, boys, we'll leave your ma to deal with him." Steering the boys by their shoulders, she marched them from the room.

Deal with him. Suddenly Coit felt as if he were the age of the twins. He waited until after the boys were gone before he asked, "How did I make Anna cry?"

"Coit Jackson, are you thicker in the head than those bedposts?"

He looked from Sara's face to the thick pine posts on each corner of the bed that were as big around as a good-sized tree, then back to Sara's face. He was about to tell her that, no, he wasn't that dense, when she blurted out.

"Anna loves you. And unless I've misjudged your character all these years, I think you love her, too."

"Anna loves me?" Coit shook his head in amazement. "She never said so."

"Men," Sara mumbled as she rolled her eyes heavenward. "Did you tell her?" Not waiting for him to answer, she continued. "I happen to know she gave you the most precious gift a woman can give a man, especially a proper lady like Anna. Here you are telling me you didn't take that gift for what it was—as a gift of her love.''

Coit felt himself blush. Although he and Sara were the best of friends, he hadn't expected her to know what had gone on between him and Anna. Or understand. Heck, if he were to admit the truth, he didn't understand either. He only knew he had wanted Anna more than any woman before her, and he still wanted her.

"If she loves me as you claim, why the devil did she go running off to Atlanta?''

"Because of all the things you both failed to mention to the other about yourselves.''

Coit was puzzled. "What are you talking about? She knew everything there was to know about me. I'd say I'm the one who had the wool pulled over my eyes.''

"Until today, Anna never knew how involved you were with the mill. I understand your brother informed everyone in the room.''

"I've never denied my ownership of the Company Store. My ten percent certainly isn't making me rich and doesn't give me much say-so in the running of the mill.''

"I don't know about percentages, but Anna said you never told her you owned the store. You told her you ran it.''

"I do run it.''

"Coit, you're being stubborn. Tell me truthfully—did you really believe that Anna was like the normal mill worker?''

Hell, no, I didn't believe it. After several moments of deliberation, he said, "I guess I did think she was a little different with all the highfalutin ideas she voiced about how the mill should be run. And I reckon there were other things about her, too.''

Sara looked disgusted. "You'd have to be deaf, dumb, and stupid, Coit Jackson, not to have realized that Anna was a bona fide lady.''

He grinned for the first time since confronting Sara. *His Anna a lady?* "That first day I met her on the train I knew she wasn't like the usual women who worked in the mill.

And after I got to know her better, I was convinced she wasn't who she claimed to be. Who is she anyway?" he asked.

"You should be asking Anna that question instead of me."

"And how in the devil am I to do that when she's gone? If you weren't so all-fired convinced that I'm the only guilty party here, you would have heard what I said when I first arrived. We had planned to talk tonight. Which is why I'm here. But seeing that the lady has fled, it makes it kinda impossible, now doesn't it?"

"Don't get feisty with me," Sara warned. She glowered at him. "I'm gonna tell you everything she told me before she left. Then if you do have the good sense that God gave a dog, you'll find her and straighten out this horrible mess before it's too late for you both."

Some half hour later, Coit emerged from the Polks' house, his emotions in a state of confusion. Anna Belle Blow didn't exist—her real name was Annabel Lowe. Not only was she an imposter, but also she was the worst kind of woman in his opinion—a rich man's daughter from Atlanta. Why, with all the women in the world, had he fallen in love with a woman who had nothing but money and time on her hands, and who had also appointed herself the personal crusader for the women of the world who were less fortunate than herself?

He met Lance and Percy in the backyard. They stopped him, refusing to allow him to pass. With their hands fisted upon their narrow hips in a show of defiance, they asked him, "You gonna bring our Anna back and make her tears go away?"

Their response tugged at Coit's heartstrings. All this time he had believed the three of them were comrades, but it seemed Anna had usurped his place. Coit ruffled their blond hair. "I'm thinking on it, boys, but a man can't rush into a decision that will affect the rest of his life. I promise when I do make my decision you two will be the first to know."

The twins exchanged glances. His answer seemed to

satisfy them, and they stepped aside. When Coit entered his own yard, they called out to him. "You know we love her, Mr. Coit."

He couldn't help but smile at the serious look on the boys' faces. "You know what, squirts, I do, too."

Annabel had been home for more than a week. She had returned to Atlanta late that Monday evening, the same day as Billie Jean's accident. Because her parents weren't expecting her return no carriage had met her at the depot, so she had hired a hack to carry her to her parents' home in Inman Park.

When Annabel arrived at the Lowe address, the dwelling had been aglow with lights and activity. Her parents were entertaining. It had been the perfect opportunity for her to slip inside the house unnoticed. Beneath the cover of darkness, she had crept to the back entrance that was usually kept unlocked for the servants. She had made her way up the back stairs and into the safe haven of her room without being discovered. Once inside her bedroom, she had locked the door, thrown herself across the bed, and cried into the wee hours. She had cried long after the guests had departed and the servants had retired for the night. Finally Annabel had fallen into an exhausted sleep and hadn't awakened until the next day.

At noontime when the maids had come upstairs to dust Annabel's room, they had found the door locked. They alerted the housekeeper, and immediately after that her mother had been notified. It was with a bevy of servants surrounding her like a small army that Evangeline Lowe had discovered that her wayward daughter had returned home.

Even now, the scene her mother had created those first few days of her return made her shudder. Her parent had raved for days about Annabel's lack of propriety, traveling unchaperoned through the city in a rented coach. Whatever would her friends say when they heard of Annabel's latest indiscretion?

She had immediately informed her mother that no one

would hear unless she chose to tell them. Annabel had been reminded repeatedly of how selfish it had been of her not to advise her parents of her travel plans, and then how cruel she had been for not notifying them immediately of her return to the premises.

If it was true what Sara had said about making a man a good wife because she knew how to nag, then her mother must be a perfect one.

Next her parent had informed her of how disappointed she was in Annabel because she had defied her mother's instructions and had not returned to Atlanta immediately after receiving a letter telling her to do just that. Mrs. Lowe had finished her tirade by announcing to Annabel that it would be over her mother's dead body before she returned again for a visit with upcountry rustics who lived in Dalworth.

Annabel had *yes ma'am'd* and *no ma'am'd* so much that she felt as if her tongue might fall out of her mouth. At least her father had been happy to see her. He had welcomed her home with open arms, never admonishing her once.

It was only yesterday that life in the Lowe home had returned to normal, primarily because Annabel had agreed to accompany her mother to the Cotton Exposition that had been in full swing for the past week, and because she had also agreed to work alongside her mother in the Women's Exhibit.

Later that morning, she would be trussed up like some Thanksgiving turkey and would have to endure all of her mother's friends, reminding her of her inadequacies because she hadn't snared a man. If they only knew, she thought.

Now Annabel sat alone and listless in her room, recalling every vivid detail of her snaring. The memory only made her long for Coit and the simple life she had led as Anna Belle Blow, a life she had much preferred to this one.

One memory led to another, and Annabel knew she would defy her mother's wishes and return to Dalworth for the christening of Sara and Jess's baby when the time came. She would stand up beside Coit and be recognized as the baby's godparent. Although she knew her visit would be brief, she looked forward to seeing her friends again. She missed those hectic days of working in the mill, the friendships she had formed with some of the workers, and most of all she missed Coit.

Her anger with him had gradually faded into a dull ache that she lived with daily. In spite of her resolve to get over Coit Jackson, she couldn't. She loved him more to-day than she had a week ago. The things he and Sara had pointed out to her about the mill had given her a new perspective. Since her return to Atlanta, she saw the mill village in a more realistic light.

Before she had left town, Sara had confirmed the truth about Coit. The things Gordy had claimed that horrible day of the accident had been true. Sara had confessed that it was only a guess as to how much of the mill and ad-joining land Coit actually owned. Everyone knew the Company Store had been left to him by his stepfather, and Coit owned it outright. A fairer man to deal with she said there could never be.

Sara had gone on to say that she suspected Gordon Hamil's outburst had probably been caused because he had been so upset about the accident. People did and said strange things when faced with a crisis, she had told Annabel. Perhaps the matter of ownership and Gordy's ac-cusations that Coit was as responsible for the accident as he was grew from Mr. Hamil's pain. Perhaps that was his way of dealing with it. Imagine, she said, how awful it would be to feel responsible for the welfare of all those many workers and then to see an innocent child hurt by one of his machines.

She had also told Annabel that she agreed that the Royal Mill wasn't perfect. But using her own poor up-bringing in Texas as an example, she had emphasized how horrible hunger could be. She and Jess had come to Geor-gia seeking a better life for themselves. They had found it in the Royal Mill. No, it wasn't a perfect system, Sara had admitted, but it was so much better than they'd ever expected to have, and she knew if Annabel questioned others who worked at the mill, they would tell her the same. Hadn't Fanny and Mona stressed similar opinions?

Once again, Coit's words surfaced in Annabel's mind. If it ain't broke, don't fix it.

Those words, along with both Coit and Sara's views, had prompted her to write her letter to Hollie Cross with information on the Royal Mill. Hollie would pass the facts on to her cousin, Miss de Graffenreid. Intending to post her letter when she accompanied her mother to Piedmont Park, she wrote the following:

My dear Hollie,

I have completed my assignment at Dalworth, and after spending several weeks employed in the Royal Mill as a weaver, I'm happy to report that I see no undue mistreatment of the women and children employed there. They are all a hard-working bunch of people who, without the mill's existence, would be forced to eke out a living by sharecropping.

The Royal Mill provides these workers with substantial housing and decent wages, and I heard that someday schools will be built for the mill children to attend. In my opinion, it is a good place for families to work and live. A feeling of community reigns high in the mill village, and on occasion they even enjoy planned socials.

In closing, I wish to say that I hope I have fulfilled my mission to your satisfaction. If you, or your cousin, find yourself in need of my services again, you may write to me at the same address.

Respectfully yours,

Annabel Lowe

*   *   *

Even Annabel was excited as she strolled in Piedmont
Park with her mother and father. It was a beautiful day
for an outing, the mid-September sky so blue it reminded
her of a crystal-clear spring. The park, with its new Lake
Clara Meer that was built especially for the Cotton States
Expo, was like a miniature city. What had once been quiet
carriage paths was now transformed into a busy midway.

The music of a marching band drifted across the
grounds. Annabel had read in this morning's newspaper
that John Philip Sousa was to premier his "King Cotton
March" at the Expo.

As they strolled, Annabel saw in the distance the
world's largest Ferris wheel, many Greek-columned
buildings, and beautiful lawns and gardens. Gardens, Annabel reflected, that in her opinion couldn't rival Coit's,
but far prettier than she expected them to be.

Their first stop, at Annabel's insistence, had been the
Pennsylvania Building. She wanted to see the Liberty Bell
that had been transported all the way from Philadelphia
and placed on exhibit for all to see.

Her mother complained as the threesome stood in front
of the historic bell. "With all the other wonderful things
to see, I can't understand your fixation for this dirty old
bell."

"Mother, I care about the bell's significance. This bell
proclaimed independence for all, and it was present at the
reading of the Declaration of Independence in 1776. At
that time it wasn't called the Liberty Bell. The name came
later with the first anti-slavery movement in 1839."

This information didn't appear to add to her mother's
pleasure. Instead of being impressed with Annabel's little
tidbit of history, she replied, "I knew there was a reason
I didn't want to see it. We all know what anti-slavery did
to the South. Besides, it's broken anyway."

Annabel ignored her mother's remark. "The bell was
fatally cracked and silenced on Washington's birthday in
1846."

"Well, I can't say I blame Washington for breaking it.

I would have done the same if someone tried to ring it on my birthday. After we reach a certain age, who of us wants to be reminded that we are growing older?"

"Mother, Washington didn't break it."

"Who cares how it got broken? Certainly not me. Have you seen enough, Annabel? There is so much more to see and do, I hate to waste any more time here."

Annabel breathed an impatient sigh. Her mother, God bless her, would never change.

"Lead the way, Mother," she said, moving away from the bell. Annabel mumbled beneath her breath, "I know you will anyway."

Her father silenced her with a stern look that plainly implied she shouldn't argue with her mother.

Soon the Liberty Bell was forgotten. They strolled over bridges and paths that led past the other exhibit buildings.

They passed the Colored Exhibition that Annabel wanted to visit. She hoped to catch a glimpse of the American Negro educator Booker T. Washington, but when Annabel suggested they go inside, her mother turned up her nose.

"Later, dear. We'll see it later. We can't see everything in one day."

"Ah, here we are," her father said.

They had reached the Woman's Building that stood in the center of the amphitheater. The building looked impressive surrounded by terraces, fountains, and parks.

"Annabel," her mother said, "did you realize that a woman designed this building?"

No, she didn't know, but because of her mother's statement, Annabel paid more attention to the building's appearance. The main front was built in the classical design and had large porticoes and galleries. Its rich ornamental friezes, cornices, and balustrades made the exterior very handsome. A large dome rose high above the roof, a statue on its very center.

"I knew you would like it when you learned a woman designed it."

Her mother looked pleased with herself because she had told Annabel something she didn't know.

"They say the statue on the top represents immortality," her mother continued. "Why they would want such a thing representing women is beyond me. We all know youth is fleeting and that we women are the first ones touched by age." She shrugged her dainty shoulders. "Come along, dear, my friends are waiting inside."

Evangeline Lowe started up the stairs, then stopped. "Oh, Henry, I completely forgot about you. What will you do while Annabel and I are working?"

"Mother, I think Father can find plenty to do. Perhaps I could stroll along with him. I could meet you here later."

"Annabel, you know that's not possible. Besides, you promised me that you would work beside me today like a proper daughter."

Henry Lowe cleared his throat. "Run along with your mother, Annabel. I assure you I'll be fine. I'll meet you here later, and we will have lunch."

Her mother walked back toward her husband. "You stay away from the Streets of Cairo, Henry. I've heard about the coochee-coochee girls. I am sure no decent man would be interested in watching those half-clad women, rotating their hips and heaven knows what else," she admonished.

Her father cleared his throat again. "Certainly not I, my dear. I'm much more interested in seeing Buffalo Bill's Wild West Show or the moving pictures."

"Oh, me, too, Father. Please allow me to join you," Annabel begged.

"No, child. You run along with your mother. You'll be able to see everything later. The Expo will run for four months."

Disappointed, she watched her father leave. He was right; she could attend the Expo many times before it ended in order to see all the exhibits. Reluctantly Annabel turned and followed her mother up the high steps leading to the interior of the building.

She paused when she reached the portico. A giant sign stood beside the entrance doors. Everyone who entered the building would be sure to stop and read the words inscribed in black on the sign's surface. The title New Woman was centered across the top with the definition of the New Woman written below. Annabel read the words:

NEITHER THE ANTAGONIST NOR THE RIVAL OF MAN, BUT HIS COWORKER AND HELPMEET ALONG BROADER, NO-BLER, AND DIVINER LINES, FOR AS HER POWERS AND FAC-ULTIES HAVE FREER SCOPE AND LARGER GROWTH, HIS BURDEN LESSENS.

"Come along, Annabel. Must you dally so? We're going to be late."

Annabel ignored her mother's summons and reread the words. She recalled that when the Expo had still been in the planning stages she had heard that Susan B. Anthony had urged that the Woman's Building be built with the purpose of paying tribute to women everywhere. Annabel wondered what the activist thought of the prose that greeted all who entered the revered halls.

In Annabel's opinion, the meaning was very clear. It said to her that the New Woman wasn't new at all. The phrase only reiterated what Annabel had always believed was true. It was a man's world and always would be.

The Expo no longer held its earlier excitement, or at least not the Women's Exhibition. Wishing she was anywhere but here, and dreading the next few hours in the company of her mother's friends, Annabel followed her mother reluctantly inside.

With Coit's arrival in Atlanta yesterday, he had gone directly to the Hotel Aragon and checked in. It was fortunate for Coit his brother Gordy had reserved rooms for himself for the last two weeks in September because the city was packed with visitors, and all the hotels were full. It seemed people had come from all over to enjoy the Cotton States Expo.

After settling in, Coit went in search of the Lowe home. With the information he had gleaned from Merelda Whitcomb before leaving Dalworth, he knew Annabel's address. He had struck up a conversation with a porter, and the man had told him Inman Park was the city's first planned suburb. There was a streetcar line connecting the area with downtown, and it was no more than a five-minute trolley ride either way.

That same evening when Coit had stepped off the trolley, he realized Inman Park was also a very prestigious address with its large ornate Victorian homes and tree-lined avenues. He had no trouble locating the Lowe home. The elegant house had been built in the Eastlake style and looked much too large for a family of three. He stood outside the iron gate hidden behind a huge boxwood shrub at the corner of the yard, trying to picture the Anna he knew in such elegant surroundings.

When he left the suburb to return to the hotel, Coit wondered if he should give up on contacting Annabel, declaring his love, and then carrying her back to Dalworth to become his wife. Although Coit lived comfortably and could afford much more than the rooms behind the store, his wealth couldn't compare with Annabel's father's. Mr. Lowe was the president of one of Atlanta's largest banks. Would Annabel be willing to give up such wealth to spend the rest of her days with him?

After a sleepless night, he decided it was best to pursue the truth instead of avoiding it. This morning he planned to return to Inman Park, go directly to the Lowe mansion, and demand an audience with Annabel. But when he stepped down from the trolley, he saw the whole Lowe family exit the mansion's yard and walk toward the trolley stop.

Instead of making his appearance known, Coit darted behind a nearby tree. He decided he would follow them and approach Annabel later when she was alone. Undetected, he jumped on the back of the trolley and followed them to Piedmont Park and the Expo grounds.

Had it only been a week since he had last seen Annabel? She looked more beautiful than he remembered. Whaleboned, he suspected, into an impossibly small-waisted corset, her waist appeared no bigger than a bee's. His Anna had never worn a corset in Dalworth, but then his Anna had never appeared so elegantly dressed as she was today.

The frock she wore was made of black pearl silk with leg-o-mutton sleeves that, in Coit's opinion, would have been more appropriate as lamp shades. He didn't like the new style, and the sleeves gave a winged appearance to the ladies who wore them. He believed if God had intended for women to have wings, he would have made them angels or perhaps butterflies.

The rust and green plaid of the bodice and wide flat collar that covered her narrow shoulders brightened what might have otherwise been a widow's ensemble. He didn't like the somber color, especially on Annabel, but he knew without a doubt that the bright plaid would complement her hair and eyes. Her hat was a black straw boater topped with black feathers and ribbon roses in the same color as the plaid of her dress. Coit preferred seeing her hair hanging loose around her shoulders, with the light of the moon casting bronze shadows in the coppery tresses.

When they left the trolley and made their way toward the park, Coit followed them at a reasonable distance so as not to be detected. He heard bits and pieces of conversation between mother and daughter who, Coit thought, looked nothing alike. Annabel looked more like the tall, silent man who was her father than the petite, flashing dark-eyed woman who was her mother.

Their walk ended at the Women's Exhibition where mother and daughter went inside and the father had left them, going his separate way. He had watched Annabel pause outside the entrance, read the sign, then follow her mother indoors.

An hour later, Coit still waited beneath the huge portico of the Women's Exhibition building. Propped against a column, he hoped to catch Annabel when she left.

People came and went, pausing at the sign, reading the

words, commenting, then making their way into the building's interior. Coit could only guess what his Anna had thought of the words written on the sign. She probably wouldn't be too happy with what the words implied.

He chuckled. *A helpmeet for man to lighten his burdens.* No, he didn't believe for a moment that his Anna would agree with such nonsense.

Coit shifted restlessly. Maybe he should go inside and find her. He began to worry he had missed her. Maybe there was a back entrance, and she had left that way. He was about to move away from the post when Annabel pushed past the entering crowd, looking mad enough to stomp a dead chicken. Unwilling to confront her when she was in such a state, Coit stepped behind the column and watched her.

She paced from one end of the portico to the next, mumbling to herself as she went. Coit only caught bits and pieces of the words flowing from her mouth, but the set of her shoulders indicated she wasn't in the best of moods.

Suddenly she stopped pacing. Her gaze focused on something hidden behind the sign, then she glanced around her as though sizing up the crowd. Appearing satisfied with her surroundings, she moved toward the sign, intent on whatever had intrigued her. When she was once again in Coit's sight, he saw she held an open can of paint with a brush still in it. Coit figured the paint can had been shoved behind the sign until the painter could return for it.

He watched Annabel check her surroundings again. Holding the can in one hand, she picked up the brush with the other and gave the paint a quick stir.

From his hiding place Coit tried to read the thoughts inside her head. She pivoted on her feet, stopped several inches in front of the sign, and nodded at the people who passed.

A group of women climbed the building's stairs. Coit heard one lady in the group ask Anna upon seeing the can of black paint in her hands, ''Did you paint this, my dear?''

Annabel smiled in acknowledgment.

The lady asked, ''Can't say I see anything new in its meaning, do you? Always been our purpose in life to help the little man.''

The woman's companions walked inside the building, but she remained a few moments longer to talk to Annabel.

''Sure beats being a coochee-coochee girl like the ones I just saw on the Streets of Cairo.'' The woman puffed up with indignation suggestive of a fluffed-up pigeon. ''It's disgraceful the way those women are carrying on. Decent folks shouldn't have to be exposed to such frolicking.'' She shook her head. ''I don't know what the world is coming to.'' Before Annabel could respond, the lady hurried inside behind her friends.

What the devil was Annabel doing with the can of paint? A moment later, Coit found out.

With her chin set in the stubborn pose Coit had come to know, Annabel said, ''I'd rather be a coochee-coochee girl than a little man's helpmeet.'' Then she walked back to the sign and began spreading black paint over the surface, obliterating the words.

Everything began to happen at once. A lady ascending the stairs screamed when she saw Annabel desecrating the sign.

''Call the police,'' a passerby shouted.

The shrieking woman attracted the attention of the people inside the building, and several women ran to the front door. On seeing Annabel smearing the sign with black paint, several of them looked as though they might swoon.

''Annabel Lowe, what are you doing now?'' The woman apparently knew Annabel because she immediately turned toward the interior and began hollering. ''Evangeline, you better get out here at once. Your daughter is losing her mind.''

From off in the distance came more shouting, the

stomping of running feet, and the shrill scream of a po-
liceman's whistle.

The whistle prompted Coit into action. He dashed from
behind the pole toward Annabel. "What in the devil do
you think you're doing?" he scolded, approaching her.

Annabel dropped the paint can. It thundered loudly to
the floor, splattering paint everywhere, and as it rolled
across the floor, it left a trail of black.

When she recognized him, Annabel looked as though
she might faint. All Coit could think of was getting her
away from the chaotic scene. When the police discovered
she was responsible for the destruction of the sign, they
would haul her to jail in the paddy wagon.

Not even thinking that he was aiding a fugitive, Coit
tackled her skirts and threw her over his shoulder like a
sack of potatoes.

He hesitated for only a moment, trying to decide which
way he should run. There weren't many options. He could
run down the steps, in sight of the approaching policemen,
or he could take his chances inside the building, fighting
the crowds. Coit chose the latter.

He darted toward the door. He pushed past the screaming and swooning women and stopped inside the large
reception hall. Annabel beat furiously on his back with
her fists and kicked her legs, demanding that he put her
down. Coit wasn't about to let her go.

The police whistles grew louder. The shrieking of the
onlookers traveled like a roaring wave throughout the
building. Coit ran for the two sets of stairs. He chose the
ones leading down to the basement instead of the ones
leading to the second floor. He rushed downward. If he
lost his balance, they both would end up with broken
limbs.

Once downstairs, he ran past the kindergarten, the day
nursery, and toward the quiet area designated for the hospital. It had been set up to serve those who needed medical services while attending the Expo.

As he approached the entrance with his baggage, he
told the woman manning the door, "I'm a doctor. This

woman needs medical assistance. Is there a private room in this clinic designated for emergencies?''

The woman looked frightened. Above their heads they heard more screeching interrupted only by the sound of police whistles.

"Madam, please," he demanded, "this woman needs immediate attention."

Coit's words jerked her into action. "This way, Doctor," she said. "Bring her in here."

Once inside the small room, Coit ordered the woman to leave. She hesitated for a moment before rushing out the door. Before dropping Annabel on the examining table, he made certain the door was locked.

"Have you lost your mind?" he asked. "Whatever possessed you to destroy that sign?" His anger rolled over him. "You just may end up in jail yet, unless your father has as much clout as I believe he does."

"You leave my father out of this," Annabel answered. Springing up from the table, she marched toward the door.

Coit jumped in front of her. "You're not leaving here until you've calmed down. Or perhaps I should say until they've calmed down." He jerked his head toward the wall where the sound of stomping feet grew louder.

Suddenly the fight went out of her. Annabel turned and slumped against the wall. She stared at him with her beautiful pickle-colored eyes.

"What are you doing here?" she asked when she could finally speak, her gaze never leaving his.

"I've come to take you home."

"I am home," she answered. "Atlanta is my home."

"Annabel Lowe might belong in Atlanta, but not my Anna. She belongs by my side in Dalworth."

Coit moved toward her. With one hand on each side of her head, he trapped her against the wall.

"I love you, Anna. I want you to be my wife."

Annabel's eyes filled with tears. "You can't love me, Coit Jackson. I'm not the woman for you. You said so yourself. Even now you've had to rescue me from the police because I vandalized public property."

"I know what I said and I know what you did, but none of those things matter. This last week without you has been hell. I want you with me for the rest of my life."

"But . . . but I'm one of those women—one of those reformers, I believe you called them. Those infamous meddlers whose single purpose in life is to save the world."

"I'll keep you busy making babies." He grinned. "You'll be too busy to reform the world. Instead I'll let you reform me."

Her arms slipped around his neck, and she turned her lips up for him to kiss. "Reform a robber baron? Is that really possible?"

He pulled back and looked deep into her eyes. Before he could respond, she said, "I owe you an apology for all the things I implied. You were right, Coit, if something isn't broken, you shouldn't try to fix it."

He massaged the back of her neck, wanting to remove her now lopsided hat, loosen her hair, and run his fingers through it. He wanted to make love to her, right here and now on the examining table.

Instead, he said, "I know there are things at the mill that can be improved upon. Gordy and I have decided to work together to make those improvements. My brother felt horrible about Billie Jean's accident, and from now on he is going to consider hiring adults first and children second. No children will work in the mill without their parents' signed consent."

Annabel looked at him with so much love in her eyes that his heart felt as though it might break. He tried to kiss her again, but she stopped him.

"I learned from Sara that you owned the store outright, but I also learned you are more than fair with all your customers. It seems you're a saint in our Sara's eyes."

"Was," he teased. "This last week I felt I was close to forfeiting my life to the knights and their mother. All of them insisted I bring you home to Dalworth, and soon."

"Lance and Percy. I do miss those boys."

"There is something else, Anna, that you must know if we're going to be married. I'm well off in my own right, but not as wealthy as your father. I do have enough money that will allow us to live very comfortably. We won't even have to live behind the store."

She looked at him hesitantly. "Not money you make from being a partner in the mill?"

"I'm not a partner. My stepfather left me ten percent ownership, non-voting shares, and gave me the store outright. I always liked the store better than the mill anyway. He knew that. I suppose that's why he left it to me. I also have a small inheritance from my mother's estate. It's like I said, I'm not rich, but we can live comfortably."

"Oh, Coit, we have so much to learn about each other." Annabel kissed him deeply and asked between nibbles, "Do you believe in long engagements? Engagements! Dear Lord in heaven, when my mother finds out about my latest imprudent behavior there will be hell to pay."

She jerked away from Coit. No longer were they alone. The outer rooms of the hospital were buzzing with activity. Several fists beat against the locked door.

They heard the woman who had admitted them to the room. "He said he was a doctor. That is why I allowed him to use the examining room."

Above the din, Annabel recognized her mother's voice. "My daughter has been kidnapped by that uncouth man, and you refuse to break down the door in order to save her? Annabel, dear, I'm coming. Don't you worry. Surely someone has a key . . ."

Her mother's voice trailed off. Annabel and Coit listened from inside the door.

"Did you say doctor?" It was Annabel's mother again. "Did you hear that, Mrs. Featherstone, my daughter is locked in that room with a doctor."

Annabel couldn't help but laugh. "She approves of you," she whispered.

"She approves because she thinks I'm a doctor. But it

doesn't matter to me whether she approves of me or not. I'm still gonna marry her daughter.''

He pulled her into his arms and really kissed her. He was feeling and touching as though he couldn't get enough of her, and she returned his embrace with the same hungry enthusiasm.

The door of the examining room flew open, and the crowd rushed inside. Annabel kept kissing Coit and peeked at her mother who stood among her bevy of socialite friends. The gazes of mother and daughter locked. Did she detect approval?

"Imagine that, Mrs. Featherstone," she heard her mother say. "My Annabel is going to marry a doctor."

❖ Author's Note ❖

The inspiration for this book came to me after reading an article in the *Atlanta Journal and Constitution* about the Cotton States and International Exposition held in Atlanta in 1895. The exhibition, which ran 104 days beginning September 18, 1895, closed its doors on New Year's Eve of that year. What a celebration it must have been.

I learned from the article that the Atlanta History Center had an exhibit of the 1895 Cotton Exposition. With notebook and pen in hand, I took myself off to visit the Center. It was there among the displays of photographs and paraphernalia that my heroine Annabel was born, the progressive Southern woman.

Since the Our Town books are set in small-town America, and because the cotton industry was so important to the South, Annabel and I traveled to the town of Dalton, Georgia, where we found Coit when we visited the Crown Gardens and Archives, the home of the Whitfield-Murray Historical Society.

The Crown Cotton Mill and Village, a mill where raw cotton was spun into yarn and later into cloth, is on the register of historical places. Most of the original buildings built in 1884 (including the Company Store) still stand today.

It was through the historical society that I learned about people such as Catherine Hart, whose cottage industry of hand-tufted spreads was the forerunner to Dalton's carpet industry. The late Victorian poet, Robert Loveman, resided in Dalton, and Georgia's first woman's literary club, the Lesche, was created in 1890 in the small town.

Another newspaper article introduced me to sacred harp, or shaped-note, singing. A sacred harp singing convention was held in Troup County, Georgia, in 1845. "Fasola" singing, as it is also called, went on to become a fixture of rural Deep South worship.

With the wealth of information available to me, I wove a little bit of history into my fictitious town of Dalworth and the Royal Mill. Mary Claire de Graffenreid was a real person who did attend Wesleyan College in Macon, Georgia. She was one of twenty special investigators appointed to the Bureau of Labor under President Cleveland. Her cousin Hollie is fictional. Annabel and Coit were the actors I used to tell my story, and I hope you glean as much pleasure from the reading as I did from the telling. I learned a great deal from my research, and I hope you, too, gain insight into what life might have been like in a cotton mill village before the turn of the century.

I'd love to hear from my readers. You can write to me at 5361 Redfield Circle, Dunwoody, GA 30338.

Our Town ...where love is always right around the corner!

■ ■

__	**Harbor Lights** by Linda Kreisel	0-515-11899-0/$5.99
__	**Humble Pie** by Deborah Lawrence	0-515-11900-8/$5.99
__	**Candy Kiss** by Ginny Aiken	0-515-11941-5/$5.99
__	**Cedar Creek** by Willa Hix	0-515-11958 X/$5.99
__	**Sugar and Spice** by DeWanna Pace	0-515-11970-9/$5.99
__	**Cross Roads** by Carol Card Otten	0-515-11985-7/$5.99
__	**Blue Ribbon** by Jessie Gray	0-515-12003-0/$5.99
__	**The Lighthouse** by Linda Eberhardt	0-515-12020-0/$5.99
__	**The Hat Box** by Deborah Lawrence	0-515-12033-2/$5.99
__	**Country Comforts** by Virginia Lee	0-515-12064-2/$5.99
__	**Grand River** by Kathryn Kent	0-515-12067-7/$5.99
__	**Beckoning Shore** by DeWanna Pace	0-515-12101-0/$5.99
__	**Whistle Stop** by Lisa Higdon	0-515-12085-5/$5.99
__	**Still Sweet** by Debra Marshall	0-515-12130-4/$5.99
__	**Dream Weaver** by Carol Card Otten	0-515-12141-X/$5.99
__	**Raspberry Island** by Willa Hix (10/97)	0-515-12160-6/$5.99

Payable in U.S. funds. No cash accepted. Postage & handling: $1.75 for one book, 75¢ for each additional. Maximum postage $5.50. Prices, postage and handling charges may change without notice. Visa, Amex, MasterCard call 1-800-788-6262, ext. 1, or fax 1-201-933-2316; refer to ad # 637b

Or, check above books
and send this order form to:
The Berkley Publishing Group
P.O. Box 12289, Dept. B
Newark, NJ 07101-5289

Bill my: ☐ Visa ☐ MasterCard ☐ Amex _____ (expires)

Card# _____

($10 minimum)

Daytime Phone # _____

Signature _____

Please allow 4-6 weeks for delivery. Or enclosed is my: ☐ check ☐ money order
Foreign and Canadian delivery 8-12 weeks.

Ship to:

Name _____

Address _____

City _____

State/ZIP _____

Book Total $_____

Applicable Sales Tax $_____
(NY, NJ, PA, CA, GST Can.)

Postage & Handling $_____

Total Amount Due $_____

Bill to: Name _____

Address _____ City _____

State/ZIP _____